Sam slid her foot behind Cullen's ankle and tugged.

Cullen managed a startled "Hey!" just before he hit the water. He retaliated by pulling Sam's legs out from under her. For the next few minutes, the water churned around them as they wrestled and tried to drown each other.

"Uncle!" Sam yelled, half choking on a mouthful of lake water.

"That's better," Cullen said, panting for breath as he stood up. "Now, would you mind telling me just how this childhood regression is supposed to make Whitney jealous? Oh."

Sam had wrapped herself around Cullen's broad back, her hands splayed in his thick mat of chest hair. "This is a physical demonstration," she murmured, "of our evolution from childhood friends to potential adult lovers."

But it didn't feel anything like the make-believe she had intended. It felt heart-stoppingly real and seductive and addictive. She loved wrapping herself around Cullen, she loved touching him and molding herself to his tall, muscular body. It felt too good and too right and impossible to stop.

He turned in her arms so that they faced each other, his arms sliding naturally around her. "Good plan," he said. "Is this where we kiss?"

Also by Michelle Martin

STOLEN HEARTS

STOLEN MOMENTS

THE
Long Shot

Michelle Martin

🐓 BANTAM BOOKS

New York Toronto London Sydney Auckland

THE LONG SHOT

A Bantam Book / August 1998

ISBN 0-553-57650-X

Published simultaneously in the United States and Canada

Bantam Books are published by Bantam Books, a division of Bantam
Doubleday Dell Publishing Group, Inc. Its trademark, consisting of the
words "Bantam Books" and the portrayal of a rooster, is Registered in U.S.
Patent and Trademark Office and in other countries. Marca Registrada.
Bantam Books, 1540 Broadway, New York, New York 10036.

PRINTED IN THE UNITED STATES OF AMERICA

OPM   10   9   8   7   6   5   4   3   2   1

One

THE TAXI'S WINDSHIELD wipers swept an accumulation of drizzle from the windshield as the cab turned onto Mackenzie Lane. Rows of towering ancient white oaks on either side of the road enfolded the cab, their rain-darkened branches and green leaves spreading over the lane to form a lush canopy. The world felt hushed and luxurious and magical and Cullen hadn't expected it.

He certainly hadn't expected to feel so . . . odd. He was aware of every drop of rain, every blade of grass in the pastures bordering the road, every swipe of the windshield wipers. Was this culture shock? He was only coming home, how could he have culture shock?

But it occurred to him that Hong Kong, with its towering skyscrapers, and noise, and packed streets, and noise, and the mixed scents of humanity, sesame oil, exhaust, cigarette smoke, and wet asphalt had acted like a sort of shield these last nine months, protecting him from the awareness of any other world, and from any other thought save business and Whitney, protecting him even from any real emotion.

But this hushed, magical world through which he was now traveling offered no shields, no protection. He was feeling again and what surprised him most was that right this minute he was feeling excited.

He hadn't been home in the summer in almost ten years. It was all Cullen could do to keep from pressing his nose to the rear passenger window to gaze at all the achingly familiar sights that seemed somehow absolutely new. He had to forcibly remind himself that he was a rich and powerful thirty-year-old man and CEOs just didn't do that sort of thing.

They were driving past the Barrisford farm now, Thoroughbreds contentedly cropping the lush green grass, their coats darkened by the mid-morning drizzle. Foals nursed or cropped grass near their mothers, or stood with newly made friends, unsure whether to play or rest. The development slowly choking out so much of Virginia's horse and hunt country with suburban houses, shopping centers, and office parks was blessedly banned in this small part of the world.

The distinctive white iron rail fence of Skylark Horse Farm appeared on the left side of the road. Cullen scooted across the taxi's backseat and stared out the cab window at the Larks' southeastern pasture which, like the rest of Skylark, resembled more than anything an English farm. Thick four- and five-foot-tall hedges, not fences, separated the different fields, creating a gentle, almost serene atmosphere so different from the high-octane vibrancy at Mackenzie Farm.

The taxi had gone almost half a mile up the road when Cullen suddenly saw movement. "Stop!" he said.

The bearded Sikh driver obligingly pulled off the road on the right and stopped the cab as Cullen watched a Lark rider school a tall, powerfully built bay over a hedge, taking him at it straight on, then looping around and coming at it from the right, then from the left, then from straight on again. Over and over in the steady drizzle.

Anyone else could have been mistaken that rider for a teenage boy, boots and jeans and short-sleeved purple shirt darkened by rain, slender five-foot-six inch body moving as one with the bay; leg position perfect; line from bit, through reins, to bent elbow perfect; back straight and pressed forward over the bay's strong neck. But Cullen knew differently.

This was no teenage boy, this was the part owner, manager, and chief trainer of the Skylark Horse Farm, Samantha Fay Lark herself. It didn't matter that the drizzle and distance and riding helmet obscured her face, or that he couldn't see her copper braid bobbing between her shoulder blades. He'd known her all of her life. He'd recognize her anywhere and at any distance.

"I'll be back in just a minute," he said, opening the cab door.

"The meter will keep running," the driver warned.

"Fine."

Cullen walked across the road, climbed through the fence's white iron bars, opened his black Hong Kong umbrella, and walked across thick wet grass toward horse and rider . . . who ignored him. Cullen grinned. Sam had to be surprised to see him, he wasn't expected until next week, but that didn't matter. Samantha Fay Lark had more sangfroid than anyone he'd ever met. It's what made her such a formidable competitor in Grand Prix and horse trials events. It's what had enabled her to beat him three poker hands out of five when they were teenagers.

He could see her clearly now and it felt as if he was stepping back in time. He could only marvel. Sam might be . . . what? Well, if he was thirty, then she was twenty-eight. But she still looked just as she had at sixteen: a scruffy tomboy who could do her job better than just about any man or woman in the country. A rush of happiness swept through him at seeing her again, catching him by surprise. He hadn't realized how much he'd missed her during these last months . . . well, years, really. The last time they had spent any real time together had probably been five years ago at her mother's funeral and wake. It had rained that day, too.

Admiration for the ballet of rider and horse taking the hedge twenty feet away turned to concern as Cullen slipped on the slick grass. Was Sam deliberately trying to break her neck?

She had the bay take the hedge at a right angle coming toward him. The horse took it cleanly, neither expending too much energy and popping over the hedge, nor too little energy and brushing the hedge with his hooves. She pulled him down immediately to a walk and then slowly circled Cullen.

"My, my, my," she said with an exaggerated drawl as she stopped the bay directly in front of him, "if it isn't Daddy Warbucks. What brings you to my humble pasturage, your High and Mightiness?"

"I'm lost," Cullen retorted. "I'm looking for the Daisy Mae Oriental Beauty Parlor and Chop Shop."

Not even a hint of a smile. "Two miles down the road and hang a right."

She had just directed him to the only gay roadhouse in the county. He couldn't hold back a low chuckle. "It's good to see you, too, Sam. You look grand, if a trifle damp. Couldn't you at least have worn a slicker?"

"Some idiot weatherman said it would be clear today. I don't mind. A little rain never hurt anyone. Except Whitney, of course. Rain wreaks havoc with those hair sculptures Stefano creates for her."

He ignored the hint, because he was determined *not* to appear eager for the teeniest tidbit of news about his beloved. Instead, he walked slowly around the bay and his rider. "Good overall proportion and consolidation," he pontificated, scanning the gelding. "Broad, deep chest. High wither with good, long, muscular shoulder. Well-shaped back. Wide, muscular loin. Good close-angled hind legs. There's some spring in them. Elegant, straight head. Eyes intelligent, honest, spirited. Small, alert ears with fine points. Very self-confident air." He stopped in front of Sam again. "I don't know what it is, but I like it."

"This is Lark Magic, you brain-dead businessman."

"That's Magic?" Cullen said in surprise. It had been a few years since he'd last visited the Lark stables. He usually split his time during his brief visits home between the Mackenzie estate and Whitney Sheridan's home . . . and luscious self. "Looks like that breeding program of yours is really paying dividends," he said. "So, why are you trying to kill off such prime horseflesh on this slick grass?"

Her slim nose rose an inch higher in the air. "Magic has to be able to take a fence under even the most treacherous conditions. I know it's not on *your* calendar, but the Mackenzie Horse Trials are only three months away, it'll be his first advanced competition, and I want him ready for anything."

"Even if it means getting yourself killed in the process? This grass is as slick as ice."

Sam shook her head in disgust. "Brain dead *and* stupid. Unlike those wet Italian clodhoppers of yours, Lark Magic has shoes with studs. So, why aren't you in Hong Kong leveraging the stock market or whatever it is you corporate giants do?"

"I was able to finish up contract negotiations with the Chinese government early," Cullen replied, the drizzle tapping lightly on his umbrella.

"Surely there was some merger breathlessly awaiting your attention in London or New York?"

"There's only one merger I'm interested in, and it's right here in Virginia."

"Think you can negotiate equitable terms?" she inquired innocently.

He smiled. "I've spent the last twelve years honing my skills."

She laughed at him. "And Whitney's spent a *lifetime* honing hers. Wake up and read the fine print, Daddy Warbucks. You're out of your depth. Whitney will have you on *her* terms or not at all. Not that that's bothered you in the past, of course."

Cullen sighed inwardly. Sam was not taking him seriously and he was used to everyone taking him seriously. But then, money—even the substantial amount he had piled up—had never impressed Sam. "I've made a career out of getting what I want. That's not about to change now."

"The business world has *not* improved your ego, Mr. Mackenzie, but it does appear to agree with you," Sam said. Dark brown eyes that had never lied to him, or flirted with him, or deceived him scanned him slowly up and down. "You look good."

She meant it. He was both amused and secretly pleased. He looked *her* up and down. "You haven't changed."

"I wish I could take that as a compliment," Sam said with a sigh.

He grinned at her. "How's the brat?"

"My little sister is currently raising hell in Rome. According to her letters, Erin hasn't stopped celebrating since she was named first cellist for the Italian Symphony Orchestra six months ago."

"And how's Calida doing?"

"Oh," Sam said, a knowing smile beginning to spread across her mouth, "she's as motherly and as pragmatic as ever, despite the Grand Affair."

"What grand affair?" Cullen demanded.

"With Bobby Craig, of course."

"You're kidding."

"Nope. My foreman and my housekeeper have been carrying on a scorching romance since your last visit. They just think that no one knows. And no one does, except for me," Sam said with a grin.

"Oh, come on! At least Miguel must know that his own sister and Bobby Craig are involved?"

"Hasn't a clue. Men are pretty oblivious to this sort of thing."

"We are not!"

Sam regarded him with open disdain. "When a woman doesn't want a man to know what she feels, the whole cretinous lot of you are in the dark, trust me."

"Sexist," he charged.

"Man," she countered.

He laughed. "And how's Whitney doing?"

Her knowing grin widened and curled into a sickening display of self-satisfied amusement. "More beautiful than ever. More voluptuous, more graceful, more—"

"All right, all right," Cullen growled, "I get the picture."

"Oh, Daddy Warbucks, you haven't even got the tintype. There is a second contender for my fair friend's hand, or at least for her body."

The world turned black. "Who?" Cullen demanded grimly.

Sam crossed one leg over the low pommel of her English cross-country saddle and studied her short fingernails. "Noel Beaumont. Tall, dark, and handsome. Very French, very rich. He wants to buy an American horse farm and your dad invited him to stay at your place and tour the glories of Virginia."

"Beaumont? As in two-time Olympic gold medalist, three-time world champion Noel Beaumont?"

"One and the same."

Cullen swore, bitterly.

Sam laughed. "Now, now. You must know that horsemanship is *not* what captures Whitney's heart."

"Beaumont and I have also crossed swords on a few Asian business deals," Cullen retorted sourly.

"Who won?"

"We've split about fifty-fifty."

"Ooh. Not good. I guess it really could go either way on this one after all. Whitney has definitely been enjoying his attentions."

"Damn!"

Sam shook her head at him. "Cullen, Cullen, Cullen, how can you even think of Whitney when you've been betrothed to me for the last twenty years?"

A chuckle escaped him as he shook his head at *her*. "We are not betrothed, as you so quaintly put it. We have never been betrothed."

"Of course we have! I declared my matrimonial intentions on a hot and humid summer day twenty years ago. You can't have forgotten."

"How can I when you constantly remind me and everyone else in the county of that childhood nonsense? *Try* to get this through your stubborn head, Young Lark: I am *not* going to marry you."

"No?"

"No!"

She looked suitably downcast. "You done me wrong, Cullen Mackenzie."

He gave it up and laughed from the sheer pleasure of her company. "*God,* I've missed you, Sam."

She grinned at him. "Sure you have. You've thought of me every day you haven't thought about Whitney. And since you think about her three hundred sixty-five days out of the year . . ."

"Hey, I'm a little obsessed, I admit, but I've got it managed."

"Sure you do. So what *are* your plans now that you're back?"

"I'm going to woo, wed, and carry off Whitney, just as I've always dreamed."

"In one summer? And with Noel Beaumont in residence? *Sure* you are."

"You might try to treat my romantic quest with a bit more respect, Sam."

"And miss out on all this fun? I'd rather ride a sloth stoned on barbiturates at the Mackenzie Horse Trials. No quarter given on *this* little romp, Daddy Warbucks."

"I wish you'd stop calling me that. I am neither bald nor right-wing, nor am I fond of grossly independent vacant-eyed redheads!"

" 'Vacant heart, and hand, and eye, Easy live and quiet die,' " she quoted.

"What?"

"*The Bride of Lammermoor,* you brain-dead businessman. Walter Scott. You used to be able to quote him by the hour. Have you given up *everything* you used to love?" Sam demanded.

"I've been a bit too busy of late to read Sir Walter Scott."

" 'Tell that to the marines—the sailors won't believe it,' " she quoted.

"*Redgauntlet,* volume two. Ha!"

She grinned. "There's hope for you yet, Daddy Warbucks."

The taxi horn blared at them from across the road. "I'm going home," Cullen said, scowling at her.

"And about time, too," she retorted, not the least affected by his scowl. "It's a good thing Whitney has the patience of a saint, otherwise you'd find yourself shut out in the rain right about now." She looked at the wet world around her in seeming surprise. "Oops. Better get a move on, Ivanhoe."

Cullen couldn't decide whether to stick his tongue out at her, or laugh. He settled for a lazy, two-fingered salute and sauntered off toward the taxi.

" 'Hail to the Chief who in triumph advances,' " she called after him.

Scott again. *The Lady of the Lake.* He tried not to laugh, and failed. Sam had always been able to make him laugh, at himself and at the world. In the first few years after Teague's death, she'd been the only one who *could* make him laugh. Trust her to laugh at his homecoming and his successes and his matrimonial intentions now. If there was a serious side to Samantha Fay Lark, he'd never met it.

He walked back to the cab through the heavy drizzle, slid onto the backseat, and watched the windows begin to fog up as the driver pulled the car back onto Mackenzie Lane and continued toward Mackenzie Farm. Toward home. And family. And soon, very soon . . .

Whitney.

Beautiful, golden, lovely, perfect, poised, elegant Whitney. He had loved her forever it seemed. He had loved her even though she had loved his brother, Teague. He had loved her even though Teague had loved her. He had loved her through Teague's death and his own self-imposed exile to Yale and then New York, London, Hong Kong. He had spent the last twelve years slaying dragons to prove himself worthy and win the prize he wanted above all others. *Whitney.* And now, finally, he had come home to claim her, no matter what plans Noel Beaumont might have for her.

Was Beaumont a real threat, or had Sam merely been teasing him? She had a habit of making it hard for people to know when she was pulling their leg and when she was serious.

Knowing Beaumont as he did, though, Cullen had to consider his presence and his pursuit of Whitney a problem. Damn! Just when he'd thought he'd surmounted every obstacle, here was another hurdle to leap.

An image of Whitney as he'd said good-bye at the end of his last trip home nine months earlier flooded his mind. Tears slowly sliding down her sweet face. Mouth hot and soft and lingering on his. Voluptuous body molded perfectly to his.

He let out a ragged sigh. One more hurdle or a hundred, Whitney was more than worth it.

The cab drove through the green wrought iron gate with "Mackenzie" emblazoned in intricate iron scrollwork at the top. The driveway slowly curved and turned and then suddenly, there before him, was the dark red brick Georgian manor standing on the site that had been home to generations of Mackenzies since Aidan Mackenzie had first come to Virginia in 1643. Cullen's heart filled his chest as the cab swung to a stop in front of the low porch and the broad white front door.

He paid the driver and stepped out of the taxi, feeling that unaccountable excitement again, even though he shouldn't be excited. He'd left his love of this place behind him long ago, buried in Teague's grave. But his happy heart would hear none of it.

Home, it said. *I'm home.*

He walked up to the front door and just stood staring at it as the driver set his suitcases on the porch behind him and then drove off. The old tension and anxiety he usually felt when he came home were beginning to reassert themselves. This white door represented everything he had been running away from for the last twelve years.

Cullen sighed with self-disgust, pushed the door open, and walked into the familiar Great Hall with its rose-colored Italian marble floor. There was no one in sight. His eyes swept the Hall once, taking in at a glance the perpetual vase of his mother's roses—pale orange today—on the delicate Regency table ahead of him, and the grand marble staircase that swept up to the second floor and the balcony there overlooking the Hall.

Knowing that his father was undoubtedly down at the stables supervising the training of the renowned Mackenzie Thoroughbreds, and that his mother would be tending her almost equally renowned gardens at the back of the house, Cullen turned to the left to make his way through the west wing and back outside, when he heard the low murmur of voices coming from the morning parlor on his right.

Shrugging, he pulled open the sliding oak-paneled doors—proclaiming "Behold! The Prodigal Son!" —just in time to see the love of his life locked in an ardent clinch with the man immediately catapulted to the top of Cullen's Most Hated List—Noel Beaumont. "Rehearsing for my homecoming, Whitney?" he politely inquired, his hands shoved into the front pockets of his gray suit pants.

"Cullen!" Whitney shrieked, jerking herself from Beaumont's too accommodating arms. "What are you doing here? We didn't expect you until next week."

"I wanted to surprise you," Cullen said walking to within three feet of the most beautiful woman on this or any other continent. "It seems I've succeeded."

Head held high, Whitney refused to blush or look guilt-stricken. Whitney Sheridan—only child of Virginia's renowned elder statesman, Senator Albert Sheridan—stood at five feet nine inches in her stocking feet and every male who came into her orbit was grateful for every inch . . . and her perfect oval face, large deep blue eyes, lush full mouth, high perfect breasts, tiny waist, and legs that went on forever. Add to that mounds of cascading golden hair, and it was a wonder she hadn't been carried off to the altar long before this.

But she had been loyal to Cullen, she had waited for him all these years. It seemed, however, based on the current evidence, that she had not been waiting alone.

"Of all the inconsiderate men," she pouted, walking up to him in her short pink dress and kissing his rigid cheek. "I've spent weeks planning our reunion and buying the perfect dress and convincing Stefano that it isn't beneath his dignity to leave that cathedral to coiffures he calls a salon to come to my house to style my hair, and *you* have to ruin it all by coming home early!"

The humor of the situation finally hit home. Trust Whitney to be caught kissing another man and then turn around and blame *him* for it. "I'm sorry, Whitney," he gravely replied as he struggled against a grin. Whitney did not like to be laughed at. "I only wanted to surprise you."

"Surprise me with a bracelet or a ring, for heaven's sake, but not your homecoming!"

"Oh, I've got the ring, too," Cullen said, unable to hold back a smile.

"Ah yes," Noel Beaumont purred from behind Whitney, "but will you have the chance to use it?"

Some of the humor left Cullen. He directed at Mr. Beaumont the glare he had used over the years to fell the hardiest deal-makers, only to find that it made not the least impression. Mr. Beaumont smiled engagingly back at him as he raised Whitney's left hand to his lips.

Cullen developed a virulent dislike of the French. "Beaumont, you're intruding," he stated.

"I fervently hope so," Noel replied.

Cullen removed Whitney's hand from Noel's lips and clasp. "Your poaching days are over," he informed the Frenchman, "get used to it."

Mr. Beaumont's smile became beatific. "But is that not for the dazzling Whitney to decide, my friend?"

"Yes," Whitney tartly retorted, "it is!"

Smiling, Cullen pulled her into his arms and gazed down into her wide blue eyes. "No coup d'etats, my love, not at this late stage of the game."

"Cullen Mackenzie, don't you dare—" she began.

"Hi, Whitney, I'm home," he murmured, just before he kissed her, long and slow and thorough, just as he'd fantasized doing every day of the last nine months he'd had to do without her in Hong Kong. She was all warm, soft, curvaceous woman in his arms, her mouth opening readily to him, her arms twining around his neck, her body molding itself to his as the top of his head spun off into the stratosphere. Still, he retained just enough sanity to ensure that she kissed him a whole lot longer than she had kissed Noel Beaumont. He'd come home to claim his woman, and no Frenchman—however, tall, dark, and handsome—was going to derail his plans.

"Cullen, you're home!" Laurel Mackenzie shrieked from the parlor doorway.

Cullen was forced to relinquish the love of his life so he could turn and give his mother the bone-cracking bear hug she insisted upon receiving every time he came home. "Don't you dare cry," he said fondly.

"I'm a mother. I'll cry when and where I choose," Laurel declared, brushing a smattering of tears from her cheek as she took a step back from her son, tilting her head back to look up at him.

Laurel Mackenzie stood no more than five feet two inches tall. Over the years, she had devoted herself to her family, to her gardens, and to the Mackenzie Thoroughbreds, not to starvation diets and obsessive exercise. She was plump and fit and surprisingly strong, which she proved by returning his bear hug and nearly breaking a half dozen of his ribs in the process. "You look wonderful! Just wonderful!" she tearfully declared.

"Thanks," he gasped. "So do you."

"And dear Whitney here to greet you," Laurel burbled, her face glowing. "Oh, it couldn't be better."

"That," Cullen said with a glance at Noel Beaumont, "is a matter of opinion."

"Oh, now don't you go getting yourself into a jealous snit over *Noel*," Laurel chided him. "Why, he's practically *family*!"

"*Madame!*" Noel said. "You move me, deeply."

"If you adopt him," Cullen said, smiling down into Laurel's brown eyes, "I will drown myself in Mackenzie Lake."

His mother dissolved into a gurgle of laughter just as his father strode into the floral-decorated morning parlor.

"Ah," said Keenan Mackenzie, hands thrust into the front pockets of his tan breeches, "Williams wasn't hallucinating. You *are* home."

Keenan was a few inches shorter than his son and all sinew, his blue eyes as unnervingly direct as they'd always been.

"Hi, Dad," Cullen said, meeting his father's gaze and feeling as he always did—that he was meeting some test of manhood. He just had never been sure exactly what that test was. "Surprise!"

Keenan chuckled as he gave him a quick hug. "Welcome home, son. You've disrupted an entire day of work, you know."

"Sure, but I'm worth it."

"Any Mackenzie is," Keenan retorted with a grin.

"Are you really going to stay the entire summer?" Laurel asked.

"Cross my heart," Cullen said with a fond smile, which grew as he glanced at Whitney. "I have all sorts of plans for how I'm going to spend my first vacation in ten years. Plans," he added with a darkling glance at Noel Beaumont, "that don't include you."

"A good general always adjusts his strategy to meet unforeseen circumstances, does he not?" Noel inquired with a grin.

Cullen turned to his father. "The milk money I've sent home each month wasn't enough? You've had to take in boarders?"

Keenan laughed. "Don't worry, Son, we've kept your room inviolate."

"Although we did show Noel all of the steeplechase and horse trials ribbons and trophies you won when you were a teenager," Laurel said.

"They were most charming," said Noel.

Cullen winced. Somehow he just couldn't see his youthful awards stacking up against two Olympic gold medals, let alone three world championships. "We Mackenzies are renowned for our skill in entertaining guests."

"To my benefit," Noel said, raising Laurel's fingers to his lips, "I assure you."

She looked as if she would coo at any moment.

Cullen nudged his father. "Shouldn't you be bellowing 'Unhand my wife!' and brandishing a gun right about now?"

Keenan chuckled. "Our French boarder has a way with women, I'll give him that. And with horses. He's already registered to ride in the Mackenzie Horse Trials. That's at the end of September, as you may recall. If you want to take him on in some honest competition, you might consider entering yourself."

"No," Cullen said firmly.

"But—"

"Dad, horses are your life, not mine. I'm a businessman now, remember? A very successful businessman. I'll meet

Beaumont in the boardroom or at Whitney's feet, but not on horseback."

"Think you're out-classed?"

"No," Cullen said, stung, "just rusty, and I intend to stay that way."

"Okay," Whitney said, hands on her delectable hips, "why are there three men in this room and not one of them paying attention to me?"

Two of the three men began making instant reparations as Laurel, laughing, was enveloped in her husband's arms.

Two

WITH A SIGH of the utmost satisfaction, Samantha let the shower wash the last of the mud from her body. She'd begun to think she'd never be clean again after a morning that had begun with her five o'clock rounds with Bobby Craig, her foreman, and Miguel Torres, her head trainer, inspecting the progress made by the sixty-three mares, geldings, colts, and fillies born from her seven-year-old breeding program and trained by Sam, and Miguel, and the five men and women under him. At seven o'clock she'd been in the saddle, schooling her four most promising six-year-olds—first Flora Lark, then Central Lark, Lark Ness, and Lark Magic—an hour each in the drizzle.

Then an hour walking among the foals and the yearlings, inspecting them for any injuries or flaws, stroking them, talking to them, leaning gently against them so they would be completely comfortable and trusting when they were finally old enough to begin training. She'd spent her afternoon schooling the four most promising five-year-olds an hour each in the rain, followed by supervising the training of the most promising four-year-olds for two hours in the indoor arena, because by then the rain had become a downpour.

She still had to toil for an hour over her hated accounting books and she had to write to Erin. She was two days late as it was. But for now, she grabbed the bar of soap for a second go-round, happily remembering her mid-morning break. Cullen was actually home for the summer and looking *very* good.

The soap squirted through her fingers and bonked against the floor of the shower.

She picked it up, laughing at herself. Oh, it was good to have him back! She had seen him walking across the pasture, she had seen him standing near the hedge watching her and Magic, and she'd felt an odd kind of reluctance to acknowledge him. Because when she did, she'd feel like she always did when he came home: she'd be eight again, and he'd be ten and perfect and her hero.

So she had waited while her informally adopted big brother had stood calmly in the rain, black umbrella shielding him, perfect gray suit molded to his six-foot-two-inch frame, strict propriety belied by his shoulder-length blond hair. When his gray eyes finally met hers, happiness had surged through her. Not that she had any intention of letting him know that. She had never gotten mushy on Cullen in her life and she wasn't about to start now.

Besides, it had felt so good to banter with him again, to fall into their old rhythm of conversation as if he had never been away, to watch him painstakingly wend his way around to asking about Whitney. Sam laughed out loud as she rinsed the soap from her body and began to shampoo her hair. Poor Cullen was as messed up about her best friend as ever. Whitney was the luckiest woman in this or any other century to win the heart of so steadfast and obsessed a man.

If only—Sam stopped, then let herself finish the

thought. If only Cullen would give up his ghosts, maybe this wouldn't be just a summer visit. Maybe he'd stay. "And maybe the Chippendale models will worship me as a goddess," she muttered in disgust.

She stepped out of the shower and had just begun to dry off when her bedroom phone rang. A towel wrapped around her wet hair, a towel wrapped around her wet body, she trotted to her bedside table and answered the phone on the third ring.

"Daisy Mae Oriental Beauty Parlor and Chop Shop."

Familiar laughter greeted her. "Samantha Fay, you are a fool," Laurel Mackenzie informed her.

"Yes, ma'am. How's Daddy Warbucks?"

"Home safe and sound, as you very well know. That's why I'm calling. I want to invite you to dinner tonight, to welcome Cullen home properly.

"I am there," Sam assured her. "I'll even wear a dress for the occasion."

"Now Samantha Fay, don't get my hopes up. I haven't seen your knees in years."

"Well, they were never much to rave about. What time's dinner?"

"Seven-thirty."

Sam glanced at her bedside clock. It was nearly seven. "Gee, thanks for thinking of me last."

Laurel's laughter bubbled across the phone line. "Keenan and I have been pumping Cullen for every detail of his life since he got in. We all just came up for air and realized it was well past dinner time. You were first and only on our list, Samantha Fay, and you know it. So stop playing coy and come eat."

"Yes, ma'am," Sam said with a grin. "Want me to pick up Whitney?"

"She's already here. She and Noel had just come back from touring some of the local horse farms with some real estate agent when Cullen arrived. It couldn't have been a better homecoming!"

"I'll bet," Samantha said, having a fairly good idea of Cullen's reaction to finding Whitney with Noel. It boded well for tonight. She'd be enjoying a little drama and romance at last, if only at second hand. "Should be a fun evening. See you soon." She hung up the phone and then used the intercom to call the kitchen. "Calida?"

"You don't have to bellow," came the response. "I can hear you perfectly well."

"If you're making dinner, stop. I've been invited over to the Mackenzies. The night is your own to do with as you like."

Humming happily—she loved furthering Calida's secret romance—Sam padded back into the bathroom. She dried her copper hair and pulled it back into her usual French braid, then dressed in a simple navy blue sleeveless knit dress that brushed her calves, slipped on a pair of sandals, and headed downstairs to the kitchen for a snack. She hadn't had anything to eat since breakfast and she was starving.

"Smells good," she said, walking through the white swinging door into the butter yellow kitchen. "Will it keep till tomorrow?"

"My stew is always better on the second day," Calida informed her as she shoved a large pot into the industrial-size refrigerator.

Calida Torres, at forty-two, was plump but solid, sturdy, and strong. She combined Filipina motherliness with a drill sergeant's demeanor. She might be an inch shorter than Sam, but sheer personality made her seem about ten feet tall. She had worked as a housekeeper for the Larks for twenty-four years, as her family had worked for the Larks since Colonel Augustus Lark had helped evacuate the Torres family and other Filipinos out of Manila following the American invasion of 1898. During those twenty-four years, Calida had funded the college education of four brothers and sisters, including Miguel, earned her own degree at night school, and had just recently begun romancing Samantha's usually taciturn foreman.

Sam hopped up onto a kitchen counter, pulled the pig-shaped cookie jar to her side, grabbed a large chocolate chip cookie, and began munching. "Cullen's back."

"So I've heard," Calida replied, scraping carrot and celery and potato scraps into the garbage disposal. "Does Whitney know?"

"Oh yeah," Sam said, grabbing a second cookie. Calida made the best chocolate chip cookies this side of the universe. "She was there when he turned up. If I know my Whitney, she's probably furious with Cullen for not giving her the chance to wear her newest best dress to welcome him home."

"Whitney could wear burlap and Cullen wouldn't care."

"He is a tad myopic where Whitney's concerned," Sam agreed.

Calida's black eyes cast her a quick glance before she began wiping down the counter nearest her. "You're wearing a dress."

"It's a special occasion," Samantha said with a shrug.

"I don't think I've seen you in a dress in the five years since Jean's funeral."

"Dresses aren't really practical for riding," Sam said, leaning against the cupboards behind her and reaching for a third cookie. "Ow!" she said as Calida slapped her hand away from the cookie jar.

"I won't have you spoiling your dinner," Calida informed her. "Rose Stewart works hard to prepare good meals for the Mackenzies. You will show her the proper appreciation."

"Okay, okay," Sam grumbled, sliding off the counter.

The kitchen screen door banged closed. Bobby Craig walked into the room.

"Evening, Sam," he said. "Hello, Calida."

The housekeeper didn't even glance at him. The lady was tough.

"Hey, Bobby," Sam said. "What's up?"

"You're wearing a dress," her foreman observed.

"So I've heard."

"I don't think I've seen you in a dress since—"

"What is this?" Sam demanded. "A conspiracy of two?" She quickly hid her smile as Bobby and Calida shared a guilty glance before Calida turned away, ostensibly to empty the dishwasher. "So, what can I do for you, Bobby, on this wet Virginia evening?"

"Chancery Farms called from California. Tom Harris wants to buy two more of our remaining Thoroughbreds."

"Bless his pea-pickin' little heart. I've always liked that man."

"He bid six thousand less than our bottom-line."

"Then Tom Harris can go whistle," Sam stated flatly.

"That's what I told him. He's sleeping on it, which means he'll call back tomorrow and, after a suitable amount of dickering, meet our price."

"Thanks, Bobby. Good work."

"My pleasure." Her African-American foreman stood in the Lark kitchen, freshly showered, in a painfully starched white shirt and crisp black slacks, boots polished, black hair cut almost to the scalp. He had not come here to chat with Sam.

"Oh my," she said, pointedly glancing at her wristwatch, "just look at the time. I've got to go. You two will have to find something other than my dress to talk about."

She sailed out of the kitchen, chuckling to herself. There was definite pleasure in furthering a secret romance, however obliquely.

She walked out to the garage, climbed into her six-year-old black Audi, and drove down Mackenzie Lane. Shaded by a canopy of ancient white oaks, Mackenzie Lane took a leisurely path through these Blue Ridge foothills of Loudoun County. It linked together some of the country's most important horse farms and families, including Sam's immediate neighbors: the Barrisfords with one thousand acres of prime land and their landmark home Cambria Hall to the south, and the massive Mackenzie Farm to the north. Skylark was sandwiched in between.

The sky was beginning to clear as the red rim of the sun sank below the western horizon, turning the Blue Ridge mountains nearly twenty miles away a dark purple. A few sparrows, cardinals, and larks were swooping from tree to tree beside the road and cruising over the Mackenzies' southern pasture. Thoroughbreds still stretched their necks down to the thick grass, contentedly cropping their way through the evening, tails occasionally whisking off a fly.

Sam loved it. She loved all of it. From the time she was four, she had always thanked God in her evening prayers for bringing Jeremiah Lark to Virginia in 1636 and guiding him to this land she loved with a ferocity she was afraid to reveal to anyone.

She drove through the green Mackenzie gates and up to the Mackenzie manor house, an amused smile tugging her lips. But then, any evidence of Mackenzie ambition always amused Sam and this was evidence in its rawest state.

There had been two previous houses on this site before Dugan Mackenzie decided it was time to make an architectural statement. He imported an English architect and began construction on the red brick Georgian manor in 1728. The central rectangular portion of the manor rose two stories to a steep hipped roof with dormers. It was flanked by a pair of story-and-a-half wings ending in a pair of tall chimneys at both ends. The long, horizontal building had a central entrance framed by pilasters that supported a frieze depicting Dugan Mackenzie with his favorite Thoroughbred.

The owners of Westover Plantation in Charles City County began construction of their remarkably similar Georgian manor house in 1730, loudly insisting that Dugan Mackenzie had stolen both their architect and their plans. Dugan took umbrage and settled the matter by soundly thrashing the Westover entry in a horse race attended by half the colony. Mackenzie Manor had appeared first in the tourist guidebooks ever since. Samantha insisted this was simply a matter of alphabetization, but the current Mackenzies ignored her.

The reed-thin Mackenzie housekeeper, Margery Thompson, let her into the house and escorted her through the wide Great Hall, turning to the right through the floral morning parlor, into the gilt-edged drawing room, and finally into the family room with its huge brick fireplace. This had always been Sam's favorite room. It lacked the usual Mackenzie determination to promote themselves as one of the first families of Virginia, and had instead all of the Mackenzie warmth.

The brick fireplace faced the double-door entrance to the room. Over-stuffed sofas and chairs in creams and greens and chocolate browns were cheerfully scattered around the floor. The walls were paneled in golden oak, the ceiling was festooned with elaborate white Georgian plasterwork. Cut flowers in vases were everywhere. Laurel Mackenzie was one of Virginia's most noted horticulturists.

But Sam didn't really see the flowers or the furniture or anything except the delicious sight of Whitney Sheridan seated regally in a cream-colored arm chair, with Cullen in doting attendance on one side, and Noel on the other. Damn! The romance and the drama she must have missed thus far! Well, the night was young. She still had a chance to get in some vicarious thrills.

"There you are!" Laurel cried, jumping up from the sofa where she had been sitting with Keenan. She trotted up to Samantha, Keenan on her heels. "Samantha, darling, you *did* wear a dress! I'm so honored"

Laurel kissed Sam on both cheeks. Keenan—his close-cropped pale blond hair so different from his son's golden mane—warmly repeated these greetings.

"Interesting evening?" Sam softly inquired.

Laughter-filled pale blue eyes looked into hers. "You know the Mackenzies' competitive spirit, Sam," Keenan said.

Sam sighed heavily. "If only you'd called me sooner."

"Ah yes." Noel Beaumont had appeared at her side. "Your company has been sorely missed, Samantha," he said, raising her hands to his lips. "You look most charming in that dress."

"Well," Sam said ruefully, glancing at Whitney's dress, "it ain't five square inches of pink silk."

"With your coloring? I should hope not!"

"My, you're good at this," Samantha said admiringly as she smiled up at Noel. Then she waved cheerfully at the couple kissing behind him. "Hi, Whitney. Hi, Cullen. Well, now that the niceties have been attended to, " she said, turning back to Laurel and Keenan, "where's the food? I'm starved."

Cullen pulled just far enough away from Whitney to frown at Sam. "Can't a man have a touching reunion with the woman he loves without you complaining about your stomach?"

"I can't help it," she retorted. "Kissing makes me hungry. Speaking of which—" she said brightly as she turned back to Laurel.

"Patience, my dear," Laurel said, "because there is our trusty butler Williams standing right behind you and trying to discreetly intimate that dinner is served. Am I right, Williams?"

"Yes, Madam," the British import replied with strict formality, amusement lurking in his hazel eyes.

"Excellent," Laurel said as she took her husband's arm. "Noel, be the perfect houseguest and escort our poor starving Samantha Fay into dinner."

"With the utmost pleasure, *Madame*," Noel replied with a slight bow.

"Poor Noel," Sam said sympathetically as they all walked back through the Great Hall and into the rosewood dining room, "Cullen isn't home even twelve hours and already you get relegated to dotty neighbor escort service."

"You are not dotty, you are a delight," Noel avowed. Black eyes began to twinkle. "And the night is still young, is it not?"

She and Noel were seated directly opposite Whitney and Cullen, with Keenan and Laurel on either side. The table was just small enough for all of them to converse easily, which meant that Noel could direct any comment he chose to Whitney and there was nothing Cullen could do about it.

Yet even with the distracting glory of Whitney Sheridan before him, Noel made a point of also engaging Samantha in conversation, occasionally flattering her, doing what he could to make her laugh. He had the best manners of any man she'd ever met, and she liked him for them. She also liked how comfortable he was in his own body, and how comfortable he was with his innate sensuality which always made her very aware in his company that she was a woman.

Tonight, however, she simply wanted to be a spectator at the Wide Wide World of Romantic Gamesmanship being conducted before her by acknowledged masters who knew the rules and would inflict no serious injury.

The general conversation in which the game was played wove in and out of the farms Noel had toured, Keenan's hopes for Mackenzie's Pride, an eight-year-old gelding, in the upcoming Mackenzie Horse Trials—a three-day event of dressage, cross-country, and show-jumping competition in the last week of September—Cullen's recent business activities in Hong Kong, Laurel's gardens, and Whitney's (by now habitual) triumph at the annual Red Cross Charity Ball.

The tools each player employed varied. Cullen deftly wielded lifelong familiarity of the woman he loved against the intoxicating newness of Noel's pursuit, while Noel exuded the Gallic charm that had served him so well in the past. Whitney, meanwhile, ran hot and cold, mostly with Cullen. She seemed determined to keep both men from making any assumptions about her intentions towards either of them.

Thus, when she wasn't talking with Keenan on her left, she was flirting with Noel opposite her, and he was flirting right back, in between asking Sam her opinion of the horse farms he had toured this week. One moment she was pointedly removing Cullen's hand from hers, and in the next moment she was feeding him an asparagus tip from her fork.

Cullen's gray eyes took on an increasingly dangerous gleam as the dinner progressed. This was not the reunion he had expected.

"I don't understand why you're looking for a horse farm in the States, Beaumont," Cullen said after a sip of red wine. "Why must you invade our once peaceful countryside? We've given France Jerry Lewis and McDonald's. Isn't that enough?"

"But no," Noel replied amiably. "I spend half of my time in America on business and I miss the horses and my training. In this way, wherever I am, I shall be home."

"A pity," Keenan said, "that you haven't found anything in Loudoun County these last two weeks to interest you."

"I dislike contradicting so amiable a host, but I have found *one* thing that interests me very much," Noel said with a significant look into Whitney's accommodating blue eyes. "But as for the farm. . . . alas, no. I want the best, you see, but you refuse to sell Mackenzie Farm."

"I'd sooner sit through a Jerry Lewis movie marathon," Keenan said with a smile.

Cullen raised his wineglass in a silent toast to his father.

"I hope you can stay for our anniversary ball in two weeks, Noel," Laurel said, laying a fond hand on his.

"*Madame,* you honor me," Noel replied. "With so much kindness and," he said, turning to Whitney, "so much beauty before me, I would stay forever if you wished it."

"We don't," Cullen cheerfully informed him.

Noel cast him an amused glance and then turned back to the matter at hand. "Have I any hope, Whitney, that you will honor me with the first dance at the ball?"

"*Whitney—*" Cullen said warningly.

She ignored him, of course. "I'd be delighted, Noel. Thank you."

"You know," Keenan complained from the head of the table, "I'd really like to have some grandchildren in the near future."

"I'm working on it, Dad," Cullen said.

"The problem is," Sam put in, "you're working on the wrong woman."

"How can you say this of your best woman friend?" Noel demanded.

"Because it's true," Sam said with a grin. "Cullen may insist that Whitney is the only woman for him, but it's all a sham. He's really going to marry me."

"*Sam,*" Cullen said wearily.

"Is this not a little sudden?" Noel inquired, his black eyes alive with curiosity.

"I don't call a twenty-year-long engagement sudden," Sam retorted.

"Ah, the childhood sweethearts! How delightful. Tell me everything."

Samantha beamed at Noel and ignored Cullen's groan and his request to Williams to refill his wineglass. "It was really very romantic. One day when I was eight and Cullen was ten and already god-like in my adoring eyes, he and his friends were jumping off Essex Bridge into Brandy Creek. Naturally, I jumped off the bridge, too. I was going down for the third time when Cullen hauled me out of the creek and pounded the water out of my lungs."

"Most impressive," Noel murmured.

"That's what I thought," Sam said with a grin. "I knew then and there that Cullen was the boy I was going to marry. He, of course, responded to my announcement of our engagement with all the horror and disbelief and ridicule of any ten-year-old boy, and," she said, casting a stern glance at Cullen, "he's never really gotten past that stage."

"The man is an imbecile," Noel pronounced.

"That's what I think. But he's bound to come to his senses sooner than later, which gives you a clear road with Whitney, so we can all be friends."

"My heartfelt thanks. But how will you bring your hero to his senses?" Noel inquired.

"Well, I've tried beating him at poker, out-riding him in every competition we've entered together—"

"You have not!" Cullen said from across the table.

"And occasionally punching him in the shoulder," Sam continued, struggling against a grin, "but nothing has worked so far. I figured next I'd try hiring some thugs to make him an offer he can't refuse."

"The plan has merit," Noel conceded, "but perhaps

you might first attempt to lure him with your feminine wiles."

"Wiles?" Sam said. "I have wiles?"

"Of the most charming," Noel assured her, raising her hand to his lips.

"Stick to one woman at a time, can't you, Beaumont?" Cullen complained from across the table.

"You see?" Noel said happily. "Already the spark of jealousy lights his eyes. Between us, we will bring *Monsieur* Mackenzie to his senses, my little one, never you fear."

Two of Whitney's slim fingers brushed Cullen's chin and turned his head to face her. "But does *Monsieur* Mackenzie want to be brought to his senses?" she murmured, her eyelids drooping seductively as she brought her lips to within scant inches of his. "Or does *Monsieur* prefer his more recent choice?"

"Game, set, and match to Miss Sheridan," Sam murmured as she watched Cullen slowly smile at his beloved with enough sensual heat to melt the chandelier above them. It was inevitable, of course. There wasn't a man breathing who didn't succumb to Whitney's charms.

Having made major inroads on a large coconut cream pie—Cullen's favorite—the dinner party adjourned to the family room for coffee and further conversation. Keenan immediately grabbed Sam and pulled her into a corner to ask her about the new line of feed she was introducing to her yearlings and that he was considering for his stock. In the middle of the conversation, she felt Cullen's gaze and looked up to see both surprise and discomfort in his gray eyes before he hastily turned his attention back to Whitney.

She understood that gaze all too well. For the last several years, she had been filling the role Cullen had once planned for himself. As a boy, he had envisioned himself becoming his father's advisor. He would be the man who would take Mackenzie Farm into the twenty-first century and make it bigger and better than ever. But he had not been around to advise his father, or to find ways to improve the farm operations, or the horses' training, or to experiment with new feed. At eighteen, he had run away from home and grief and guilt to build the career and the life his brother would have had if he had not died. It seemed he'd succeeded, right down to claiming Teague's bride as his own.

To Sam's surprise, as Keenan left her to return to his wife's side, Whitney abandoned both suitors to join *her*.

"Hello, Stranger," Whitney said coolly, leaning casually back against the fireplace.

Sam cringed. "Oh come on, Whitney. You saw me two weeks ago at your father's fund-raiser and you know it."

"Sam, dear, the fund-raiser was last *month*."

"Oh," Samantha said in a small voice.

"I think most people," Whitney said as she studied her expert manicure, "consider me more important than a horse."

"Hors*es*, Whitney. Plural. Lots of them. I know I'm working a lot, but I've got a lot of horses that need a lot of attention."

"And I don't?" Whitney demanded.

Sam burst out laughing. "*God,* you're shameless."

"I know," Whitney said with a grin. "That's why I'm so popular. I've missed you, Sam."

"I'm sorry, Whitney. Really I am. Things have been a little crazy, that's all."

"So, when are you going to start remembering to call me for a late-night chat, or invite me out to one of those macho-hero-against-the-world movies we've vowed never to tell men we like?"

"Soon, Whitney," Sam said, chuckling, "I promise. Getting ready for the Mackenzie Horse Trials has got me a bit preoccupied, but after that—"

"The Horse Trials?" Whitney sputtered. "My dear Sam, the Horse Trials are three long months away. Don't you foresee needing a best friend sometime this summer?"

"Of course I do, Whitney," Sam said, squeezing her friend's hand in hers. "But let's get realistic here. You're going to be juggling two determined men this summer. Just how much time do you really think you'll have left over for me?"

Whitney tried not to grin and failed. "True," she conceded.

"So, exactly what are your intentions toward Cullen now that he's back home?"

Whitney shrugged. "I'm going to marry him, of course. I'm not going to make it easy for him, mind you. Men appreciate a wife more when they have to work to get her."

Sam shook her head in bemusement. Whitney's lifelong use of feminine stratagems to win boyfriend after boyfriend, and Cullen Mackenzie's obsessed devotion, had been honed over the years to Machiavellian quality. She didn't envy Cullen these coming weeks. "And what about Noel Beaumont?" she asked as they watched the two men verbally fencing across the room.

"Oh, he's marvelous fun, and I have every intention of enjoying his attentions. I just don't intend to succumb to them. I mean, honestly, Sam, Noel just wants a roll in the hay. Cullen is a sure thing."

It had always impressed Samantha that, lovely as her friend was, she was absolutely clear-sighted when it came to men and what they wanted from her. And she was always very practical about what she wanted in return. "So, you'll be sending Noel away?"

"Good heavens no! I'll enjoy letting him try to seduce me and succeed only in making Cullen jealous instead."

"I get it," Sam said, nodding wisely. "You've always secretly wanted to have two men duel over you."

Whitney grinned at her. "This is my chance to fulfill a major feminine fantasy and I have no intention of letting down the side. I owe it to women everywhere."

Samantha smiled, but in her heart of hearts she just didn't get it. She had never understood the game of love. She had never considered love a game. But Whitney did, and she had turned the game into high art. It might be wise to have Keenan and Laurel hide the Mackenzie family dueling pistols—and swords—until Cullen finally got a ring on Whitney's finger.

"Thank *God* Cullen has finally come back," Whitney said, staring out the French doors at the damp gardens. "If I have to spend one more year surrounded by grass and horses and horse *riders*, I think I'll go mad."

"But you've got to admit that it's beautiful here," Sam said.

"*New York* is beautiful. *Paris* is beautiful. All of this greenery is just mind-numbingly dull."

"Sometimes, I think you must be a changeling left by the Fairy People."

"Oh come on, Sam. Every letter you wrote me when you were at the Sorbonne was filled with superlatives about how beautiful Paris was."

"Sure. But this is better."

"Only for some."

Samantha smiled at her friend. "Okay, I admit that Cullen's new jet set lifestyle perfectly complements your girlhood dreams."

"I'm going to be a player, Sam," Whitney said with barely suppressed excitement. "In the big leagues. An intimate of royalty and presidents and the real power brokers of this world. Daddy may have the respect of his peers for being such a stickler for honesty and morality in his *highly* unethical line of work, but it hasn't done *anything* for our bank account.

"Whitney, the Senator isn't exactly hurting for cash."

"Nor is he on the list of America's ten wealthiest men."

"You mean, Cullen is?" Sam said in surprise.

Whitney regarded her pityingly. "You see what living in the stable has cost you? Cullen has been in the top *five* for two years running, Sam."

"Wow," Sam said, staring at her outrageously wealthy neighbor as he took a sip of coffee. The Larks had never had much money, just enough to live comfortably and show well in company. Sam couldn't have gone to the Sorbonne if she hadn't earned a full scholarship. She couldn't have traveled across Europe the year after graduation if she hadn't worked her way through every country.

Cullen, on the other hand, had fulfilled Teague's dream of riches and power with a vengeance. But he didn't look like one of America's wealthiest men, the intimate of royalty, presidents, and power brokers. He looked like. . . . Cullen. Troubled, loving, loyal Cullen. "So what are you doing hanging around with me?" she asked Whitney. "Go hog-tie that masculine bank account and get him to the altar."

"In due time," Whitney said with a satisfied smile as she began strolling toward Cullen. "In due time."

Sam watched her friend insinuate herself between Cullen and Noel and begin the games anew. With a sigh, she turned and looked up at the portrait above the brick fireplace of fourteen-year-old Teague and sixteen-year-old Cullen. Both blond and blue-eyed like their father, they had their mother's infectious smile and their parents' *joie de vivre*. Love and happiness radiated out from the painting, warming the room on this warm Virginia night.

But not Samantha, because she knew that Cullen never

looked at that portrait. Ever. Nor, during his rare visits home in the last twelve years, had his gaze ever rested on any of the pictures that included Teague which Laurel had scattered throughout the house. Laurel and Keenan and everyone else all believed Cullen had recovered from the loss of his beloved younger brother, but Samantha knew her friend too well. The pain of Teague's death still gnawed at him. She had seen it this morning in the depths of his quiet gray eyes and even at dinner tonight. The unreasonable guilt he had taken on when Teague was killed still overshadowed every thought, every plan, every dream.

He couldn't escape that shadow. How could he, when all he had to do was look in a mirror when he shaved each morning to see the thin white crescent scar that ran from the outside edge of his high cheekbone to within an inch of the corner of his mouth? It was like a brand, forever burning into him that horrible evening twelve years ago when a drunk driver had plowed into the car Cullen was driving, nearly killing him, and crushing Teague in the passenger seat.

"He is very different." Noel Beaumont had materialized at her side and was gazing up at the portrait.

"But the core of him has held true," Sam replied. "I hope."

Noel considered her a moment. "It is a close connection between your two families, I think."

"I've always felt like we're one big extended family," Sam said, turning away from the portrait to watch Laurel and Keenan flirt by a large vase of lilies. "Cullen and Teague and I were the Three Musketeers and, when we could pry my sister Erin away from her cello, we were four adventurers romping across the vast Mackenzie estate on horseback, jumping hedges and fences in pursuit of dastardly villains, crossing over onto Lark land, and back to Mackenzie land. I think we were born blind to any borders or divisions or separation."

"But what of Whitney?"

"Surely, Noel, you must realize that Miss Sheridan does not *romp*. Usually she spent her time with Missy Barrisford dissecting the most recent issue of *Vogue*. But sometimes she'd join us for swimming forays into Mackenzie Lake, or for summer picnics in the old-growth woods the Mackenzies have maintained for generations. It was all so . . . wonderful. When Teague died," Sam glanced back at the portrait, "I lost a brother."

"Not a future husband?"

"Oh no," she said with a smile. "I'd set my sights on Cullen, remember? Besides, *Whitney* had staked her claim on Teague, so what chance did I have? She's always wanted the best and that was pretty much Teague in a nutshell."

"The younger brother was very handsome," Noel observed.

"Teague was *gorgeous*," Sam said frankly. "And he knew it. Fortunately, he had sensible parents who never let it go to his head."

"A most attractive family," Noel said with a smile as Laurel ten feet away laughed at something Keenan had whispered in her ear.

"The Mackenzies have always bred for beauty."

"They are not the only ones to do so, Samantha."

She laughed up at him. "You have had too much wine tonight, *Monsieur*. So, where is my gorgeous best friend?" she inquired in fluent French, smiling at his startled look.

"Cullen has taken her outside for some fresh air and long-denied amorous attentions," he replied in French.

"And you've come to pay attention to me," she continued in French, "rather than going out to battle Cullen for Whitney's favors? *Monsieur*, you are too good."

Noel laughed. "As it is Cullen's first night back, I do not mind conceding the field this one time. And it is no sacrifice spending my time with you. There is more to you, I think, my little one, than most people realize."

This amused Sam. "Do you flirt with every woman you meet?"

"I am not flirting. I am speaking the truth. I am glad I have not found the farm I seek, for it gives me more time to uncover the many gifts you hide away."

"Gee," Sam said wistfully, "I hope that's a double entendre, and I hope you mean it."

Noel laughed and raised her hand to his lips. "You have but to say the word, Samantha."

"Or I could just save time and hand my head on a platter to Whitney now."

Noel raised one dark eyebrow. "I believe I am still a free agent."

Sam stared up at Noel in amazement. "Have you learned *nothing* about Whitney these last two weeks?"

Three

"HEY, ANDY," Sam said as she slid off Lark Magic in the bright heat of late morning. "Give him a few sugar-dipped carrots once he's cooled down. He came through with a clean cross-country ride."

"That's my boy," said Magic's groom, Andy Bream, a punk rocker wannabe, as he patted the bay's neck. He clipped a lead shank to Magic's bridle and then handed Sam the reins to Flora Lark, a roan mare standing quietly behind him. Like the other Lark grooms, Andy was responsible for six horses. On any other horse farm, it would have been no more than three. "Flora's all warmed up. She's feeling a bit nervy. Wanted to dance on the longe line today, not walk."

Sam gave the mare a stern look. "Get over it," she commanded.

Flora blew air through her lips.

"I used to be the boss around here," Sam said with a sigh as she walked to the side of the roan to check the tightness of the girth around her belly.

"That's right, ignore me. I've only flown thousands of miles to get here."

With a startled cry, Sam spun around. There was her sister perched jauntily on the white paddock fence facing the stableyard, looking tan and chic and at least half-Italian in her white capri pants and top, her long brown hair tumbling past her shoulders.

"Erin!" Sam shrieked, not caring that she had just destroyed the delicate nervous systems of two of her best horses as she flung herself at her sister and dragged her down into her arms. "My God, my God, I can't believe it," she babbled, squeezing her sister breathless. "What are you doing here? When did you get here? Oh, I can't *believe* this!"

Laughing helplessly, Erin squeezed her back just as tight. "Now that's a proper welcome home."

"But what are you *doing* here?" Sam demanded, holding her younger sister at arm's length. "You're supposed to be in Rome raising hell, breaking lots of Italian hearts, and playing the cello now and then."

"Ah, but that was just Stage One of my master plan, Sammy. It has led to Stage Two, and Stage Two will answer all of your questions. Remember I've told you how through the years different organizations have talked about founding a National Symphony Orchestra in Washington, D.C.? Well, they've finally done it. I flew in yesterday and passed the first two rounds of auditions, which means I am definitely in. Next week, there'll be a third round of auditions to determine which musicians get which chairs."

"You'll get first! I *know* you'll get first!" Samantha said, hugging her sister ferociously.

"Well, of course I will," Erin said, grinning from ear to ear, "despite some pretty daunting competition. And all of this means, of course, that I am finally home to stay for good."

Samantha stared at her sister. "You're kidding."

"Nope," Erin said smugly. "It'll be an easy commute. So, you're stuck with me until I finally decide to marry myself off to some stud muffin gifted both sexually and intellectually, which means I'm here for the long haul."

"The world is spinning round and round," Sam said wonderingly.

Erin laughed as she slipped an arm around her sister's waist. "Now there's a call for champagne if ever I heard one. Come on," she said, pulling Sam toward the house, "let's go find us a magnum or two."

"I'll have one of the other grooms keep Flora warmed up, Miss Lark," Andy called after them.

Startled, Sam turned and stared at Andy holding the two horses. She'd actually forgotten about work for a whole two minutes! There was too much to do today to take any time off, of course, but . . . She looked at Erin standing happily beside her. But how many times did your younger sister come home to stay for good? "Thanks, Andy," she said as she pulled Erin toward the house. "Come on. Let's see if we can freak out Calida for once in our lives."

They succeeded. The unflappable Calida did not shriek as Sam had, but she did gape at Erin's sudden appearance and speak Spanish for a good ten seconds before she realized what she was doing. She hurriedly collected herself, but the victory was still sweet. More than satisfied, Erin and Sam collected a magnum of champagne and two glasses before trooping into the main room on the first floor— an open-plan combination living, dining, and family room backed by the kitchen and pantry.

Erin sprawled on the green Edwardian sofa while Sam took the matching chair opposite her and poured the first round of champagne.

"Mud in your eye," Erin said as she raised her glass to her sister.

"L'chaim," Sam said, completing their traditional toast.

They drank their champagne with a single swallow and Samantha promptly refilled their glasses, grinning from ear to ear. Erin was *home*.

Just three years separated them, but they were probably as different as two sisters could be. For the longest time, Erin had been an enigma to Sam. As a child, she had preferred sitting inside listening to music, or playing the cello, all day long rather than spending her day on horseback. But Sam had finally found a touchstone when she ran against the steel beneath her sister's musical exterior. Erin was as strong as they came, and Sam respected and liked that. Erin also had a robust sense of humor that had added hours of laughter to Sam's childhood and girlhood. Erin also knew her way around all the masculine wiles ever directed at womankind and had been an invaluable resource when Sam had finally broken out of her self-imposed shell at the Sorbonne.

"You realize, of course," Sam said, "that I just mailed you a five-page letter *yesterday*."

Erin grinned happily at her. "So tell me all the news, at least about the Romantic Triangle. Your last letter was better than a suspense novel. I'm all aquiver with anticipation."

Sam ruefully shook her head. "This last week has been quite an education, let me tell you. It's been like watching a dramatization of Sun-tzu's *The Art of War*. Cullen has turned the Sheridan house into a jungle. Every available table and mantel is crowded with every color and kind of flower you can name. Then, of course, there are the European chocolates, the very expensive little trinkets Cartier and Tiffany's love to supply, plus teddy bears and Barbie and Ken dolls in full wedding regalia, *and* an honest-to-God Mystery Date board game with Cullen's picture and stats on every card. Meanwhile, *Noel* has gone in for personally authored poetry, which isn't half-bad, I grant you, plus picnic baskets with racy invitations, and last night a serenade by some local Irish fiddlers and singers."

Erin was laughing so hard she began to hiccup. "Oh, I'm *so* glad I've come home! We need to have a party to welcome me back and then some kind of group riding foray so I can watch the romantic gamesmanship up close and personal."

Erin Lark never said what she didn't mean. At the end of an hour, several stories of her Italian triumphs (musical and romantic), one magnum of champagne, and a plentiful lunch to counteract some of the effects of the champagne, Erin was helping Calida prepare a gourmet repast as she held a phone against one ear burbling to Keenan, whom she had adored from infancy. In short order, the Mackenzies and Noel Beaumont, the Sheridans, and the Barrisfords agreed to come to dinner that night. Samantha, happy in seeing her sister happy, headed back to the stables.

THE NEXT MORNING, Sam forced herself to think again of her sister's happiness and not of the work demanding her attention as she cantered Lark Ness beside Erin, who rode Lark Nocturne, one of Skylark's few remaining Thoroughbreds. Her sister hadn't even been home a full twenty-four hours, after all. This was no time to be getting petty about work.

They pulled their horses down to a walk in a lush meadow to avoid crashing into Cullen and Noel, who were also on horseback, but riding on either side of Whitney ahead of them. Cullen and Sam and Erin were casually dressed in jeans and short-sleeved shirts. Whitney, however, wore jodhpurs, as she always wore jodhpurs when she rode, because she thought they flattered her figure. And they did. Noel, too, was in jodhpurs, in a deliberate attempt, he had informed Erin and Sam, to outshine his rival.

"Gamesmanship," Sam said, shaking her head as she and Erin let the trio pull farther ahead of them.

Erin was grinning like a kid given free rein in F.A.O. Schwartz. "I've gotta admit, Sammy, that Whitney is playing Cullen beautifully. He is miserable, and poor Noel isn't much better off. If Whitney has let him kiss her in the last twelve hours, I'll eat my riding helmet."

Sam laughed. "She's got grit, I'll give her that. Not many women could resist Noel Beaumont wanting to kiss them."

"I think it's more a use of brains than restraint. She's probably figured out that Noel's the kind of man who loves the chase, but becomes immediately bored once he's caught what he was chasing. As long as she holds him at arm's length, he'll stay interested."

"You seem to have figured out the Mackenzies' French houseguest pretty quickly."

"Hey, who wrote *you* dating tips during your three debauched years at the Sorbonne?"

Sam sighed. "I keep forgetting that you're a woman of the world. You just look so damn *innocent*."

Erin laughed. "Think of me as a wolf in lamb's clothing. Heaven bless genetics. I like catching men off guard. Actually, I like catching men. You used to, too. So, why haven't you done anything about Noel?"

"Noel?" Samantha said in the utmost surprise.

"Sure. I've seen him watching you. He's interested. You should take advantage of his interest. Have some fun. Have a fling."

Ahead of them, Noel deliberately brought his chestnut gelding closer to Whitney so he could brush his knee against her knee.

Samantha grimaced at her sister. "Erin, get real. He's after Whitney."

"He's the kind of man who's happy to be side-tracked," Erin blithely insisted, "and you're just the woman who could sidetrack him."

"You must be on serious drugs."

"Nope. I just have a lot of confidence in my big sister, and I'm not quite so blinded by Whitney's beauty as you are. You could take her, Sammy."

"Only in an alternate universe," Sam retorted.

A half hour later, she handed Lark Ness over to her groom and asked for Flora Lark. Andy Bream brought the roan mare up to her and, cupping his hands, tossed her up onto Flora's back. The small knot in Sam's stomach eased a little. She was working again.

IT WAS NEARLY ten o'clock that night when Sam started the long walk from the stables back to the three-hundred-fifty-year-old white frame house with its green shutters and steep pitched roof that had, through various expansions and renovations, been home to the Larks since Jeremiah Lark first claimed the land for his family and all their descendants.

Jeremiah had been one of the first to settle in what had become Loudoun County, but he had taken only a relatively modest tract of eight thousand acres, which had through the centuries been whittled down to three thousand acres. The generations of Larks after Jeremiah had also never been overly ambitious, preferring to keep to themselves and to live on, work, and make a comfortable living from their land.

The Mackenzies, on the other hand, had insisted on making their mark from the moment Aidan Mackenzie claimed the adjacent twenty thousand acres of prime colonial real estate. Farming and horse breeding could not sustain their ambition for long. They quickly branched out into politics, shipping, and banking. Then Cullen's grandfather had gone on a buying spree, making the Mackenzies one of the major landholders in Florida, Texas, and southern California. Now Cullen had expanded the family business on a global scale, creating an intricate corporate network that seemed to pump cash into the Mackenzie bank accounts like rain during a monsoon.

This primal difference in ambition had helped the Larks and the Mackenzies get along through the centuries, basically because the Larks never went after anything the Mackenzies wanted. In fact, the Larks, Samantha included, had never been able to fully understand the Mackenzie brand of ambition. As far as they were concerned, they had more than anyone could ask, so why want more? But they had tolerated the Mackenzie ambition through the years, just as the Mackenzies had tolerated the equally incomprehensible Lark lack of ambition through the years.

That peaceful coexistence was now shattered as an open BMW convertible roared angrily up Mackenzie Lane. Sam sighed. Poor Cullen. Whitney sure knew what buttons to push.

She continued walking through the hot, humid night up to the house as a red Mercedes 450 SL drove leisurely up the Lark driveway. Whitney had come calling.

By the time Samantha reached the front porch, Whitney was curled up comfortably on the white porch swing, sipping an iced tea that Calida had undoubtedly provided. "Howdy, Miss Sheridan," Sam said as she settled onto the top porch step and leaned back against a white porch post.

"Evenin', Miss Lark," Whitney lazily greeted her.

"Make yourself to home."

"Thank you kindly. Don't mind if I do."

"I saw Cullen driving up the lane," Sam said. "He looked pissed."

"I wish you wouldn't be so crass," Whitney complained. "Cullen was peeved. He asked me to marry him and I refused."

"You *what?*" Sam ejaculated in honest horror.

"You don't think I'd accept him the first time he asks me, do you?" Whitney said nonchalantly.

"The first . . . ? Whitney, what if he is so *peeved* at being turned down that he doesn't ask you a *second* time?"

Whitney's laughter was like music. "Oh Sam, you are so *ignorant* when it comes to men. Of course he'll ask me again, and again, until I finally decide to accept him."

White-hot anger suddenly fried Samantha's brain. "Are you *insane*? How *dare* you treat Cullen like that?" she exploded, startling her friend. "He has worked and slaved these last twelve years just to create the kind of life *you* want. He deserves your love and support, not these ever-lasting *games*. He deserves some happiness, Whitney, and that means a quick engagement and a quicker wedding. Why are you insisting on making this so difficult? You must know he's the best thing that's ever happened to you. Why are you fending off your own happiness?"

Whitney flushed with equal anger. "How dare *you* challenge *me* on how I choose to conduct my romances?" she demanded. "Cullen, and Noel for that matter, like the game and know the rules. If they didn't, they wouldn't still be playing."

"Love is not a game!"

"Oh, of course it is," Whitney said impatiently. "It's the most important game going and I intend to win it on my terms. Missy Barrisford understands me, why can't you? Cullen has made me wait six long years before deciding he is finally ready to marry me. *Six years!* I've had to sit on the sidelines and watch all of my friends get married. Good God, Sam, Missy has already been married *and* divorced! Well, now it's my turn to make Cullen wait a little bit, and I will, and *you* can just keep your nose out of *my* business!"

Whitney stormed off the porch toward her car, a glorious headstrong goddess certain in her righteous anger.

Sam watched her go, not angry anymore, just depressed. She and Whitney seldom argued. Even as kids, they had gotten along so well. So, what had just happened? Why had she blown her top like that?"

"It's late," she muttered as she stood up, using that as both an excuse for her anger and as a reason not to explore it any further. She walked from the hot, humid night into the air-conditioned common room, the door banging closed behind her, just in time to see Calida and Bobby hurriedly jump out of a clinch. Sam clamped her jaws shut. Love was in the air on this June evening and for some reason it put her in a foul mood.

"Evening, Sam," Bobby said.

"Evening, Bobby," she said.

"You missed your dinner," Calida informed her, smoothing back her black hair.

"I had some work I had to make up," Samantha said, heading for her office on the western side of the house. "I'll just have a sandwich."

She walked into the tiny office and there was Erin lying on the old green leather couch, music sheets in her hand. "That was some storm," Erin commented from behind the music sheets. "I could hear it all the way in here."

"Swell," Sam muttered, plopping into her office chair and staring at her roll-top desk. *Cullen had proposed to Whitney* . . . "I just don't understand the games Whitney plays, Erin."

Erin peered at her over her music sheets. "I think it's all a matter of priorities. You don't understand her, because Whitney's priorities have always been different from yours."

"Oh, they have not!"

Erin smiled in amusement. "Whitney, for all her machinations, prefers to follow, not lead. She judges herself by how others judge her. She believes marrying the right man *in the right way* will be her ultimate glory and fulfillment.

You, on the other hand, don't value yourself by how others value you, you don't think marriage defines you, and you don't understand Whitney, because *your* priority is to be independent, while Whitney prefers to be dependent on others."

"*Whitney?* Don't make me laugh."

"Have it your own way then, which, by the by, is one way you and Whitney are *very* much alike. You got in late tonight."

"I had some work to make up. Sorry," Sam said guiltily. "I wish we could just spend weeks doing shopping sprees and eating out and ogling the guys in the malls, but this is a working farm and on a working farm—"

"You work," Erin said, sitting up. "I know, I know. I had that phrase hammered into my head, too. Don't worry, Sammy. I'm going to be so busy practicing for next week's final audition that I'll probably forget you're even around."

"Ah, the obsessed Larks."

"That's us," said Erin with a grin. "Must be something in the genes."

"Or maybe the food," Sam quipped as Calida walked into the office carrying her dinner tray.

Sam carefully kept the conversation light and easy until Erin finally went off to bed. Then she leaned back in her chair and sat staring at the black spines of her accounting ledgers, hating them and everything they represented.

Four

HANDS SHOVED INTO the front pockets of his jeans, Cullen strolled to the first of the Mackenzies' three outdoor dressage rings, birds singing happily around him, the rich scents of earth and horse filling his lungs. Keenan stood in the center of the ring, ripcord-lean in the tan breeches and white long-sleeved shirt he always wore when he was working. Right now, he was longeing Mackenzie's Pride, directing him with his voice and the long longe line into a slow canter, smiling as the eight-year-old gelding bucked, more from the pleasure of moving than as any protest against the command. He was a magnificent animal. Cullen climbed up onto the fence and just sat there, drinking in the gelding's power and grace.

"Still keeping banker's hours I see," Keenan greeted him, eyes never leaving the blue roan.

Cullen grinned. His father had never minced words. "Give me a break, Dad. I've been on the phone with our London office for the last hour."

"You lead a rough life, Son."

"It has its moments. Mom said you wanted to see me."

"Actually, I've wanted to see you these last nine years and more. It's good to have you back for more than a flying visit."

"Thanks."

Keenan led Mackenzie's Pride through a tightly controlled change of direction and set him to trotting, ears pricked forward eagerly to detect what this new view of the world would bring. "Your mother and I, of course, have no complaints about you expanding the business and the family fortune."

"That's a load off my mind."

Keenan shot him a quelling glance. "But there comes a time," he continued, "when even a Mackenzie must say enough is enough. I mean, what in hell are we supposed to *do* with all that money you've made us? Unlike the Sultan of Brunei, we don't go in for solid gold toilet seats."

"I have always admired your good taste."

Keenan brought Mackenzie's Pride to a sudden stop and then turned, arms akimbo, to glare at Cullen. "The Mackenzies have always been ambitious, but we've never been *driven*. But you *are* driven, Son, and it's been worrying your mother and frankly, it's worried me these last few years. So, stop it."

Yes, sir!" Cullen said, unable to hide his grin.

"There's more to life than money," Keenan grimly continued, *"and,"* he said before Cullen could interject, "there's more to life than Whitney Sheridan. So, were you planning to sit around on your rich butt all summer long, or were you actually planning to lend a hand now and then?"

"Hey, come on, Dad, I'm on vacation. Besides, getting Whitney to marry me is turning into an around-the-clock job. Any slacking off on my part could ruin your chances of becoming a grandparent any time soon."

"Mendacity," Keenan said in disgust as Mackenzie's Pride pawed at the soft dirt, impatient with just standing around. "I know for a fact that Missy Barrisford carried Whitney off this last Friday for a weekend in New York, leaving you to sit around on your rich butt, twiddling your thumbs."

"Dad, get real. You've built a superb staff and crew who do every task on this farm well. There isn't a blade of grass out of place or a horse unattended. I'm just excess baggage. I'm unnecessary here." A cold knife sliced through Cullen's heart as he said these words. It was hard for a moment to speak. "I'd only get in the way."

Keenan was silent for a moment as he set Mackenzie's Pride into a trot. "Your mother and I were hoping that now that you've finally decided to get married, you'd settle back here. This *is* your home, Son."

"My family is here, but my life isn't." *God,* why was this so hard? "Whitney and I will live abroad for the most part, Dad, you know that. I've talked about it often enough."

"We hoped this summer would change your mind."

"Our New York, London, and Hong Kong offices would object. Not to mention Whitney. Do you have any idea what she'd *do* to me if I told her we're staying in Virginia?"

"Vivisection comes to mind."

"Exactly!"

"You may not have your ring on her finger yet, but that woman has certainly got *her* ring through *your* nose."

"The man who becomes a quivering mass of jelly whenever Mom starts to cry shouldn't be casting the first stone," Cullen pronounced.

"Jelly, sir? *Jelly?*" Keenan trumpeted as he glared at his son.

"*Quivering* jelly," Cullen smugly corrected as he hopped

down from the fence. "Glad we could have this little father-and-son chat."

More than content with this rare victory over his father, Cullen sauntered off to the garage, climbed into his red BMW convertible, and drove the two miles down Mackenzie Lane to Senator Sheridan's antebellum house. It was one of the few in the district that actually fit the stereotype of a southern mansion, complete with four towering white columns across the front of the house, a renowned ballroom, and trellises festooned with wisteria. It was a palatial house on just thirty-four acres, but it suited the Sheridans and they carried it off well. The Senator had an excellent staff that kept his house, grounds, horses, dogs, wife, and daughter in superb condition while he argued tax increases and social spending on Capitol Hill.

As Cullen drove up the brick-paved driveway he saw the daughter in question standing at the front door with her friend and confidante, Missy Barrisford.

Missy was a year older than Whitney and an inch shorter, less voluptuous, but still nicely put together, and she knew it. Missy was nobody's fool. Her short, wheat-colored hair gave her a gamin quality that was in direct contrast to the shrewd business mind that had founded and now ran Barrisford Inns, high-end resorts in St. Moritz, Taos, Kenya, and the Cayman Islands that served only the upper reaches of the world's upper echelons.

"I had the most wonderful weekend!" Whitney was saying, enveloping her friend in a good-bye hug as Cullen turned off his car.

"So did I," Missy said, her voice strictly mid-Atlantic. "We should do it more often."

"You won't have to bend my arm," Whitney said, releasing Missy and finally spying Cullen. "Darling! You're right on time and I'm running late. Give me just five minutes to change. Bye, Missy!" she called, dashing into the house.

"Ciao," Missy called after her. Then she turned to Cullen with a smile. "First out of the blocks today, I see. Noel isn't here yet."

"Probably because I put sugar in his gas tank. You're looking well, Missy."

"It's always nice to be noticed," Missy said, walking down the few porch steps to the driveway, her long paisley skirt brushing the tops of her ankle boots. A slim gold chain around her throat glinted in the sunlight. "You're looking well yourself. Massive infusions of cash agree with you."

Cullen laughed. "I still think you should partner with me in Hong Kong. The Chinese takeover hasn't changed the city's lust for luxury and prestige, a Barrisford Inn trademark, I believe."

"You're such a sweet man. The Mackenzies always had the best manners. Except for Keenan, of course. But then Keenan is the exception to everything."

"Occasionally annoying, but true. So, Missy," Cullen said, draping a friendly arm around her shoulders, "I don't suppose I could count on you to put in a good word with Whitney for me and matrimony, could I?"

"Hardly," Missy said with a laugh as she shrugged off his arm and began walking to her gold Mercedes sedan. "I've been trying for *years* to convince her that you're just deadweight."

"Thanks a lot."

"Hey, what are neighbors for?" she called to him, her laughter hanging in the humid air.

Whitney had said five minutes, which meant, of course, ten, so Cullen leaned back against his BMW trying to decide how best to turn a morning and afternoon of antiquing into a successful assault on her determination to string his courtship out through the entire summer.

By the time Whitney appeared, radiant in white Calvin Klein slacks and sleeveless vest, he had his plans fixed firmly in his mind. But it seemed that once again Whitney had plans of her own.

While knowledgeably examining warming pans and white pine dressers, Whitney would not discuss their oft-discussed plans of a future together. She would only burble about her wonderful weekend with Missy. Pewter table-ware, silver tea sets, and Georgian goblets did not remind her that the time had come to sign the bridal registry at Tiffany. They reminded her of the risqué story Missy had told over dinner at Zoe's, a chic Soho restaurant. She would not kiss him. She would not even flirt with him.

Frustration began building in Cullen, like bricks being added to a wall.

In the late afternoon, he took Whitney to Chasers, a restored colonial tavern of yellow fieldstone in Leesburg that served elaborate high teas with every conceivable pastry to every tradition-loving gastronome in a fifty-mile radius. It was a mistake. Cullen knew it the minute he followed Whitney into the sunlit common room and spied amongst the packed tables Noel Beaumont sitting in a corner and flirting with Erin and Samantha Lark, who seemed to be enjoying his attentions.

Frustration turned to low-burning anger.

"Let's go to the Tuscarora Mill instead," Cullen said, tugging on Whitney's elbow.

"Don't be ridiculous," Whitney said. "I *love* Chasers."

"Especially when Beaumont's in-house," Cullen snapped.

Whitney turned on him, blue eyes glittering. "I won't have you dictating who I may and may not have as friends, Cullen Mackenzie! You'd best get that into your thick head right now."

"And I won't have *you* demoting me to spear carrier or whipping boy every time we're in public with Noel Beaumont!"

• • •

"THAT DOESN'T LOOK GOOD," Erin said she set down her sangria.

"No," Sam said quietly as she stared at the furious couple in the middle of Chasers, "it doesn't." Cullen wasn't the kind of man to lose his temper, but Whitney possessed an unerring skill for finding just the right buttons to push.

"How good of Cullen to create his own setbacks," Noel said as Whitney started toward their table. "It gives me more time to pursue a more pleasurable line of attack. Ah, Whitney, how enchanting you look today!" he said, standing up. "Won't you join us?"

"Noel, how sweet," Whitney purred, just before pulling him into a full body contact kiss, tongue and all, in front of over fifty witnesses.

Sam stared at the couple, honestly appalled that Whitney would deliberately and publicly dig her spurs into Cullen like this.

"This would be the take-no-prisoners approach to romance," Erin informed her with a grin from across the table.

Frowning at her sister and blushing for her friend, Samantha glanced toward Cullen and saw that he was stalking toward them, mouth hard and set, face rigid, gray eyes darkened with fury. If only there was something she could say or do to stop the coming storm. . . . but her brain felt like sludge.

"Hello, Erin," Cullen said as he reached their table. "Hi, Sam."

"Hey, Neighbor, how's it hangin'?" Erin said happily.

One sharp glance erased her smile just as Noel and Whitney came up for air.

"Cullen, please don't—" Sam began.

"If you really are so intent on furthering Franco-American relations, Whitney," Cullen said pleasantly as his beloved turned in Noel's arms to face him, "I know of a good street corner in Paris you could use."

Whitney gasped and then slapped Cullen, hard, the sound ricocheting off the restaurant's fieldstone walls and silencing every conversation in the room.

Cullen laughed. It was a fatal mistake. Whitney had never been able to tolerate anyone laughing at her.

Color high in her cheeks, she grabbed a deep-dish cherry pie from a nearby dessert cart and rammed it into his face.

Everyone in Chasers erupted into gasps and laughter and shocked, delighted comments as Whitney took Noel by the hand and pulled him outside. But Sam wasn't watching them. She was looking at Cullen and seeing, not the remains of the cherry pie, but the pain in his gray eyes that even his rueful smile couldn't diguise as he used the cloth napkin Erin had handed him to start cleaning himself off. Those anguished gray eyes shredded her heart. Oh God, what was Whitney *doing* to the man?

THREE HOURS LATER, Sam threw her pen onto her roll-top desk and leaned back in her office chair, heaving a huge sigh that encompassed Whitney's stratagems, Cullen's poor judgment, and why some people had to take a simple matter like love and make it so damned complicated.

"Looks like you hate accounting minutiae as much as I do."

Sam hurriedly turned to find Cullen standing in her office doorway. His immaculate white shirt was open at the throat, blond tufts of chest hair peeking over the white cotton. Black jeans molded themselves to his long legs. Sam's heart unaccountably began to beat faster. " 'Can she bake a cherry pie? Yes, she can. Yes, she can,' " she hurriedly sang.

Cullen burst out laughing.

Sam grinned at him. *God*, he was gorgeous. "You clean up good," she said.

"Gee, thanks," he said as he sat down on the top of her desk.

"I just wish the light of reason in your eyes now had been around a few hours ago."

Cullen winced. "It was not one of my better moments," he agreed. "I succumbed to a fit of temporary insanity and let Whitney get to me."

"That *was* her intention," Sam pointed out.

"I know," he said with a sigh. "Whitney's like a barb under a saddle pad. There's just so much irritation you can take, and then you start bucking around like a damn fool."

"Have you groveled at the pie thrower's feet and begged her forgiveness yet?"

"It seems to be my lot in life. She's currently doing her interpretation of the Snow Queen."

Sam grimaced. "Miss Sheridan is playing you like a finely tuned flugelhorn."

"Well, sure," he said with a grin, "but she's worth it, Sam."

"I know," she said with a smile, happy that some of the pain had left his eyes. "You're worth it, too, you know. 'So faithful in love, and so dauntless in war, There never was knight like the young Lochinvar.'"

Cullen laughed, his crescent scar becoming nearly invisible. "Scott again, and *Marmion* of all things. I don't get no respect."

"Let's not quibble here, your High and Mightiness. You don't even get my *sympathy*. Of all the brain-dead businessmen," Sam said, shaking her head. "Whitney is not serious about Noel, Cullen."

He smiled into her eyes, warming her all over. "I know that. Hell, *Noel* knows that. He just likes having fun at my expense. I only wish Whitney would stop all these games and get serious about *me*."

"Oh, she will, Daddy Warbucks," Sam assured him, shoving her accounting books into a drawer, "when she's good and ready."

Cullen laughed. "Sanity in the midst of madness. Bless you, Sam."

"I live but to serve the course of true love."

"Maybe you should just shoot me now and put me out of my misery."

"You stumbled badly with the Paris street corner crack, I grant you." Samantha said, smiling up at him, "but there's nothing vital broken, at least not yet. We really should hold off on mercy killing until you commit a major boo-boo, like forgetting to genuflect when Whitney walks into the room, something like that."

"I do not genuflect," Cullen huffily informed her. "I may hyperventilate, but I have not yet become obsequious."

"Men are so blind," Samantha said with a sigh.

"That's right, bludgeon me when I'm down, see if I care."

"Your problem is that you care too much. You should not be letting Whitney get to you like this. Can't you see that she's stringing you along?"

"Of course I can!" Cullen said. "But at this rate, the string won't play out until I'm old and gray and struck with senility and I want to get married *now*. I can finally give Whitney the fortune and the status and the life Teague would have given her. What more does she want?"

Sam laughed. "Complete and absolute power over you, of course, you dolt."

"Well, she can't have it," Cullen replied flatly. "I've always believed in an equal balance of power in a marriage. Something has got to be done to knock Whitney off her high-horse and get her to the altar."

"Agreed." They sat silently together for a few minutes pondering the possibilities, the rich tones of Erin's cello as she practiced upstairs for her final audition providing muted background music. Then Sam's eyes suddenly widened. "By George, I've got it!"

"What?"

"You just turn Whitney's own weapons against her! Jealousy is working on you, why shouldn't it work on her?"

"I think I like that."

"All you have to do," Samantha said with growing excitement, "is present *Whitney* with some competition. We'll get someone to pretend to pursue you in earnest, you'll pretend to be interested, that will make Whitney jealous, she'll obligingly fall into your arms, and you'll get her to the altar before you're senile!"

"That is brilliant," Cullen declared.

Samantha's glee turned glum as she sank back into her chair. "But who can compete with *Whitney*, for crying out loud?"

Gray eyes met hers and knocked the breath from her lungs. "You can," Cullen said.

"What?"

"Sam, we've been friends all our lives," Cullen continued. "You've got to help me!"

Samantha had never been more taken aback in her life. "Cullen, no one would consider me *any* kind of competition for Whitney."

"Sure they would," Cullen said, looking her up and down and bringing an unaccountable blush to her cheek. "All you have to do is clean yourself up a little so you don't look like a scruffy tomboy—"

"I beg your pardon?"

"Wear something other than jeans and slacks," Cullen continued, "do something with your hair, cut it or curl it or *something* different than that everlasting braid of yours, and Whitney is bound to see you as a threat."

For some reason, an image of Phillippe Valentin sprang into Sam's mind. Tall, blond, and beautiful, he had had half the females in the Sorbonne, and at least a third of the men, pursuing him. But Samantha had got him, reducing him to rubble in just two Parisian hours. And she had enjoyed him, too. He had been her first lover, an excellent tutor in the art of lovemaking, and a killer Scrabble player. Phillippe Valentin. She hadn't thought of him in ages.

"Besides," Cullen continued, "you've been saying for the last twenty years that you're going to marry me. That gives us the perfect set-up. It would seem perfectly *reasonable* for you to pursue me and, since we've known each other all our lives, it would seem perfectly reasonable for me to be interested. . . . particularly if you avoid shoving a cherry pie into my face."

"True," Samantha conceded, "but—"

"Come on, Sam, it'll be fun," Cullen coaxed with the boyish grin that had led her into many a childhood adventure.

The grin got her. It was impossible to resist. But there were also added incentives. This whole crazy plot would help bring Whitney to her senses, end so much of Cullen's pain, assuage her own guilt at ignoring Whitney in favor of work, and basically create the fairy tale ending she thought her friends' romance deserved.

And Cullen was right. It *would* be fun to make a public spectacle of herself chasing after him.

"You've got yourself a cohort," she said, holding out her hand.

Cullen shook it vigorously, grinning from ear to ear. "Sam, you're a *pal*!"

"*Just* what a femme fatale loves to hear," Sam said with a sigh. "So, when do we start? What do we do?"

"How about starting at Mom and Dad's anniversary ball tomorrow night?" Cullen suggested.

"That's awfully public," Sam said, feeling a distinct chill in her feet.

"That's the whole idea!" Cullen said. "The more public your pursuit and my supposed interest in it, the more Whitney will get her back up."

"She'll be boiling mad," Sam corrected. She took a breath. "Okay, tomorrow night we launch the Great Plot."

"Thatta girl!" Cullen said happily as he pulled a slim scheduling book from his shirt pocket and snagged a pen off her desk.

"What are you doing?"

"We have to do more than launch the Great Plot. We have to plan the follow-through. We need to arrange to be thrown together a lot so Whitney will buy the act. I figure," he said, beginning to write in the little book, "that I can start dropping by for lunch every day."

"Lunch?" Sam said. My God, between Calida's four-course meals, and the way Cullen and she loved to talk, she'd be lucky to get through lunch in under two hours.

"We all have to eat, Sam," Cullen said. "Now, I figure the best way for us to do lunch is for me to come over in the morning and then just sort of segue into noontime eating. We should also plan some picnics and dinners out and—"

"Hold it, hold it, hold it!" Sam said, yanking the scheduling book from his hand. "Some of us still have to work to earn our living. You may be on vacation, but I'm not. I've got way too much to do, particularly with the Horse Trials coming up, to go gallivanting off with you."

"Sorry," he said a bit sheepishly. "I guess I got carried away."

"Look, it's only fair that if this plot on your behalf takes time out of my day, that you should make it up."

"How?"

"You could work for me. Do some of the stuff I won't be able to get to otherwise."

"Like what?"

"Oh, I don't know," Sam said, leaning back in her chair and crossing one leg over the other. "Some of the morning longe work and cross-country and jump training would be great."

"You are out of your mind," Cullen said flatly. "Couldn't I just do your bookkeeping?"

"*No.*"

"Sam, it's been years since I schooled a horse."

"Then it's time you got back to it."

"I'm too rusty. I'd undo all the good work you've done."

It was the unexpected glint of fear in his gray eyes that made Sam sit up.

"Cullen," she said gently, "you're a *horseman.* I know you're a High Mucky-Muck businessman now, but you're also a horseman. You were a top rider and trainer when you were just seventeen. That's still in you. It's a part of your bones and the beat of your heart and it always will be. We'll start you off easy. No dressage work, just cross-country and jumping. I've got four horses scheduled for the upcoming intermediate competition at Morven Park, so I'm only working them over intermediate courses and jumps now. That's kindergarten stuff for you. You'll do great, I promise."

"Well," Cullen said with a wry smile that tugged at her heart, "I suppose if you can go head to head with Whitney, I can school a horse or two."

Sam covered his large hand with hers. "It'll be just like old times."

His warm gaze engulfed her and for a moment the

office disappeared. There was only Cullen's clear gray eyes and the staccato beat of her heart and his hand beneath hers.

"You're the best friend anyone could have, Sam."

"You can name your first child after me," she said, a little breathless from the sudden return to reality.

A few minutes later, she stood at her office window watching Cullen as he walked with the grace of a Thoroughbred through the boxwood gardens toward the driveway.

She had always liked watching Cullen, even as a little girl, though she'd never let him know that. His ego was big enough as it was. Still, when it was safe, she liked to watch the breeze catch and tease wisps of his shoulder-length blond hair, as it did now. She liked to trace his tall frame from broad shoulders, across finely honed muscles to narrow hips, over muscular buttocks, down long legs to large feet currently encased, sans socks, in dark brown loafers.

Even with loafers, he reminded her of a Celtic warrior. There was an air of danger about him, a feeling of physical power precariously held in check. The thin crescent scar along his cheek—erotic and disturbing—only added to the effect. Anyone seeing him would instantly have visions of him wielding a massive ax or sword in battle, fighting on oblivious to his wounds . . . and Cullen was wounded.

Why couldn't Whitney see that and cut him some slack? Why couldn't she see that Teague's death still darkened every hope, every dream? Why wouldn't she give him the love and happiness he deserved, instead of making him crawl over barbed wire to get it? Much as Sam loved her friend, Whitney was wrong in what she was doing to Cullen. Noel could take it, he liked the game and he didn't care about the outcome. But Cullen was in earnest. The outcome was vital to his heart.

Sam sighed as he disappeared from view. She might

joke about it now, but Cullen *had* seemed like a god to her child self. Adolescence had helped her restore him to being a mere mortal, but he was the best mortal she knew. To see him grieve day in and day out after Teague's death had torn her apart. To know how savagely he blamed himself for the accident had twisted her heart. To run full-tilt into a dark place in Cullen she had never felt before had been shocking, and frightening, because at sixteen she had never encountered a shadow side in anyone before. Heat burned her cheeks as she remembered her sixteen-year-old vow to grow up fast so she could learn some way to help Cullen.

Well, she was grown up now, but she had singularly failed to help him put that shadow side back in its place lo these many years of adulthood. It didn't matter that he'd scarcely been around, giving her little opportunity to help. She had failed, and Samantha wasn't used to failing at anything, particularly at anything as important as Cullen. Maybe the Great Plot was her second chance to make good on her promise.

She glanced at the phone on her desk. And maybe now was a good time to get the Great Plot in gear. Returning memories of just exactly *how* she had reduced Phillipe Valentin to rubble reminded her that prep work was vital to any romantic plot. She picked up the phone and dialed Whitney's private line.

"Has Noel managed to soothe your shattered nerves?" she asked when Whitney answered.

"He's been wonderful," Whitney replied.

"You haven't been so wonderful to Cullen."

"Don't tell me you're taking *his* side? You're *my* best friend, not his! You should be defending *me* after he was so horrible in Chasers."

"The Paris street corner crack was inexcusable," Sam said, leaning against her desk. "But I figure the cherry pie in the face made you even. And he's groveled at your feet since then. So, why freeze him out for the rest of the day?"

"He's much too sure of himself," Whitney replied. "I won't have any man taking me for granted. I particularly won't have Cullen *assuming* I'll just fall into his arms the minute he snaps his fingers."

"He doesn't assume that. He just believes what you've told him: that you love him and you want to marry him."

"A little uncertainty is good for any man's ego, just ask Missy."

Samantha blinked. "I'm warning you, Whitney," she said, "that if you don't start treating Cullen better, I'll go after him myself *and* do my damnedest to shut you out."

Whitney burst into musical laughter. "Do you honestly think Cullen will pay you the least little bit of notice when I'm everything he wants?"

"Withhold what he wants from a man, and he'll start to look elsewhere."

"Perhaps, but he won't look at *you*," Whitney said, laughing even harder. "Good God, Sam, Cullen thinks you're his kid sister."

Sam's hand gripped the phone hard. She didn't know why the truth angered her so much, but it did. "He won't think that for much longer."

"Old habits die hard, and you aren't exactly equipped to help kill them off."

Sam felt hard and grim and sick all at the same time, because she was realizing for the first time that her best friend looked down on her, that she had always looked down on her because she considered her inferior as a woman. It was clear that as far as Whitney was concerned, Samantha Fay Lark was the last woman in the world who could pose a threat to her happy status quo.

Sam felt like someone had just wiggled a red cape in

front of her face. "What you fail to realize is that I love Cullen," she lied without a blush. "I have always loved Cullen. I haven't done anything about it, because he loves you and you love him. But I won't stand idly by and watch you make him unhappy any longer. If going after him myself can make him happy, then I will."

"Good luck," Whitney said on a laugh, "you'll need it!"

Images of Cullen salivating at her feet while Whitney fumed in a jealous rage danced in Samantha's head as the line went dead.

She hung up the phone and stalked upstairs to her bedroom, angry and unsettled and wishing there was something she could hit, or throw, or trample that would help her feel better.

She settled for putting Chopin on her CD player. Then she stripped off her jeans and workshirt. Tossing her clothes on an Edwardian arm chair in a corner of her room, she caught a glimpse of herself in the wardrobe mirror. Slowly she walked across the room until she stood in beige panties and bra in front of the mirror, staring at herself.

She got a little angry, not at Whitney, but at Cullen for still thinking of her as a kid, as a tomboy who needed a make-over. She had a decent figure. Well, all right, she was a bit too thin just now, but that could be easily rectified. Besides, other men had been attracted to her. Other men had desired her and enjoyed her, both in bed and out. Phillippe Valentin was a very satisfying example.

Chopin on the CD player mingled with memories of the three lovers she had taken in Europe. She had felt so alive in those years. There had always been too much to do and say and think and feel. Every day had been a joy. Every day had been an adventure. Music and philosophy had mingled with politics, film debates, huge cups of latte, laughter, arguments about the evolution of civilization, and blush-filled critiques of some of the racier romance novels. Maybe the Great Plot would return a little of that joy to her life.

Sam pulled open the oak wardrobe doors and stared at the clothes she had bought in Europe and hadn't worn since. They were gorgeous, sexy, inspiring. She had loved wearing them seven years ago, loved feeling the silks and satins and lace against her skin. Loved the way men had looked at her. Loved feeling alive in them.

How would she feel tomorrow night when she stopped being a horse trainer and let herself look and feel like a woman again? Would she feel the fun and the excitement? Or would she feel like a fool? Sam grimaced. She'd have to pull out all the stops tomorrow night, because the *really* scary part of the Great Plot was that she was basically going to have to out-Whitney Whitney to make it succeed. It was both an impossible and an exciting idea. She had never tried to openly compete with her friend on any level before, and certainly not on a woman-to-woman level.

A smile began to curl the corners of Samantha Fay Lark's mouth. It would be fun to show Whitney up just once. It would be fun to make Cullen excise the word 'scruffy' from his vocabulary.

"You're looking downright dangerous," Erin commented from her doorway.

Sam turned to find her sister leaning against the doorjamb. "I'm feeling downright dangerous."

Erin's long eyebrows arched up. "Are you plotting, Big Sister?"

"I am."

"Can I help?" Erin asked eagerly.

"Strap on a hump and call yourself Igor. We're gonna breathe new life into the old girl."

"Oh *boy*!" Erin said, gleefully rubbing her hands together. Her smile growing, Sam turned to stare again at her couture dresses. She would not look scruffy in *these*. Yes, they were seven years out of date, but still, she thought as she fingered whisper-thin green chiffon, they would do just fine in her initial campaign to make Cullen—that is, to make *Whitney*—start seeing her as a threat.

Five

CULLEN WAS TYING his bow tie and thinking what fun it was to be plotting with Sam again. It had been too long. He only hoped she had retained enough of the adventurous spirit that had propelled her through childhood and adolescence to inaugurate the Great Plot tonight. Half measures wouldn't do, not where Whitney was concerned.

He slipped a white rosebud into the boutonniere of his black tuxedo, ran a brush through his hair a few times, and then tied his hair back at the nape of his neck in a thick pony-tail. This was a formal occasion, after all. He glanced in his dressing room mirror. He never did more than glance in a mirror, any mirror, because the crescent scar on his face always raised too many bitter memories. He caught a glimpse of his confident smile and then looked away. Between the Great Plot and the usual attention he got from the opposite sex at these affairs, he had every hope of stirring a strong case of jealousy in Whitney's delectable breast tonight. It wasn't time to start sending out the wedding invitations just yet, but there was definitely reason for optimism.

He walked out of his room onto the gleaming second-floor landing and watched the servants dashing about below in a flurry of last-minute preparations for his parents' anniversary ball. Eagerness had made him early, of course. The first guests weren't due for another hour, which meant it would be a good thirty minutes before he saw Noel or his father, and fifty-five minutes before he saw his mother. He was on his own and feeling restless.

He walked downstairs, across the rose marble Great Hall, and into the Mackenzie ballroom at the back of the house. Two hundred people could dance in it at a pinch. The other hundred guests would have to shift for themselves at the supper buffet being set up in the dining room, or at the card tables in the drawing room and family room, or on an evening stroll through the west gardens leading off from the ballroom.

The Mackenzie housekeeper, Margery Thompson, was giving a few final touches to the opulent floral display on the side table with its welter of liquid refreshments for the dancers. Williams, their slyly humorous butler, was escorting the first of the musicians to arrive up a narrow spiral staircase to the gallery above Cullen.

Three eighteenth century chandeliers hanging from the carved oak ceiling dripped with crystals as they shone upon the gleaming oak floor. Cullen breathed in the elegant beauty of this room and told himself for the thousandth time in a little over two weeks that he shouldn't be this happy to be home again when he'd expended so much energy these last twelve years trying to avoid it.

He glanced into the dining room, but it was swarming with Rose Stewart's kitchen staff and four maids and he was feeling much too content for so much activity, so he wandered into the gilt drawing room. This was better. All was still and silent. No rushing about, no urgent orders, no one at all. It was usually not his favorite room in the house, but its regal beauty suited his mood tonight. There was something about formal occasions . . .

The family meals, the casual conversations with his parents, the teasing interplay were all lovely and surprising because he hadn't expected the two people he had avoided like the plague for so long to be so welcoming. But it took a formal occasion like this ball to really emphasize that he truly had come home again, if only for a little while.

In the past, Teague's ghost had haunted every brief visit home, driving Cullen back to Yale and then New York and London and Hong Kong to escape the dark memories. That was why he had announced in his senior year at college that he wanted to separate the family business from the farm and take over the business from Keenan. The farm was tainted with everything he had loved before the car crash. He couldn't bear to see it, let alone help run it.

Fortunately, it was a reasonable plan which his father welcomed, because Keenan would rather devote himself to the Thoroughbreds anyway. Still, his parents *had* been openly shocked when he had announced after graduate school that he would be running the business from New York, not Virginia. But they had finally accepted even that, and he had what he wanted: freedom from the constant pain and guilt and reminders in every room in this house of what might have been if Teague had lived.

But somehow something had changed. It was easier to stay now, maybe because Cullen believed he had achieved everything Teague would have achieved if he had lived. Marrying Whitney would slide the final piece of that life into place. Maybe then he'd reclaim some of the real happiness he had known before Teague died. Heaven knew that Whitney, for all her games, had it in her to make a man happy.

Cullen had fallen in love with Whitney when he was seventeen. She had been fifteen—young, yes, but already beautiful and perfectly poised and sure of herself. And in love with Teague. But then, everyone loved Teague. He was perfect: beautiful, loving, generous, brilliant, funny, and completely self-assured. There was no one in the world like Teague and Cullen had known it. But rather than making him jealous, it had only made him love his younger brother more.

So when Teague, at fifteen, had fallen as madly in love with Whitney as she with him, Cullen had accepted that the two most perfect people in the world must love each other and should be together. He had stepped aside, keeping his own love secret as he watched his brother romance the only girl he had ever wanted.

He had thought it would be for a lifetime. It had only been for a year.

For the first time since Teague's death, Cullen made himself look at the group of framed family photographs his mother had arranged on the fireplace mantel. There was Teague at six and nine and twelve. So beautiful and perfect and loving. No wonder Whitney had loved him, no wonder his parents had adored him, no wonder Sam and Erin had basically adopted him. A small shudder rippled through Cullen as he looked into the gold-framed mirror above the mantel and saw once more the thin white crescent scar that had branded him for all time.

He strode abruptly to the nearby sideboard, poured whiskey into cut crystal, and drank half of it in a single swallow.

He had spent the last twelve agonizing years trying to recompense them all for Teague's loss. He had worked his butt off to do it and it was time—it had to be time—to move into his own life now. To marry Whitney and carry her off into the perfect world he had made for her and finally be happy again. He'd give her New York, London, Paris, and Hong Kong. In the last year, he had bought an eleven-mile-long Caribbean island and built a winter house on it just for her. He'd decorated the penthouse at the top of the Mackenzie Hong Kong Development Corporation headquarters tower to suit her tastes. He had purchased and renovated an English castle with five hundred acres of grounds just half an hour from London so she could have the best of both worlds whenever they were in England.

Everything was ready. He could elope with Whitney to Maryland tonight if she'd only cooperate. But she wouldn't, at least not yet. Hopefully, though, Sam could do a convincing job tonight and get the wheels moving. He had even briefed his parents on the Great Plot and they had agreed to help nudge Whitney into jealousy and matrimony, too. The stage was set. All he needed now was for the damn curtain to go up.

"You're looking grim. Thinking of Whitney?" Erin inquired from the doorway.

Cullen finished his drink and turned to his informally adopted little sister with a smile. She had styled her hair into a mass of silky brown curls that tumbled about her head and down to her shoulder blades. She wore a strapless black velvet sheath that molded itself to her body like a second skin.

"Hello, Brat. You like you're hunting big game tonight," he said.

"I'll take that as a compliment," she said, walking into the room. "You're looking sleek and dangerous yourself. Even Whitney won't be able to ignore you tonight."

"One can only hope."

Erin laughed and kissed him on the cheek. "She's got you tied up in more knots than even the Navy knows about. Have you no self-respect? Be a man. Turn her over your knee and give her the spanking she deserves."

"She'd put me in the hospital and you know it. Where the hell is your sister?"

"Waiting for the perfect moment to make a Grand Entrance, of course."

"No jeans, right?"

"Right," Erin said with a secret smile. "I came early to provide moral support. Toppling Whitney off her high-horse is a noble undertaking, but no easy task."

"It can't be any harder than convincing three hundred people tonight that Sam is a femme fatale."

"Ah, ah, ah," Erin said, her secret smile growing. "Assumptions will only get you into trouble. Rid yourself of the little devils right now."

Cullen regarded Erin with interest. "Just what exactly is Sam up to?"

Erin radiated glee. "Wait and see."

"Ah, what a delightful way to begin the evening," Noel Beaumont said from the doorway. Cullen sighed. His rival was looking tall, dark, and debonair in a black Armani tuxedo. No woman breathing could fail to find him attractive. Cullen would have some stiff competition holding Whitney's attention tonight. "Ah, my musician of love," Noel said, raising Erin's hand to his lips, "you are divine. I worship at your feet."

Erin wrinkled her nose. "Trust me, Noel, they are *not* my best feature."

Noel burst out laughing and then shook his head at her, black eyes twinkling. "Always you laugh at my ardent admiration. How am I to flirt with you properly if you will not cooperate?"

"But I don't want you to flirt with me, Noel, properly or otherwise."

"But when a man is in the company of so much beauty and charm, what else is he to do?"

"Converse like a rational adult," Erin retorted.

"Now don't go asking the impossible, Erin," Cullen broke in.

"What?" Noel said, glancing at him. "Are you here?"

"There you are, my dears," Laurel Mackenzie cried, bustling into the room in a gown of aquamarine satin, the full skirt billowing around her. "Erin, darling, thank you for coming early. So sweet of you. You can support me in my hour of need. Williams has informed me that the Finch-Burtons have just driven up. The two most boring people in Virginia and always the first to arrive and the last to leave, heaven help us all. You all look splendid, simply splendid. Erin, if that dress doesn't get you a husband, nothing will."

"I'm still on the green side of thirty, Laurel," Erin said with a smile and a fond kiss. "There's plenty of time left to find a mate."

"*Never* assume that matrimony is a simple matter," Laurel warned. "Only look at all the trouble Cullen is having."

"Perhaps it is his technique," Noel said. "I could offer you a few tips, my friend."

"I've had lovers, *my friend*," Cullen riposted. "I want a *wife*."

"That, I think, is your first mistake."

"And what have you got against marriage?" Laurel demanded of her guest.

"Nothing, I assure you, *Madame*," Noel said. "I only object to treating a woman like a wife instead of a lover. A marriage of two lovers is a union of creativity and fun and passion. A marriage of husband and wife, however, is a humdrum affair with no spark, no joy of life. After thirty-three years, yours is still a marriage of two lovers, is it not so? Your son could learn much from your example if he would but open his eyes."

Keenan Mackenzie leaned through the doorway. "The Finch-Burtons are at the front door!" he hissed at his wife. "Come rescue me!"

"Certainly, my love," Laurel replied with an arch smile at Noel.

"Great Caesar's ghost!" Keenan gasped. "Erin Lark, is that you?"

"In the flesh," Erin replied, turning in place to provide the full effect.

"So I see," Keenan retorted. "Marry me!"

"I'd love to, Keenan, but Laurel would object."

"Yes," said Laurel, "she would."

"Well, at least save me the second dance," Keenan said, taking Laurel's hand in his. "Got to dance the first one with the wife, you know."

"Yes," said the wife, "you do."

Laughing, he led her from the room.

"Well," said Erin, squaring her shoulders, "into the fray."

"Allow me," said Noel, offering his arm.

An hour later, a brassy instrumental version of "Luck Be a Lady Tonight" poured from the musicians' gallery. The Mackenzie ballroom was half-full. A glass of champagne in his hand, Cullen stood conversing with Mrs. Helena Carmichael, a hearty and distant cousin, as well as one of the judges of the dressage competition in the Mackenzie Horse Trials, and with Emily Barrisford, Missy's older sister and a noted equestrian. They were, of course, discussing horses, with Mrs. Carmichael, as always, doing most of the talking.

Cullen was content. The less attention he had to give to Mrs. Carmichael and to Emily, the more attention he could give to waiting for Whitney and Sam to arrive. He was feeling oddly excited, as if something important was going to happen tonight. He thought it must be because he was finally going to nudge Whitney toward the altar, and when she walked into the room, he was certain of it.

He heard several people gasp, and he couldn't blame them. Whitney was breathtaking as she stood at the entrance to the ballroom, blond hair piled sensuously on top of her head, leaving her white shoulders bare. The tight-fitting bodice of her shimmering golden gown barely covered her magnificent breasts and molded her narrow waist above a full skirt that flowed down to her golden shoes.

She greeted Laurel and Keenan fondly and then looked around the room until her gaze met his and, to his surprise, stopped. She even smiled. It was a warm, lovely smile that became a glow within him as she walked slowly and deliberately toward him.

"Excuse me," he said to Mrs. Carmichael and to Emily as he began to walk slowly and deliberately toward Whitney.

They stopped within a foot of each other.

"You're too beautiful tonight, Whitney," he said.

She smiled with pleasure. "What? This old thing? I must have had it in my closet for years."

"I didn't mean the dress. I meant you. *You* are—"

He didn't get any further, because at that moment Samantha Fay Lark made her Grand Entrance into the ballroom. He heard a roaring in his ears, like Niagara Falls on fast forward. Under the right conditions, Sam could be mistaken for a teenage boy. . . . but she didn't look anything like a boy tonight.

Freed from its habitual French braid, her hair was a copper flame she had pulled back from her forehead to sweep down just past the nape of her neck. Her gown was diaphanous emerald green chiffon with a V-shaped halter bodice that dipped precariously over her breasts before swirling down in airy layers around her shapely legs. The layered material was so sheer that it created the illusion that Sam was nearly naked. The illusion was furthered by her slim white back, bare between halter and the skirt that began at her hips.

So this was Sam's version of a femme fatale. Lord have mercy. Dimly, Cullen was aware that Whitney, on his left, had turned grim. But then, she always turned grim when she was no longer the center of attention. And she wasn't. Almost everyone in the room was staring at her friend in amazement, because no one in the state of Virginia had ever seen Samantha Lark look like *this*. As for Cullen, he was badly unnerved. He didn't quite know where to look. There was just so much of *Sam* that was exposed.

"A remarkable transformation," Noel Beaumont commented in a low voice on his right. "I have long suspected she had it in her. I am happy to be proven so right."

"Well, I wish you'd confided your suspicions to *me*," Cullen complained.

Noel laughed. "My friend, you would not have believed me. If you will excuse me, I think that I shall lead the masculine stampede to her side."

Cullen watched in amazement as most of the eligible bachelors in the room made a rush towards Sam. *Sam!* Noel, of course, got there first, but soon a gaggle of tuxedos had joined him and had blocked her from view.

"Where on earth did she get that. . . . that *dress*?" Whitney demanded.

Cullen glanced at the love of his life. "Is this is the first time you've seen it?"

"Of course it's the first time! She's lived in jeans for years. What in the world is she playing at?"

"Whatever it is," Cullen murmured, "she's playing to win." He made a mental note never to assume anything about Samantha Fay Lark ever again.

For the next half hour, and for the first time in thirteen years, Cullen found his attention continually wandering from Whitney. It insisted on following Samantha as she slowly made her way around the room flirting, in a perfectly friendly fashion, with any willing man—and every man she met was willing. It was disconcerting how much the overwhelmingly positive masculine reaction to her bothered him. It was downright surprising how much he resented every happy smile she gave Noel Beaumont who had, of course, permanently attached himself to her side.

"I want some champagne," Whitney said, for the second time, an edge to her voice.

"Hm?" Cullen said, dragging his gaze from diaphanous green chiffon. "Oh, sorry, Whitney. Of course. Just a minute." He didn't even take the first step, because just then his parents reached the head of the room. They stood hand in hand, Keenan lean and vibrant in his tuxedo, Laurel plump and glowing in aquamarine satin.

"Ladies and gentlemen," Keenan called out. Instantly the dull roar of conversation in the room became hushed. "My bride and I would like to thank you all for helping us to celebrate our thirty-third anniversary and we hope that you will be able to join us for thirty-three more. We'd like to start this ball off with the waltz we danced at our wedding. Maestro, if you please," he called up the musicians' gallery.

A lush Viennese waltz filled the ballroom as Keenan took Laurel in his arms.

"I believe," Whitney said, turning to Cullen, "that this is our dance."

"But no, my dear one," Noel, with Sam on his arm, had materialized before them. "You had promised me this first dance. I have witnesses. You are mine for these few minutes at least."

"Besides," Sam added jauntily as she grabbed Cullen's hand and tugged him to her side, "Cullen promised *me* the first dance tonight since you didn't want it."

Whitney hesitated just a moment and then decided to make the best of things. She flashed Cullen her most brilliant smile, took Noel's arm, and walked with him to the dance floor, her body pressed against his side.

"Now there's a disgusting sight," Cullen muttered.

"So look at me instead," Sam advised.

He turned and stared appreciatively at her from head to toe. "You clean up good."

She laughed, a slight hint of pink in her cheeks. "I hired a top special effects crew."

"That entrance of yours was brilliant," Cullen said, enjoying the view much more up close and personal.

Sam grinned at him. "I was lurking in the bushes so I could time it right after Whitney made *her* entrance. Come on, let's start some tongues wagging."

"You did that just by walking into the room," Cullen said as he began leading her to the dance floor. "What'd you do? Meet your Fairy Godmother on the way to the ball?"

"You said you wanted me to give Whitney a little competition. I'm only trying to oblige."

"Oblige? That's like saying Isaac Stern can scrape a few notes out of a fiddle," Cullen said as they reached the dance floor. He pulled Sam into his arms and into the waltz and it felt almost like an out-of-body experience. He had danced primarily with Whitney these last several years, and Sam was different. She was a good three inches shorter than Whitney, which meant eight inches shorter than he. She was slender, not voluptuous. But it wasn't just the physical differences. Her grace and fluidity as he swirled her around the room surprised him. He had only associated them with Sam on horseback before. But it was even more than that. She had a quality . . . she felt like coming home to Virginia after being gone too long.

She shivered slightly as he smiled down into her up-turned face, so familiar, and yet somehow different. "You're full of surprises tonight."

"I've decided to be guided by the words of the immortal Scott: ' "Charge, Chester, charge! On, Stanley, on!" were the last words of Marmion.' " She shook her head, copper hair brushing the nape of her neck, making him wish he could touch that fiery silk. "This has got to be the craziest adventure I've ever agreed to."

"That's what you said about our midnight foray to the Barrisford estate to steal Mrs. Barrisford's prize-winning rose bush on Mom's behalf. And it's what you said before *that* about putting red light bulbs in all of the Finch-Burtons' outdoor light fixtures."

Her sweet smile disrupted his steady heartbeat. "Most people wouldn't know it to look at you, particularly now when you're all decked out and on your best behavior, but you really are the most *outrageous* man. That must be why you've been such a success in the business world. Your competition just can't figure out what you'll do next."

"Oh, Noel Beaumont figured it out once or twice."

"He did? I must say I'm liking that man more and more."

"Well, if you like him so much, and if the Great Plot doesn't succeed, you can switch to Plan B: seducing Noel away from Whitney so I can have a clear field."

"There's a word for men like you," Sam said darkly.

"Inventive?"

"Hardly. Think one syllable. Starts with a *P*."

"So how is your training coming along?" Cullen inquired brightly. "Think you've got any stock that can offer some competition at the Trials?"

"I've got four promising six-year-olds, and the eight others are no slouches."

"Four? *Four?* Are you seriously considering entering *four* horses in the Trials?"

"Why not? It's a good round number."

"Are you out of your mind?" Cullen sputtered. "You're going to ride four green horses in an advanced competition? That's insane. That's suicidal. You'll land yourself in the hospital, Young Lark."

"No, I'll just place all of them in the top thirty," Sam sunnily countered.

"There's a word for women like you," Cullen informed her.

"Brazen?" Sam asked hopefully.

"Hardly. Think four syllables. Starts with a *P*."

"Promiscuous?"

"Pixilated," Cullen grimly corrected.

"Oh," Sam said with a grin. "Well, that's entirely possible. Not that the other isn't, too."

"Sam," Cullen said wearily, "don't go shattering all of my preconceptions about you in one night, I beg you."

"Sorry," she said, her engaging grin broadening. "I guess I've never really been promiscuous. Except, perhaps, in Europe."

"What?" Cullen said faintly.

"Well," Sam said, gnawing on her full lower lip, "I don't suppose three lovers in four years is really promiscuous, do you?"

"Lovers? As in. . . . um . . ."

"Sleeping together?" she supplied helpfully. "Well of course! I didn't reduce Phillippe Valentin to rubble just for the heck of it."

"Who?" Cullen quavered.

"Phillippe Valentin. He was my first deliberate attempt at seducing a man, and a very successful attempt, I might add."

Cullen stared down at her. "Who are you and what have you done with Samantha Lark?"

She laughed up at him and Cullen understood in that moment how Sam had successfully reduced Phillippe Valentin to rubble.

"Shoots my scruffy tomboy image all to hell, doesn't it?"

"I believe *I* was the one who told *you* you could compete with Whitney."

"You're also the one who looked like a horse had just kicked you in the head when I walked into the room," Sam retorted sunnily.

The dance ended in the next moment. She rose on tiptoes and kissed his cheek. The soft heat of her lips felt like butter melting into him. "Go claim your prize," she said. "*I* have work to do. I have to convince half of Virginia *and* Whitney that there's more to thee and me than just childhood chums."

Bemused, he watched her stroll off, almost able to trace the outline of her legs through the green chiffon. He flushed when he realized he was *trying* to trace his oldest friend's partially revealed figure. Maybe the Great Plot wasn't such a great idea after all.

He watched Sam as she insinuated herself into one conversational grouping after another, dance with Noel—*twice*—and with Eric Langton, the oil heir, and with Donovan Streik, the international architect. She was pulling off a role he'd never expected to see her play—the Belle of the Ball—and she was doing it on her own terms. To compete with Whitney, she hadn't tried to act like Whitney, or look like Whitney, or dress like Whitney.

Instead, she seemed to have stripped off an old mask. She was just being herself, fully herself. That, he thought, was the key to her success, and she *was* successful tonight. He knew it by the way everyone in the ballroom surreptitiously watched her and tried to eavesdrop on her conversations. And he knew it by Whitney's growing testiness whenever he danced with her or stood talking with her, his gaze wandering repeatedly back to Sam.

Well before midnight, Whitney's regal nose was royally out of joint. "Let's hear if for the Revolution," Cullen murmured as Noel reclaimed her for a dance.

"Self-satisfaction is so unappetizing in men."

Cullen turned with a smile to find Samantha at his side.

Ach, she was lovely. "This is not self-satisfaction, this is pride in a job well done. The Great Plot is a roaring success. Whitney is in a snit."

Sam guffawed. "If she's let herself sink so low in a room full of adoring men, we *are* a success. Come on," she said, taking his arm just as if they had always been a couple, "let's go turn up the heat on our supposedly burgeoning romance."

They walked out onto the dance floor for a slow rumba, dancers all around them, music pressing against the walls, but Cullen's vision had telescoped. He only saw Sam. Her sweet engaging smile, the fiery sweep of copper silk to the nape of her neck, dark brown eyes lit from within.

"I've warmed up the audience, so on with the show," she murmured as she stepped so naturally into his arms. She raised her voice so the couples nearby could easily eavesdrop as she launched into a survey of foreign cuisines she and Cullen both liked, European cities they both loved, and romantic movies that turned them both to mush.

But Cullen wasn't paying strict attention. He was distracted by the stunning discovery that Sam had curves that knew how to move caressingly into him and around him and against him. When had she gotten curves? When had she learned to move like this and look like this and smile so seductively? How could his childhood chum feel so womanly and desirable and delicious in his arms?

"Cullen, pay attention!" Sam hissed.

"Hm?" Cullen said, and then hurriedly regrouped. "Oh, sorry, Sam. What's my line?"

"I've just been complimenting your dancing. So say something about me."

Cullen's smile grew. The Great Plot was turning out to be a whole lot easier than he had imagined. "Careful, Miss Lark," he said, raising his voice, "dancing like that could get you arrested."

"For what?"

"For looking like you know exactly what to do with a man when you get him alone."

"But I do know! I'm not the kid of your golden childhood, Mr. Mackenzie. I'm all grown up."

"And a lovely job you made of it, too."

"Why, Mr. Mackenzie! Are you flirting with me?"

"No, no. Only telling truths."

"Now you sound like Noel."

"There's no need to be insulting."

She laughed. It went all the way up into her luminous brown eyes and stopped his heart for a moment. "You really must get over thinking that Noel is any kind of competition for the best man Virginia ever bred."

"And *you* should consider registering yourself in that dress as a lethal weapon."

She grinned up at him, dazzling him. "I don't think the girl who once put a frog down your back could ever make you putty in her hands."

"Oh Miss Lark, you'd be surprised." He looked around the ballroom. "Where's a frog when you really need one?"

She laughed. "No need to panic. I've developed much more sophisticated ways of conveying my affection." She dragged him to a stop in the middle of the dance and dropped him into a dip. "Come with me to the Casbah," she said in a hideous French accent. "We will make beautiful music together!"

"Not if my back goes out on me," Cullen gasped as the couples dancing around them laughed, staring openly at these antics. Cullen was laughing, too, and realizing in the middle of the Mackenzie ballroom, and Sam's dip, just how much fun he was having. And when was the last time he had really had fun?

The dance ended, to be immediately replaced by a merengue. Sam placed a hand on his shoulder and slithered around him in a blatantly erotic fashion that was hypnotizing. She had promised to put on a show tonight and she was making a good job of it. Too good. The world had telescoped again.

"Well?" she said when she stopped in front of him again, her arm resting on his shoulder.

Time stopped. His gaze never leaving her face, Cullen took her hand in his and then slid his other hand slowly across the silky warmth of her bare back and pulled her against him, loving the heat of her body and the slight tremor that rippled through her. He loved that she felt fluid and lyrical when he began dancing with her, hip to hip. She was a heady combination of fire and delicacy, silliness and strength. He loved staring down into brown eyes that never shied from his. He loved that she ran the fingers of one hand through his hair, dislodging the pony-tail tie, setting his hair free.

"I've always wanted to do that," she murmured.

Sam's habit of making it hard for anyone to know when she was serious held full sway. Was this an act or was it for real? Cullen didn't know. He only knew in the strange haze of the small circle they had claimed on the dance floor that it was shocking to feel her body pressed evocatively against his, to stare down into her flirtatious smile and return it, and to be hyper-conscious of her every touch as he guided her into chassés, pivots, and maxixe rocks as if they had danced together always, when in fact—now that he thought about it—they had never danced together, even though they had known each other forever.

At his parents' parties and balls, he had danced with Whitney most of the time, and with some of the daughters of his parents' friends as a courtesy to them. But he hadn't danced with Sam. They had talked together, drunk champagne together, joked together, but never danced together.

Until now. Until this moment that he was enjoying much too much . . . and perhaps that was the reason they had never danced before.

He ended the merengue by dipping her. She came up laughing, which made him laugh with a happiness he hadn't felt in years. *God,* what a wonderful evening!

"I trust you are quite finished making spectacles of yourselves," an icy voice broke into their laughter. Whitney stood almost at Sam's side, glaring at Cullen. "I would take it as a personal favor, Sam, if you would stop parading around the ballroom like a whore!"

Sam didn't flinch, she smiled. "I was dancing, not parading. And I don't recall asking you for your opinion." She traced Cullen's ear with her index finger. "You enjoyed the dance, didn't you, Mr. Mackenzie?"

"Sam, that is enough!" Whitney hissed, distracting Cullen from his burning ear. "A *lady* knows to keep her hands off another woman's man."

"There's no ring on your finger, Whitney, and no engagement announcement in the papers," Sam purred, "so Cullen is fair game. Aren't you?"

"I've always believed in being fair," Cullen said.

He feared in that moment that Whitney would explode.

"You will stop pretending to be interested in Cullen right now, do you hear me? Right now!"

"Oh, I'm not pretending," Sam calmly replied. "I warned you, Whitney, that if you continued to abuse Cullen I'd have to step in and do something about it, and I am."

"And I," Cullen murmured as he brushed his fingers through copper silk, "am eternally grateful."

"It looks like you'll have to find some other poor man to abuse, Whitney," Samantha said, snuggling against him, "because Cullen is otherwise engaged."

"Oh, stop it!" Whitney hissed, her golden gown practically emitting sparks. "This is some stupid game you've created and for some infantile reason Cullen is going along, probably because *he's* jealous about Noel."

"Like Samantha said," Cullen coolly interposed, "there's no ring on your finger, Whitney. That's your choice, remember? You're free to enjoy the company of any man you choose. Just as I'm free to enjoy the company of any woman I choose, and I choose Sam."

"Your standards *have* dropped," Whitney sneered.

Cullen heard Sam's sharp intake of breath. "Actually, they've improved," he retorted. "Samantha has more kindness and consideration and loyalty in her than I've ever found in you or anyone else, Whitney."

She gasped, first with shock and then with anger. "If that's the thanks I get after waiting for you for *six years*, then you're welcome to the little androgyne!"

She spun around and stalked off to Noel Beaumont's accommodating arms.

"Well, that was an unpleasant little interchange, but effective," Sam said lightly. "But you misread your script. What in the world were you doing sticking up for me, rather than Whitney?"

"Like I said, I believe in being fair," Cullen retorted grimly. That Whitney could so cruel to her best friend . . . this is what came of being so damned self-absorbed. All he'd thought about when he'd dragged Sam into the Great Plot was winning Whitney. He hadn't thought about making Sam a target for Whitney's abuse. If Whitney had destroyed any of the pleasure Sam had found in the evening, he'd—

"Hey," she said softly, tugging on his sleeve. "Hey," she said again until he finally looked down at her and saw the mingled concern and whimsy. "You just won a major victory here, don't you realize that, you big dolt? Whitney's so mad, she could spit bullets. I haven't seen her this passionate in years. You've hooked her, Daddy Warbucks. Now all you've got to do is reel her in by ignoring her for the rest of the night and you *will* get that summer wedding."

"But you—"

"I'm fine. I told you from the start this charade would make her boiling mad. Except for the cherry pie episode, you haven't had much experience of her temper, so it came as a bit of a surprise, that's all."

He looked down at her curiously. "And you *have* had some experience?"

"Now and then. We're *friends*, for crying out loud. Friends fight. It's just that long ago Whitney made it a policy never to fight with prospective husbands. The fact that she broke that rule tonight makes me want to start picking out a bridesmaid's dress. Something in satin fuchsia with big hoops and *tons* of puffy bows."

He smiled down at her. "You're a good friend, Sam."

"The best," she agreed. "Now go mingle or something while I advance the Great Plot."

Cullen mingled, but his eyes and his thoughts were constantly on Sam as she laughed and chatted and danced her way around the room. Lovely and charming and delightful. Cullen now knew fully what it was to feel boggled.

His mother and father suddenly began waltzing in a circle around him.

"Hello, Son," said Keenan.

"Evening, Dad."

"I'm having the most wonderful time," Laurel said happily. "Are you having a wonderful evening, Cullen?"

"The best," he assured her.

"I'm so glad," Laurel called back to him as Keenan whirled her away.

He stood watching them dance, assailed suddenly by a rush of memories of Keenan and Laurel teasing each other on a Fourth of July picnic when he was eight, kissing and cuddling together on the family room sofa when he was eleven, arguing politics at the dinner table when he was fourteen, dancing together on the back patio beneath the stars when he was seventeen, mourning Teague when he was eighteen, dancing together now, so obviously in love even after thirty-three years of marriage.

But it was more than that. They genuinely *liked* each other. They seemed in that moment to embody everything marriage was about. Loving and working and living together through bad times and good. Being strong enough to survive even the worst tragedy. Coming through it still capable of the fullest love and happiness.

Was it at all possible that he had somehow inherited the same capability?

Cullen turned again to Sam, to find her laughing at something his parents had said as they danced by her. A bright flame in sheer green chiffon. A woman he'd never met before and yet knew as well as he knew his own soul.

The small orchestra in the musicians' gallery began playing the Beach Boys' "Fun, Fun, Fun," which kept most of the guests on the dance floor. Some walked into the dining room, others headed back into the drawing room or outside into the gardens. Whitney had pulled Noel out onto the dance floor, her glittering glance briefly meeting Cullen's, before turning back to her handsome partner. Sam was right, she looked like she *could* spit bullets. "Let's hear it for the Great Plot," he murmured with a smile.

He walked up to his parents, who stood sipping champagne with Sam near the garden doors, gave them each a kiss on the cheek, and wished them happy anniversary.

"We must thank you two for making this our most *entertaining* anniversary," Keenan said, grinning at him and Sam.

"If Whitney doesn't break down soon," Laurel said with a wicked gleam in her eyes, "you may well find yourself married to *Samantha Fay* after the performance you two have put on tonight."

"We have been pretty splendid, haven't we?" Sam said happily.

"*Everyone* is talking about you," Laurel said.

"The entire county," said Keenan, "is waiting with bated breath to see Whitney and Samantha duke it out for your hand, Son."

"Ah, the Ladies," Cullen said, clapping his hand to his heart and striking a pose, "how they love me!"

Sam folded her arms over her chest. "Trust me, it ain't you, it's your *money*."

Cullen staggered back and pretended to pull out an arrow lodged in his chest. "Medic!" he gasped, which sent Sam off into a fit of giggles.

"Oh, heaven bless the Great Plot," she gasped. "I haven't had this much fun in years!"

"You haven't?" Cullen said. "Why not?"

"Oh, you know me. I like to keep my nose to the grindstone," she said with a shrug.

"Okay," Cullen said, surprised as he felt Sam emotionally withdraw from their little group, "but why?"

Six

SAM'S MIND WENT BLANK, just as it always did when she was caught between a rock and a hard place. She wasn't about to say "Because if I don't, Erin and I will lose Skylark forever" and Cullen's steely gray eyes would see through every lie, every joke. So what on earth could she say?

Then a knight in shining armor came to her rescue.

"Ah, my little one," Noel Beaumont said as he reached her side, "I have come to claim you for the waltz you promised me."

"Right. Sure. Thanks," she said gratefully. "Please excuse me. Previous engagement. Give my apologies to the host. Unavoidably detained. You understand," she said in a rush, like Bugs Bunny on amphetamines. Then she grabbed Noel's hand and practically ran onto the dance floor. "You have just earned my undying gratitude," she informed him as he swept her into the waltz.

"I am honored," Noel replied smoothly. "What precisely have I done?"

Sam looked surreptitiously left and then right. "You

have just rescued me," she said in a conspiratorial voice, "from having to reveal certain top secret information about the best equestrian in the ballroom."

"Ah, the mysterious Samantha Lark. Always so much hidden beneath the surface. I must commend you, however, for revealing at least some of your hidden treasures tonight. The gown, it is magnificent."

"Thanks," Sam said, feeling naked in his arms. Noel had a way of looking at a woman . . .

"I told you that using your feminine wiles would bring you success," he said, continuing in French. "This new strategy of yours to win Cullen Mackenzie's heart is much more effective than defeating him at poker or hitting him on the shoulder. He has been looking dazed most of this evening."

Sam laughed happily. "I *have* enjoyed turning all of his preconceptions about me upside down," she said, also switching to French.

"It is a great pleasure to see you reveal the fire I have long suspected dwelled within you."

Sam frowned up at him. "You're starting to rhapsodize again, Noel."

"What man would not with so much perfection before him?"

"Uh huh. You're drunk as a skunk, aren't you?"

"On one glass of champagne? *Don't* be insulting!"

"Sorry," Samantha said with a grin as Erin and Keenan danced by them. "It's just that you do go on at an alarming rate. Can't you see *any* of my faults?"

"Certainly. But a gentleman would never be so unkind or so foolish as to speak them aloud to the lady receiving his attentions."

"Then be a lout."

Noel laughed. "Very well. You are unaware of your

true charms, you keep too many of your troubles secret, you refuse to lean on even your closest friends for help and support, and you do not understand your own heart. You think, for example, that it is only a game you are playing tonight, this supposed pursuit of Cullen Mackenzie."

Sam gasped. "Who told you about the Great Plot?"

"No one," he said. "Knowing the play and the actors performing it, I was able to quickly guess the strategy designed to make Whitney jealous and get her to accept Cullen's next proposal. But my little one, is this wise to help bring together two people who will not best serve each other?"

"Of course it's wise! Cullen and Whitney are perfect together."

"Standing on the outside of your little circle, I perhaps see things a little differently and so, though it pains me, I must disagree with you on this one matter."

"Why?" Sam said with a teasing smile. "Because you want Whitney for yourself, or because you'd like defeating Cullen in head-to-head competition?"

Noel's dark eyes smiled down at her. "Such a fascinating combination of innocence, intelligence, and cynicism."

"I am not innocent!"

"Ah my little one, you do not know yourself at all."

He swirled her effortlessly around the dance floor, making her feel graceful and lovely and feminine. In Cullen's arms, she had felt too self-conscious. Nonstop jokes had been her only safety net. But with Noel, she felt attractive and desirable for the first time in too long a time.

At the end of the dance, she sank into a low curtsy as Noel, laughter in his black eyes, raised her hand to his lips.

"All right, stop groveling at the man's feet, Sammy," Erin commanded behind her. "His ego's already the size of Jupiter."

"But with just cause, no?" Noel said with an arch smile as he raised both of Samantha's hands to his lips.

"That's enough of nibbling on my big sister for one night," Erin informed Noel as she pulled Sam's hands free. "Go off and find some poor female willing to be duped by all your flattery."

"Hey!" Sam complained. "*I* was willing to be duped!"

"Noel Beaumont does not dupe the beautiful women," Noel corrected Erin. "He speaks only the truth."

"Enough!" Erin said sternly. "Go make goo-goo eyes at Whitney or some other gullible female, Noel, and let Sammy and me enjoy a little private girl talk."

"You will be talking about me, yes?" Noel said hopefully.

"We will be talking about you *no!*"

Noel sighed heavily and looked downcast. "You have a heart of stone."

"Go!"

Noel went.

"All right," Sam said, arms akimbo, "what's all this about?"

"The Great Plot, of course, Sammy," Erin said, shaking her head, brown curls bouncing in the chandelier light, "you cannot convince people that you're serious about pursuing Cullen if you dance around the room looking half in love with Noel Beaumont!"

"Oops," Sam said with a grin.

"Don't worry," Erin said with an answering grin. "No major damage done. Everyone really is convinced that you're pursuing Cullen and that he's more than half-interested in being pursued by you. I only wish it wasn't all a sham, because I'd love having Cullen as a brother-in-law."

"Excuse me."

The two women turned to find Noel standing behind them, looking humble.

"Yes?" Erin coolly inquired.

"It has occurred to me that I have been singularly boorish this evening. I have yet to dance with my musician of love."

"That would be you," Sam informed Erin. "Think you'll be safe?"

"It's okay," Erin assured her. "I'm wearing my Gallic-proof corset."

"Well, it's a relief to know you've got *something* on under that dress of yours."

"It is not a relief to all of us," Noel countered, which made both women laugh as he led Erin off to the dance floor.

Samantha turned around in place, wondering what to do next, when she saw Cullen walking purposefully towards her, his mane of blond hair making him look wild and dangerous. Ah, would she ever get tired of watching the man move? What was wrong with Whitney anyway? Had she no appreciation of perfection?

"Time to set tongues wagging again," Cullen announced, stopping a foot in front of her. "May I have this dance?"

She hesitated a moment. It had been disconcerting dancing with him this evening—she had felt too aware of her body, and of his. Her pleasure in dancing with him had been too rich, and now the orchestra was playing a slow dance. *What's the matter with me?* she wondered. *This is Cullen, for crying out loud. There's nothing scary about Cullen.*

"I thought you'd never ask," she said, surprised again at how easily she stepped into his arms, at how naturally her head rested against his broad shoulder as they moved in time to the languid music, at how good his warm hand felt resting against her bare back.

"Whitney's watching us," Cullen whispered in her ear.

"I wondered why I felt like a quiver of arrows had just been lodged in my spine," she replied, snuggling closer.

She was feeling sensual and desirable and invincible and decided it was all because of the champagne and the Great Plot, and she was glad. She was Cinderella at the ball and she had triumphed. The night felt delicious. *Cullen* felt delicious. The world was wrapped in a sensual haze. She laughed a little at herself. My, she *had* immersed herself in this role, hadn't she?

THE SKY WAS just beginning to lighten as Sam followed Erin into their house, resigned to the fact that she would not be going to bed.

"I love dancing till dawn," Erin said before a huge yawn overtook her.

"But wasn't it murder being strapped into that dress all night long?" Sam asked as they began to climb the stairs together.

"It was only murder on the men," Erin said with a grin. "I tell you, Sammy, there's nothing like slobbering male adoration to give a girl confidence."

"Confidence is not something you've ever lacked," Sam wryly retorted. "Noel told me he thought you were the most formidable female he'd ever met."

A yawn overcame Erin's laugh. "Our Noel seems to have been blessed with an intuitive understanding of women. 'Night, Sammy," she said, walking into her bedroom.

" 'Night," Sam said as she walked into her own room and languidly began undressing, loving the way her chiffon dress slid over her skin. The ball *had* been wonderful and she had felt more than just a touch like Cinderella, but without the time constraint or the undoubtedly painful glass slippers.

Once again in her work clothes, she shoved her feet into her old black riding boots, brushed out her hair and tied it into her habitual French braid, grabbed her battered black riding helmet, and headed downstairs. Stepping outside, she stopped for a moment just to drink in the beauty of her world. The Potomac River was a few miles to the east, the Blue Ridge mountains were several miles to the west. In between was God's most perfect horse country.

Half a dozen exercise boys and girls were atop some of the three-year-olds, riding to the west for a conditioning gallop up the long gradual rise of Bluegrass Hill. Smiling in comradeship, Sam walked into the largest paddock—five acres of fenced grass—to spend some time with the newest additions to Skylark, getting the foals used to her scent, her voice, her touch as she fed them and their mothers sugar lumps, stroking slender, ungainly bodies, marveling as she always did at their beauty.

Then she walked the farm with Bobby Craig and Miguel Torres, Bobby talking fences and stock rotation for the different fields and the bumper crop of alfalfa they were cultivating, while Miguel focused on the horses, their personalities, their strengths, their training programs. He slipped away for a meeting with his training staff while Sam finished with Bobby, going over the intermediate show-jumping and cross-country courses she needed built for her six-year-olds. Finally, she left him, stifling a yawn as she walked back toward the main stable.

"Have you even been to bed?"

Startled, Sam turned to find Cullen sitting on the paddock fence to her right. Her gaze swept over his broad chest pushing against the limits of a black T-shirt, and black jeans that molded themselves to his narrow hips and long, muscular legs. "What are you doing here?" she asked, walking over to him, disconcerted by the odd staccato rhythm of her heart.

"You scratch my back, I scratch yours, remember? I'm reporting for duty, ma'am," he said, jumping down from the fence. He yawned ferociously. "God, what a horrible hour. We should be in bed."

"That is *not* part of the Great Plot!" she quipped, which earned her a smile.

"*Have* you been to bed?" Cullen demanded.

"I've never been able to sleep with shoes on, and those damn glass slippers just would not come off. Besides, this is a working farm," she said, slipping her arm through his and pulling him toward the main stable, "and on a working farm—"

"You work," Cullen said with a groan. "I know. I know. But do we have to work so early?"

"The horses kind of insist on keeping to a schedule. Oh, I love the aroma of fresh hay and horse in the morning," Sam rhapsodized as they walked into the cool stable. And she loved that the horses all looked towards her, whickering softly. "Come on, let me introduce you to everybody."

All of her four-, five-, and six-year-old cross-breeds had stalls in this stable. She and Cullen slowly walked down the line of stalls, handing each horse a piece of apple, stroking soft dark muzzles, murmuring their greetings, and saying a cheerful good morning to the two stable girls responsible for the morning feeding.

"Let's start you on Central Lark," she said, opening a stall door and pushing Cullen toward the golden dun gelding with zebra-striped legs. "I'll be right next door," she said, closing the door behind him.

She walked into Lark Magic's stall, taking in at a glance that Andy Bream had already thoroughly groomed him. She ran her hand over Magic's glossy dark brown coat, marveling once again at his perfect composition. He was everything she had imagined the union of America's Morgan and Germany's Holstein (from the Schleswig-Holstein region) would create. The well-crested neck, prominent withers, sloping shoulders, and broad, deep chest of the Morgan, along with its tremendous air of importance, had been augmented by the Holstein's height and elegance, stamina and power, to create spirited but well-mannered horses that excelled at every event she threw at them because they had inherited the genetic blessings of handiness—the ability to get out of any trouble in a show-jumping arena or on a cross-country course. Sam prayed her own DNA had the same genetic code. She'd need it in the Mackenzie Horse Trials.

She examined Magic for any nicks or strains or soreness he might have acquired during the night, but he was perfect, as always. If Cullen hadn't been here, she'd have done some basic longe work to warm Magic up, then dressage, jumping, and finally a cross-country workout, before returning him to his stall and repeating the process with his half-sister, Flora Lark. And then Central Lark, before finishing out the morning with Lark Ness and some of the five-year-olds. The afternoon's schedule was even more tightly packed.

It was an insane regimen. She knew she was nuts. But she was also desperate, so a reasonable work schedule could just take a hike. She was grateful for Cullen's help, but it wouldn't make her schedule any more reasonable. It would simply make up for the time she'd lose each day helping him further the Great Plot. So she shouldn't be feeling like a weight had been lifted from her shoulders, but for some reason she did.

"Central's a real beauty." Cullen stood with Central Lark outside Magic's stall.

"Isn't he?" Sam said as she threw on Magic's tack—his bridle, saddle pad, and saddle—having to stretch.

"Your new stock looks like they're all coming in at around sixteen hands tall."

"You haven't lost your eye, and you're right," Sam said, tightening the saddle girth. "It's the low end for Holsteins, but taller than purebred Morgans, just as I planned when I selected the stallions and brood mares. Anything higher would have added additional weight and size that could lead to awkwardness and injury in competition. But at sixteen hands, give or take a few inches, they should make great stadium jumpers. They should make great steeplechasers. They should make great three-day-eventers. On top of all that," Sam said, gazing proudly into Magic's dark eyes, "they look marvelous."

"That they do," Cullen said as she led Magic out of his stall.

Grabbing longe lines and whips from the tack room, she and Cullen led their horses down to her outdoor dressage ring. She clipped the longe line to Magic's bridle and led him to the far end of the ring while Cullen, looking a little stiff, began to work Central.

She remembered the fear in his eyes when she'd first suggested he help her with her training schedule. Part of her didn't understand. For the Cullen she knew to be afraid of schooling a horse was like a fish being afraid to swim in water. But after twelve years of his living Teague's life, how well did she really know this Cullen? "Relax," she called to him. "It's like riding a bicycle. You never forget how."

Watching him a moment, she saw with relief that the stiffness quickly left Cullen, to be replaced with the ease and assurance he had always had around horses, as Central responded to every command. She'd been right, then. The core of him *had* held true, despite Teague. After just a quarter-hour's work, she and Cullen were in the saddle riding toward Bluegrass Hill.

"We'll do a conditioning gallop, and then some cross-country work, and finally some show-jumping," Sam said. "Central used to you yet?"

"We're best buds," Cullen assured her with a grin as he patted the dun's neck. "I'm beginning to understand why you're so obsessed with this breeding program. What got you started?"

The question startled Sam. Cullen had carefully refrained from asking her about her program, or discussing his father's stock, or talking horses at all since he'd first left for college. "Well, after I graduated from the Sorbonne, I spent a year traveling through France and Austria, Italy, Belgium, the Netherlands, and Germany, studying European methods of breeding, raising, and training some of the finest horses in the world. I know, I know," she said with a wry smile. "Any reasonable twenty-one-year-old woman on her own for the first time in her life would have been exploring European castles. But *I* got to talk for hours with some of the world's foremost experts about the one thing I love most—horses. When you come right down to it, though, it was probably Kaspar Reinhart who got me thinking about the breeding program."

"I rode against Kaspar once in a Grand Prix event," Cullen said. "Very formidable competitor. You knew him?"

"Well," Sam said modestly, "in the biblical sense, yes."

"Samantha!"

She burst out laughing. "Well, I did! He was the third of my three European lovers, you see. During the course of our grand passion, Kaspar took me to visit his family home. You've heard of Abelard Farms in Germany's Schleswig-Holstein region, haven't you?"

"Vaguely," Cullen muttered, apparently still not fully recovered from her newest bombshell.

Oh, how she loved shredding his misconceptions about her! "Well, I fell in love with the Reinhart family's champion Holsteins at first sight. Kaspar even talked me into riding one of his geldings in the Hamburg Grand Prix. I made it into the final jump-off, which ironically came down to Kaspar and me. I won, and not only did Kaspar not hold it against me, he helped me celebrate my victory." In ways she chose not to reveal to Cullen. "The money I won for that day's work paid for the rest of my European travels and for my couture wardrobe.

"I think," she said as Cullen slid off Central to open the white gate before them, "that that may have been the happiest summer of my life." She looked away from Cullen, shaken by a sudden surge of bitterness. "But all good things come to an end."

"You still miss them, don't you?" he said quietly as he stepped back into the saddle.

She didn't even consider playing obtuse. "Every morning I walk into the kitchen and expect to see Mom and Dad sitting there, drinking their coffee and teasing each other." They walked through the gate and continued toward Bluegrass Hill.

"It's that way with me and Teague. I wake up in the morning and think I hear him singing as he gets dressed."

Shadows again. She longed to reach over and touch Cullen, free him somehow from those dark clutches.

"I don't suppose you'll ever let yourself accept that the crash wasn't your fault."

"No." Cullen's face was hard, closed.

Tears stung Samantha's eyes for a moment. That so good a man should insist on torturing himself to the grave for something he couldn't have prevented . . .

"Laurel and Keenan are so thrilled to have you back, you know, even if it is just for the summer."

"I'm every parent's dream," Cullen quipped. "Eldest son makes good. Parental nest egg assured."

"Oh, stop it!" Sam said angrily. "They don't give a damn about the money you made and you know it. They love *you*, Cullen Mackenzie, and they respect you, not for what you've done but for who you are, and *you are not Teague*! Haven't you figured out yet that you're fine by yourself, that you don't need to be Teague, too?"

"Of all the ridiculous—"

"Don't patronize me, Cullen," Sam said sharply.

He was silent a moment. An enraged Celtic warrior on a dun gelding. "I took Teague from my family and from Whitney," he said. "It's important to me that I give them back as much of him as I can. I feel better when I do."

"But all of that has nothing to do with what *they* want from you," Sam said, reaching out and grasping his muscular arm to make him look at her, feeling his heat, forcing herself not to jerk her hand away. "Have you even bothered to ask them what they want? What they need?"

"*Whitney* needs the life I'm finally able to give her," he retorted, pulling his arm free.

"Whitney needs *you,*" Sam countered. "There's a difference. A huge difference."

"No," Cullen said with disturbing certainty. "For Whitney, it's a package deal. It always has been. She's been my biggest cheerleader these last six years while the rest of you kept trying to convince me to chuck the business and come home."

"That's only because she loves you. She'd support you in anything you wanted to accomplish."

"There's no need to sound so defensive. I'm grateful to Whitney, I really am. Because of her, I became much more than I ever thought possible."

"How could you think for a minute that you weren't enough just the way you were?" Sam demanded.

Murderous gray eyes bored into her. "Because who I was was never as good as Teague, and because who I was got Teague killed."

"That has nothing to do with the truth," Samantha retorted, heart pounding in her chest. "That's just some more of your shadow lies."

He looked at her curiously. "What do you know about shadows?"

Sam forcibly hauled herself back from the edge. "Keep it light" had been her lifelong mantra. "I'm an observant kind of gal. You've taught me a lot these last twelve years. I can't tell you how much I wish you hadn't."

He looked away as a half dozen exercise boys and girls rode past them back toward the stables, greeting Sam, smiling at Cullen. "You were telling me how you started your breeding program," he said.

"Oh yeah. Right," Sam said, forcing herself to retrench. "Well, riding the Abelard Holsteins, working with them every day, watching them calmly taking six-foot jumps, the brainstorm just sort of hit me. It proceeded to rule every thought and plan and dream and feeling for the next two months while I negotiated with Kaspar and another Holstein breeder face to face, and over the phone with Ridgeback Horse Farm for the best Morgans America had to offer. When I was sure I had the best deals on the best Morgan stallions and Holstein mares that money could buy, I called home."

"How did Rufus take it?" Cullen asked with a knowing smile.

It was hard to make herself smile back. The consequences of that phone call still haunted her. "Oh, he balked, of course. It took hours of steady reasoned argument to convince Dad that the breeding program would work, that Skylark Horse Farm could create a new American breed that would become champions in Grand Prix, steeplechase, and three-day-event competitions. It took several more hours to convince him that we needed three Morgan stallions and twelve Holstein brood mares if we were going to have any chance of really pushing the cross-breed forward." Rufus had trusted her knowledge and judgment to make the right purchases, but the expense—

She had talked him into even that. She shuddered slightly as she and Cullen began a steady gallop up Blue-grass Hill. Three-quarters of a million dollars for fifteen horses, because she had to have the best bloodlines, proven studs, champion mares. She had personally chaperoned the Holstein mares across the Atlantic to their new home, the home she hadn't seen herself in nearly four years. The Morgan stallions had been waiting for them.

It had all felt like a wonderful dream her first summer home: starting the breeding program, sitting up night after night to plan and organize and plan again. The dream ended when the first generation of new stock were just yearlings. She was twenty-three. Her father was felled by a massive stroke as they walked the farm together. It took Rufus al-most a month to die—the hardest month of her life, she thought. Then she took on the responsibility of running Skylark and made the shocking discovery that, long before the purchase of the new stock, her father had run the farm's finances into the ground.

She had never even *suspected* it, and she should have. Rufus Lark had always been much more of a dreamer than a practical businessman. Each of his moneymaking schemes had ended in disaster, because he always went off half-cocked without the buildings and the equipment and the staff and the knowledge in place to do the job properly. The farm that had been in their family since 1636 had paid the consequences. A mortgage couldn't cover Rufus Lark's pipe dreams. There was a second mortgage, and several bank loans, and a maxed-out line of credit. And then Sam had come along with a pipe dream of her own.

Five years ago, her father newly buried, she had stared at Skylark's accounts, nausea and horror roiling within her.

Because *she knew*. She *knew* that the intolerable burden of carrying the enormous debt of her precious breeding program day after day, month after month, had caused her father's stroke. It had killed him. *She* had killed him.

And her mother, too. Rufus and Jean Lark had shared a very symbiotic relationship. Sam had known on the day of her father's funeral that her mother would die soon, too. Jean Lark hadn't the strength or even the desire to withstand grief and loneliness and a world without Rufus. Four months later, she was buried beside her husband. The death certificate had said heart failure, but Sam knew the truth. She and she alone had taken away her mother's reason for living.

Sam had blood on her hands, and a sister to support at Juilliard, and creditors demanding payment on mortgages, bank loans, and lines of credit.

She had been left with nothing to cover those debts except some very expensive horses and her father's persuasive powers which she had inherited and which she now wielded mercilessly to talk her way out of foreclosure and receivership. She fired the accountant whose only advice was to sell and sell now. She went to Virginia's largest bank, talked her way into the senior vice president's office, and seven hours later walked out with a consolidation loan that paid off all of Skylark's creditors. She now had only the one bank to pay off and no way to do it.

For two days, she had walked the farm she loved more than her life before reaching her wrenching decision. She would cut her staff in half. She would sell off most of her older stock, Thoroughbreds she had helped to deliver and train, horses she had competed on and had won on. With that money, and by cutting expenses to the bone, she could make her monthly loan payment, and pay her remaining staff, and keep her new breeding program going for three years. She held some Thoroughbred stock back, to be sold off carefully in the following two years, and also took in stud fees on her Morgans to raise additional funds.

Five years. That was her timeline. There wasn't a penny to keep the farm alive after that. She would have to push the first generation of new stock harder and faster than she normally would, and put them into advanced competition as six-year-olds, which was insanity, and pray that they would show well, which was even greater insanity, knowing the kind of competitors they would face.

But everything hinged on those six-year-olds shining in the midst of much more experienced ten- and twelve-year-old internationally seasoned horses—and their world-class riders. If Magic and Flora and Nessie and Central did well in their first advanced (and televised) competition, they would generate the kind of interest and sales of her new stock she needed to pay off her crushing debt and keep the farm afloat. It was her only chance. She was wagering every-thing she had on this one throw of the dice.

And the Mackenzie Horse Trials were the crap table.

God, what a mess, Sam thought as she and Cullen pulled their horses back down to a walk.

She had been terrified every day of these last five years and had hidden it because she had to be strong for every-one else, and because it was imperative that no one know how bad Skylark's finances were. If word got out, vultures around the world would insist on paying wholesale prices for her stock, and that would be the final nail in the farm's coffin. She needed top dollar for every horse and every stud fee or her desperate plan wouldn't work. She had had to deceive everyone except her foreman, Bobby Craig. He and he alone had to understand why she was pushing the new stock so hard, because she couldn't pull it off without Bobby's help.

She hadn't even told Erin, partly for fear her sister would let the secret leak out, and partly from guilt. She had caused this mess and Erin could lose her home because of it. Fearful her sister would see the guilt and the stress if she stayed too close to home, Sam had encouraged her to follow in her own footsteps and work her way through Europe, first with the Paris Opera, then with the Berlin Philharmonic, and finally in Rome. Knowing Erin was happy in her career and ignorant of Skylark's troubles had been the only peace Sam had known these last five years.

She glanced across at Cullen sitting so easily on Central Lark. The Mackenzie fortune had often been the bane of her existence during these last five years. Two or three times a year, Bobby Craig pleaded with her to ask the Mackenzies for a loan, knowing just as well as she did that they would give her the money outright if she asked.

But she wouldn't. She couldn't. *She* had nearly destroyed Skylark Horse Farm. *She* had filled the last two years of her parents' lives with unbearable stress and fear. She had killed them. It was her fault, her burden, her penance. She was, she reminded Bobby every time he begged her to go to the Mackenzies, an old-fashioned moralist. For every wrong-doing there was a punishment, and this was hers.

"Another ten minutes to rest Magic and Central and then we'll hit the cross-country course," she said, turning Magic to the northwest. Cullen rode into place beside her.

"Swell," he said. "I know I've been out of the loop these last twelve years, but it seems to me you've got your stock on an incredibly fast track."

"Tell me something I don't know," Sam said, shuddering inwardly. "I worry about it nonstop. I can't push them too hard because I have to keep them healthy. No pulled tendons. No splints or sprained ligaments or windgall. At the same time, they have to be as well prepared as I can make them. I had to enter them into preliminary competitions last year to earn enough points for each to qualify for intermediate competitions this spring, so they could, in turn, rack up enough points to qualify for advanced competition this fall."

"But what if they finish badly at Morven Park and don't earn enough points?"

Samantha regarded him pityingly. "We are riding two of the four horses that blew every single one of their competitors out of the water last year and this spring."

"They're that good?"

"They're better," Sam assured him. "I only hope the intermediate competitions will have seasoned them enough so they don't freak on the advanced tests at the Trials." She'd done what she could to squeeze in very possible moment of training to give them the best chance to show well. But it was a tightrope act that had begun to make even her precious six hours of sleep at night difficult.

"There's a hint of desperation about all of this," Cullen commented, watching her closely.

Sam made herself laugh carelessly. "No, just impatience. It's time the wee beasties began paying their own way."

They reached the start of the cross-country course. Sam described each jump to Cullen in detail. Then they walked the course while their horses enjoyed a quick grassy snack. They climbed back into their saddles and gathered their reins.

"Ready?" Sam asked.

"Let's do it," he said, looking grim, not eager. Sam began to realize just how much these last twelve years had stolen from him.

They set out on the course at an easy gallop, Cullen following Sam and staying close enough behind so that each could call to the other if there was any trouble.

There wasn't. Cullen rode as if he hadn't had a twelve-*minute* sabbatical from competitive riding. Seeing immediately that she didn't have to worry about him, Sam didn't.

She focused all of her attention and energy on Magic and the course, loving that the bay moved confidently and easily beneath her. She rode Magic down the steep right bank of Brandy Creek—home to bass and catfish, turtles and salamanders—jumped him over the eight-foot-wide expanse of water, and sent him charging up the left bank.

She turned him toward the next obstacle, a four-foot-tall timber fence ten yards away, the red flag on the right side of the jump and the white flag on the left side hanging limp in the still air. She glanced at her large digital wristwatch. A little under five minutes, and three-quarters of the way through the course. Magic hadn't refused a jump or shied or tried to run away with her once. Maybe he was finally beginning to gain a little maturity. Maybe . . . She made herself refocus on the course. Magic needed her complete attention, not her desperate hopes.

The gelding easily cleared the final jump, a four-foot-tall post and rails. She pulled him down to a walk. He moved easily beneath her, still strong after the grueling thirty-jump cross-country course. Stamina, strength, agility, brains—they were everything she had hoped for when the breeding program had first captured her imagination seven years ago.

She laughed as the gelding tossed his dark head in protest at the walk she forced on him. He still wanted to run, bless his youthful heart.

"God, that was wonderful!" Cullen said breathlessly as he and Central caught up with them. "Let's do it again."

"No problem. You get to do it all over again on Nessie," Sam said with a grin as they rode through shin-high grass back toward the main Skylark buildings.

"I'd forgotten how much *fun* this is," Cullen said, happily stretching toward the sun.

"You'd *forgotten* . . . ?" Sam stared at her friend. How could the horseman she knew him to be forget about this joy?

He shrugged. "The only time I ride is when I come home, and since I don't do much of that, I ride very little. I mean, think about it, Sam. This is only the second time I've been on horseback since I've been home this summer."

"The Great Plot will soon remedy *that*."

"Yeah," he said, looking oddly torn, as if he didn't want to be glad, but was.

They worked easily and comfortably together all morning, Cullen asking her more and more questions about her new stock, she catching him up on all of the changes at Mackenzie Farm, as they galloped and jumped and didn't land on their butts once.

It was just before one o'clock that hot afternoon when Sam rode Lark Honor, a black five-year-old gelding, into the stableyard. Cullen was on Desdemona, Magic's five-year-old bay sister.

Sam jumped to the ground, ran the stirrups up their leathers, and began leading Honor toward the main stable. Marybeth Hill, the young and very promising African-American groom responsible for Honor, Central Lark, Lark Ness, and three others, came running up.

"I'll take Honor, Miss Lark," she said.

"Thanks, Marybeth," Sam said as the groom clipped a lead shank onto the bridle. "Cool him down carefully. He had quite a workout today. And give him an extra apple for me."

"Yes, ma'am," Marybeth said with a grin before leading Honor away.

"Andy, bring Sigfreda over here," Sam called.

Andy, wearing only tattered jeans and boots, his blond mohawk swaying in the slight breeze, his nose ring glinting in the sunlight, obligingly turned around and led a very large blood bay mare over to Sam and Cullen.

"She looks ready to explode," Cullen said, gently stroking the mare's extended belly. "When's she due?"

"Two days ago," Sam said. "How's my little beauty doing, hm?" she crooned to her favorite brood mare as she stroked the soft muzzle.

"She had a good workout and actually managed to roll onto her back afterwards," Andy said.

"An Herculean task," Cullen said with a grin.

"She's a very determined lady, aren't you, Sigfreda?" Sam crooned as stroked the mare's head. "Has Bobby checked her over?"

"Yep," Andy said. "Everything looks good. Bobby says she and the foal are just trying to coordinate their schedules."

"Well, put a light blanket on her when you're done grooming her," Sam said. "My best brood mare gets hypersensitive care."

"Yes, ma'am," Andy said.

"Where on earth did you dig *him* up?" Cullen demanded as they watched the boy lead Sigfreda away.

Sam chuckled. Andy *was* an incongruity in Virginia horse country. "I noticed him hanging around the horses at the National Horse Show in Madison Square Garden about four years ago. When he turned up the year after that, and then the year after *that*, I sort of struck up a conversation with him. The poor kid is mad about equines. So I hired him. Andy's been working for me for almost a year now. He may be from Queens, but he's got a real feel for horses. There's a lot of potential there, maybe as a trainer, maybe as a rider. Maybe both. Bobby's taken him under his wing to help him figure out which direction he should go."

"This is an improbable world," Cullen said. His stomach suddenly growled, loudly and at length. He looked at Sam. "You want to help me out here?"

She laughed and looped her arm through his. "You've scratched my back, now I'll scratch yours. Let's have lunch." She suddenly stopped. "Oh, crud. I forgot to say anything to Calida. I only hope we have something to feed you."

"Sam, get real," Cullen said, pulling her toward the house. "Calida could feed the President of the United States *and* his Cabinet on five minutes' notice."

He was right, of course. All Sam had to do was stick her head in the kitchen and tell Calida that Cullen had come to lunch, and she hoped that was all right, and five minutes later Calida was setting cold cucumber soup, a curried chicken salad, fresh bread, and a still warm peach pie on the dining table.

"It's a pleasure to see you sit down to lunch for once," she told Sam as she set a pitcher of iced tea in the middle of the table. She glanced at Cullen. "You should come around more often."

"I intend to," Cullen said with a grin. Calida gave him a curt nod of approval and then headed back into the kitchen. "A formidable woman," he said as he helped himself to the chicken salad.

"Practically her own little junta," Sam grimly retorted as she buttered a piece of bread. She did not need Calida taking her to task in front of Cullen for her poor eating habits.

"Do you really skip eating lunch?"

"No, of course not. It's just that Calida doesn't think those organic meals in a bottle constitute food. You know her: if it isn't set on a proper dining table and have at least four courses, then it's not a meal."

Gray eyes caught her gaze and held her with sudden hypnotic intensity. "Dad said that I was driven. I'm getting the idea that I could turn around and say the same thing about you."

"We all have our causes," Sam said a little breathlessly.

"Hey, don't start without me!" Erin yelled as she hurtled herself down the stairs and threw herself onto a dining chair. "I'm starved!"

"How goes practice?" Sam asked with a grin as she handed her sister the bowl of curried chicken salad.

"Splendidly, thank you," Erin said, putting two helpings onto her plate.

"When's the final audition?" Cullen asked.

"Tomorrow," Erin said, reaching for the soup tureen.

"Luck to you," he said.

"Thanks."

Calida walked back to the table, shoved an open box of long-stemmed white roses into Sam's startled hands, and headed back to the kitchen.

"What in the world are these?" Sam demanded.

"They're called flowers. They're for you," Cullen said.

"Huh?"

"A thank you for such a terrific kickoff to the Great Plot last night."

Sam blushed with pleasure.

"And a barb to drive Whitney mad with jealousy, of course," Cullen concluded.

Sam fell off her pink cloud with a thud and tried hurriedly to cover. "So," she said, setting the flowers down beside her on the table, "find any glass slippers last night?"

He laughed at her and then turned the conversation to his parents' anniversary ball, to how happy they had been last night, and how successful the Great Plot had been.

"Sammy *was* brilliant last night," Erin said proudly.

"Well, Cullen didn't do too badly himself," Sam said.

"He had *you* for inspiration," Erin said.

She was immediately distracted by the peach pie and left Cullen and Sam to carry on the conversation without her. So, of course, they talked about horses. Sam's horses, the Mackenzie horses, the Barrisfords' horses, even Noel's two champion French Anglo-Arabs he had recently had shipped to him from his farm in France. They talked as if Cullen hadn't spent the last twelve years avoiding anything and everything having to do with horses.

"About the Great Plot," Cullen said over their peach pie.

"Yes?" Sam said.

"We made a good start last night, but to really sell the scheme, we need to put on another public display. That is why I've sold my folks on having a group picnic at Mackenzie Lake this coming Sunday. You know: invite twenty or thirty of their nearest and dearest, horseback riding, picnicking, swimming, romping about. The perfect setting for romantic pursuits."

God, she'd lose *hours* from her Sunday. Sam forced herself to smile. "Fine by me."

"There is just one other thing."

"Yes?"

"We should probably kiss."

"Huh?"

"Each other. In front of Whitney. At the picnic."

Erin burst out laughing. "God, Whitney will burst a gut!"

"Exactly," Cullen said with a pleased smile.

"This will push Whitney over the edge for sure," Sam agreed. "But what kind of a kiss should it be, to achieve maximum effect, I mean. Long or short? Gentle or hard? Should we be standing, or sitting, or lying down?"

"Hm," Cullen said, adopting a scholarly pose. "Long, hard, standing."

Sam laughed. "Okay, but how do we get to it? I can't just walk up to you in the middle of the picnic and kiss you. No one would buy it."

"True," Cullen said. He considered things a moment. "We'd better rehearse," he said, shoving back his chair.

"Right," Sam said happily as she stood up. She hadn't done any acting since high school. This was going to be fun.

"I'll be your audience," Erin said, adjusting her chair. "The curtain goes up on a quiet country setting, beautifully lit and decorated. The audience applauds." She clapped robustly.

Cullen cast her a wry glance and then got down to work. "I suppose we could be standing and talking, making sure, of course, to be where *everyone* can see us."

"We could pretend to be arguing about our budding romance!" Sam said excitedly. "You could pretend to be back-pedaling or something, I could counter by saying I'll *prove* to you that we're more than friends, and *then* we can kiss!"

"Great. Now, should I go with the Errol Flynn approach?" Cullen asked, suddenly grabbing her and dropping her into a low dip and making loud kissing sounds.

"No!" Sam gasped, giggling helplessly.

"It was the accent that sold him anyway," Erin said.

"The Bing Crosby arm-around-your-shoulders buss?" Cullen asked, hauling Sam upright and enveloping her between his arms as he puckered up.

"Ick, no!"

"Ditto!" Erin hollered.

"Picky, picky, picky," Cullen said with a sigh.

"Look, Romeo, *I'll* kiss *you*," Sam said. "I'll grab your head," she said, grabbing his head, "ignore the spinach caught between your teeth, look deep into your eyes, rise to the tippy-top of my toes—*do* you think you could bend down just a tad?—and then proceed to suck out your teeth."

"Well, that sounds appetizing," Cullen said, grinning down into her laughter-filled eyes.

"Stop!"

Still in each other's arms, they turned to find a horrified Whitney standing in the doorway, an actual blush creeping into her cheeks. "I-I-I mean, don't you dare kiss her, Cullen Mackenzie."

"Why not?" Cullen said, his grin growing as Sam hitched a leg onto his hip.

Erin turned hurriedly away to hide her laughter.

"Why," Whitney sputtered, "because she's just the sort of woman to actually believe you mean it. Sam, stop acting like a teenager hopped up on hormones and *let him go*!"

"Yes, ma'am," Sam said meekly, releasing Cullen.

"What are you even doing here?" Whitney demanded as she marched into the room, glaring at Cullen.

"Samantha invited me to lunch," he replied innocently.

"It's been years since Cullen and I have had a chance to sit down and really talk together," Sam said with a smile that only added fuel to the fire in Whitney's blue eyes. "I realized last night that we hardly know each other after all these years of living and working apart. Before last night's ball, he was still treating me like the adolescent tagalong who was forever harassing him fifteen years ago. Can you imagine?"

"I'm sure last night corrected *that* little misconception," Whitney replied brittlely.

"And how," Cullen chimed in. "Samantha is full of surprises."

"Yes," Whitney said with a silky smile as Erin watched avidly from the sidelines, "I noticed. But then, I've got a few of my own." She twined her arms around his neck and arched her body into his. "I've tracked you down to ask you if you'll come to dinner tonight. There's a reward for the right answer."

"Really?" Cullen said, staring down into her bedroom eyes and realizing with something like chagrin that he wasn't enjoying her deliberate seduction half as much as he'd enjoyed Sam's silliness. "There's no need to bribe me, Whitney. I'd love to come to dinner."

"Wonderful," Whitney said, pressing her full mouth to his for the briefest second before pulling away. "Come, walk me to my car." She glanced back at Sam. "You're through with him, aren't you, Sam?"

"For now," Sam replied.

Whitney's blue eyes narrowed for a moment, then she laughed lightly and pulled Cullen to the front door.

"Y'all come back now, y'hear," Erin yelled.

"See you tomorrow, Cullen," Sam cheerfully called after him.

Whitney became suddenly rigid. "What does she mean by that?" she demanded as Cullen, impressed by Sam's perfect sense of timing, opened the front door for her.

"I'm helping Samantha out with a few horses," he said as they walked outside into the heavy heat of mid-afternoon.

"Oh," Whitney said, unable to hide her relief, *"horses."*

CULLEN WAS CONVINCED, thanks to horses and the hours of physical work he'd done that morning, plus Whitney's delightful attentions at dinner that night, that he'd fall asleep the minute his head hit the pillow just after midnight.

But he didn't.

Instead, his mind kept replaying over and over again Sam's laughter as they had practiced for their forthcoming kiss. Ah, the Queen of Silliness. A smile tugged at his lips as her giggles filled his ears once more. Then he remembered the way Sam had looked so completely in love as she'd greeted her horses in the stable this morning. He'd be happy if Whitney would look at him with even half as much love in her eyes. Had Sam looked with as much love at Phillippe Valentin and Kaspar Reinhart and whoever her third lover had been when she had shared their beds?

It was an uncomfortable train of thought. He didn't like the idea of Sam in *any* man's bed.

Cullen rolled over onto his stomach and shoved his hands under his pillow. It was strange, really, how little he knew about the adult Samantha Lark, when he'd known

her all of her life. In just twelve hours he'd learned so much
that he hadn't known yesterday morning. Important things.
Things like Samantha was a sensual, beautiful, driven woman.
He wondered about that last. What was driving her? Ambition? Cullen smiled. She'd laugh herself silly if he ever suggested it.

Maybe she wasn't driven or desperate. Maybe he'd
misread her. Maybe she was just wholly engrossed in her
work and in her vision of what her breeding program could
accomplish.

That's what she'd said. Why couldn't he quite believe
her?

Cullen's mind continued spinning around Samantha as
he began to slowly drift asleep. Lord, he was tired, and he
liked it, because it was a tired that had come from stretching his muscles as well as his brain. He hadn't sat behind a
desk once today. Or had a phone glued to his ear for hours
at a time. It felt, Cullen thought sleepily as a long line of
horses began jumping over Brandy Creek, like this was the
best day he'd ever had.

Seven

THE TWENTY-SIX CELEBRANTS of the first week of July in all its glory, heat, and humidity rode at an easy lope across a lush Mackenzie pasture towards twelve acres of a clear blue lake bordered by bluegrass, crape myrtle trees in full bloom, brown-eyed susans, birch trees, blue lobelia, and dogwoods. Sam had expertly maneuvered Central Lark so that she began the ride at Cullen's side and stayed there, knowing full well that Whitney would never lower herself to ride on Cullen's other side in clear competition with her friend for his attention.

Whitney had turned, naturally enough, to Noel Beaumont, only to find that, as she had secretly promised her sister, Erin had claimed Noel's attentions for herself. Fuming, Whitney turned to Missy Barrisford for comfort and companionship on the thirty-minute ride to the lake, complaining all the way about the fickleness of men, the stupid competitiveness of women, and the insulting gossip loping around her. Missy finally broke in to advise patience and a change in strategy, and Whitney listened, as she always listened to her longtime friend.

Sam, meanwhile, was actually enjoying herself, despite the work waiting for her at Skylark. Thank heaven for the Great Plot! Because of it, she was remembering that she was a person who knew how to have fun. She chatted with Cullen, recalling childhood adventures at Mackenzie Lake, and pretended to flirt with him by wielding some of the games she had seen Whitney use over the years. She smiled at the appreciative gleam in Cullen's gray eyes. Apparently, just because Whitney's games had worked didn't mean that Cullen hadn't known he was being played.

They topped a grassy hillock and Mackenzie Lake sprang out before them, gently rounded, blue, and still.

Under Keenan Mackenzie's autocratic supervision, it took only fifteen minutes to create a rope corral for the horses, with a section of the lake providing the fourth side, so the horses had grass to crop and water to drink while the humans frolicked around them. A rock-lined fire pit, built years before, was filled with charcoal and wood chips, and a fire lit to cook lunch.

Whitney expertly maneuvered herself beside Cullen and then led him away to the picnic blanket she had spread out under a tree near the lake. No longer distracted, Sam's thoughts flitted back once again to Skylark as she helped to set up the makeshift day camp, two dozen people laughing and chatting nonstop around her. Tomorrow she had to ride her top four six-year-olds in the first of two intermediate eventing competitions that should earn them the last of the points they needed to become eligible for the advanced competition at the Mackenzie Horse Trials. Lark Magic needed more dressage work, Lark Ness had to be helped through her sudden aversion to water jumps, Sigfreda was ready to foal any second now, and—

Horses were suddenly relegated to the far back burner of Sam's brain. Just ten feet away, a small clutch of people were stripping down to their bathing suits.

People like Cullen.

He was all rippling muscles and sinews in a taut package of broad shoulders, narrow hips, and long, beautifully proportioned legs. A large square mat of thick golden hair covered his chest before tapering down in a thin arrow to disappear within a white Speedo swimsuit. Standing there, he was pure, primal man, shocking in the power of his masculinity. It radiated out and enveloped her, caught her, stirring something equally primal and shocking within herself. She was assailed by a barrage of sexual fantasies. She could actually feel her naked body sliding down over that thick, crinkly chest hair and down those long legs to—

Clarity and truth slammed into her, knocking the air from her lungs. She wanted the man! She was physically, sexually, mesmerizingly attracted to the man. In fact, she had *always* been attracted to Cullen. She had just never let herself know it until now, because it was too dangerous to their friendship, and because Whitney wanted him and he wanted Whitney. There was no way she could change that equation. Why acknowledge something she could do nothing about?

Unfortunately, thanks to the Great Plot, illumination *had* struck. The truth was, if she could take Cullen to bed right now—without him laughing himself silly, of course—she would. In a heartbeat.

God, what a mess! She'd promised to help Cullen win Whitney, and that meant she had to keep flirting with him, throwing herself at him, and letting him catch her, and all the while somehow fend off this desire burning through her, hotter, deeper than she'd ever felt for any man before.

Cullen's eyes met hers. He started walking toward her, almost naked, taut skin practically steaming in the sunlight.

"You're drooling," he said.

Oh God, he knows! "I-I-I'm playing a part, remember? The Great Plot," she said hastily. "We're supposed to be a burgeoning romance, which means I'm supposed to ogle you."

"Right," he said, smiling.

Her hormones began to sizzle. Oh, *why* hadn't she clung to her fourteen-hour workdays and told Cullen to find himself another partner for the Great Plot? She felt shy and awkward with the man for the first time in her life and she didn't know what to do about it except pretend that she didn't feel awkward and shy and to keep playing the game full tilt and pray that he, or anyone else for that matter, didn't notice that she wasn't acting nearly as much as she pretended.

"Why . . . . white?" she asked.

His smile grew. "I remembered the feminine uproar when Greg Louganis wore a white swimsuit at the 1988 Olympics. I figured I needed every edge I could get with Whitney. Think it'll work?"

"If Whitney doesn't drag you to the altar by the end of today, she has no right to call herself a woman."

Cullen laughed. "Let's see if we can add another successful chapter the Great Plot today," he said just before Whitney walked up to them wearing a black bikini that looked ready to burst its seams at any moment. She draped herself against Cullen's side. His arm went around her waist, bronzed skin against white flesh.

"Nice suit," she said to Sam with a feline smile.

Sam ordered herself not to blush. Her midnight blue bikini wasn't as skimpy or as well filled out as Whitney's black bikini, but it was perfectly adequate. Or was it?

"Yes," Cullen said, open admiration in his eyes, "it is."

She blushed. *Was he reading her mind?* And did he really like her suit, or was he just furthering the Great Plot?

Oh hell! she silently railed to herself. *I shouldn't care!*

Her inner turmoil left her outwardly mute and uncertain what to do or say next to get the Great Plot back on track. Whitney took advantage of her rival's hesitation by tugging Cullen toward the lake.

"Come on, darling," she said, infusing each word with a world of meaning, "let's get wet."

Sam watched helplessly as Whitney pulled Cullen into the lake, she laughing up at him, he gazing admiringly down at her. Something horribly like jealousy stabbed into Sam. "Oh, well, that's the end," she muttered in disgust as she stood, arms akimbo, on her red plaid picnic blanket watching Whitney, thigh-deep in water, methodically seduce Cullen. "I've gone stark, raving mad, that's all. The nice young men with the butterfly nets should be along any minute."

"But no, it is only me."

Sam turned to find Noel standing beside her, quite naked except for a microscopic black swimsuit. Her eyes traveled over dark tanned flesh that rippled with the after-effects of countless strenuous hours of weight lifting. His washboard belly was a work of art. His stunningly defined thighs looked good enough to eat. His smile could melt Antarctica. A lock of black hair brushed his forehead, tempting feminine fingers to stroke it back into place. Michelangelo would have insisted on sculpting him. *People* magazine would have named him "Sexiest Man Alive" in perpetuity. Every female in a hundred-mile radius would have thrown herself at his beautifully shaped feet.

Samantha's heart didn't even skip a beat.

"Oh, Noel!" she wailed, throwing herself on his sympathetic chest. "I'm such an *idiot*!"

"But what is wrong, my little one?" Noel asked in the greatest confusion.

She stared up at him in agony. "I don't want you!"

"What?"

"I can't even work up casual interest in going to bed with you."

"You are not well."

"I *know*!" she wailed.

"This calls for drastic measures." Noel picked her up and began carrying her to the lake.

"Just what drastic measures were you thinking of?" Sam asked uneasily.

"I am going to drown you," he cheerfully replied.

Sam burst out laughing. "No, really, Noel. Noel!" she shrieked as he carried her into the lake and kept walking. She tried to wriggle out of his arms, but Noel had vast experience with wriggling women. He was like a human straitjacket. "Can't we just be friends?" she pleaded, hiccuping with laughter.

"I'm sorry, my little one, but I have my reputation to think of."

"Oh, well yes, of course. How silly of me. Cullen, *help*!" she shouted as Noel carried her past the source of her current predicament.

Whitney was just leaning in for the big kiss she had so carefully been working up to, only to find herself kissing lake water as Cullen leapt to Sam's rescue with a gallantry even Sir Walter Scott would admire. His flying tackle submerged Noel, Samantha, and himself. He got his feet back under him, caught Sam's wrist in his hand, and hauled her upright just as Noel was stumbling to his knees.

"Ta da!" Cullen said with a boyish grin.

"My hero!" Sam said, coughing. "Except for the near-drowning, you were great."

"Gee, thanks."

"Was that necessary?" Noel demanded.

"Very," Cullen said with a satisfied grin.

"Cullen, you *monster*!" Whitney shrieked as she hauled herself upright, blond hair plastered to her face.

"Whitney's watching," Cullen whispered to Sam, his arms sliding around her. "We should probably do something about that."

"Right," Sam said, suppressing a shiver, her heart pounding harder and harder as she wrapped her arms around Cullen's broad naked back. "I live to serve the Great Plot."

But this didn't feel anything like make-believe. This was her wet, nearly naked body molding itself to Cullen's wet, nearly naked body, chest to chest, hip to hip, leg to leg. She was hyper-aware of his long fingers pressing into her back, of each breath that he took, of the water drops sliding between their bellies. Her heart was pounding faster and faster, her nipples eagerly hardening against the thick golden mat of his chest hair.

"I think this," he murmured as he slid one hand to the back of her head, "is where we kiss."

Oh, she wanted to kiss him more than she wanted to breathe! She wanted to devour him. She wanted his warm, wet tongue to invade her mouth and claim her, caress her, until she went stark, raving mad.

Gray eyes held her spellbound. A whole world she had never even imagined stirred in their smoky depths. They were coming closer, and closer, as he lowered his head to hers. She was stretching up to meet him halfway, lips aching in anticipation of this first brush of his mouth against hers.

"Lunch! Come and get it!"

The exuberant clanging of several cowbells shattered the sensual fog that had held the rest of the world at bay only a moment before. Sam was plunged back into the cool water of Mackenzie Lake, the hot July sun overhead, people splashing and laughing all around her, Whitney spitting mad just ten feet away.

Cullen was staring down at her, looking like a man who'd just discovered that there really *were* monsters under his bed.

Sam had never felt more painfully aware of another human being in her life. She hastily backed out of Cullen's arms. "Hooray, lunch," she said weakly. "I'm starved."

"Yeah," Cullen said, staring at their fellow picnickers who were beginning to gather around the fire pit on shore. "Me, too."

"We'd better get a move on, or there'll be nothing left to eat." Sam said, already beginning to walk toward shore, silently repeating *Thank God, thank God, thank God* to herself over and over again.

Thank *God* they'd been interrupted! She had wanted that near-kiss way too much. Cullen was a smart guy. He'd have known immediately that that kiss meant more to her than just another way to further the Great Plot. He'd have known all the secrets she was just learning about herself. She'd have been left standing there feeling exposed to the world while their lifelong friendship disappeared forever beneath the blue water of Mackenzie Lake.

She had to get some clothes on fast to help bullet-proof herself from any knowing gazes, and particularly from Cullen's X-ray eyes.

She reached her plaid picnic blanket and immediately pulled her lavender polo shirt over her head and dragged on her pair of jeans over her wet swimsuit. She let out an audible sigh of relief. There, that felt better.

She glanced surreptitiously around and saw Cullen ankle-deep in the lake as Whitney stood before him, berating him, her breasts swelling her damp bikini top to the near-breaking point.

"Look what you've done to my hair!" she yelled.

Cullen seemed puzzled. "Well, what did you think would happen if you went swimming?"

"I didn't *intend* to go swimming!" Whitney shouted. "And I don't call falling flat on my face in the lake *swimming*! Of all the inconsiderate men . . ."

Wet blond hair swept back from his forehead, powerful body glowing in the sunlight, Cullen devoted himself to making amends and very soon had made significant headway. Whitney allowed him to put his arms around her. She even went so far as to twine her arms around his neck and smile up at him.

Samantha watched it all, knowing that she should be rejoicing in this happy change in Cullen's romantic fortune, and knowing that she felt very differently. *Cullen was holding Whitney like he had just held her.* Pain and anger knotted her belly.

She turned hurriedly away from the pair to pull on her boots. The Great Plot would certainly call for her to disrupt that intimate conversation, but the Great Plot could go hang. Safety first. It had just become Sam's motto. Safety first. It meant backing off and letting Whitney have the field today so Samantha could remind her heart and her brain that this was all just a silly game and not real and nothing to go having ugly feelings about. She looked a little desperately for Noel to distract her, and spied him flirting with Erin as her sister towel-dried her brown hair. She strode off toward that safe haven, forcing herself not to glance back at Cullen and Whitney.

Safety first.

FORTUNATELY, SAMANTHA WAS able to hide from Cullen the next two days by riding in the intermediate competition at Morven Park a few miles away. Magic, Nessie, Flora, and Central all came through with flying colors and Sam— in the pleasure of demonstrating the superiority of her hybrid stock four times in a row—got to remember what all of her hard work and sacrifices were for. It was just the confidence boost she needed.

But to be safe, she juggled her training schedule on Wednesday so she could school Magic in the dressage ring while Cullen rode Central over the new advanced cross-country course and show-jumping course Bobby Craig designed.

Then she took Central into the dressage ring while Cullen rode Magic over the cross-country and show-jumping courses. The juggling worked well all morning long. At lunch, she kept the conversation strictly on horses, refusing to mention the picnic, or the lake, or when they should reschedule The Kiss.

She was grateful, and a little surprised, that Cullen didn't call her on these tactics. Perhaps he hadn't noticed. Or perhaps he didn't care. *That doesn't matter,* she told herself sternly over and over again. It seemed to work.

By the time she waved good-bye to Cullen at the end of Wednesday lunch, she felt like she'd completely regained her equilibrium and her sanity. Letting one near-kiss wreak havoc on her nervous system. What idiocy! Cullen was an attractive man. Any woman would desire him. There was nothing to fear or worry about in that. She had been attracted to lots of men when she had been in Europe and she'd done just fine then. There was no reason why she wouldn't do just fine now.

She'd probably overreacted badly at the lake because it had been six years since she'd found herself in anything resembling a clinch and her hormones had gone haywire. The Great Plot had forcibly reminded her that she was far from being asexual, and in the end that was a good thing. She was a hot-blooded Lark woman who'd been living in the deep freeze for too long. Well, she'd thawed out now, her hormones were back in working order, and so was her brain. She felt more than ready to take up the standards of the Great Plot at the dinner party Whitney was hosting that night

HONOR, A FIVE-YEAR-OLD black gelding, sailed over the final hedge on the 4,155-yard advanced cross-country course he wouldn't be able to compete on until he was six. He felt ready now. Oh, sometimes she thought her breeding program could conquer the world. She jumped from the saddle and handed Honor over to his groom, Marybeth Hill, to be cooled down and groomed and fed.

She was running late, of course. She had to leg it from the stables back to the Lark house with just thirty minutes left for a quick shower and shampoo, blow-drying her hair and dressing in an off-the-shoulder teal blue mini-dress. Remembering Cullen's crack about her habitual French braid, she left her copper hair loose, added just enough makeup to hide the shadows under her eyes, and then headed for her car.

From the day Whitney had given her first party, Sam had always made it a point to turn up early to offer moral support and reassurance. Whitney always stressed around the tiniest details of every party she gave.

A Sheridan maid let Sam into the antebellum mansion. She walked across black and white checkerboard marble tiles and into the oak-paneled Victorian dining room where Whitney was making minuscule adjustments to the tableware. Tonight she wore black silk, her hair a cascade of blond curls. Her blue eyes narrowed when she looked up and that secretly thrilled Sam, because it was the look of a woman coming face to face with a dangerous rival, which meant for all the briefness of her ablutions, Samantha was looking good tonight.

"Good for me," she murmured. "Everything looks great, Whitney."

"Thank you," Whitney coolly replied as she continued her inspection walk around the long oval table. "I'm surprised you could take time from your busy schedule to come tonight."

The temperature in the room was definitely icy. "I've never missed one of your parties, Whitney, and I'm not about to start now."

"But your horses and Cullen are so much more important than little old me."

"Whitney—"

"How could you, Sam?" Whitney demanded, turning on her, startling her with the tears shimmering in her blue eyes. "You ignore me for months on end because of your damn *horses*, and then Cullen comes home and suddenly you've got hours and hours to spend with *him* but not with me!"

Sam felt lower than bread mold. She repeated to herself over and over again that the Great Plot was designed to ultimately benefit Whitney as much as Cullen, but it didn't help much. "Whitney, honey, I'm so sorry. I never meant to hurt you."

"Well, you have," she said with a sniff. "I never thought you'd let a *man* come between us."

"He hasn't! He won't," Sam insisted. "If Cullen walked through that door and put an engagement ring on your finger, I'd step aside in a hot minute, I swear I would."

"Well . . ." Whitney said, her finger drawing circles on the dining table. The doorbell rang in the next moment. "Oh lord, my guests, and I'm not *near* ready!"

"Of course you are," Sam said heartily as she walked up to her friend and slipped an arm around her slender waist. "You look more than gorgeous, the room is lovely, your cook undoubtedly has everything under control, and I'm here to distract your more boring guests. That sounds ready to me."

"Except for Erin's welcome-home dinner, which *she* organized, you haven't had a party at Skylark since your parents died. So what do you know?"

"Well, for one, I know that you've been prowling the house for the last hour, triple-checking everything that you triple-checked the hour before that and driving most if not all of your staff nutso."

"Oh, stop knowing me so well," Whitney complained as she headed out of the dining room.

Samantha trailed discreetly behind her.

"Is that our guests, Whitney?" Senator Sheridan asked as he walked downstairs arm in arm with his wife. He was a tall man of sixty-two with a shock of white hair and a hawk-like nose that endeared him to political cartoonists around the country. Olivia Sheridan, at forty-seven, looked thirty-five thanks to the devoted attentions of massage therapists, facialists, private trainers, and a wonderfully discreet plastic surgeon. At eighteen, she had fulfilled her lifelong ambition of marrying the greatest catch in all of Virginia and had never regretted her choice.

"I think so, Daddy," Whitney said.

"Oh, Samantha, are you here?" Mrs. Sheridan murmured. She never spoke, or yelled. She only murmured.

"Yes, ma'am," Samantha replied. "What a lovely dress."

"Versace," Mrs. Sheridan murmured with a pleased smile as she smoothed peach silk.

The Henley twins—two voluptuous brunettes—had arrived first, a major disappointment for Whitney. Eric Langton, the oil heir, came next, but he had brought Erin. Not good. Samantha exchanged a wry glance with her sister as Whitney took in this unappetizing sight. Fortunately, Donovan Streik, the architect, and Garrick Jennings, the English airline tycoon, arrived next, followed by the Mackenzies and Noel Beaumont, so Whitney had plenty of masculine attention to juggle at the same time. She made a point of flirting with every man except Cullen.

His eyes met Sam's gaze from across the room and they shared a smile. Whitney had never been known for pulling her punches.

They were all gathered in the Sheridan living room, which was a study in white, from the tiled floor, to the furniture, to the diaphanous curtains. Half a dozen vases of flowers and the guests added the only color to the room. With a shrug, Cullen abandoned the frosty love of his life and made his way to Sam's side, a Celtic warrior in a dinner jacket, his crescent scar a stark counterpoint to the chic civility of the room.

Sam was sure she saw a tightening in Whitney's jaw as Cullen smiled down at her. She felt a telltale tightening of her own, in a far different part of her anatomy.

"Banned from Whitney's inner circle, I see," she hurriedly said.

"She's doing everything she can to make me jealous," Cullen said, brushing copper hair back behind Sam's ear. Fire streaked through her brain. "I thought it best to retaliate. You might help out by laughing loud enough for Whitney to overhear, as if I'd just said something scintillating."

Samantha obliged with a low, seductive laugh.

Startled, Cullen stared at her. "Very good," he said. "Where in heaven's name did you learn to laugh like that?"

"Paris, of course," Sam replied, regrouping from his brief touch.

"You aren't anything like the scruffy tomboy I used to know, are you?"

She smiled pityingly upon him.

"Erin's still glowing, I see," Cullen said, glancing at Erin as she chatted happily with Eric Langton on a plump love seat. Noel Beaumont, who had been walking past with a wine glass in one hand, leaned over the back of the love seat and whispered something in Erin's ear that made her laugh uncontrollably.

"Glowing? She's been *burbling* ever since she was named first cellist of the National Symphony Orchestra. If there was a way to bottle her high, we'd make a fortune."

"You haven't been doing too badly yourself. People are still talking about your recent triumph at Morven Park," he said.

"We *were* rather spectacular."

"I'm beginning to think you just may pull off competing at the Horse Trials."

"My dear sir," she haughtily replied, "I intend to be *dazzling* at the Horse Trials."

"My dear Miss Lark, you are dazzling *anywhere*."

Sam stared up at him. "Wow. That was great. Flatter me some more."

He laughed, ancient pain receding to the farthest depths of his eyes. "Surely you've had men flatter you before."

"With the exception of Noel—and of course, Noel is the exception to everything—I've had to do without masculine flattery for way too long. I'd even forgotten how much I like it. Tell me about my eyes."

"Ah," he said, sweeping her into his arms in an excellent imitation of a swashbuckling Errol Flynn, "your eyes! Your eyes are like two limpid pools of hot cocoa lit from within."

Samantha choked on a gurgle of laughter. "A poet you ain't."

"But I'm 'Steady of heart, and stout of hand,' " he said brightly as he brought her upright.

"Ah, good, you haven't entirely forgotten Sir Walter Scott."

"I've begun rereading him, thanks to your constant hounding."

She cocked her head. "What other loves did you give up in the name of Big Business?"

"None."

"Uh huh. You gave up horses," she said, ticking the list off on her fingers, "and Scott, your family, your friends, your home. What about karaoke?"

"Fortune 500 executives do *not* sing karaoke," he said severely.

"That's what I thought. Has the local prep school's star first baseman played any baseball?"

"No."

"Have you hiked across Maui?"

"No."

"Swum in the Pacific?"

"No," Cullen said slowly, looking puzzled. "I've worked, and thought about Whitney, of course, and done hundreds of business lunches, and business dinners . . ."

"Have you been to one opera in the last ten years?"

"Oh, I must have!" He thought a moment, then looked at Sam. "No, I haven't. Isn't that awful?"

"Yes," she said quietly, "it is." Pursuing Teague's dream may have built the life Whitney wanted, but it seemed to have eradicated any joy in Cullen's life. He couldn't keep existing like that, could he? Should he?

Across the room, Whitney had half her male guests in doting attendance, but her eyes kept straying to Cullen, who seemed so enraptured with Sam's conversation that he hadn't even bothered to glance at her *once*. She shooed her masculine admirers away and sought solace in a glass of white wine and Missy Barrisford's company.

"Of all the stupid, sickening displays!" she erupted.

Missy, in a sleeveless maroon panne jumpsuit, followed her gaze to Cullen and Samantha, who were standing close enough to each other to share the same breath. "Come on, Whitney," she said soothingly. "You're not going to let Sam, of all people, get to you, are you?"

"Not Sam, *Cullen*. Do you see the way he's looking at her? Like someone about to dive into a giant bowl of chocolate pudding. I've never been so hurt and so angry in my life! How can he treat me like this, and in public? He knows I love him."

Missy laughed in honest amusement. "Oh, what

nonsense, Whitney. The only person you've ever loved in your entire life is yourself. Your pride's just been hurt, that's all."

"How could you, Missy? How *could* you?" Whitney demanded, blue eyes brimming with tears. "After all these years of my depending on Cullen and sticking by him and telling you *everything*, how *could* you say such an awful thing about me?"

Missy smiled fondly. "Because I know you too well, Whitney, to trust what you say over what you feel."

Disconcerted, Whitney sought safety in action. She walked back across the room, making each step more languid and seductive, until she stood beside Cullen, who was standing beside Sam. After ten minutes of surprisingly hard going, she had just gotten him to turn completely from Sam, when a maid entered the room to announce that dinner was ready.

Whitney cursed under her breath. The timing was all wrong, and she had been too clever by half. To make Cullen jealous, she had already agreed to let Noel lead her into the dining room, and she had arranged the place cards herself to punish Cullen for even pretending to be interested in another woman. She had Noel on her left side, and Garrick Jennings on her right, with Cullen at the opposite end of the table. She had had the foresight to keep him equally distant from Sam, but that was little recompense for having to give up the advantage she had just worked so hard to gain.

During dinner, Noel was as attentive as ever, Garrick did his best to charm her away from Noel, but Cullen was happily devoting himself to Laurel on his left and to Erin on his right. He never even bothered to glance at Whitney during the entire meal. For the first time in their long romance, Whitney felt fear begin to whisper through her.

But she would not lower herself to actually changing

her strategy. Rather than turning the full force of her powers on Cullen after dinner, Whitney surrounded herself once again with the rest of her male coterie and ignored Cullen as completely as he had ignored her at dinner.

"Poor Cullen," Samantha said with a sigh as she and Cullen stood near the open doors of the garden veranda, a crescent moon in the night sky. "There's Whitney, practically in arm's reach, and here you are stuck with *my* company all night."

"No sympathy is needed," he said with a smile. "I like your company."

"You are the sweetest man, and Whitney is such a fool."

"I'd never realized before that courtship is really just a battle of wills," he said ruefully.

"But it's not! Or at least, it doesn't have to be," Sam said, biting her full lower lip. It did strange things to Cullen's equilibrium. "I think courtship is all about exploration. You know, finding out your different likes and dislikes, particularly when it comes to kissing and hand holding and cuddling on the couch with a bowl of popcorn and an MGM musical on the TV. It's all about finding out how honest you can be with each other and still be safe, and what personal habits make your teeth grate, and discovering just how eager your family is to get you off their hands. Mostly, though, it's all about love, and growing that love until it's strong enough to get you down the aisle without fainting, or throwing up, or turning tail and running. From what I've seen, it takes a *lot* of love to survive a wedding."

Cullen smiled as he brushed his long fingers through her silky hair. "I like your courtship. You seem to have given it a lot of thought."

"Twenty-year-long engagements give you lots of time to think things through," Sam said, oddly breathless.

He chuckled. "You are the most darling woman," he

said, leaning toward her to kiss her brow, his hand still at the back of her head.

She looked up at him at just the wrong moment. His lips brushed her mouth instead. That soft sweet heat was the most addictive sensation he'd ever known. His lips brushed her mouth again, and again, and then stayed of their own accord, submerging him in warm burgundy, the wine filling his head and heating his lips, and enveloping his body in the most delicious heat. Sam's hands at the back of his head knotted in his hair and pulled him in even deeper, her burgundy mouth soft and hungry against his and suddenly he just wanted to *devour* her. He wanted to carry her off to his bed and spend hours drinking his fill of her.

His arms enfolded her and lifted her off the ground as her soft moan filled his throat.

Eight

SAMANTHA'S MOAN FILLED his body as he slid into her, loving the way she arched up to welcome all of him, loving the strength of her fingers digging into his back, loving her expression of agonized pleasure as he began to move in her, her moan changing to a heated, urgent *"Yes!"*

Cullen jerked awake, sitting upright in bed in his dark bedroom, his heart hammering in his chest. What the *hell* was he doing having a sexual dream about *Sam* instead of Whitney? Even now he could feel Samantha's mouth on his, her arching body drawing him in deeper and deeper—

Cullen dragged both hands through his hair. He was having sensual fantasies about a girl—a woman, *Sam*—he'd known all his life. Who would have thought one kiss could creak such havoc?

But then, who would have thought Sam could kiss like *that*?

If it hadn't been for Whitney's wineglass shattering on the white tiled floor, he'd probably still be kissing her. But the glass *had* slipped from Whitney's fingers when she'd seen him kissing Samantha and that had interrupted the kiss and jerked them both apart. He'd never felt more frustrated in his life. He hadn't wanted to be interrupted!

That had returned him to sanity with a vengeance. He had stared with something like horror into Sam's wide brown eyes and then back-pedaled for all he was worth.

"I knew giving our all for the Great Plot would work," he said, looking everywhere but at Sam. "Whitney looks ready to murder us both."

"I'll kiss you in the name of the Great Plot, Cullen Mackenzie, but I will not die for you," Sam retorted. "I'm going to go hide with Laurel and Keenan. You're on your own."

She had walked across the room, ensconced herself on the white sofa with his parents, and had stayed there the rest of the night.

Whitney, meanwhile, had walked stiffly from the living room and Cullen, sanity fully restored, had followed her, catching her arm in the entrance hall and pulling her to a stop.

"Whitney—"

"How *could* you?" she demanded, whirling around on him, startling him with the tears shimmering in her blue eyes. "How could you kiss Sam, of all people, and in front of all my guests? You made me look like a fool!"

"And you've made *me* look like a fool every time we've been in public for the last *month.* There's just so much a man can take, Whitney, before he lets himself enjoy more sympathetic company."

"But you *know* how I feel about you!"

"And just how is that?" Cullen inquired.

"I love you, you miserable cretin!" Whitney shouted.

"Then why won't you marry me?"

"I *will* marry you—"

"Are you accepting my proposal?" Cullen asked.

Whitney stopped. Some of the color left her cheeks. "I

will not be tricked into marrying you before I'm good and ready to marry you, Cullen Mackenzie, and don't you forget it!"

She had stormed off into the pale yellow morning parlor and Cullen had followed, determined to push the advantage he had gained. He got himself slapped for his pains, and then Whitney had burst into tears.

It had taken a good ten minutes to calm her down and they had been more than worth it. Whitney had actually said the words "love" and "jealousy." She had even agreed—after her usual number of refusals—to let him take her to a play at the Kennedy Center for the Performing Arts in D.C. tomorrow night. It was one of those gala grand opening events that bored him silly, but he knew it was just the sort of thing to tempt Whitney into forgiving him. It would also further the Great Plot, which seemed to be turning into a roaring success.

Who would have thought one kiss—one incredible, mind-searing, volcanic kiss—could do so much? Cullen groaned aloud. Thinking about the wrong woman *again*. Naked, he walked into the small sitting room adjoining his bedroom, found the rosewood sidebar in the shadows, and splashed some scotch into a glass. He downed the drink with a single swallow and then grimly headed back to bed.

Whitney had had him riding an emotional roller coaster these last few weeks, that was why he was in such bad shape. Tonight's pyrotechnics had simply pushed him over the edge, that's all. He'd reclaimed his equilibrium. He would go back to sleep and he would dream about Whitney, not Samantha, and that was final.

He dreamt the rest of the night about riding for the U.S. equestrian team in the Olympics which, when he woke up the next morning, felt almost as disturbing as dreaming about Sam.

He sat up in bed in his sunlit room and hugged his

knees as he realized just how dangerous Samantha Fay Lark really was. Not only did she have a sanity-shredding kiss, she was also directly responsible for his growing understanding of just how much he'd missed working with horses these last twelve years. Helping her train and school Magic and Nessie and the others day after day was simply supposed to serve the Great Plot by keeping him in Sam's company and fueling Whitney's growing jealousy.

But now when he cleared a hedge on Flora or jumped Central over Brandy Creek, he didn't think about Whitney or the Great Plot. He thought only about how best to take the next fence. Galloping up Bluegrass Hill, he felt suffused with love, not for Whitney, but for the powerful horse beneath him and the heady euphoria of being one with such a perfect animal.

Even the pleasure of simply longeing a horse again felt as if he was pulling on a single thread of the life tapestry he had woven for himself these last twelve years, only to see that tapestry start to unravel. He should stop, he should back-pedal. He shouldn't let himself get caught back up in the love of horses and work he had deliberately left behind. He should call Sam and tell her he was reneging on his part of the deal and then avoid Skylark and those marvelous horses like the plague.

But he'd given his word to help, and she needed his help, and it felt good to be needed. The world he had so carefully built didn't have to come crashing down around his ears because of *that*. He could return to New York and London and Hong Kong unscathed at the end of the summer. All he had to do was get Whitney to accept his proposal and marry him and everything was bound to fall into place after that.

But doubt nagged at the back of his mind. When this summer was over and Whitney was finally his wife—and she *would* be his wife—would he be able to turn his back once more on the horses and the parents and the home that he loved, to return to ten- and twelve-hour days locked up in offices that stirred nothing in his heart or soul?

"Oh *hell*," Cullen muttered as he got out of bed and stalked to a nearby window. He stared out at the pastures and the leggy Thoroughbreds that had dominated his first eighteen years. "This is not my life anymore!" he said, hands clenched in fists against the window frame. The choices he'd made these last twelve years were the right ones. They'd accomplished every goal he'd set himself. They were giving him everything he wanted. He'd grown beyond horses and Grand Prix events and breeding programs. They weren't important.

They weren't.

With an oath, Cullen headed for his bathroom and a shower to wash doubt away.

SAM WAS HER usual self as they worked together that morning: cracking jokes, teasing him, letting nothing of a serious nature intrude on the very serious work of training her superb horses. Clearly *she* had had no disturbing dreams the night before. The world was on its proper axis and he had badly overreacted.

When he and Sam walked through the Lark front door that afternoon, Cullen felt as if everything *had* fallen into place, because there was Whitney. She had invited herself to lunch, finally taking direct and serious action to distract him from her supposedly amorous best friend.

Over lunch, she slid her fingers over his hand or his arm, brushed some hair back from his ear, slid her foot against his under the table, leaned invitingly toward him, smiled into his eyes, all the while asking him about the greatly diversified family company (and fortune) he attended to via phone and fax machine and e-mail, and about his last Hong Kong trip, and about how much she was looking forward to the theater that night, and inviting him to play tennis with her at the local country club tomorrow.

She had stopped treating him like a toy and was treating him like a lover. He was grateful, he was ecstatic, and he was also aware all through lunch that Samantha scarcely touched her food. Erin was still burbling, Whitney was cooing, and Sam just sat there dabbing at her food with her fork. She seemed shut down, pulled within herself, leaving no forwarding address. Something was troubling her deeply.

What was wrong? Why wouldn't she confide in him? Why, when she had promised to give her all to the Great Plot, did she only make two half-hearted attempts to distract him from Whitney during lunch? And why was he thinking nonstop about her instead of Whitney?

He got no answers. Samantha was up and gone before he and Whitney had even finished dessert, while Erin headed back upstairs to continue practicing on her cello.

"I thought they'd never leave," Whitney murmured, startling him by exchanging her chair for his lap, and her dish of chocolate mousse for his lips.

Her mouth was full and warm and soft on his, as it had always been. Whitney didn't like hard kisses or rough kisses or anything that smacked of passion gone just a little bit wild. Still, her kiss felt different and for the life of him, Cullen couldn't figure out why. Disconcerted, he tried to compensate by sliding his arms around her waist and deepening the kiss.

But she pulled free with a low, satisfied laugh and stood up. "Behave yourself," she chided, her fingers cupping his jaw. "We still have tonight."

Cullen stared up into blue eyes full of seductive promises he knew Whitney had no intention of keeping. She was too skilled at the game to give him everything he wanted all at once. Yes, she had tacitly agreed to play him on a more level playing field, but her rules still held full sway.

He made himself smile and look forward to an evening of sitting in a darkened theater beside a newly attentive Whitney. It was what he had wanted. It was what the Great Plot was designed to achieve. It should be enough.

But it wasn't.

Something disturbingly like unhappiness crept into him that evening, even though Whitney was everything he loved about her: beautiful, charming, knowledgeable about the play and many of the theater patrons in the audience. She flirted with him, and teased, and caressed. She was the embodiment of romance and all that was lovely in the world. At intermission, she was surrounded by half the men in the audience. She treated each man as if he was the most handsome, most enthralling man in the theater, but all the while she made it clear that she preferred Cullen.

She was no longer Helen of Troy—an unobtainable object of desire—she was flesh and blood and his as she rested in the half circle of his arm in the midst of this adoring throng. She even let him take a full half hour to say goodnight when he drove her home after the play and their late super.

It should have been more than enough. But somehow it wasn't.

It was not lost on him that Whitney chose another public forum in which to display their mutual devotion the next day: tennis at the Blue Ridge Country Club. Saturday, she cajoled him into attending the Finch–Burtons' popular high tea, to which half the county's leading families came to sip tea, eat a wealth of delectable pastries and miniature sandwiches, and gossip about each other.

She might say that she merely wanted him to be her

escort, but Cullen knew better. She was courting him, publicly, at last. She had permanently ensconced herself in his days and nights, whether it was taking him to an art gallery opening, dancing with him until closing at Alexandria's hottest night club, or attending a champagne brunch charity auction. But for some reason, having Whitney fully in his life wasn't as satisfying as he'd long imagined it would be.

What was wrong with him? Why couldn't he be happy having everything he'd ever wanted?

Cullen continued to help Sam and have lunch with her and Erin every day—continuing the Great Plot so Whitney wouldn't get suspicious. She didn't. She simply insisted on insinuating herself into each meal and each conversation to claim his full attention.

But only a week after a single kiss had changed so much in his life, Cullen wasn't giving Whitney his full attention. He was looking at the empty chair on his right in the Lark dining room, and then at his watch for the tenth time in as many minutes. He'd had to renege on helping Sam with this morning's workouts so he could spend the morning talking with his London and Hong Kong offices. But they had agreed to still meet for lunch. "Where is she?"

"Honestly, Cullen," Whitney said on his left, looking a trifle peeved, "you know what Sam is like. She's probably mucking about with one of her precious horses. She'll probably turn up in an hour or two. Stop worrying and let's eat. This chicken pot pie looks wonderful."

"She promised she'd be here and Samantha doesn't break her promises. So where the hell is she?"

"She's in the foaling shed with Bobby Craig and Dr. McClaren," Erin said, helping herself to some salad from a teak bowl on the table. "She's been there all morning, and part of the night, from what I can tell."

"That girl is a martyr to this farm," Whitney said, looking bored. "I wish she'd realize there's more to life than work."

"There may have been complications," Cullen said, standing up. "I'll go see."

"Oh honestly, Cullen," Whitney pouted. "You don't have to go anywhere."

"Yes, Whitney, I do," he said quietly, a little startled by such a truth. He wasn't doing this as his part of the Great Plot. He was going to Sam and the brood mare because he wanted to, because he cared, because even Whitney wasn't more important than a mare in labor, and he'd worry about all of that later. "I'll just be a minute," he said, giving Whitney a reassuring smile before striding from the dining room and the house, across the yard and past the main stable.

The foaling shed was actually a small red barn with its own three-acre paddock, separated from the rest of the stables and paddocks so that mares and their newborns could have some necessary privacy. Cullen felt the tension ten feet from the barn door. He heard a mare's agonized groan two steps later and shuddered. He'd heard that sound before. The mare was dying.

He pulled open the door and stepped into the cool shadows of the stable. Following the low murmur of people talking, he came to the fourth foaling box and looked through the small window in the door. The box was bedded down deeply with straw, with straw banked on all four sides to protect the mare and her foal, and to prevent drafts. Three people were huddled around a lathered blood bay Holstein mare lying in the box.

Sigfreda.

Bobby Craig and Dr. McClaren, a fiftyish veterinarian, were covered in sweat, their faces tight with worry and strain as Dr. McClaren stretched his gloved hands into the mare's womb. It was a breech birth, then, and the vet was trying to untangle the foal. "Dammit!" Dr. McClaren said. "It slipped back again."

Samantha knelt in the straw, holding the mare's head in her hands. Normally, there would be someone holding a mare's head and neck to keep her down, but that clearly was no longer a concern. The Holstein looked like she'd never move again. Sam stared into huge dark eyes dulled by pain and exhaustion, using her voice and the sheer force of her willpower to keep the mare clinging to life.

"Don't you give up on me," Sam was telling the mare in a low, urgent voice. "You've got too much pride to give up now, Sigfreda. Come on, baby, hang in there just a little bit more. I won't put you through this again, I swear it. Stay with me, girl. You can't die now. Your foal needs a chance. Your foal's gonna need *you*. Come on, dammit, *live!*"

Cullen slipped into the box, closing the door behind him. "Need any help?" he offered quietly. He doubted if Sam even heard him or was aware of anything save the agonized gaze she held with her own.

But Dr. McClaren looked up. "Glad to have you, Cullen. We need all the help we can get. Wash your hands with carbolic soap and disinfectant. There's not much time left. If I can't shift the foal out of breech *and* keep it from getting lodged against the pelvic brim this time, I'll have to do a cesarean, and I'll have to do it fast."

Ten minutes of tense effort and Dr. McClaren suddenly sat back with a satisfied "Ah!" Bobby handed him a vial of oxytocin and a syringe. The vet injected the drug into the mare to make her uterus contract tighter. She no longer had the strength to help with the birth. Almost immediately, the foal's front hooves appeared, then its legs, one foreleg slightly leading the other as it should, then its head straight and slightly behind the forelegs, and suddenly the entire foal slid out with a final moan from its mother.

Cullen helped break open the still intact amnion. The vet raised the foal's head out of the amniotic fluid and suctioned out its nostrils and mouth. He placed a stethoscope to the chest. "Still breathing *and* a decent heartbeat," he marveled, sitting back on his heels. "It's a bloody miracle."

"I'll take care of the foal," Bobby said, beginning to wipe down the dark wet mass on the straw that was still attached to its mother by the umbilical cord. "You worry about Sigfreda."

The mare's head lay in Sam's lap as she stroked and crooned to her, urging her to not slip away now that the worst was over. The vet quickly injected antibiotics into Sigfreda, checked her heart, and then began drying her to prevent a chill.

Cullen helped Bobby with the foal, not because Bobby needed help, but because he couldn't stand helplessly by and do nothing, and because he couldn't watch Sam give the last ounce of her strength to keep the mare clinging to life. There were no jokes and banter and laughter to hide behind now. Samantha had been stripped bare, enabling Cullen to finally see the fear and anger and exhaustion that blanketed her soul. He had thought he'd seen Sam being fully herself at his parents' anniversary ball, but he'd been wrong. He hadn't seen this side of her. He'd never seen this side of her before.

While Bobby filled him in on the difficult eight-hour labor, he helped rub down the foal to dry it and to stimulate its circulation. Half an hour after his birth, the foal broke the umbilical cord as he tried to get up and stand on wobbly legs. They gave out twice before finally keeping him upright, a miracle in itself after the ordeal he had just survived.

"That's better," Dr. McClaren said into the quiet stall.

"What do you mean?" Samantha said, speaking to someone other than Sigfreda for the first time since Cullen had walked into the barn. The mare's head was still in her lap. Dr. McClaren was kneeling beside her.

"Her heartbeat's stronger," the vet said, sitting back on his heels. "And her eyes look more alert. Let's give her a few minutes and then see if we can use her foal as an incentive to get her on her feet."

"You mean . . ." Sam said, her voice wobbling badly as she looked up at Dr. McClaren, "she'll make it?"

"No promises," he warned. "But I am feeling the first bit of hope I've felt these last two hours."

She looked back at the mare. "Come *on*, Sigfreda," she urged. "You can do it, I know you can!"

The vet began massaging the mare from neck to tail, talking to her as Sam spoke to her, creating a cheerleading duet that Cullen silently echoed as he and Bobby began to move the foal towards his mother. The mare caught its scent, her head jerking in Sam's lap, her ears coming forward.

"Thatta girl," Dr. McClaren said. "Out of the way, Samantha. Don't make lying down so comfortable for her."

Sam scrambled to her feet as Bobby and Cullen led the foal around the mare. Four large hooves scraped against the straw-covered floor.

"Oh, you can do better than that, Sigfreda," Sam insisted. "Come on, stop lazing about. You've got a job to do."

With Samantha urging her and the scent of her foal in her nostrils, Sigfreda heaved herself upright in a lumbering, graceless effort that nonetheless left her standing. She was shaking and breathing heavily from the effort, but she was upright.

"Oh, my beautiful, brave girl," Sam said, wrapping her arms around the mare's neck and hugging her even as Dr. McClaren covered Sigfreda in a horse blanket and Bobby and Cullen brought the foal up to her head. Sigfreda nuzzled the foal who had nearly killed her, first weakly, but then with growing interest and strength. She began licking her son. Cullen wanted to cheer.

Fifteen minutes later, the foal was greedily nursing, his tail whisking side to side with frenetic speed, while the mare delivered the afterbirth intact. "The only complication we *didn't* have with this birth," Bobby muttered as he set down a pail of warm bran mash with linseed oil in front of Sigfreda. She considered it a moment and then began to eat as Sam continued stroking her and speaking softly to her.

"Was this her first?" Cullen asked quietly.

"Her fourth," Bobby said, shaking his head. "The other three went like clockwork. We never expected this. Not in a million years."

"It's a bloody miracle," Dr. McClaren repeated to Bobby and Cullen as he rolled down his shirt sleeves and put on his jacket. "Well, I'll be back to check on your newest addition and his mother this evening," he informed Bobby as he picked up his medical bag.

"Hopefully it will be a short visit," Bobby said.

The vet smiled, nodded at them, and walked out of the barn.

"I love happy endings," Cullen murmured as he and Bobby watched Samantha crooning to the mare and her foal.

"Particularly when they're so unexpected."

Cullen looked at Bobby.

"There were half a dozen times when that mare should have just given up and died," Bobby quietly explained. "There's only one reason on God's green earth that she didn't, and you're looking at her."

Cullen looked at Sam a moment as she stroked the mare's neck and whispered secrets in her ear. "Samantha's always been a fighter."

"Yeah. But this mare's death could well have killed even that in her."

Startled, Cullen looked into Bobby's serious black eyes. "Coming, as it would, on the heels of . . . what?"

Bobby looked away. "Everything else," he said disgustedly.

Sam was keeping secrets. What were they, and why had she confided them to Bobby and to no one else? Something nagged at Cullen's chest, something almost like jealousy. Why hadn't Samantha turned to *him*? He stopped. When had he been around to hear any secrets she might have wanted to share?

Oh good, he thought, *something else to feel guilty about.*

He walked over to Samantha as the foal finished his first meal. Together with Bobby they led Sigfreda and her son into a large, clean stall.

"I'll stay with them, Bobby," Sam said. "You go get some well-earned rest."

"The hell I will," Bobby retorted. "*You* look shakier than that foal did an hour ago. If McClaren left, that means he's not worried about them and that means *you* don't have to worry about them." He held up a broad hand to fend off her protest. "I'll have Miguel stay with them. You know you trust Miguel and you trust me, so trust me when I tell you that you are not staying in this shed one more minute."

She started to sputter in outrage, but Cullen grabbed her arm and began pulling her out the door. "Come on, Sam. Bobby's right and you know it. You are going to take a shower and then you are going to bed."

"The hell I am," Samantha retorted, struggling without success to free herself as he dragged her out into the muggy afternoon heat. "I've got a farm to run and horses to train and a near-dead mare to look after and I am not—"

"Oh yes you are," Cullen interrupted grimly as he pulled her toward the house. "You are going to bed and you are going to sleep, even if I have to tie you to the bedposts myself!"

"Cullen, we don't need to advance the Great Plot *that* far."

"And you don't have to carry the weight of the world on your shoulders, Samantha Lark. There are plenty of skilled, knowledgeable people on this farm who can run things just fine without you," he said, pulling her through the front door and into the house. Erin's music as she practiced her cello provided a muted background to their battle. "So you will walk up those stairs and into your room, or I will carry you up."

"You wouldn't dare."

"Oh, wouldn't I?"

She took a hasty step back and then clasped her hands under her chin. "Oh *please*, let me just stay up to see *Creature Features*," she implored, sounding like a seven-year-old TV addict. "I promise it won't give me nightmares."

"Shut up and go to bed," Cullen said, struggling against a grin.

"I'll bet you've wanted to say that to Whitney a million times."

"Go!" he ordered, swatting her behind.

If she'd been in anything like normal condition, she'd have turned around and decked him for that. The fact that she didn't told him just how far gone she really was, and that worried him. A lot. He watched Samantha, her physical strength long gone, as she marched up the stairs on sheer pride and willpower. What the hell was going on in her world?

"You certainly have a way with women."

Cullen turned to find Calida laconically regarding him from the kitchen doorway. "Trust me," he said with a smile, "if she wasn't so exhausted, that scene would probably have ended with at least a broken nose, mine, and permanent banishment from this house, mine as well."

"Still, you're one for two today."

"What does that mean?"

"You lost a round to Whitney. You made her wait nearly two hours for your company. Whitney waits no more than a minute for any man, I thought you knew that."

"I was distracted," Cullen said, looking down at himself for the first time and seeing the blood and sweat and grime that had been a part of those lost two hours.

"How are they?"

He looked up at Calida. Concerned dark eyes met his. On a horse farm, when a mare was in labor, there was only one understanding of *they*. "They should both pull through with flying colors."

"Thank God for that. Hungry?"

The tension of the hard labor and its aftermath washed away and Cullen was left with a very disgruntled stomach. "Yeah," he said in surprise, "I am!"

"Come on in the kitchen, then. I kept everything warm for you."

After lunch, Cullen headed back to the stables. Samantha was getting some hard-earned sleep, there were horses to train, he was available, and he didn't care that this had nothing to do with the Great Plot.

IT TOOK a few hours of hard, consistent work, but by the time Cullen led Whitney into the Barrisfords' colonial house that night for a dinner party, she had forgiven him for deserting her at lunch.

Cullen had always liked the Barrisfords. Except for Missy, they were not prone to putting on airs and imagining themselves better than anyone else in the county. They were first and foremost horsemen. They were not interested in breeding horses, only in buying, training, and riding them well. A Barrisford from each of the last three generations had won a place on the Olympic team, a secret goal Cullen had once had for himself before Teague had died.

Once upon a time, he and the Barrisfords had had a lot in common and he was surprised to find that they still had a lot to talk about, while Whitney alternated between arguing the merits of French versus Italian fashions with Missy, and flirting with him. Erin was there, with Noel of all people, but Samantha was nowhere to be seen. She had been invited, of course, but had declined, claiming she had too much work to make up, despite Cullen's help that afternoon.

But she was far from absent. Cullen was surprised to find that she was a favorite topic of conversation with the Barrisfords, or at least her horses were.

"I told Rufus Lark flat out he was a fool to spend so much money on that stock," old Matthew Barrisford, the eighty-one-year-old patriarch, informed him, "but it looks like he may be having himself the last laugh, even from the grave. The Larks' south pasture borders our property and many's the time I've just stood out by the fence and admired those colts and fillies. They seem to have inherited the best of both the Morgans and the Holsteins. I'll see how they prove out in the next year or so. If they turn out half as well as Samantha Lark insists they will, I just may buy a few for my great-grandchildren."

"If you want a good price, you may want to buy sooner than later," Cullen advised him. "Samantha is entering some of her six-year-olds in the Mackenzie Horse Trials and from what I've seen, they stand a good chance of garnering serious interest."

"That girl's nuttier than my Aunt Mabel's pecan pie," Matthew Barrisford declared. "No one enters a green six-year-old in a three-day trial like that! The youngest horse any Barrisford ever rode in an event was seven, and that was a disaster. Poor thing was so panicked that he tried to gallop through the dressage course and then knocked down damn near every fence in the stadium jumping."

"Don't sell Samantha short," Cullen advised. "She's a very determined woman, and she's working with some very talented horses."

Matthew Barrisford pursed his lips. "I was thinking about visiting my grandson Peter in Seattle this September, but maybe I'll postpone that trip and stick around for the Trials instead."

"I think you'll find it worth your while," Cullen said with a smile. "You could get in on the ground floor of a new American breed."

Matthew's bushy white eyebrows shot up. "Is that what Samantha's up to?"

"It is. She keeps saying, 'If Justin Morgan could do it, why can't I?' and from what I've seen, she *can*. I've ridden about a dozen of her four-, five-, and six-year-olds. Steady, strong, and smart pretty much describes them all. Sam's building a very impressive base."

Whitney turned to him, a frown creasing her lovely brow as she directed his conversation away from Samantha and back to her, where it belonged. Cullen winced. What the hell was wrong with him? Why did he keep going off track like this?

He devoted himself to Whitney for the rest of the evening.

It was just after midnight when he drove Whitney back to the Sheridan house. They were chatting about the changes in Hong Kong since China had reclaimed sovereignty of the city from Great Britain, a safe topic. There were dangerous shoals—like horses and Samantha and marriage—that both wanted to avoid.

"How about a nightcap?" Whitney asked as he opened the car door for her and handed her out of the BMW.

"You're on," he said.

They walked arm in arm into the antebellum mansion and then into the Victorian dining room where a host of crystal decanters lay in wait on a huge mahogany sideboard.

"Brandy all right?" Whitney asked.

"Fine. I'm worried about Sam," Cullen said before he could stop himself. "I think she's working much too hard."

"Oh, nonsense," Whitney replied, pouring the brandy into two snifters. "Sam isn't working any harder than she usually does."

"If this is usual, then she *is* in trouble."

"Don't be absurd. Sam works hard because she likes to work hard."

Cullen took his glass of brandy from Whitney and stared at the aromatic liquid for a moment. "I think she's running scared," he said quietly.

"Sam? That's a laugh. Sam isn't afraid of anything. She's simply doing what she loves and setting a very good example for the both of us." Whitney kissed him long and sweet and pulled away with a smile. "That's what *I* love doing."

Cullen stared at her, badly disconcerted by the sudden memory of Samantha's kiss a week ago and how different his response was to Whitney's kiss tonight. He polished off his brandy with a single swallow.

"Mm, brandy kisses. My favorite." Whitney kissed him again and then turned to the sideboard. "Would you like a refill?"

Cullen stared at his glass. He didn't remember emptying it. He looked at the woman he loved and felt something like dismay. "Um, no thanks, Whitney. I should get going. I've got to get up early tomorrow. I've got a conference call scheduled with my London and Hong Kong offices."

"I'll see you for lunch tomorrow, then," she said, walking back to him and offering her mouth for a good-bye kiss.

For the first time in the thirteen years he had loved her. Cullen didn't want to kiss Whitney. He couldn't kiss her, not when comparisons were raging in his brain, comparisons that shouldn't be there and most definitely shouldn't be unfavorable.

He hurriedly raised her hand to his lips. "Good-night, Whitney," he said and then made his escape while he could still lay claim to sanity.

Nine

SAMANTHA GROANED in her sleep. She was having *that* dream again and she didn't want to, but it kept playing.

She was standing just a foot from Cullen, her gaze tracing his beautifully shaped gray eyes, and the thin crescent scar, and his very male, very tempting, mouth. She was aware of every centimeter of his tall, powerful body. She could actually feel the heat of his skin even though they weren't touching.

Gray eyes caught her gaze and held her with sudden hypnotic intensity. She could hear the hammering of her heart, feel the blood turning to flames beneath her skin, as desire heated her in all the wrong places, curling through her with traitorous glee. Vaguely she remembered the desire she had felt for Phillippe Valentin, her first lover, and for Kaspar Reinhart, her last lover. It felt like junior high school stuff in comparison to these rippling flames. But this was *Cullen*, for heaven's sake! Her second-best friend! This shouldn't be happening to her. But it was.

She looked away, seeking refuge by studying Whitney as she stood in the middle of her male coterie. *I'm trying to help Whitney get married,* she reminded herself over and over again as Cullen's fingers brushed through her hair. Oh, how she loved his touch!

"You are the most darling woman," he said, leaning toward her to kiss her brow, his hand still at the back of her head.

She looked up at him at just the wrong moment. His lips brushed her mouth and she was lost.

None of her boyfriends had prepared her for this. She felt sucked into a heated vortex, gale-force winds rushing around her, forcing her even deeper into Cullen's hard body. There was no floor beneath her feet, no walls, no ceiling. There was only this magical rush of joy as Cullen kissed her like a famished man coming upon a feast. It was a masterful performance. Sam was caught hook, line, and sinker. He couldn't seem to get enough of her, and she certainly couldn't get enough of him. He was life, vibrant life, and more joy than she had known existed in the world.

The sound of shattering glass jerked her back into sanity and away from the man who felt too good and too right in her arms.

Sam jerked herself awake. Her lips felt hot, her breasts swollen, her pulse hammering in her wrists. "Oh, *dammit,*" she moaned, pounding her fist into her pillow again and again.

Almost every night for nearly two weeks. Would she *never* stop dreaming about that damn kiss? It was wreaking havoc with her sleep and her waking thoughts and her ability to act like a rational adult whenever she was around Cullen.

"It was just a *kiss,*" she said aloud.

The most incredible, soul-stirring, heart-expanding, dizzying, addictive kiss she'd ever known.

"Oh, for crying out loud," she said disgustedly as she threw back her comforter and slid out of bed. She glanced at her bedside clock. Four-thirty. She had time for a quick shower to wash away desire that just kept growing, and then two hours of work to distract her and help her get her mask in place before Cullen turned up to help with her morning training sessions.

It always tore her in two, working with him in the mornings. She needed his help and was grateful for it, but spending so much time with him day after day only seemed to build the hunger within her more and erode the cavalier mask she wore so he'd never know about that hunger, or about a kiss that for her at least had had nothing to do with the Great Plot and everything to do with desire.

During her cool shower, she made herself think about horses, not Cullen, which created a different kind of knot in her stomach. She was beginning to have a crisis of confidence as the summer advanced toward September. She was beginning to second-guess herself.

She was pushing Magic and Flora and Nessie and Central too hard. She was asking too much of them. It was too much of a long shot. They'd fall to pieces at the Mackenzie Horse Trials and no one would see their beauty and strength and potential. She and Erin would lose Skylark. She'd end up working in an office or on an assembly line because no owner worth his or her salt would let her train their horses after her colossal failure at the Trials.

She tried to stop imagining worst-case scenarios as she dressed and braided her hair, but it was hard. There was just so much that could go wrong. She could be making mistakes she didn't even know about. She felt like she didn't know anything anymore.

Moving carefully through the dim, hushed house so she wouldn't wake Erin, Sam walked out into a Saturday morning just touched by dawn, the sky a spectacular azure blue that always filled her heart with love no matter what imaginary disasters she was obsessing about.

She walked the farm with Bobby and Miguel, inspecting

the fields and hedges and paddocks and each of her sixty-three horses, including Sigfreda and her rambunctious foal. They discussed rotating the horses into different pastures, and this year's alfalfa crop, training schedules, feed supplies, and the two dozen people on Skylark's staff.

Then Cullen was there, long blond hair glowing in the morning sunlight, crescent scar nearly invisible as he smiled at her. Jeans seemed only to emphasize his long, powerful legs. A maroon, long-sleeved, V-necked Henley shirt couldn't disguise his broad chest and hard male nipples or hide all of the crinkly golden chest hair that seemed to demand to be stroked by Sam's fingers.

Oh, why couldn't Whitney just give in and marry the man and end this damn fever once and for all?

"Ready to work?" he asked.

"Always," she said, refusing to let her gaze focus on his mouth. His wonderful, addictive mouth. "I want to start with the five-year-olds this morning so we can work the six-year-olds when it's hotter and more humid. They've got to perform well no matter what the conditions."

"Right," he said, falling into step beside her as they walked into the main stable.

She could feel his heat, smell his masculine scent, hear his breath. *Help!* she silently wailed.

Working with the horses was her safety net, because she *had* to focus on them, which meant she couldn't think about, let alone moon over, Cullen. Even when he was galloping up Bluegrass Hill with her, or jumping the tent-shaped chicken-coop jump right behind her, she was thinking about her mount's gait and form, and the next obstacle, and the condition of the ground, and her own position in the saddle. Not Cullen.

And that, even in the midst of too much work, was a blessing.

They walked up to the house together just before one

o'clock, talking about her horses and that morning's training. She felt almost safe, even though for the first time in over a week Whitney wouldn't be having lunch with them. The Sheridans were sharing a family meal with some of the Senator's most important backers. Fortunately, this was Saturday, which meant no rehearsals in D.C. for Erin, so she would be there. Since there was no need at this lunch to further the Great Plot. Sam would be able to sit back and relax. No flirting with Cullen for Whitney's benefit, no touching him, no smiling into his eyes and getting caught in their gray depths.

It would be a nice, quiet, safe lunch for a change.

Unfortunately, that meant that her mind could dwell once again on the growing stack of bills in her office, the caliber of competition she and her horses would be facing at the Mackenzie Horse Trials, the worn-out tack that needed to be replaced, the loan payment due at the bank next week, the sudden lameness of one of her most promising four-year-olds . . .

"I mean, our premiere is two whole months away," Erin was saying as she sat across the table from Sam in a rainbow-striped thigh-length jumpsuit, her brown hair held in a jaunty ponytail, "but there are all these hunky Secret Service guys checking out the concert hall anyway because practically the entire Administration will be at the premiere, this being the national orchestra and all, and they need to start securing the place now, and there's poor Weaver, the conductor, trying to get us through Beethoven's Fifth, but he's not having much luck because about half the orchestra is female, and a quarter is gay, so three-quarters of the musicians are checking out the hunky Secret Service guys."

"What, no Secret Service gals?" Cullen asked.

"Sure. I mean, I guess so. I mean, who notices when you've got beefcake in suits right at your fingertips?"

"Careful, Erin. Look but don't touch," Samantha cautioned as she forced back her worries and re-entered the conversation. "Those guys have solemnly sworn to take a bullet for the politicos they're guarding. Never date a guy with a death wish."

"Look who's giving *me* dating advice," Erin retorted with a grin. "The Vestal Virgin of Skylark Farm."

"Celibacy is a virtue," Cullen piously informed her.

"Trust me," Sam said before she could stop herself, "celibacy is highly over-rated." *Oh crud, would she never learn to keep her big mouth shut?*

Cullen's smile faded as he studied her. "Hey," he said softly, "what gives? You look whipped, Sam." Heat flamed into her face as Cullen's fingers tilted her chin up so he could study her better. "There are shadows under your eyes, Young Lark. And from what I've seen of you since I've been home, they aren't a temporary phenomenon. You're also too thin, which makes no sense because Calida is a great cook. What's going on?"

"I'm leading a double life," she retorted, heartbeat erratic as she pulled her chin free. "Horse trainer by day, owner and head girl at the Daisy Mae Oriental Beauty Parlor and Chop Shop by night."

"Sam—"

"On Tuesdays we run a Roman orgy shampoo and cut special. Come on down."

Gray eyes narrowed at her. "Cute. From what I can tell, you aren't sleeping, you aren't eating, and you're working yourself harder than a prisoner on a chain gang. What's going on, Sam?" he demanded in a low, commanding voice. "And no generalities, and no jokes, and no running away. I want the truth and I want it now."

"Tough patooties. This disgusting display of masculine dominance has no effect on the more evolved female. That would be me."

"*Sam*—"

"There's a blueberry pie on the table, Cullen, and I'm not afraid to use it." She hefted the pie plate in one hand and gave him her most threatening glare as Erin looked on.

His expression gentled, catching her off guard. "Sam, are you in trouble?"

"No." She hurriedly set the pie down and stabbed a piece of grilled chicken with her fork.

"You're lying, Sam."

"Did you hear the one about the porcupine lost in a nudist camp?"

He reached out and covered her clenched fist with his warm hand. "We've been friends all our lives," he said softly, forcing her to meet his gaze. "Won't you trust me? Won't you let me help you if I can?"

Oh, it was so tempting as she stared into gentle gray eyes and felt the warmth of his large hand seep into her. How lovely to lean on him for a little while, to share a little of the burden she bore. But she didn't dare. Cullen was too well connected. One slip of his tongue, and the whole country would know her fiscal problems by the next day, because he *was* well connected.

She pulled her hand free, forcing it not to tremble as she reached for her glass of iced tea. "You're letting your imagination carry you off into dungeons and disaster where none exist," she said lightly. "I'm just a little stressed preparing for the Trials. Once they're over, I'll be right as rain."

He considered her a moment and then leaned back in his chair. "Sam, working a great horse on familiar ground is one thing, but working a green horse in high-end competition on unfamiliar ground is something else entirely. You may be far too optimistic about what you can accomplish at the Trials."

"My horses are good enough to pull it off," she retorted. She glanced out the window at brood mares contentedly cropping their own lunches in the lush distant pastures, their newest foals close beside them. "They have to be."

Cullen looked as if he was going to question her about that, then changed his mind. "I only hope your efforts are half as successful at the Trials as they've been in the Great Plot. You make a surprisingly convincing femme fatale, you know."

"Ah, but you've never seen Erin in action," Sam said, grateful for the change to a safer topic of conversation.

"The world is my oyster," Erin agreed.

"According to her letters," Sam informed Cullen, "Erin-mania swept Europe the minute she stepped foot on the Continent."

"Popular, were you, Brat?" he asked Erin.

"I've always played well with others," Erin said demurely.

"You two are destroying my belief in the purity of Lark womanhood," Cullen complained.

"Cullen, get real," Samantha chided him. "For three hundred and fifty years, the Lark women have been the most hot-blooded females in this or any other Virginia county."

"We have a proud tradition to uphold," Erin said, "and *you*," she said, directing a stern glance at Sam, "need to start doing your fair share."

Sam forced herself not to glance at Cullen. "Yes, Erin," she said.

SAM SHUFFLED INTO the house just after eight o'clock that evening, bone tired, with her accounting books still to face. Would the last of Skylark's funds last to September? The stud season was pretty much over. There would be no more stud fees to augment her bank balance. And she'd sold the last of her Thoroughbreds last week to Rosewood Farms in Connecticut.

She'd run out of income. She had nothing left to sell or pawn. She was down to her last horse trailer. All of the tack was old and worn. The furniture and curios that generations of Larks had bought over the years were inviolate. She was fighting to protect her heritage, not sell it off. She felt like the lowest form of pond scum for even considering it, but if worse came to worst, she might have to ask Bobby and Calida and Miguel to forgo their salaries for a month or two and pray that the Mackenzie Horse Trials garnered enough interest in and sales of her horses to pay them back double.

"There you are," Calida said, walking through the swinging door that led to the kitchen. "I kept your dinner warm."

"Thanks. Where's Erin?"

"She ate an hour ago."

"Oh," Sam said, feeling guilty. It seemed the only time she saw her sister nowadays was at lunch, and that was just on the weekends now that Erin was rehearsing during the week in D.C. "Well, I'll just eat in my office then."

She pushed open the door and walked into her office and there was Erin sitting in her old green leather desk chair and leafing through her accounting ledgers.

Every muscle Sam owned turned to jello.

"W-w-what are you doing?" she said weakly.

Erin slowly placed the ledgers on the desk, turned the chair to face Sam, and glared at her sister. "I've been solving the mystery Cullen raised at lunch today. If I hadn't been so preoccupied with the orchestra, and if I'd seen a bit more of you these last few weeks, I might have tumbled to it a whole lot sooner."

"Erin—"

"Now I know why you practically packed me in a crate and shipped me off to Europe after I graduated from

Juilliard. You didn't want me to find out how bad things are. You didn't want me to see you forgoing even the basics, like a new pair of jeans now and then, or a night on the town. You didn't want me to see you sell off everything on this farm that wasn't nailed down. You didn't want me to see you working yourself to total collapse. That was swell of you, Sammy, really. *Didn't it ever cross your mind that someday I was going to grow up and want to help?*"

"There's nothing you can do," Sam said with a shrug.

"I've saved some money—"

"No."

"Sam—"

"This is my mess and my fix."

"And Skylark is my home, too!" Erin said, standing up, grabbing Sam's shoulders, and shaking her a little. "I'm twenty-five and all grown up and I can pull my fair share."

"Look, everything will be fine once I get through the Horse Trials. Magic and Flora and the others are bound to garner the interest and the sales we need to get into the black once and for all."

"And if they don't?"

"They will," Sam said a little desperately. "They have to. We'll pull it off somehow."

"If you don't run yourself into an early grave first," Erin countered. "Cullen's right. You're so overworked you can't even think straight. I may not have the skills to train the stock, but there are other things I can do around here to relieve some of the burden you're carrying. I can take over the bookkeeping, for one."

"Erin—"

"*And* I can pay off the feed and vet bills."

"You can?" Sam said, her voice wobbling badly.

Erin pulled her into her arms and hugged her tight. "I forbid you to even think about accounts payable until after the Trials, is that clear?"

"It's not the easiest habit to break."

"Try."

"Okay," Sam said, pulling far enough away so she could look into her sister's serious face. "And you've got to swear on everything you consider holy that you won't tell a soul about Skylark's problems, particularly Cullen. Bobby is the only one who knows and it's got to stay that way. The last thing we need is bargain hunters sniffing around our stock."

"No problem. Mum's the word."

Calida walked up to them, carrying a dinner tray. "You want this on your desk?" she asked Samantha.

"Nope," Erin said, pulling the tray from Calida's hands. "Sammy is going to eat her dinner at the dinner table like a human being and I am going to have a second dessert to keep her company."

"Don't go power mad on me, Erin," Sam warned.

Erin nudged her with the tray. "March!"

Sam marched. It was better than dissolving into a grateful puddle of tears at her sister's feet. She hadn't realized until that moment how much she dreaded looking at Skylark's growing stack of bills every night. To forgo that torture in the coming weeks felt like Nirvana. "You're the best sister a girl ever had," she informed Erin as she sat down at the dinner table.

"I'm a saint," Erin said as she set the tray down in front of Sam. "Eat!"

Thanks to Erin, the perpetual knot in Samantha's stomach had eased enough that she *could* eat. She even had seconds.

When she finally crawled into bed that night just after ten o'clock she felt as if she had been up three days without so much as a catnap. Oh, how she had been looking forward to stretching out her weary body and letting it sink into her mattress! She was certain she'd fall asleep thirty seconds after pulling the summer comforter up to her chin.

But she didn't. Her perverse brain began conjuring memories of Cullen. Memories of dancing with him, laughing with him, feeling his gray gaze warm her heart, and of how much she had liked feeling his hand on hers at lunch today. She felt again his strong arms around her, his long hard body pressed against her, his hot mouth on hers. She heard a low moan and realized in the same moment she felt the frenetic beat of her heart that it was hers.

It took her another hour to fall asleep.

CULLEN STOOD at his bedroom window just after dawn the next morning, seeing nothing of the verdant landscape that extended to the horizon. He thought of dinner parties and charity auctions and felt like he was going mad.

"One hour of life, crowded to the full with glorious action, and filled with noble risks, is worth whole years of those mean observances of paltry decorum." Scott, of course. *Count Robert of Paris.* No wonder Cullen had once devoured every word the man had ever written. Scott knew some important truths.

Cullen pulled from his jacket pocket a small velvet box he'd been carrying around like a talisman since he'd stepped off the plane at Dulles Airport. Flicking it open with his thumb, he stared at the large marquise diamond engagement ring he had bought for Whitney months ago in Hong Kong. She would love this ring, he was certain of it. Samantha, of course, would want something small and elegant, an emerald perhaps, or—

Cullen caught himself thinking of the wrong woman again. What the hell was going on? Why was his mind betraying Whitney just when he was getting ready to propose to her again? His heart was outraged. *He* was outraged. And yet, every time he saw Samantha now, he compared her to

Whitney when there should be no comparison. Whitney should be enough. She should be everything that he wanted and needed in a woman.

But what if she wasn't?

"Oh, of course she is!" he growled, crushing the small velvet box in his fist. She hadn't changed. She was everything he had loved at seventeen and more. She was a stunning, provocative woman who would never let herself be taken for granted and who would always keep him on his toes. He smiled at that. His life would never be dull, for all the boring cocktail parties and charity balls she dragged him to.

So what was wrong with him? Why did he feel agitated and restless? Why was something suspiciously like misery growing in the depths of his soul? *There was nothing wrong with his life!* Whitney was on the verge of saying yes to his proposal, business was good, even Noel wasn't around to plague him because he'd had to fly off to France to attend to some corporate emergency.

Cullen suddenly realized he was pacing. With an oath, he stalked from his room. He couldn't stay cooped up a minute longer.

It was just before seven o'clock when he reached Skylark. One of the Lark grooms directed him to the dressage ring just beyond the main stable. In the distance, he saw half a dozen Lark exercise boys and girls riding a conditioning gallop up the long Bluegrass Hill. He walked on, assailed by all the emotions that had been surging within him recently. He grimly shoved them back down. He would not let them get the better of him. He wouldn't.

He climbed up the white iron railing that surrounded the dressage ring, perched himself on the top rail, and watched Samantha school a leggy roan, turning exercise and training into a graceful ballet. The mare obeyed every leg, voice, and rein cue Sam gave her, her ears pricked forward, her eyes bright, every part of her alert and eager. Though young, the mare showed an excellent mastery of balance and body control as she executed a perfect half pirouette to the left. Six steps later, she stopped, backed up four steps, and then broke into an immediate working canter. Lovely.

Slowly Cullen became aware that he was watching Samantha more than the nimble roan. She moved as one with the horse, supple and graceful and in complete control, the cues she gave the mare nearly invisible. Why had he been lazy and content to stuff her in a narrow pigeonhole and leave her there all these years? Why had he insisted on seeing a one-dimensional woman when she had clearly and always been so much more?

On this already hot Virginia morning, he saw her so clearly. Samantha Fay Lark was lovely and sexy and multitalented and unaware that she was any of those things. He wondered why. Rufus and Jean Lark had been loving parents who had consistently taught their daughter that she could become anything she wanted. Sam had lived that ideal, she just somehow hadn't believed in it.

Something was blocking the view. She had spoken once of his shadow side. Watching her dark eyes yesterday at lunch, he had seen Samantha's shadow side and for the life of him he didn't know why it was there . . . and that was most troubling of all.

He caught his breath as Sam and the mare executed a perfect flying change of lead. Beautiful! A smile touched his lips as his eyes followed them around the ring. Samantha was beautiful on a horse or off. Stupid of him not to have seen it long before this.

She walked the roan to within five feet of him, then bowed as if he was the judge at a competition. "You're looking stressed. You need a vacation."

"I'm *on* my first vacation in twelve years. You're due, too."

"Every day is a holiday on Skylark Horse Farm," she said brightly.

"Trust me, you should bring your travel agent up on charges of fraud."

She stuck her tongue out at him.

He grinned at her and hopped down from the fence. "I'll get the gate for you."

"Thanks." She guided the young mare through the gate, then jumped to the ground and ran the stirrups up the leathers. "Guadalupe!" she called.

A younger, slimmer version of Calida came out of the main stable on the run. Cullen recognized her as one of the many Torres cousins. "Yes, Miss Lark?" she said.

"Keep Sky Rocket warmed up for me for a few minutes, will you?" Sam said.

"Sure thing," Guadalupe said, leading the roan mare away.

"Aren't we going to be working this morning?" Cullen asked, puzzled.

"In a minute," Sam said. "First, tell me what's wrong."

"Nothing's wrong," he said, avoiding her gaze by looking up at the serene vista of the seventeenth century frame house and its distinctive green shutters. A gardener was tending a thick bank of wisteria.

"And I'm a one-eyed, one-horned, flying purple people eater."

Cullen sighed heavily. Trust Samantha to put him in his place.

"Whitney isn't acting up again, is she?" Sam asked.

"No, Whitney's been wonderful," he replied. "I may actually get her to accept my next proposal sooner than later."

"Great!" She caught his arm and then suddenly released it, shoving her hands into the back pockets of her jeans. "So why are you so miserable?"

"I'm not!"

She looked derisively up at him. "Balderdash. I haven't seen you look this miserable since you were seventeen and placed second at the Virginia Gold Cup. What's going on, Daddy Warbucks? Someone trying a hostile takeover of one of your precious corporations?"

Cullen sighed with resignation. She had always been able to see right through him, even in the first years after Teague's death when he'd done such a good job convincing his parents that he'd fully recovered from that horror. Sam had known better, and had called him on it, and had gotten him to talk for hours as she listened for hours. Not judging, not advising, just listening. It was what he had needed most then. Maybe it was what he needed now. Even if she didn't understand, he knew that at least his secrets would be safe with her.

"I don't *know* what's wrong," he said in exasperation as they walked onto the lush front lawn of the Lark house. "I only know that everything looks and feels different to me—my life, my world—and it's all . . . wrong. On the surface, my life is everything I wanted and chose," he said as they sat down on the wooden bench that encircled an ancient oak. "On the surface, I'm a successful man. I'm proud of my business accomplishments. I'm proud that a woman like Whitney wants and loves me. But . . . I'm not happy and I feel both guilty, because I *should* be happy, and angry. I've done everything that the world and Whitney expected of me and by all rights that should bequeath happiness. But it hasn't. Instead"— he shook his head in bewilderment— "there's this storm of emotions roiling inside of me and I don't know how to make them *stop*."

"Years of dissatisfaction are roiling within you," Samantha countered.

"What have I got to be dissatisfied about?"

Her smile was gentle. "*Everything,* you ninny! I've tried to tell you before that no good can come from trying to live someone else's life. You've spent the last twelve years denying all of who you are and what you want. It was bound to boomerang on you sooner or later."

"I'm *good* at business," Cullen mulishly retorted.

"Hey, let's not quibble. You're *great* at business, but you're also a horseman, and that's something you've brutally ignored for twelve long years."

"I am not miserable because of horses!" he insisted.

"Oh, of course you are," she said, laughing at him. "Horses are as much a part of you as they are of me. Just as the land is as much a part of you as it is of me. If I didn't have this farm, I'd wither up and die. You've avoided Mackenzie Farm like the plague these last twelve years, and so a big part of you *has* tried to wither up and die. Being back for more than just a flying visit was bound to stir up that hornet's nest sooner than later."

"You're talking through your hat," Cullen growled, standing up and beginning to pace, because he couldn't sit still and listen to this nonsense. "Mucking about with horses may be fun, but it's kid stuff. I'm playing in the big leagues now and it is *very* satisfying!"

"Cullen," she said gently, "it's time to stop letting guilt about Teague's death manipulate your life. Let go of him and get on with your own dreams and the life you were born to."

Frustration and confusion and fear filled his chest and his shoulders and his throat. "The business is as much a part of my heritage as those damn horses and *far* more important!" he said harshly. "I left behind my childhood dreams long ago because that's what grown-ups do! You play around with horses all day long and for what? So a few rich people can buy them and ride them in competition and maybe win a ribbon or two? Come on, Sam, get real. Who are you really benefiting? What good does this breed of horse or that breed of horse do in the great scheme of things? It's all irrelevant. Your *life* is irrelevant. *My* work and *my* companies affect the lives of thousands of people every day and *that* means something!"

She stood up stiffly, hands clenched in fists at her sides, her face tight with a barely suppressed fury he had never seen in her before. "Get off my land," she said in a low, choked voice.

"What?" he said, thinking she was teasing him.

Her hands grabbed fistfuls of his green polo shirt and shoved him backwards. "Get off my land!"

"Sam——" he said, dumbfounded. She was serious!

"You dim-witted, wooden-headed, money-grubbing *moron*," she said, shoving him back again. "You can't see the truth even when it's spread out all around you in glorious living Technicolor! The land is *everything*! It is all you or I or anyone else on this planet *has*. It is more important than your precious mergers or the stock market or *you*. You used to know that. You used to love it as fiercely as I do. But *you*, in your infinite wisdom, chose to turn your back on the land, and your family, and your dreams, and on *me*, dammit!"

"What?"

"*Not* because that's what grown-ups do," she continued bitterly, "but because you were a self-absorbed coward."

"Now wait just a——"

"This land you are *defiling* merely by standing on it is my *heritage*. It represents three hundred and fifty years of my history and love and commitment. I am its custodian. I am responsible for every wildflower, tree, and blade of grass, not to mention the two dozen people whose livelihoods depend upon it." She shoved him backwards again. "And if you would stop wallowing in guilt and self-pity, you would see that you used to know that basic truth and believe in it as fiercely as I do. You would understand that the land is everything. You would understand that horses are a part of us and they bring joy to so many others and there is *nothing* irrelevant about *joy*! Now *get off my land*!"

Slowly he backed away—confused and shocked and just plain mad—then he turned and walked to his car. He slid onto the leather driver's seat, feeling Sam's glare burning into him, put the key in the ignition, and got the hell out before he threw something at her. He would not succumb to her insane logic, or to the misery burrowing deep within him. He would not betray the last twelve years of his life. He would not betray Teague.

Sure, his life was incomplete, but it was incomplete because he hadn't gotten Whitney to the altar yet, that was all. This damned malaise had nothing to do with land or horses and everything to do with matrimony. It was time he started planning a September wedding and some real happiness at last. It was time he introduced Whitney to the perfect world he had created for her.

Cullen slowed the red BMW and turned into the long Mackenzie driveway. Noel had called last night to announce his return to Virginia at the end of next week. His parents, who loved any excuse to throw a party, were giving a welcome-back party for him next Friday. That would give Cullen plenty of time to remove the last of Whitney's roadblocks to matrimony. After the party, he would get her alone and propose and get on with the life he had always wanted, and to hell with Samantha Lark.

Still furious, he slammed on the brakes in front of the Mackenzie front door, turned off the ignition, and climbed out of his BMW. He wanted to hit something. Why wasn't Noel around when he really needed him?

Then Cullen realized that this fight with Sam meant he wasn't going to be around at Skylark just when she needed him to help her get ready for the second intermediate eventing competition that was supposed to earn Magic, Nessie, Flora, and Central enough points to qualify for the Mackenzie Horse Trials in September.

"She threw me out, she can take the consequences," he muttered. It didn't help. He still felt like a rat.

THE MACKENZIES' GOLDEN drawing room, which Erin Lark had loved from childhood, was filled with light and laughter and conversation as Williams, the Mackenzie butler, walked with stately grace among four dozen guests, amusement rigidly held in check, a silver tray perfectly balanced on his hand as he offered the newest delicacies from Rose Stewart's kitchen.

Erin sipped her glass of French champagne—served in Noel's honor—and watched Whitney, in black Ralph Lauren slacks and sleeveless knit shirt, sitting with Missy on a drawing room love seat, holding court with a good dozen masculine admirers. Cullen wasn't among them.

He stood beside a cabinet of ancient Chinese curios, lost in thought. Something had been troubling him for over a week. Erin wanted to blame it on Whitney, but then, she wanted to blame the national debt, Steven Seagal films, and processed cheese on Whitney too, and she suspected it was something other than the blond bombshell that was bothering Cullen now. Perhaps it was this startling little feud he and Sammy seemed to have cooked up between them despite the higher claims of the Great Plot.

Erin frowned a little as she saw her sister chatting with the very tall, very old, and slightly stooped Matthew Barrisford, both of them seemingly oblivious to anyone else in the room. Sammy had dressed up in a lavender Chanel pantsuit with an elaborately embroidered jacket, her copper hair pulled back from her forehead and then left to tumble to her shoulders, makeup skillfully applied to hide the shadows under her eyes and other telltale signs of exhaustion.

Erin frowned because Sammy had been avoiding every single one of the Mackenzies all night long, and that wasn't like her. Nor was her feud with Cullen. Something was wrong with her big sister, very wrong, and it seemed to be about more than Skylark's financial problems. Most troubling of all was that she wasn't telling, and she was pulling off *that* Herculean accomplishment by using work to avoid Erin and turning down every proposal she put forth for fun or food or both. In their teenage years, such proposals would have had Sammy dragging *her* out the front door. Until last week, Sammy would at least have given in to keep Erin from worrying about her. Yep, something was definitely wrong.

Thus far, teasing, complaining, and bullying had failed Erin miserably. The time had come to find herself a two-by-four and use it for Sammy's own good.

Musical laughter drew Erin's gaze. She grimaced as she watched Whitney rise from the love seat to drape herself seductively against Cullen. Maybe she could find other uses for that two-by-four.

"A beautiful woman should never drink champagne alone."

Erin turned to find Noel at her side, looking even more than his usual drop-dead-gorgeous self in an Armani dress suit that reminded her of Walter Farley's Black Stallion: sleek, and powerful, and dangerous. She smiled. How could she not smile at such a man? "All the men have been otherwise engaged," she informed him.

"Whitney is diverting," he conceded with a slow smile.

"Don't sell yourself short. She's not the only diversion in the room."

Black eyebrows shot up. "My God! Can you finally be paying me a compliment after all these weeks of your blatant disregard for all my remarkable qualities?"

Erin laughed, shaking her head at the Frenchman. Somehow, Noel could always make her laugh. "Your ego is big enough without me running off at the mouth about your remarkable qualities. You looked like you were enjoying yourself just now."

"Whitney is always enjoyable when she is happy, and she is very happy when she is manipulating the game to her satisfaction."

Erin regarded Noel in some surprise. "If you know you're being manipulated, why play along?"

He shrugged, looking wonderfully Gallic. "The game has its amusements, though there are fewer of them now that Cullen has foresaken homicidal tendencies for tolerance."

"Cullen is a sap," Erin said frankly.

"Because he will not engage me in battle for the fair Whitney?"

"No, he's a sap because he *wants* the fair Whitney," Erin retorted.

"You disapprove of his choice of a bride?" Noel inquired, gracefully swirling the champagne in his glass.

"That's putting it mildly. Most people, including Sammy and Cullen, are fooled by Whitney's beauty. They think it reflects an inner beauty. It doesn't."

"No?" Noel said with hooded eyes.

"No," Erin flatly retorted. Noel was a big boy, he could handle the truth, particularly when it seemed he wasn't half as interested in the neighborhood goddess as she had once believed. "I'm not sure if she's even capable of truly loving Cullen, or anyone else for that matter, which of course makes her seem even more desirable. No man can resist pursuing an unobtainable female."

"True," Noel conceded. "You surprise me, I confess. I had not known your dislike of Whitney ran so deep."

Erin shrugged. "You know what they say: familiarity breeds contempt. Whitney has spent her life cultivating the fine art of manipulation, pretending to be a delicate flower to avoid hard work and harsh realities, playing Sammy for all she's worth, pitting one man against another to get what she wants. With Cullen back home, you in doting attendance, and all the games in play, Whitney is in her element. It's enough to drive any sane person to drink." She swallowed the last of her champagne, to Noel's open amusement.

"I, too, do not believe she is the best choice for Cullen."

"That's only because you hate to lose in any competition, particularly when competing for a woman's favors."

"But no," Noel replied quietly, "I am being perfectly altruistic. Certainly I am attracted to Whitney, for I am yet still breathing, but I have become bored pretending she may actually succumb to my palpable charms. I think I shall look elsewhere for more entertaining game." He glanced at Samantha as she suddenly laughed at something Matthew Barrisford had said.

"Oh, I wish you would!" Erin said.

"What?" Noel said with the utmost surprise.

"A torrid fling is just what Sammy needs right now. *Something* has to put her back on course, and I'd really hate to have to use the two-by-four."

Noel regarded her with consternation. "You would not object to the breaking of your sister's heart?"

"Oh, Sammy is much too sensible to fall in love with you," Erin assured him.

He regarded her in some outrage. "And what of my heart? It would be a simple thing to love a woman like Samantha. I believe I am half in love with her already."

"Noel," Erin said kindly, placing a hand on his broad shoulder, "it's my understanding that you've been half in love with most of the female populations of Europe and America!"

"Ah, the prosaic American," Noel said sadly, taking her hand and placing it on his chest. "Do you not believe I have a full heart to give?"

"Maybe in ten or twenty years," Erin riposted, feeling suddenly light-headed, "when the chase no longer amuses you."

"Amusement," he said, black eyes holding her gaze captive as he raised her hand to his lips, "is not all that I want."

"Keenan, what's wrong?" Laurel Mackenzie screamed.

The room was suddenly silent. Everyone turned to Laurel, her arms around her husband as he collapsed to the floor.

"Keenan!"

Cullen and Noel reached them at the same moment.

"He's not breathing!" Laurel cried, tears streaming down her face as she stared helplessly up at her son. "Cullen, *he's not breathing!*"

"I'll call nine-one-one," Sammy said, running to the phone in the far corner of the room.

"Dad? *Dad!*" Cullen shouted, checking Keenan's lifeless eyes as Erin wrapped Laurel in her arms.

Noel's ear was pressed to Keenan's chest, his fingers clasped against Keenan's wrist. "I hear no heartbeat. I can find no pulse."

Cullen was already straightening Keenan out on the floor. "Do you know CPR?" he tersely demanded.

"But yes."

"You do the heart compressions, I'll take respiration."

Heart pounding against her ribs, Laurel sobbing in her arms, Erin watched as if from far, far away as Noel began rhythmically pressing his clasped hands against Keenan's still chest to Cullen's count of five. Cullen pinched his father's distinctive nose shut, blew twice into his slack mouth, and then Noel continued the heart compressions.

"Paramedics are on their way," Sammy said at her side. "I've got Williams watching for them."

"It's too late," Erin whispered, tears sliding down her cheeks. "It's too late."

Ten

CULLEN SAT ON the most uncomfortable chair in God's creation in the emergency room waiting room. Others were there—a teenage mother and her crying baby waiting to find out if her teenage husband had survived a motorcycle crash, and an elderly man whose equally elderly wife had fallen off a step and had broken her hip—but Cullen had developed tunnel vision. He only saw and heard the frightened little group around him, and even they were a little out of focus.

He was actually using automatic pilot to comfort Whitney, who sat beside him repeating again and again how she hated hospitals. It was very hard to think and feel in this moment while doctors worked behind a closed door just a few feet away trying to save his father's life. He glanced at Erin, who sat on his left, her face taut and devoid of all color, her hand clasped tightly in Noel Beaumont's hand as he spoke to her in French in a soft undertone. Directly across from them, Samantha sat with Laurel, her arms wrapped around his mother, gently rocking her and stroking her and lulling away some of the terror. For a moment, his eyes met Sam's brown gaze and he started feeling again.

"I hate this. I just hate this!" Whitney said angrily. "Why are they keeping us in suspense like this? Why don't they tell us something?"

"They'll tell us something when they have something to tell us," Cullen replied.

"I shouldn't be here. I've never been good in a crisis. Never."

"You're stronger than you think, Whitney."

"This is all just so awful," she said, shuddering beside him. "It reminds me of that terrible car crash that killed Teague and nearly killed you. The doctors had to keep me under sedation for *days*."

"You're not going to need sedation, because Dad's going to be fine, just fine," Cullen said soothingly.

"It's not fair," Whitney complained. "Things were going so well. Why did this have to ruin everything?"

Cullen didn't answer. He was on his feet, watching an angular young woman in scrub greens walk out of the room where his father lay dead or alive. She stopped in front of Laurel.

"Mrs. Mackenzie? I'm Doctor Devereaux."

Sam helped Laurel to her feet. "Is my husband . . . alive?" Laurel quavered.

"We've been able to stabilize him, for the moment," the doctor replied. "I'm afraid Mr. Mackenzie has suffered a massive heart attack. We've got to find out why and then repair as much of the damage as we can. It will be a couple of hours before we can tell you anything more."

"What are his chances?" Cullen demanded.

Doctor Devereaux turned to him. "He should have died twenty minutes ago," she said gently. "Your father's a fighter, Mr. Mackenzie, and he was in superb physical condition for a man his age. That's all in his favor. But like I said, it *was* a massive coronary. I can't give you any odds or projections or clues about what will happen, because I just don't know. If he can survive the next couple of hours, I should be able to give you something stronger to pin your hopes on."

"May I see him?" Laurel asked, barely audible.

"I'm afraid not, Mrs. Mackenzie," Dr. Devereaux replied. "He's still unconscious. We're moving him up to the cardiac unit now. We've got our best people working on him. We need to stay out of their way."

"But you'll tell us—"

"As soon as I know anything," Dr. Devereaux assured her. She nodded at Cullen and the others and then strode back to work.

"I wish someone would hit *me* over the head with a two-by-four so I could be unconscious for the next few hours," Erin muttered as she sat back down with Noel.

"This is the worst night of my life," Whitney said as she tugged Cullen back down beside her.

"Come on, guys, you heard what the doctor said," Sam broke in. "Keenan's tough as nails, *and* he's stubborn. He won't let a little thing like a massive coronary beat him and neither should we. We've got a couple of hours, so let's use them to Keenan's advantage. Sending him our prayers and our love could only help."

Cullen flashed her a grateful smile. "Samantha's right," he said to the others. "Dad hasn't given up, he hasn't stopped fighting, and neither should we. I mean, look at you, Mom. He'd be appalled to see you wimping out like this."

Laurel gave him a watery smile, then straightened her shoulders a little bit, took the tissue Sam offered her, blew her nose, and said with greater force in her voice, "You're right, Cullen. I've lived through worse, and so has he. I've never doubted your father before and I'm not going to start now. The Mackenzies have always lived into their eighties and nineties and you know how devoted Keenan is to up-holding tradition."

"That's right," Erin said with equal firmness. "He's got another twenty or thirty years left to try to run your lives. He's not about to pass that up."

"He has often expressed to me his unquenchable determination to teach his grandchildren how to ride," Noel offered. "He will not forgo such a dream so easily, I think."

Erin smiled at him and squeezed his hand, which still held hers. "Keenan has never reneged on a promise in his life. He's not about to start now."

They spent the next three hours alternately cheering each other up and praying to every god in creation to keep Keenan alive for the next twenty or thirty years.

At last, Dr. Devereaux reappeared. Everyone was instantly on their feet. "He's still alive," she said, before they could bombard her with questions.

"Thank God," Laurel said.

"We found the problem," Dr. Devereaux continued, pulling the green scrub cap off her short brown hair. "It appears to be a congenital defect of the aortic valve. It just simply stopped working and that stopped Mr. Mackenzie's heart. We're taking him into surgery now to repair the defect and what damage we can from the heart attack."

"But Keenan's never had a heart problem in his life," Laurel protested. "None of his checkups showed the least trouble."

"It's the kind of thing only a cardiologist would detect, so don't go suing your family doctor just yet," Dr. Devereaux replied.

"Will he make it?" Cullen demanded, skin ice-cold, heart battering his throat.

"All I can do is tell you our best guess," Dr. Devereaux said. "At this point, he's got about a thirty percent chance of surviving the surgery—"

"Oh my God," Laurel moaned.

Dr. Devereaux gave her a reassuring smile. "Mrs. Mackenzie, he had less than a two percent chance of surviving when he was first wheeled into the place, so think of this as a major improvement in his prognosis."

"Yes, you're right," Laurel said. "I'm sorry."

"No, you're just worried, and you have every right to be. The best answer I can give you all is this: If Keenan Mackenzie survives the next twelve hours, he has a better than fair chance of walking away from this in the end."

"*More* waiting?" Whitney complained.

"I'm afraid so," Dr. Devereaux replied. "If Mr. Mackenzie survives the surgery, they'll keep him in the surgical unit for a few hours and then move him into ICU on the fourth floor. ICU has its own, and much more comfortable, waiting room. I recommend you wait up there."

"Thank you, Doctor," Cullen said.

She gave him a brief smile. "I only wish I could offer you more hope."

"Trust me," Sam said. "We're doing a lot better than when we first arrived."

Ten minutes later, they were resettled on the dark blue upholstered couches and chairs in the ICU waiting room.

Time stretched ahead of Cullen like a century-long famine. He hated hospitals more than Whitney did. Much more. He hadn't been in one since Teague had died.

Teague.

Being in this hospital again brought up dark memories and a pain so deep and so old it seemed to be in his DNA.

Cullen stood up because he couldn't sit still. He hid his shaking hands by shoving them into the pockets of his charcoal gray suit. "I'll be right back," he said hoarsely as he headed for the bathroom.

The door closed behind him and he leaned against it,

shaking all over now. Stumbling, he leaned on the pale blue basin, turned on the cold water, and brought it up to his face once, twice, and then made himself stare into the mirror above the sink at the crescent brand that proclaimed his guilt.

Teague had died on a beautiful summer day, much like this one. Cullen had been eighteen and had somehow cajoled Keenan into lending him the keys to his beloved Jaguar convertible to drive sixteen-year-old Teague into town for a guy's day of fun and girl watching.

And they had had fun. They had taken the Jaguar on a one-hundred-mile-an-hour joyride over the county's back roads. They had stuffed themselves with all the greasy fast food Rose Stewart abhorred. They had canvassed the regional mall for the latest in athletic shoes, tight jeans, and sexy briefs neither was willing to let any female see them wear. They had flirted with girls, taken in the newest Clint Eastwood flick, talked about family and career and dreams, and than at dusk they had started for home.

They never made it.

Gossiping about the less than perfect reputation of the prep school's drill squad, Cullen had braked at a stop sign just three miles from home, and put his foot back on the accelerator. They were halfway through the crossroads when a pickup truck plowed into the passenger side of the Jaguar.

The noise of the crash consumed Cullen for a moment, deafening him, blinding him. Then his head was aching and his right leg shrieking with pain and his left arm feeling like it had been cut off at the elbow. Blood was streaming into his eyes. He could barely see. The pickup's horn was blaring. And all he could think about was Teague.

He turned his throbbing head. "Teague?" he croaked. "Teague, are you okay?"

Then he saw the front end of the pickup where the

passenger door should be, and Teague crumpled beneath it and against it, blood streaming over him.

"Teague!" he screamed.

"C-C-Cullen?" his brother whispered.

He was alive! His brother was alive! "I'm right here, Teague. Right here."

"God, Cullen, it hurts so much," Teague whispered, tears trickling down his blood-streaked face.

Cullen tried to move to him, even just to touch him, but the Jaguar's front carriage had been twisted around by the impact of the crash, imprisoning him in his seat. He couldn't move.

"Hang in there, Teague. I think I hear sirens already. The paramedics will get us out of here and to the hospital and get us all patched up."

"It hurts too much, Cullen," Teague whispered, starting to lose consciousness.

"Don't you dare pass out!" Cullen shouted desperately. "Stay with me, Bro. Hang in there just a little longer. We're going to be fine. Just fine."

But they weren't. Five minutes after the crash, two ambulances, a fire engine, and three police cars had surrounded them, but the Jaguar was so badly twisted that it took another ten minutes to pry enough metal away to get Cullen and Teague out of the car, and that was ten minutes too long. With sirens blaring and people shouting and his body raging with pain, Cullen watched his brother die and he couldn't reach him, couldn't touch him, couldn't help him. He had always looked after Teague and now, when it mattered so much, he could do nothing, nothing to save his beloved brother.

For all of his enraged shouts to leave him alone and let him stay with Teague, the paramedics and the firefighters hauled Cullen out of the Jaguar and got him on a backboard, and then on a gurney, and were shoving him into the back of an ambulance when other paramedics and other fire-fighters finally hauled his brother's lifeless body from the car.

They had both been brought to this hospital, except Teague went to the morgue while Cullen was taken first to the emergency room, and then to neurology for a CAT scan, and then into surgery to repair his broken right femur and left arm and the gash on his face.

He kept telling them not to bother, but they wouldn't listen, damn them. What was the point of getting well when Teague was dead and it was his fault? If he hadn't been so interested in salacious gossip, if he'd been paying more attention to the road, if he had *really* looked both ways, he'd have seen the drunk driver barreling toward them in his pickup. He'd have been able to avoid the crash.

Instead, he had betrayed his brother and his parents and Whitney and himself. He spent a week in the hospital trying to die, and failing, before being released just in time to attend Teague's funeral.

Cullen shuddered in the blue-tiled bathroom. Was he going to lose his father, too? Was he going to attend yet one more funeral that he might have prevented? Guilt washed through him for all the years he might have spent with his father instead of working in New York and London and Hong Kong trying to live Teague's dream. He bitterly remembered Sam saying only last week that the last twelve years were boomeranging on him for living Teague's life instead of his own. This was payback with a vengeance.

He heard the door open behind him.

"All right, you can just stop it right now!"

Samantha Lark stood in the ICU men's room in a lavender pantsuit, glaring at him.

"You're in the men's room," he pointed out.

"And you're wallowing in your own personal little hell,"

she retorted. "Don't think I don't know what's running through that cockeyed brain of yours, Cullen Mackenzie, because I do! You're flagellating yourself over a car accident you couldn't have prevented and probably for a heart attack that had nothing to do with you!"

"Sam—"

"Well, you can just stop the stupidity right now, do you hear me?" Sam said as she marched up to him, practically spitting fire. "I am not going to stand idly by and watch the best man I've ever known destroy himself with guilt over something that wasn't his fault. Wasting twelve years of your life trying to prove yourself worthy of your family's love when you already had it, and of Whitney's love when you already deserved it," she said in disgust. "What idiocy! You are a good man, Cullen. You have always been a good man, you will always *be* a good man, so you can just cut the crap right now, because I won't put up with it. I won't let you bludgeon yourself with Teague's death and then use that to magnify your fears for Keenan. I won't! Your father needs your strength and your love right now, not your guilt and self-pity."

"Are you done?"

"No! I'm here and I'm gonna speak my mind, your shadow side be damned!"

"When have you ever *not* spoken your mind?"

"*Shut up,*" she said, jabbing a finger into his sternum. "Did you ever once ask Keenan or Laurel if they blame you for Teague's death? No, of course not! You just *assumed,* like the blithering idiot you are. Well, I happen to know them a helluva lot more than you do because, unlike you, I stuck around and I can tell you for a fact, Cullen Mackenzie, that they *don't* blame you and they never have. They blame the drunk driver, as they should. They blame him for drinking and driving, they blame him for driving too fast, they blame him for blowing through the stop sign and colliding with you.

"You're a smart guy. Try using your brain on your own behalf just this once and figure it out. Were you drunk? No! Did you stop at the crossroads? Yes! Did you look both ways? Yes! Could you have possibly seen him coming at you at over one hundred miles an hour as you started across the road? No! The police conducted all sorts of tests and *proved* that. Now, stop being so in love with guilt and self-flagellation and try being in love with life for a change. That's what Keenan needs from you right now. That's what Laurel needs from you right now. So, cut the Hamlet crap and get out there and do the job that needs to be done!"

"Are you done now?"

She folded her arms over her chest and glowered at him. "Yes."

"Good. Thanks for the two-by-four," he said, kissing her on the forehead and strolling out of the bathroom. He could feel her staring at him in shock and he almost laughed out loud. Clearly, Samantha was not fully conversant with the efficacy of a two-by-four when applied to the thick head of the Mackenzie male.

He walked over to his mother, sat down beside her, hugged her hard, and then held her hand fast in his own as he talked her through visualizing Keenan healthy and strong once again.

"EVERYBODY EATS, or you answer to me," Samantha announced thirty minutes later.

Cullen looked up to find her holding a tray loaded with food. Apparently she'd been off scavenging and he hadn't known it. Her unbeatable sangfroid holding full sway, she handed out coffee and tea, sandwiches, huge chocolate chip cookies, and apples to Laurel and Erin, Noel and Whitney, and a large Styrofoam bowl of chocolate pudding—his childhood favorite—to him.

"Thanks," he said with a startled smile. "You remembered."

"I ate chocolate pudding at your house every day for years as a kid. Of course I remembered," Samantha retorted, sitting in the chair beside the couch he shared once again with Whitney. "I called home to let everyone know what's happening," she announced to the others. "We should be getting a care package from Rose Stewart within the hour. But I figured we needed something to tide us over till then."

"Thank you, Samantha Fay, this is wonderful," Laurel said, sipping her tea beside Noel in the chairs opposite them.

"For American hospital food, it is almost palatable," Noel conceded, taking a bite of a chicken salad sandwich.

"Hey, I'm no sadist," Samantha said. "This stuff came from the diner across the street."

"For American cafe food, it is almost palatable," Noel amended, which made even Laurel smile. He followed up his advantage by beginning to tell her the absurd story of a bad fall he'd taken in a Grand Prix competition some years back, the delicacies that had found their way into his hospital room in the aftermath, and the six pounds and two jealous lovers—nurses—he had gained as a result.

Cullen turned to Whitney, only to find her curled up on the couch by his side, fast asleep.

"Best survival skills of anyone I know," Samantha commented on his left. "You save a lot of wear and tear on your nerves if you can sleep through a crisis. She slept for two days straight when you delayed calling to ask if you could escort her to her college graduation prom."

Cullen smiled. "You don't do too badly in a crisis yourself."

"Nah. I'm just no good at sitting around and waiting. I'm an action kind of gal. Give me an M16 and a hostage crisis and I'm happy as a clam."

"Not a lark?"

"I didn't want to be obvious."

"You're incorrigible."

"*That's* what the parole board said."

Cullen smiled at her. "You're supposed to be eating, too."

"You're right, I am," she said and promptly took a bite of her turkey sandwich. Then she launched into a whimsical discussion of his press coverage in *Time* and *Newsweek* and *The Wall Street Journal*, making him sound like a cross between Donald Trump and Sun-Tzu and getting him to laugh more than once.

He knew what she was doing, of course. She was deliberately trying to raise his spirits, and succeeding, and he was grateful. It reminded him of the immediate aftermath of Teague's death, and the following few years when he'd come home from college on holidays and occasional weekends. Samantha had been sixteen and seventeen and as strong-willed then as now. She had deliberately bullied him out of his room and outside into the beautiful world he loved, and then she had let him be.

For that reason alone, he'd been able to talk to her about all of the guilt and pain that only seemed to keep growing within him as the days and the months passed. She had listened and somehow, though saying very little, managed each time to lighten his heart so that he always returned home at the end of the day happier than when he had left it. He was grateful then, and through all the succeeding years when, even on his brief visits home, she had done or said something to ease the pain and the guilt that had only seemed to keep growing. And he was grateful now.

He glanced down at Whitney, curled trustingly against him and looking unbearably lovely as she slept. It had always nagged at him . . . He'd never before let it become a conscious thought . . . but now, as his father struggled for life, Cullen wondered why it was Sam, and not Whitney, who had always connected with him on that deep level of pain and guilt Teague's death had created. Why had Whitney never figured out or understood that the happy mask he put on for public consumption hid an agonizing turmoil within? If she really loved him, wouldn't she at least have picked up that he was troubled?

He covered his face with his hands for a moment to try to recover some semblance of sanity, then pulled them away and looked across the room at his mother. He had fooled his parents all these years, and they loved him, so it was only reasonable that Whitney had been fooled, too. End of story, end of stupidity. Except, why had Sam never been fooled?

He felt a slim hand cup his cheek and he turned to Samantha, her steady brown gaze meeting his. "Keenan's going to make it, Cullen. Just hang in there."

He pulled her hand to his lips and kissed it. "I'm sorry we fought the other day," he said quietly.

Big brown eyes widened and gentled and seemed to melt into him, warming his heart and banishing some of the shadows. "I'm sorry, too," she said softly, before tugging her hand free. "It was all my fault. I seem to be losing it more and more nowadays. Work must finally be getting to me."

"*Over*work," he corrected. "And I was as much to blame as you."

"Friends?" she asked softly.

"Friends," he said, brushing his fingertips across her cheek.

Her smile wavered a moment, and then she began reminiscing about the week-long fight they'd had in prep school when he was a junior and she a freshman and he, as any junior would, did his darndest to ignore the existence of a mere freshman, even though he had known her all his life. Samantha had retaliated by hanging large paper banners throughout the school proclaiming his various idiosyncrasies and loves, like chocolate pudding, as proof that she knew him and he knew her. The war had escalated from there until both got themselves hauled into the principal's office for a major lecture on the proper behavior she expected from the representatives of two of the county's most notable families.

Dr. Devereaux appeared a few hours later to announce that Keenan had survived the heart surgery and then they settled back to wait some more, a hamper of Rose Stewart's best offerings now on hand to keep them fortified. Noel and Sam and Erin quietly traded places to keep Laurel and Cullen occupied and distracted and more hopeful than they would have let themselves be if left on their own.

The numbingly long night turned into morning. Rose Stewart appeared with a hamper stuffed with breakfast delicacies. Williams accompanied her. He had brought toiletries and changes of clothes for everyone, even Whitney and Sam and Erin. This was a welcome diversion. Evening clothes and dinner jackets were gratefully shed.

As everyone consumed Rose Stewart's buttery croissants and strong coffee, Samantha began recalling some of the sillier episodes in Keenan's life, like the time he'd attended a Lark Halloween party dressed in a flouncy pink crinoline. Noel countered with the even sillier escapades of some of Europe's rich and famous, and so the morning trudged slowly by.

Just before noon, Dr. Devereaux entered the waiting room, a stocky man in his late forties at her side.

"This is Doctor Moorlock," she said, introducing him, "the head of our cardiology unit. I thought he should give you the update on Mr. Mackenzie's condition."

"I am happy to confirm what I have so often heard about Keenan Mackenzie," Dr. Moorlock began. "He's as tough as they come. I've just removed him from the critical list."

"He'll live?" Laurel quavered.

"Barring any further complications, yes."

The waiting room was filled with shrieks and yells and laughter and everyone talking all at once as Laurel hugged Dr. Moorlock and then Dr. Devereaux, and Noel hugged Erin, and Cullen hugged Samantha, and she hugged him back.

"Thank God," he whispered fervently. "Thank God, thank God, thank God."

Then he realized what he was doing and abruptly pulled away, badly embarrassed. The wrong woman again, dammit. He compensated by turning to Whitney and kissing her and saying how wonderful it was and how glad he was that she'd been there with him through this ordeal.

"I'm just glad it's over," she said, resting her head on his shoulder, worrying him anew. Cullen knew just enough about heart attacks to know that this was far from over.

When everyone had returned to a semblance of calm, Dr. Moorlock continued.

"Mr. Mackenzie has been badly weakened and his heart sustained enough damage to require two bypasses. If he will submit to a slow recovery, then I see no need for anything as radical as a heart transplant. But I'm talking a very slow recovery period, probably one lasting six months. Once he leaves here, he'll need home nursing care for at least the first few months, and very carefully regimented rest, diet, and exercise. As I understand it, Mr. Mackenzie is used to being an extremely active man. He may simply not be able to tolerate this course of treatment."

"Oh, he'll tolerate it, Doctor," Laurel grimly assured him. "I'll see to it."

Dr. Moorlock considered her a moment. "With you on our side, Mrs. Mackenzie, I don't think I'll have to worry about seeing your husband on my operating table again."

"May we see him, Doctor?" Laurel asked.

"He's conscious and asking for you," Dr. Moorlock began. Everyone made a rush to the door. He just barely managed to fend them off. "But you may see him for a few minutes only!"

They gave him their solemn word before trampling him on their way out of the waiting room.

Keenan had been moved into a private room already packed with flowers. Word of his heart attack must have spread fast, Cullen thought as, his arm around Laurel's shoulders, he led her into the room. He realized that he was afraid to look at his father. Keenan, though two inches shorter than he, had been like a towering oak in his life, tall and strong and commanding all that he surveyed.

He heard the reassuring repetitive beep of the heart monitor, saw the IV's clustered by the bed, and then he saw his father. For a moment, his arm spasmed around his mother's shoulders. In just sixteen hours, Keenan had become frail and emaciated and devoid of all color as he lay limp beneath white sheets, his head resting in the center of a white pillow, his eyes closed.

"You are the most annoying man, scaring us half to death like that," Laurel stated as she walked up to her husband, kissed his forehead, and clasped his right hand in hers.

Keenan's eyes opened and he smiled faintly. Suddenly he no longer seemed frail. All of his old strength and pugnaciousness were there for anyone to see in his blue eyes. "I must apologize for ruining your party, my dear," he said, his voice softer than usual, but the dry wit still coming through.

"Hey, Dad, not to worry," Cullen said, kissing Keenan's forehead. "I mean, it was just a party for *Noel*. It's not like it was for anything important."

Keenan uttered a faint chuckle as Erin on the other side of the bed took his left hand, and kissed him, and told him to expect a lot of coddling for a long time to come.

"Now there's something to look forward to," he said with a tinge of disgust.

"You'll love all the attention and you know it, Keenan," Samantha said from the foot of his bed. "You've got just the right kind of ego to appreciate being waited on hand and foot."

"And with such a lovely attendant as *Madame* Mackenzie doing the waiting upon, what is there to object to?" Noel inquired at her side.

"You are a rogue, sir," Kennan informed him.

"But not as charming a rogue as you, sir," Whitney informed Keenan as she stood at Cullen's side.

She won a smile from Keenan even as Samantha discreetly led Noel and Erin and Whitney out of the room so the Mackenzies could have a few private moments together. She was, Cullen thought, the perfect friend to have around in a crisis.

He walked back into the waiting room five minutes later with Laurel to find Whitney talking happily with Noel and Erin. It took a moment to find Samantha. She stood in a far corner of the room, her back to them, her arms wrapped around herself. It was the first time since Keenan had collapsed that he thought beyond his father and Teague and remembered that Samantha and Erin had endured other hospital vigils: with Rufus and later with Jean. Concerned, he started toward Sam, but before he could reach her she had already turned, her arms dropping to her sides, a smile fixed on her mouth, dark memories and fears for Keenan hidden deep inside.

It made Cullen wonder about the other things she might be hiding.

They were all distracted as Dr. Devereaux, Dr. Moorlock, and the head nurse of the ICU joined them to more fully brief them on Keenan's condition and treatment.

"Cullen, I can't listen to one more word of this," Whitney said as Dr. Moorlock explained Keenan's recent surgery. "I've been cooped up in this place for *weeks* it seems. We've done the vigil bit, Keenan is going to be fine, and now it's time to go home and bathe, and eat a real meal, and sleep in a proper bed."

"Whitney, I can't," Cullen said. "I'm staying here. You heard what Doctor Moorlock said. Dad's not out of the woods yet."

Steely blue eyes bored into him. "He's going to be fine, Cullen, and you know it. I want you to take me home now."

"I'm staying, Whitney."

"So am I," Laurel stated. "Doctor, is there any way we can set up a cot for me in Keenan's room?"

"I'm staying, too," Erin said.

"In that case, I must make the hospital my home as well," Noel said.

"It's ridiculous for all of you to stay," Dr. Moorlock said.

"The hospital has some rollaway beds we sometimes use for the spouses of our patients," the ICU nurse was saying to Laurel.

"You can't all stay," Dr. Devereaux insisted. "Mr. Mackenzie can't have more than one or two visitors at a time, at least for the next few days."

They were all talking at once, their voices rising as

they argued about who was staying and who was leaving and what Keenan really needed.

Samantha's piercing whistle brought a sudden, stunned silence to the room. She was standing, arms akimbo, on one of the blue arm chairs. "Since I seem to be the only sane person here, *I'll* tell you what we're all going to do," she announced. "A gaggle of family and friends in the waiting room will do Keenan no good. Since we all want to stay close by, we'll sit with Keenan in shifts, so he's not left alone, and we all get the breaks we need, because Whitney is perfectly right: we *all* need to shower and eat and sleep in real beds. So, Laurel stays for the first shift, since she's the wife and she's got priority. I'll stick around to help her out. Cullen, Whitney is also perfectly right that she needs to go home now, and so do you. You and Erin can pull the second shift, say, at four o'clock this afternoon. Then Laurel can come back at ten o'clock and spend the night."

"I can provide transportation for the ladies to and from the hospital," Noel broke in, "and stay with Keenan at times as well."

"Wonderful," Samantha said. "So that's all settled. Cullen, take Whitney home. Noel, take Erin home. Laurel, go sit with your husband. Doctor Moorlock, why don't you go with her so you can fill them both in on the treatment Keenan's going to need over the next six months. Doctor Devereaux and Nurse Jamison, you can fill me in on what Keenan's going to need in the next few weeks and I'll write it all down, copy it, and distribute it to the appropriate family and friends."

To his bemusement, five minutes later, Cullen found himself stepping into his car and taking Whitney home, while Noel bundled Erin into a taxi on a similar errand.

Thirty minutes after he had left the hospital, Cullen

was back home, but unable to sleep. The house was too empty, his father too ill, his thoughts too crowded to permit sleep. Still, as Samantha had pointed out, much of Whitney's advice made sense. So, he shucked off his clothes and headed for his shower.

The hot water felt wonderful as it washed away hours of fear and the hospital smell and the terrible hospital memories. He dressed in jeans, sandals, and a green Yale Business School sweatshirt and felt even better. He picked up the dinner jacket he had tossed on his bed, along with the rest of last night's and this morning's clothes, and felt the ring box he had so carefully hidden in the outside pocket early last night. He pulled it out and opened it, staring at the large marquise diamond. The night had ended so very differently from what he had planned.

He snapped the box shut and tucked it into his top bureau drawer. This was not a time to be thinking about love and marriage. Now there was only his father and whatever it took to help him get home and well. Cullen put the rest of his clothes in his clothes hamper, looked around his sunlit bedroom, and knew he couldn't stay confined a moment longer. He'd take a walk, then call his New York office to see if any crises had arisen during these last horrible hours he'd been incommunicado.

He headed downstairs and met Williams at the bottom of the gently curving staircase. "Miss Stewart has laid out a most tantalizing luncheon in the dining room, sir."

"I'm not hungry," Cullen replied.

"If I may be so bold, sir," Williams said, effectively and surprisingly blocking his exit, "nourishment is necessary if you are to be of any use to your family in this difficult time."

Cullen's eyes narrowed. "You wouldn't by any chance be telling me what to do, now, would you, Williams?"

"Yes, sir, I would."

First Whitney, then Samantha, now Williams. Cullen was beginning to miss the days when he was the high-powered CEO and everyone did what *he* told them to do. Still, he was able to recognize good advice when he heard it.

"Okay, okay, you win," he said, heading for the dining room, "but only because you're right."

He walked into the dining room and found Noel seated at the table and taking a bite of quiche.

"You could not sleep as well, I see," he commented.

"Maybe tonight," Cullen said, sitting down across from him. "How's Erin?"

"She was already sound asleep by the time I left Skylark. She is the only sensible one among us, my friend."

"I've noticed that about her," Cullen said, cutting into the quiche in the center of the table and putting a slice on his plate. He followed that with salad in his salad bowl and French onion soup in his soup bowl. It seemed Mr. Beaumont had Rose Stewart wrapped around his little finger. "I've noticed you, too. You mess with the brat, Beaumont, and I'll break you into itty-bitty French pieces."

Noel smiled. "But that is a given."

Cullen smiled back. "You've been a good friend, Noel. I don't know how to thank you for all the help you've given my family since Dad collapsed."

Noel shrugged with perfect Gallic self-deprecation. "Do not concern yourself. Friends help each other in times of crisis, no?"

"Some friends more than others," Cullen said, thinking for a moment of Whitney, and then hurriedly banishing the traitorous thought from his mind. "It's really annoying how much I've come to like you."

"There, there, do not let it prey on you," Noel said soothingly. "You'll get over it soon enough."

Cullen laughed and they spent the rest of the meal in easy conversation with each other, talking about business and travel and even horses.

He walked back into the hospital at ten minutes to four, forcing himself not to recoil from the smell, and the incessant intercom pages for doctors, and the sick and infirm being moved through the hallways. He stepped out of the elevator onto his father's floor and saw Samantha leaving Keenan's room. She saw him, and stopped, and smiled with such warmth that his heart ached. He was swamped by a sudden yearning to be in her arms and to hold her in his. Badly rattled, Cullen forced himself to smile back and walk up to her.

"How's Dad?" he asked.

"He slept through a lot of the afternoon, but he's awake now," she replied. "Laurel's already put some color back in his cheeks."

"She's always had that effect on him," Cullen said with a grin, which Samantha mirrored.

Cullen searched her wan face and tired brown eyes and found nothing but exhaustion, and relief, and love for her surrogate parents. She had looked far different five years ago.

It had taken a month for Rufus Lark to die after his stroke. Cullen had flown in from London to attend the funeral held beneath a leaden sky in the rain, ragged rows of black umbrellas unable to shield the mourners from this terrible loss. Rufus had always been so vibrant, so alive. His death seemed to have stolen life from the world. Erin and Jean had been hysterical. Samantha, too, had openly grieved. She didn't wail and sob, but she did cry steadily, as she had cried at Teague's funeral. For the first time in their lives, he had seen despair in her brown eyes and a pain so deep, it seemed to be embedded in her soul. At the wake, however, she joined in telling funny stories about her father, and reassuring grief-stricken friends, and getting the somber farm staff to remember the good times. She had been, in many ways, incomprehensible to Cullen.

Just four months later, it felt like God was showing a rerun as they buried Jean Lark in the rain, Erin hysterical, Samantha silently weeping and then rallying at the wake to help friends and co-workers get through this newest loss and to help Cullen fend off his memories of Teague's death and the guilt that was as much a part of him as breathing.

He wondered suddenly if guilt was the cause of her manic overwork now. But what could Samantha possibly feel guilty about?

He studied her a moment as she stood at his father's hospital room door in beige slacks and a beige short-sleeved cotton sweater. There was no color in her face. The shadows under her eyes were black. Any sane person would strap her down on the nearest available hospital bed and not let her out for a month.

"You're done in," he said gently, tucking a strand of copper hair behind her ear, loving that brief feeling of silk between his fingers. "The swing shift is here. Go home and go to bed and don't you dare come back until tomorrow."

"Who put *you* in charge? Al Haig?"

"Go home, Sam."

"But Erin isn't here yet," she protested.

"Noel's bringing her right behind me, and then he'll take Mom home. You can't help Dad if you don't take care of yourself, Sam."

"Okay, okay," she muttered. Such swift capitulation surprised him. She must be at death's door. "Let me just go say good-bye to Keenan."

"Nope," he said, grabbing her shoulders and steering her toward the elevator. "You'll make that good-bye last at least another hour. I know you too well, Samantha Lark. You're going home and you're going now."

"Tyrant," she charged.

"Sure. But I'm right, and you know it."

They stood waiting for the elevator, Cullen's eyes never leaving her. Sam looked as frail as Keenan had this morning. He couldn't bear it. Without a word, he bundled her into his arms, holding her close, absorbing her fragility and trying to give her some of his strength in return. Did she have any idea how precious she was?

"You do anything resembling work today or tomorrow, and I will personally hang you out to dry," he threatened.

"Yes, sir," she murmured into his sweatshirt.

He was so stunned that he just stood there as the elevator doors opened and two orderlies got off. She'd never said those two words to him in her entire life.

"Go," he said, giving her a little push, more because he didn't want to let her go than because she needed an impetus. She walked onto the elevator and turned to face him. "Thank you, Samantha," he said as the doors slid closed.

He stood staring at them a moment, then turned and walked to his father's room. He wasn't scared this time. He pushed open the door, walked into the room, and found his father still lying against the white pillow. Laurel was in a chair beside him, holding his hand, and apparently telling him something both private and salacious, judging from the twinkle in his blue eyes and the color in his cheeks.

"Hey, Dad," Cullen said, walking to the bed, "you still here?"

A low chuckle greeted him. "That's right, treat my near-death experience with cavalier disregard, see if I care."

Smiling, Cullen leaned over and kissed him. "Scare me like that again, and I'll hack up every pair of riding boots you own."

"You are a tyrant, son."

"So I've been told.'

"I don't know where you get it from."

"Of course you don't," Cullen said with a grin. He glanced at Laurel. "Erin will be here any minute, Mom. You'd best get ready to go."

She squeezed Keenan's hand. "I'll go talk to the nurses about your meals, then. I'll be right back." She left the room, quietly closing the door behind her.

"That woman gets more beautiful every time I see her," Keenan said with something like his old strength.

Cullen took his mother's chair. "She has amazing recuperative powers. Let's hope you have the same."

"Hell yes, I do! I'm a Mackenzie, for crying out loud. Six months," Keenan said disgustedly. "Six months the doctors tell me I have to lie around being waited on hand and foot, and your mother is going right along with them!"

"Mom was always the sensible one."

Keenan scowled at him. "I will go stark raving mad in under two weeks, you know that, don't you?"

"It's a concern," Cullen conceded. "But I think we'll be able to find enough ways to keep you entertained and on the recovery program Doctor Moorlock has mapped out."

"Six months," Keenan muttered. Then his blue eyes locked on Cullen. "I'm going to need your help, Son."

"Anything, Dad," Cullen said, clasping his hand, "you know that."

"Even if I ask you to take over running the farm for me during these next six months?"

"Piece of cake," Cullen assured him.

"But the business—"

"I'll telecommute. Hell, I am already. Modern technology is a wonderful thing, Dad. I just need a computer, a modem, a fax machine, and a good long distance phone carrier and I'll be able to keep on top of things. I'll need to fly to New York for the quarterly Board meetings, but the rest of the time you're stuck with me."

"But—"

"Dad, this is a great opportunity to finally wrestle some control away from the Mackenzie Patriarch and still keep life and limb intact."

Keenan smiled. "Tom Pratt is relatively new as foreman, but he's a good man, and he'll be of some help, as will Frank Tolland. Of course, I won't exactly be incommunicado, so between us—"

"I'll be fine, Dad, and so will the farm. You'll see. You might even get to like taking it easy. Stranger things have happened."

"Get real, Son."

"Sorry, Dad," Cullen said with a grin.

Keenan squeezed his hand. "There's one more thing. I need you to take my place riding in the Trials."

"You are out of your ever-lovin' mind," Cullen retorted.

Keenan frowned at him. "A Mackenzie always rides in the Trials. It's tradition."

"Dad, I haven't ridden in competition in twelve years. David and Karen O'Connor, Bruce Davidson, and Arianna Shepard will be competing. The entire U.S. Equestrian Team will be competing! So will representatives from the British, the French, and the German teams. I'd make a fool of myself, you, and the Trials, not to mention the poor horse."

Stern blue eyes regarded him. "Cullen, you've got the gift, you've got eighteen years of solid training behind you, and that will stand you in good stead. Frank Tolland will help you get ready and so will Samantha, so you have nothing to worry about."

"Samantha already has too much on her plate. She doesn't have time to help me."

"I'll make time."

Cullen turned to find Sam walking into the room. "You threw me out before I could get my things," she said, picking up a bag of clothes in a corner chair. "And as for helping you prepare for the Trials, you won't be able to get rid of me, so get used to it. Bye Keenan, see you tomorrow," she said, giving Keenan a quick kiss.

"You're a darling girl, Samantha," Keenan said.

"Ain't it the truth? You will note, you blowhard," she said, directing a quelling glance at Cullen, "that I am out of here in under a minute, not an hour." She blew Keenan a kiss as she walked back out the door.

"That woman has no understanding of her own physical limits," Cullen muttered.

"She's the strongest woman I know, and that's saying something," Keenan retorted. "She'll be fine, and so will you. Finish in the top five at the Trials and I'll be satisfied."

Cullen stared at his father, aghast. "Just the top five? Why not the top three?"

"I'm a reasonable man, Cullen, you know that."

"Sure I do," Cullen said with a grin.

When Laurel returned, Cullen walked into the hall to give them a few minutes alone together before she left. He leaned back against the pale peach wall, folded his arms across his chest, and thought he had to be the biggest fool in all of creation.

He had just promised away six months of his life. He had just promised to hurtle himself back into the world he had desperately avoided for so long. The world of childhood dreams.

But he was trapped. He'd given his word, and to his father, which made his word doubly binding. Cullen shook his head in disgust. Well and truly trapped. Keenan couldn't have planned it better if he'd tried.

How on earth was he going to run the farm *and* the business at the same time? He'd gotten by so far this summer with a fax machine and long distance calls in his sitting room. That arrangement would have to be greatly expanded. He'd need a real office. And he should probably bring his executive assistant down from New York.

Cullen had long prided himself on being a practical man. A situation had been created, he would deal with it, practically, rationally, efficiently. He stood in the hospital hallway rapidly making plans, when it suddenly hit him. *Whitney!*

What was he going to tell Whitney?

Eleven

As the new, albeit temporary, boss of Mackenzie Farm, Cullen ruefully borrowed a page from Samantha's schedule. He was up before dawn, walking the farm with Tom Pratt and the Mackenzies' trainer, Frank Tolland, learning all they could teach him, and then working with the horses, riding them, studying them, learning them. He spent two hours on the phone with his New York, London, and Hong Kong offices. Then he was off to the hospital to spend four hours with Keenan, watching his father grow stronger each minute they talked about the farm and Keenan imparted his own lessons.

Then back to the farm to train for the Trials on Mackenzie's Pride, his father's promising Thoroughbred, with Frank Tolland working with him for two hours, and even Noel helping him as he trained, every muscle aching, every muscle glorying in being in training once again. With Sam's horses, he'd just been helping out. Now he had to build his own stamina and skill and reflexes to avoid making a fool of himself in September.

Samantha also worked with him as promised, not on Pride, but on strategy, at least for the first week. In the second week, she began working with him on the dressage test, which often racked up the most penalty points in a three-day competition, keeping up a steady stream of commentary—much of it not complimentary—and advice.

At six o'clock, he went back to the hospital for a private family dinner with Keenan and Laurel. Then, with Laurel staying the night at the hospital, he drove home to inspect the renovation of the downstairs south parlor into a new master bedroom and bath for his parents that Noel was supervising. Then he went over the farm books and plans for the next day's work with Tom Pratt.

Sometimes, when all the work was done, he'd sit up with Noel over a small snifter of brandy and they'd talk horses and business. Galling though it was, he was no longer even annoyed by how much he liked the Frenchman.

Ten days after his father's heart attack, Cullen walked out on the broad front porch of his home at five o'clock in the morning, the multitude of robins, cardinals, bluebirds, larks, and swallows that lived in the surrounding woods already madly singing awake the new day as the sun brightened the azure sky of early dawn. "My foot is on my native heath, and my name is Mackenzie," he murmured, paraphrasing Scott.

He had forgotten how much he loved the early morning. He had forgotten the perfect quality of the air and the miraculous clarity of light. He stared out across the five thousand acres that were his heritage, his birthright: the dressage rings and jumping arenas, the red-roofed stables and sheds behind them, the lush pastures and the dark clouds of Thoroughbreds contentedly grazing, foals springing about on spindly legs as they began their daily games with each other and their mothers, the ancient woods of oak and pine and hickory beyond the pastures where he and Teague and Sam and Erin had skulked about, pretending to be Indians, or homesteaders, or pirates.

Everything Sam had said before throwing him off Skylark was true.

Love, pure love, swelled within him as he gazed out at the dawn-bathed landscape.

> *"Breathes there the man,"* Sir Walter Scott had written,
> 　*"with soul so dead,*
> *Who never to himself hath said,*
> *This is my own, my native land!*
> *Whose heart hath ne'er within him burned*
> *As home his footsteps he hath turned from wandering on a*
> 　*foreign strand!"*

The power of *The Lay of the Last Minstrel* made Cullen's heart ache. It seemed almost incomprehensible to him that he had struggled every day of the last twelve years to burn from his heart the love of this land that now swelled within him.

> *"If such there breathe, go, mark him well;*
> *For him no Minstrel raptures swell;*
> *High though his titles, proud his name,*
> *Boundless his wealth as wish can claim;*
> *Despite those titles, power, and pelf,*
> *The wretch, concentered all in self,*
> *Living, shall forfeit fair renown,*
> *And, double dying, shall go down,*
> *To the vile dust, from when he sprung,*
> *Unwept, unhonored, and unsung."*

Cullen felt as if Scott had been writing expressly about him two hundred years ago, for the poet and the novelist had described his faults and follies, grandiosities and soul death as if he had stood in the same room studying him. Samantha had tried to tell him that a lifetime ago when she had thrown him off Skylark, but he had been too deafened by his own self-absorption and self-pity to hear her. He had been too busy running away to even hear the truth of his own heart. Sam was right. He loved this farm, these horses, this land, more than his own life. He always had.

Staying and working the farm again after so many years of acquiring his "boundless wealth" had finally pierced the deafness and the blindness until Cullen could hear the truth again, feel it, remember old dreams of riding in the Olympics and building Mackenzie Farm into the next century. They filled his mind and his heart once again.

As Samantha had said, he had been living Teague's life, not his own. It had taken nearly losing his father to get him back on the path—his own path—that he had strayed away from for too long.

It was exhilarating to feel his body remember the training of his childhood and adolescence, it was soul-satisfying to walk every inch of the farm with Tom Pratt and remember and relearn all that he used to know about caring for each building and tree and blade of grass. It moved him to tears to walk among the horses—his horses—in pastures and paddocks, stroking them, talking to them, learning them as they learned him. It was even exciting to discover that high-technology really did make it possible to run the family business successfully from the farm with the help of his recently relocated executive assistant, and that he enjoyed running it. The business no longer felt like a penance or the arbiter of his worth, it was simply a challenge, and fun, like taking a five-foot-tall wood-and-brush hurdle coming off a downward slope.

Cullen had never been so challenged and so satisfied and so fulfilled in his life. He scarcely had time to notice all of the friends rallying to the Mackenzies' support. Keenan's hospital room was stocked daily with new bouquets of flowers, as was the house. Friends called him. Friends visited him, and visited his family, too, offering their help and their comfort and their own assurances that Keenan would make a full recovery.

Noel had made good on his promise. He drove Erin and Laurel to and from the hospital every day, carried out every commission Keenan gave him, and took his own daily shift at the hospital, beating Keenan three chess games out of five. The irritation, and the challenge, he assured Cullen, were guaranteed to speed Keenan to full health.

Even Samantha, with all the work she had to do on her own farm, and the training she helped him through, turned up at the hospital every day for her four-hour shift with Keenan, even though everyone assured her it wasn't necessary. She scoffed at them all and then settled down with Keenan to talk horses, or watch a Grand Prix event on television, or play some hands of five card stud, usually roping at least one nurse and an orderly or two into their game. Sometimes even Dr. Moorlock played a hand.

Only a solitary barb kept Cullen from perfect satisfaction. Claiming a morbid fear of hospitals—and the torture she had known waiting those sixteen hours to learn if Keenan would live or die—Whitney had not returned to the hospital to visit Keenan. This was shocking to Cullen. Fortunately, old survival tactics came to his rescue. He made himself too busy learning and running the farm, training for the Trials, managing the family business, and watching over Keenan to think much about Whitney or wonder exactly how he was going to tell her about the major changes in his life's plans.

Two weeks after he had collapsed at Noel's party, Keenan Mackenzie came home from the hospital to a party of his own. Though his termagant of a home care nurse—personally selected by Laurel to make sure her husband stayed on the regimented recovery program, no matter what tricks he played—refused to let him stay up for more than an hour, Keenan enjoyed himself thoroughly as he sat in his wheelchair surrounded by family and a good two dozen friends.

There were presents to open, including an assemble-it-yourself plastic model of the human heart from Samantha and a silver bell from Noel to summon servants or family to his bidding day and night. There was cake and sparkling apple cider (Keenan was not allowed alcohol). There were silly stories and laughter and repeated exclamations about how well he looked, and then Nurse Morgan wheeled the star of the party into his new ground-floor master bedroom despite his objections that he was fit as a fiddle and ready for fun.

Slowly the party guests trickled away until only the Larks and Whitney remained, Sam with Laurel and Erin and Noel, while Whitney in a white ankle-length cotton knit dress grabbed Cullen's arm and tugged him outside to walk through his mother's celebrated rose garden.

Whitney heaved a happy sigh and snuggled close as they strolled through the fragrant roses. "It seems like years since we were last alone together. I've missed you."

"Life has been pretty frantic these last few weeks," Cullen said, uneasy because he was having a hard time directing his thoughts completely away from work and back to Whitney, where they belonged just now.

"It's been insane," she said. "Laurel has scarcely been home, Noel has turned himself into the Master Builder and forsaken all social functions, and I heard Erin say that Samantha has stopped sleeping entirely, just so she can squeeze everything she has to do into twenty-four hours. And *you,*" she said with a playful nudge, "you might just as well have dropped off the face of the earth. You missed Matthew Barrisford's birthday party *and* the chamber music festival."

"I'm sure you enjoyed them enough for the both of us."

"How could I enjoy them when you weren't there? Well, now that Keenan is home, we can finally get our lives back to normal."

"Not . . . exactly," Cullen said, feeling more than a little uneasy. He should have prepared her for the change in his life's direction, laid the groundwork, *something*.

Whitney stiffened beside him. "What do you mean?"

He turned and gave her a hapless shrug. "I mean that we're living a new version of normal. The way things have been these last two weeks is pretty much the way things are going to be, Whitney, at least for the next six months. I promised Dad I'd run the farm for him until he fully recuperates *and* ride in the Mackenzie Trials next month, and I still have to take care of the family business a few hours a day. I'm pretty well booked. Of course, things will get a bit better once the Trials are over—"

Blue eyes glittered at him. "They will get better now. Tom Pratt and Frank Tolland are perfectly capable of running this place until Keenan is back on his feet and you know it! You don't have to be a martyr to your father's heart attack, Cullen."

"Whitney, honey," Cullen said gently, placing his hands on her shoulders, "you don't understand. I'm no martyr. I'm finally doing what I've always secretly longed to do. I'm doing what I love. I'm doing what I want to do for the rest of my life."

"I won't have you throw away *me* and every plan we made together just so you can play Gentleman Farmer," Whitney said coldly. "What about all those promises you made these last six years? What about the traveling we were going to do, the cities we were going to visit, the people we were going to meet?"

"We can still do all of that," Cullen assured her, trying to pull her into his arms, but she jerked herself free. "Whitney, honey, I promise you that we'll get away from here three or four times a year. We'll travel the world, just like you want. But for now—"

"I don't want *excursions*," she grimly informed him. "I am going to live abroad, Cullen Mackenzie, with people who care about art and music and fashion. My associates are going to be *people* with long pedigrees, not horses. People who know how to appreciate me. I will agree to *visit* this backwater a few times a year, but the rest of the time I will live in Europe or the Caribbean, and that's final!"

"Whitney—"

"Cullen, you're just not thinking clearly," she said, softening her voice, placing a placating hand on his chest. "Nearly losing Keenan has got you all muddled. But I'm not muddled. I can see clearly what has to be done."

"And what is that, Whitney?"

"The most reasonable course is for you to sell Mackenzie Farm to Noel Beaumont, not run it," she said.

"*What?*" Cullen gasped.

"Now, now, don't get your back up," she said with a smile. "Selling the farm makes good sense for everyone. It *benefits* everyone. It's good for Keenan, because he'll recover faster if he doesn't have to worry about the farm, and it's good for Laurel, because she won't have to worry about the farm weighing down Keenan's recovery. It's good for Noel because he'll have a farm that reflects his wealth and stature. It's good for you, because you'll be able to return to the world you belong in *and* you'll be able to keep your promises to me. And it's good for me, because without the farm weighing *you* down, I'll be able to get the life I've always wanted with a man who pays more attention to me than to his work."

Something cold and solid lodged itself in Cullen's heart as he took a step back. "And what about the life *I* want?" he demanded.

Twelve

"Evenin', Miss Lark," Whitney said as she breezed through the Larks' front door in a swirl of black chiffon, the slim gold and diamond chain Cullen had given her at the beginning of this summer visit glittering against her slender throat. Since Sam was finding it harder and harder to make time to visit her friend, Whitney had begun calling on her.

"Make yourself to home," Sam said, gratefully stretching out her weary body on the Edwardian sofa.

"Thank you kindly. Don't mind if I do."

Whitney sat down in the chair opposite her as Calida set down Samantha's dinner tray on the coffee table.

"Late dinner," Whitney observed.

"I stayed late at the office," Sam said, sitting up.

"I said it before and I'll say it again: there is more to life than work. Speaking of which, I don't suppose Cullen has asked for your advice."

"About what?"

"About how best to apologize to me, of course," Whitney said.

"He won't apologize," Sam wearily informed her friend as she took a sip of lemonade.

"Of course he will, even if he is the most stubborn man in Virginia."

"He's not stubborn," Samantha countered. "He's just right, and he knows it."

"You two always stick together," Whitney complained, crossing one shapely leg over the other. "There is more to life than *horses*, Sam. When are you going to realize that it's not possible for a man who has shone in the international limelight to be happy hiding that light on a Virginia horse farm? Cullen will miss the excitement and the challenge of that larger world, and he'll be grateful to me for helping him get back into it. Don't you see? I'm saving him from himself and from his idiotic notions of duty to the family homestead."

"Whitney, that farm is his heritage, it's his *family*. How on earth could you think he'd just up and sell it? How could you even *suggest* it to him?"

"It's the most reasonable solution to everyone's problems and you know it!" Whitney insisted.

"It's the most *appalling* solution and if you'd only look beyond the end of your own nose, *you'd* know it!"

"Are you saying I'm being selfish?" Whitney demanded.

All of her anger and jealousy poured out of Sam, leaving her limp. She felt too exhausted and too fragile to argue with her friend, something they seemed to be doing more and more of lately. "I just don't think you see the larger picture," she said quietly.

She buttered a slice of bread and let Whitney ramble on about the wonderful dinner party she had just attended with Missy Barrisford, about all the people who were there, what they wore, what they said. Sam heard none of it.

All she could think about was Cullen and this desire that kept growing stronger in her each day and how much harder it was becoming to hide it from him and from everyone else. The combination of nearly losing Keenan, seeing Cullen every day, working too hard, and getting only four hours of sleep a night had left her walls paper thin. She had no resistance left to this hunger that gnawed at the depths of her soul or to this longing to spend every moment of every day with a man who loved her best friend.

Most dangerous of all, however, was that Cullen now treated her as his confidante. She helped him train for the Trials every day and part of that time was always spent in conversation, usually about his current fight with Whitney. He was miserable and guilt-ridden and angry all at the same time. It took everything she had in her not to pull him into her arms and kiss him and make the world and guilt and misery go away, for the both of them.

Her honor had grown threadbare as she struggled to reassure Cullen that he and Whitney were right and best for each other, that Whitney would come around, that he would have the life he deserved. But she wasn't so sure anymore. The life Whitney wanted was the life that had made Cullen miserable for years. The life *he* now wanted was anathema to Whitney. Sam was caught in the middle. She wanted them both to be happy, but how could they be happy together? And how could they be happy apart?

Bobby Craig walked through the front door dressed in a suit and a tie. He only had eyes for Calida, who had just walked in from the kitchen. "You ready, darlin'?" he asked.

Bobby and Calida had brought their romance out of the closet the week before.

Calida took off her apron, draped it over a chair, and went to him, beaming. "Ready," she said.

He took her arm, nodded at Whitney and Samantha, and led his darlin' out the door.

"They are so cute together," Whitney said with an amused smile.

"Yeah," Samantha muttered. If they had to be blissfully in love, so be it. But did they have to rub her nose in it?

"Where's Erin?"

"Asleep. Rehearsal lasted more than ten hours today. She was whipped."

"Well," Whitney said, standing up and stretching like a sleek cat, "I'm going to follow her excellent example and go home and go to bed. You ought to do the same."

"I will."

"I meant in this century, Sam."

"I'll pencil it in," Samantha said with a wry smile.

"What is this?" Whitney demanded, hands on her shapely hips. "Some slow form of suicide?"

"The Trials are just a week away," Sam said soothingly. "I'll be able to slow way down after that." One way or the other. The farm would finally clear its debt, or the bank would take it over. Either way, she'd have less work to do.

"If you make it to next week. Honestly, Sam, you look like death warmed over."

"Thank you for helping me to feel good about myself."

"If a friend can't be honest with you, who can?"

"Erin, Bobby, Calida, Cullen, Keenan, Laurel, Noel, every Skylark groom and exercise boy and girl, Nurse Morgan—"

"Okay, okay, I get the picture," Whitney said, laughing. "But Sam, just because we all agree doesn't mean we're wrong."

"I never said you were."

Whitney cocked her head and studied her for a moment. "You mean, you agree that you're killing yourself with this insane work schedule?"

"Of course I agree. I may be obsessed, but I'm not stupid."

"Then go to bed."

"In a minute."

Whitney sighed and waved good-bye and walked back outside to her car.

Sam stared at her dinner tray, unable to eat. She hadn't the strength to eat. How was she going to survive this next week with her secrets intact if she had no strength left to keep them safe?

How could she fairly and honestly advise Cullen when every part of her ached with wanting him?

Slowly she stood up, swayed a moment on her feet, and then started for the stairs. She only had to fend off this madness for one more week. She could do it. She had to. There really wasn't any other option.

TWO DAYS LATER, Samantha slid off Lark Ness feeling downright hopeful. The mare had been jumping beautifully all week. Her strength and stamina were in peak condition. She might actually have a chance of placing well at the Trials.

"Look's like Mackenzie's Pride has got some serious competition."

Samantha looked up and saw Cullen sitting on Pride, a tall powerful blue roan Thoroughbred, just a few feet away. He was dazzling with the late morning sun shining on the long blond hair flowing from beneath his riding helmet, a white peasant shirt doing nothing to disguise his broad chest and shoulders, the tan breeches he wore leaving nothing to the imagination. *God,* how she wanted him!

She turned hurriedly back to Nessie and began running the stirrup irons up their leathers to hide her blush. "She's got potential."

"She's got it all, Sam, and you know it. She could well be part of the founding generation of America's best steeplechase and eventer breed."

"That's the general idea."

Cullen appeared shocked. "Heaven help us! Can this actually be *ambition* rearing its ugly head in the Larks at last? I think I hear a dozen generations of your progenitors spinning in their graves."

"Unlike *you*," Samantha retorted, sticking out her tongue, "I don't want to own the world. I just want to breed great horses, a far more humble ambition than anything the Mackenzies ever contemplated."

"Nonsense! We Mackenzies pride ourselves on the superiority of our Thoroughbreds to any of their so-called cousins raised in this or any other country. Dad is maniacal on the subject, you know that."

"I know a few dozen horse farms in Kentucky, Great Britain, Germany, and even Australia that would quibble with the Mackenzie claims to superiority."

"Slander!" cried Cullen, a hand to his forehead, his head turned away in horror.

Samantha grinned at him. "The Mackenzies never were fond of a little wholesome competition. Didn't your great-grandfather Struther fund a small private pirate fleet to raid your shipping competitors?"

Cullen grinned right back at her. "He did, and built a tidy little shipping monopoly for himself, too. I try to live by his sterling example. Ready for a cross-country romp? Rose Stewart will have lunch waiting for us. She promises pecan pie."

Samantha's favorite. "Marybeth!" she called to the groom thirty yards away. "Come cool down Nessie. Where's Flora?"

"She's right here, Miss Lark," Andy said, bringing the roan mare up to her at a trot as Marybeth led Lark Ness away. "All warmed up and ready to go."

"You're a prince, Andy," Sam said as she stepped into his cupped hands and vaulted into the cross-country saddle.

He unclipped the lead shank from the bridle. "Think I can ride her in next year's Mackenzie Trials?" Andy asked, his face eager as he looked up at her.

She smiled down at him. "It all depends on what Bobby says . . . and Bobby says you're shaping up into a top rider."

"Yes!" Andy exulted, thrusting a fist into the air before turning and trotting back to the stable.

"You'd put a green rider into next year's Trials?" Cullen demanded as they began to walk their horses to the start of the cross-country course Bobby had created for them yesterday.

Samantha had walked it that morning, calculating pace and number of strides between jumps and the angles at which to take the jumps, as well as checking for any treacherous groundhog holes that plagued the Virginia horse and hunt country and threatened the health and safety of both horse and rider. She had a (much reduced) grounds crew to do this, of course, but it was her neck and her horse's legs and she would take no chances with either.

"Of course not," Sam retorted. "Andy will be a seasoned pro by next September, you wait and see."

"Expanding your breeding farm into a training farm as well, then?"

"I hadn't really thought that far ahead. You get clearance yet from the USCTA rules committee to ride in the Trials?"

"Of course. Dad has a lot of pull. Besides, placing tenth last week at Fair Hill helped to reassure the committee members."

"It was a tolerable ride," Samantha conceded. Actually, it had been a superb ride, especially for someone who hadn't been in competition for twelve years. But she wasn't going to tell him that. Besides the fact that he already knew, she had never gotten mushy on Cullen and wanting to ravish him wasn't going to change that.

"You're too kind."

"You ready?"

"After you, Miss Lark."

Sam started Flora at an easy gallop on the two-and-a-half mile course that would loop through Skylark Horse Farm and then, by the simple expedient of jumping a hedge, continue onto Mackenzie Farm, ending a quarter of a mile from the Mackenzie stables, and less than half a mile from Rose Stewart's pecan pie.

It was a completely new course for Flora. Sam continually changed her training routine to sharpen her horses and keep them interested in the work that was so critical to the farm's survival.

Cullen started a minute behind her, far enough behind not to crash into her if she had trouble, and close enough to watch her every move and learn from her vast store of tricks. He might have stopped competing twelve years ago, but she had not, and she had the cups and the ribbons and the trophies to prove it. She didn't compete enough to be a contender for Rider of the Year, but she rode enough so that everyone knew her and knew she was a talent to be reckoned with.

She and Flora Lark easily cleared the starting coop, a white-painted, tent-shaped jump, and then headed downhill, the roan momentarily fighting for her head, Sam holding her firmly back. They took a hog's back, a low-high-low log configuration going downhill, jumped a small rock fence going uphill, and cleared a triple spread combination that allowed only one stride between each wide jump. Then Sam let Flora have her head a little as they galloped towards a series of obstacles Bobby had called Solomon's Hill, because every jump and stride decision was treacherous.

It was a miniature maze of tall log fences, all interconnected, on three levels, going downhill to a small pond they would have to jump into, ride through, and then jump out of to clear another fence before galloping twenty yards to the four-foot-tall hedge where they would cross onto Mackenzie land.

Sam had spent a good fifteen minutes studying Solomon's Hill this morning, deciding at what angle to take each of the jumps, which jumps she would avoid, which ones she would take, to make up time. She had her strategy well in mind as she set Flora at the maze, feeling the mare tremble with fear and excitement before leaping over the first jump, a little too high. Sam pulled her down and back, calming her, steadying her for the second jump, and the third. Flora tried to balk at jumping down into the pond, but Sam kept her going, pushing her into the water, where the young roan steadied again.

They splashed to the other side of the pond. Flora jumped out, a little ungainly, but steady on her hooves. They rode up the slight incline to the three-and-a-half-foot-tall yellow gate, Flora moving easily, an ear cocked to listen to Sam's words of encouragement. Then she just simply stopped dead in front of the jump. Sam, caught by surprise, was thrown over the gate.

Twenty-three years of experiences made her automatically tuck in mid-air so that she landed with a slight roll and ended on her back, gazing up at the cloud-dappled sky, the wind knocked out of her. Flora's reins were still clasped in one hand. Her head within her riding helmet was spinning. The mare stared down at her over the gate, looking both surprised and curious, as if saying "What in the world are you doing down there?"

"Samantha!" Cullen yelled as Pride splashed through the pond. "Are you all right?"

There wasn't sufficient oxygen in the world to answer him, so Sam just lay there and said nothing, willing her paralyzed lungs to start functioning again.

Cullen was kneeling beside her, Pride's reins in one hand. "Can't breathe?" he asked, gray eyes anxious.

She managed to shake her head.

"Thought so," he said, one hand applying pressure to her diaphragm, easing back, then pressing again.

Oxygen swooped into her starved lungs. "Thank you," she gasped.

"You're welcome. Don't get up just yet," Cullen advised, his hand holding her down. "Give yourself a chance."

With two more lungfuls of air, Sam insisted on sitting up.

"That was some fall," Cullen said, sitting back. "I learned a lot."

"I'm so glad," Sam retorted.

"Wish I had it on videotape," Cullen continued wistfully. "It'd be something to show the grandkids. Samantha Lark blows it big time."

"You really know how to cheer a girl up," Sam said disgustedly as she got to her feet. Cullen wouldn't tell *Whitney* that she'd blown it big time if *she'd* taken a similar fall. He'd be yelling hysterically for an ambulance and fifteen different doctors. "I haven't had a fall like that in over three years," she said defensively.

"Then you were due," Cullen said, standing up. "Maybe you got it out of your system today so you won't have to embarrass yourself at the Trials next week."

"There's a comforting thought," Sam muttered, climbing over the gate and running the reins back over Flora's head. "Give me a hand."

Cullen vaulted over the gate, obligingly cupped his

hands, and tossed her back into the saddle. "Derek di Grazia has designed something just like this for the Trials, you know."

"I heard. That's why Bobby built this damn thing. Come on," she said, turning Flora back toward the pond, "let's hit it again."

"The whole thing?"

"Of course the whole thing."

"I barely got through the jumps with life and limb intact the first time. Why don't I just start from the pond?"

"Because it's the series of jumps and water and jump that make the obstacle so challenging and you know it. Up and at 'em, Cullen."

Sighing, Cullen swung himself back up onto Mackenzie's Pride and followed Samantha back through the pond, up onto the opposite bank, and then a good fifteen yards past the log maze. "I should have stuck to Board meetings," he said, looking at Solomon's Hill.

"And miss all this fun and excitement? Nonsense," Sam said heartily just before she set Flora at the log jumps again.

The roan took them with greater confidence, didn't even think about balking at the pond, and cantered easily up the opposite bank. Sam felt just a whisper of doubt in the mare and used her heels to send Flora over the yellow gate before she had a chance to change her mind.

They rode the rest of the course without incident, although Flora Lark insisted on contorting herself over the triple post-and-rails combination and knocked down a rail at a ramped oxer, a jump where the front rail was set one level higher than the back rail—the easiest of all the fences on the course. Sam, mentally sighing, made a note to revise tomorrow's training schedule so she could work with Flora on the course twice, once in the morning and once at the end of the day when the mare was fully rested again. She didn't feel she could count on Flora yet, and to get through an advanced three-day event, horse and rider had to trust each other implicitly.

Cullen galloped across the finish line as she ran up her stirrups and then loosened the girth a little. He jumped down off of Pride just a few feet from Sam and Flora and ran his stirrup irons up their leathers.

"Not bad. Not bad at all, if I do say so myself," he said, pulling the reins over Pride's head. He and Samantha walked together, shoulders nearly bumping, as their horses shambled beside them through the green pasture and the quarter-mile to the Mackenzie stables. "I should be tired, I know, but I feel like I could ride like that all day long. God, I love cross-country!"

Sam laughed from the sheer pleasure of hearing Cullen so happy. "You look pretty exuberant," she commented.

"I *feel* pretty exuberant!" he retorted with a grin. "I'm riding well again and I've rediscovered how much I *love* training for competition. Dad is doing well. The farm is doing well and I love running it, even though I still have a lot to learn. I've even discovered that I actually enjoy running the family business and can do it well from the farm. What's there not to be exuberant about?"

"Well," Sam said, hating to dampen his happiness, "there is Whitney."

"Right," Cullen said, and then he sighed. "Whitney."

Samantha cast him a sideways glance. *Why* did he have to love Whitney so much? He didn't deserve this misery.

"You really should talk to her."

"I've tried, but we keep ending up on the opposite side of the same damn fence. I can understand where she's coming from, I understand what she wants. But dammit, Sam," Cullen burst out, "why can't she understand what *I* want? Why can't she understand how important the farm is to me?"

"She will, Cullen, I promise," Sam said soothingly. "She'll come around. She'll see that the life you want is what's best for both of you. You'll get your happily ever after and I'll get to wear a fuchsia bridesmaid's gown."

Cullen smiled and brushed her cheek with his knuckles. "You're so sweet, Sam."

That brief touch fogged her vision. She thought she saw Cullen bending down to kiss her and she was so tired, and her protective walls so weakened, that she swayed toward him and nearly kissed *him*.

She caught herself just in time. He wasn't trying to kiss her, she just wanted him to! The blood draining from her face, she took a step sideways, bumping into Flora.

"God, Sam, you're done in," Cullen said gently, badly misinterpreting her actions. He reached out his hand, his fingers cupping the back of her neck, his thumb brushing across her cheek. "I can't stand seeing you like this. Tell me what's got you running so scared, Sam. Please tell me."

She was so rattled by this simple caress, she was so breathless and defenseless and brain-dead, that she told him everything about the debt her father had accumulated, the crushing burden he had taken on with her breeding program that had killed him, the creditors hounding her for payment, her arrangement with the bank, the need to keep her finances secret, pinning all of her hopes on the Mackenzie Trials, everything. Cullen listened, tight-lipped and grim, not interrupting her until she had finished.

And then he exploded.

"Are you out of your mind?" he yelled, startling the two horses. "You've been systematically killing yourself these last five years when all it would have taken was ten seconds for me to write a check and make this hell and this insanity go away!"

"Why, you arrogant bastard! How dare you?" she sputtered. "I've kept Skylark going for five years all by myself and I've done a damn good job and you want to negate all that with a *check*?"

"Sam—"

"*No!* I'm not Whitney. I don't need to be rescued by a white knight, so just back off, Cullen!"

"I'm not trying to rescue you. . . . Well, all right, I am. But Sam, it would just be a loan. You could pay me back with much better terms than the bank has given you. You could have some breathing room, a little peace. You wouldn't have to continue this slow suicide of yours. You could actually have a life again."

"No. I've got to do this myself."

"*Why?*"

Five years of grief and pain and guilt welled within her. "Don't you see? It's all my fault. *I'm* the one who got the brilliant idea for the breeding program. *I'm* the one who spent a solid month talking Dad into it even though I could see he didn't want to go along with it. *I'm* the one who insisted on purchasing the very best, which meant the most expensive, studs and brood stock. *I'm* the one who saddled Skylark with three-quarters of a million dollars of debt *on top* of the debt Dad had piled up. I nearly destroyed Erin's legacy, and my own. I'm the one who burdened Mom and Dad with the most awful stress during the last year of their lives. I killed them with that stress, Cullen. I did. I've got to make amends. I've *got* to be the one who puts Skylark back into the black."

"Of all the self-absorbed, half-blind, fuzz-brained *idiots*," Cullen spat out, pulling Pride to a stop. He grabbed her arm and made her stop as well. "You're no more to blame for Skylark's problems than I am! Rufus had big dreams and little business sense, *you* know that. He saddled Skylark with a crushing debt long before the breeding program ever entered your pea brain. That debt was *his* responsibility, not yours. He knew the problems he had caused, not you. While you were touring Europe, you thought everything was hunky-dory back home, didn't you? *Didn't you?*"

"Well . . . yes, but—"

"*Exactly.* How could you have avoided a problem if you didn't know the problem existed? Don't you see, Sam?" he said, grabbing her upper arms and making her look at him, making her focus on his words. "It was Rufus's responsibility to turn down your breeding program until Skylark was back on its feet. *He* was responsible for it, not you, no matter how much you loved the farm, no matter that you would be responsible for it some day. He and he alone knew the true financial situation and, rather than acting responsibly, he chose to bankrupt Skylark, destroy his own health, and nearly deny his children their rightful legacy. I loved Rufus as much as anyone, Sam, but he was wrong, not you. Never you."

The tears she had been struggling against spilled down her face. She saw his surprise, just before he pulled her into his arms, his free hand patting her back and stroking her.

"There now," he crooned. "Let go of all that guilt. It doesn't belong to you, Sam. It never did."

"But don't you see?" she wept. "My breeding program destroyed any hope Dad had of getting out from under. He c-c-couldn't handle the intolerable stress *I* heaped on his shoulders. I killed him, Cullen, just as surely as I'm standing here. And Mom, too. You know I did."

"I know no such thing," Cullen said gently, even as his arms held her fiercely. "You're taking on guilt that doesn't belong to you, Sam. You no more killed your parents than I—" He stopped suddenly. She looked up at him, startled by his rueful smile. "You no more killed your parents than I killed Teague," he said. "Rufus screwed up, Sam. That's all there is to it. He lied to you through omission and forgot what was most important to you and Erin—your home. The land. Give the guilt back to its rightful owner. He can handle it now."

She only cried harder. Was Cullen right? Had her father betrayed her, and not the other way around? There was no answer. Sobbing, she clung to Cullen, because if she didn't, she would disintegrate into a million tiny pieces.

Thirteen

SAMANTHA SAT ACROSS from Cullen at the Mackenzie dining table, all masks and jokes and subterfuge washed away with her recent tears. He couldn't seem to get his fill of her. All during lunch, they had talked about Rufus and Jean and Teague, and about using work to hide from the pain of loss, and using work to hide from life. Odd that they suffered from similar afflictions. Odd that he'd never before let himself fully recognize the kinship and understanding that existed between them. He'd missed her so *much* these last too many years.

With Sam, he could talk about how different it was being home this summer compared to all of his previous visits. Maybe it was simply the length of his stay, maybe he'd been changing in the last year and hadn't known it. Maybe it was Sam's constant challenges to his status quo. Whatever the reason, the urge to flee this house, his parents, even his memories, was gone.

"I'm glad," Sam said with a warm smile as she covered his hand with hers.

An odd series of electric shocks cascaded over his body.

"Did you ever want to run away these last five years?" he asked.

"*Constantly,*" she wryly replied. "But I was stuck. I had responsibilities up the wazoo. But I think, more important than that, I wasn't afraid to love the land, or the horses, or even the work. Unlike you, I had that to hold on to and that, in return, kept me going."

"*I,* on the other hand, held a tiger by the tail."

"Were you miserable the whole time?"

Cullen leaned back in his chair and shoved his hands into the front pockets of his jeans. "I don't think so," he said slowly. "I liked the challenge of the work, and the accomplishments. I had tangible proof that I was doing well and that was *very* reassuring. But living only for work, and working at what I didn't love, that *was* misery."

"Success cost you a lot," Sam said quietly.

"I'm still figuring out just how much," Cullen admitted. "But it taught me a lot, too. I think in a lot of ways that I'm a better man for it."

"And how's life now?" Sam asked, taking the final bite of her slice of pecan pie.

"A bit messy. I don't have everything in place yet. Integrating the business and the farm again means tying up a lot more loose ends than I knew existed. I'm a lot closer, but I'm still not there. At the same time, I *am* happy so, truth to tell, I don't mind that things are still messy. You know, I don't think I ever thanked you."

"For what?" Sam said in surprise.

"For speaking truths to me all summer long, even when I didn't want to hear them. I think they must have had a cumulative effect, because I sure seem to be living them now."

"I'm glad, and you're welcome, and that's what friends are for."

They finally finished lunch and walked back outside toward the main Mackenzie stable where a groom had cooled down Flora Lark. They were silent, lost in their separate thoughts, but it was a companionable silence. Neither felt the need to entertain the other, or to distract the other.

It struck Cullen that he always went into Sam's company with a sense of relief. There were no games, no standards to measure up to. He could talk about the things he really cared about and know, even if Sam disagreed with him, that she would hear him and hear all the things behind his words, too. The dynamic between Sam and him was so incredibly different from the dynamic between Whitney and him.

Whitney.

He'd thought about her constantly since their argument at his father's welcome home party. Half a dozen times a day he caught himself reaching for the phone to call her. But he didn't, because he didn't know what to say, because he didn't know what he felt anymore.

It bothered him that, since he'd been home, she had treated his love as a game she would win on her own terms. It bothered him that for all of her tears and seemingly reasonable excuses, she had not visited his father in the hospital once after that first awful night. It gnawed at his soul that she didn't understand how important it was for him to stay and keep the farm going while his father recuperated. It stirred long threads of disquiet within him that she planned to live her married life in New York and London and Paris, wintering in the Caribbean or the Mediterranean, when he had reclaimed the home and the life he loved.

An older Mackenzie groom led Flora out to Sam. Cullen cupped his hands and tossed her up into the saddle. "Thanks for the ride, and the shoulder to cry on, and the lunch," she said.

"My pleasure," he said, smiling up at her. "I'll see you tomorrow."

"Right," she said, tapping her riding helmet in salute. Then she and Flora cantered down the dirt road separating a long series of paddocks.

Cullen watched her go and then let his gaze wander over gently rolling fields, over the Thoroughbreds that had been his family's life's work, and the stables and barns he had practically lived in as a boy. He strolled into the shadowed main stable and down the line of stalls until he came to Mackenzie's Pride.

"Hi, boy," he said, pulling half a carrot from his pocket. Large, soft horse lips gently brushed against the palm of his hand, making him smile. Then the carrot disappeared. "It's good to be home," he said quietly, stroking the gelding's head as Pride crunched up the carrot.

Did he love his home more than he loved Whitney? The thought made his hand spasm on Pride's cheek. The blue roan jerked his head up in protest. "Sorry, boy," Cullen murmured, automatically stroking the gelding's neck as his mind danced tentatively around the question.

Was Mackenzie Farm more important to him than spending his life with Whitney?

Whitney had beauty and brains, but he saw now that she had adopted her mother's notions of womanhood and taken the easy way out. She had waited for him to rescue her like some knight on a white horse, rather than getting her own butt out into the world she wanted. She wanted to live her life in New York and London and Paris? Fine. Why hadn't she done it? She was twenty-eight years old with a good education and the internal fortitude to make a success of anything she undertook, and she had squandered all of it on her merry round of dinner parties and charity events and country club tennis while she waited for him, counting on him to give her what she could have created with her own two hands.

Beautiful as she was, persuasive as she was, Cullen saw

clearly, really for the first time, that Whitney was not at all the perfect woman he had thought her even six months ago. In fact, she might actually be an incredibly shallow woman.

Just when the right words of conciliation meant he could have Whitney for the taking, Cullen began to think he didn't want her.

"Here's another fine mess you've gotten me into," he muttered to himself.

He stared down at the concrete floor for a moment. Then he looked up and out the far end of the long stable to the small rise of land two hundred yards away. It held the family cemetery and the graves of the first Mackenzie, Aidan, and all the Mackenzies after him.

He hadn't visited the cemetery in twelve years, not even for his grandparents' funerals. Even thinking about it had been too painful. But somehow, it wasn't too painful now.

He walked from the stable through ankle-high grass, loving the sun on his head. A soft breeze blew through his hair, holding some of the late summer humidity at bay. But he even liked the humidity. The damp heat filled his lungs and his muscles and every part of him, down to his toes, easing him out of the cramped box he had consigned himself to for so long.

His heart beat only a little faster as he pushed open the green wrought iron gate and stepped into the family cemetery. Mackenzie gardeners had kept the grass lush and neatly trimmed. There were flowers at every grave. Monuments, marble angels, and simple headstones were lined up in neat rows, creating a tapestry that was his history. There was Confederate General Brady Mackenzie and his Yankee captain son Ryan, both killed at Appomattox. Nearby were great-grandfather Struther Mackenzie, the shipping tycoon and pirate sponsor, and his wife Tullia.

Their daughter Alanna, buried beside them, had been the greatest beauty of her day. She had refused to marry and instead had led a life of continual scandal, delighting in shocking anyone she could. She had been a noted women's suffragist, and a spiritualist who led weekly seances for her friends. She had acted on the stage, posed nude for Picasso, published two books of purple prose that were banned from every library in the state, and was said to have taken as many women lovers as men. She had even written her own epitaph: "I lived as I chose, and I lived well."

Cullen smiled at Alanna's monument, crowned by a white marble statue of her nude pose for Picasso. She had lived for nearly a century and held a permanent place in his heart as his favorite relative after his parents. His smile faded as he looked across the graveyard. There were too many graves of children who had never lived to see even their tenth year, including Aidan's first two sons and Alanna's four stillborn siblings. And then there was his great-uncle Balfour and his wife Mary who had raised eleven healthy children, and adopted five more, more than half of whom had stayed on the land and were buried here. The most recent graves were of his grandparents, who were buried as they had lived: side by side.

And there was Teague.

Cullen steadied himself with a deep breath and walked up to Teague's grave. His parents had chosen a thick, four-foot-tall marble headstone that bore his brother's name, the dates of his birth and his death, and the single word "Beloved." Cullen brushed his fingers over the carved letters. "Hey, Bro," he said softly.

He thought about Teague and his own life, not just in these last twelve years, but in the last thirty years. The world tilted slightly on its axis beneath his feet, giving him a new perspective on this hot Virginia afternoon. He suddenly saw that he was very different from the guilt-riddled eighteen-year-old boy he had been, and even different from the driven man he had been these last twelve years. Perhaps the reason he was seeing Whitney differently now was because *he* was different.

Speaking truths to Samantha had begun to show him his own truths.

He stayed at Teague's grave for over an hour, sharing those truths with his brother. Then he walked home with long strides, his heart lighter than it had been in years.

THE NEXT MORNING at seven o'clock he sat atop Central Lark as Sam parted from Miguel Torres and Bobby Craig and started for the main stable. She stopped. She stared at him.

"What on earth are you doing here?" she demanded.

"I told you I'd see you today."

"But that's to help you with your dressage training this afternoon."

"You won't take my check, so you'll just have to accept more practical help in your drive to the Horse Trials."

"But you've got so much to do—"

"And you didn't when Dad was in the hospital?"

"But—"

"No buts. I'm just as stubborn as you are, Samantha Lark, and I *am* going to help. So get a move on. Grab Magic and I'll race you up Bluegrass Hill."

A grin curled the corners of her mouth. "You're crazy, but you're wonderful. Andy!" she hollered. "Where's Magic?"

THE MACKENZIE HORSE Trials were held at the end of September to avoid the intense heat of the summer months and to fire the opening shot in the fall competitions, beating out nearby Morven Park by a week. The evening before the start of the Trials, the Mackenzies always threw an outdoor barbecue party for all of the competing riders, some of whom claimed the Mackenzies deliberately stuffed them with the most delectable food this side of the Continental Divide to make them sluggish on the first day of competition. But they stuffed themselves anyway. There wasn't a human being alive who didn't succumb to Rose Stewart's cooking.

Cullen, in jeans and a full white shirt he called his pirate shirt, in honor of great-grandfather Struther, wandered across the massive back brick patio and surveyed the acre of lawn with its white gazebo and marble fountain imported from Italy more than a century ago. The evening was warm, but cooler than it had been these last summer months. Over one hundred casually dressed guests were grouped in packs of twos and threes and fours and spread across the brick patio and close-cropped lawn. Paper lanterns glowed in the early evening shadows. A fiddler, bass player, and banjo player stationed near an old dogwood filled the air with lightness and joy, while the tables of food lining the patio, and the mouthwatering aroma from the barbecue pit to the left, scented the night with family and fun.

Cullen recognized a few people from his teenage steeplechase and eventing years, and a few more from occasional glimpses of Grand Prix events on television. But most were strangers, except they didn't feel like strangers, because they all shared a common bond: horses—loving them, riding them, caring for them, debating their qualities, confessing their follies, rehashing their successes and failures on courses and in arenas around the world.

He was in his element. It was the first time in years he'd fully enjoyed a party. Unfortunately, that pleasure evaporated

as he watched a Teutonic god by the name of Kaspar Reinhart monopolize Samantha's company and conversation,
standing with her by the fountain in an easy, intimate fashion that made Cullen's teeth grate. What right did Reinhart have to monopolize Sam like this? And what on earth
did she see in him? Surely she wouldn't succumb to a pair
of bulging biceps and perfect teeth?

Of course, Reinhart *was* a top German rider, *and* he
bred champion Holsteins, and Sam *had* succumbed seven
years ago. Damn!

Cullen's mouth settled into a hard, grim line as the
German made Sam, in her tight red midriff shirt and pedal
pushers, laugh and blush. Cullen's hand curled into a fist as
she brushed a blond lock of hair from the muscle-bound
he-man's forehead. The fact that Reinhart couldn't seem to
keep his hands off of Sam only made matters worse.

Then Cullen saw Whitney.

Her voluptuous body wrapped in a silver spandex jumpsuit with aquamarine accents to match her eyes—an out-
fit that any moral society would ban outright—she stood
in the middle of her usual crowd of masculine admirers,
Missy Barrisford in a short gold muslin dress at her side.
Whitney's gaze shifted to him once, and then again, making sure that he fully appreciated how desirable she was to
other men.

They had made up. Actually, it was Whitney who had
made up. For the first time in their relationship, she had
sought his forgiveness, not the reverse.

It wasn't that he had held back from pique or residual
anger, it was just that he had changed and she had not and
he couldn't find the words to bridge that chasm. But Whitney had words. Lots of them as she insisted the most reasonable solution to their newest argument was to live half
of the year in Virginia and the other half of the year on the

Continent. She would be happy and, she vowed, he would be happy too.

But he wasn't. He was a grown-up and he loved her, and that should have been enough to carry him over any troubled waters. But his love felt different, too, as if it had changed in ways he didn't fully understand, and that had changed everything.

He had tried telling Whitney how much he didn't like charity balls and cocktail parties and lunching at the country club. He had tried reminding her how much she really hated living in a sea of Virginia horse farms and how much happier she'd be shining in the firmament of the world's upper echelons. He had tried getting her to be honest with herself, and with him, but she nimbly dodged every attempt.

Basically, Whitney was running scared, actively seeking compromise and reconciliation. He just didn't know why.

"Why so glum, my friend?" Noel Beaumont inquired, slapping him heartily on the back and jarring two back molars. "Contemplating your forthcoming humiliation at my hands in the Trials?"

"No, no, no, *I'm* the one who's going to humiliate him tomorrow," Samantha said, walking up to them, "and you, too, *Monsieur.*"

"Ah, my poor little one," Noel said, chucking her under the chin, "you live in fantasy."

"Fantasies? Did someone say fantasies?" Erin inquired eagerly as she shouldered her way into the threesome. "X-rated or children's literature?"

"Actually," Sam said after a sip of wine, "we were discussing a thousand and one ways to quell the Male Ego."

"My *favorite* subject!" Erin fluttered.

"This I know," said Noel bitterly.

"Making life hard on you, is she?" Cullen inquired sympathetically.

"You have *no* idea," Noel said with a sigh.

"*That's* my girl," Samantha said fondly, as she slid an arm around Erin's waist and hugged her. "Always the first to enter the fray and the one to capture the most heads."

"I consider it my civic duty," Erin said modestly as she smoothed her sunflower sundress.

"Ha!" said Noel Beaumont. "She considers it the greatest entertainment, the highest sport!"

"That, too," Erin said with a grin.

"Any reasonable woman would," Samantha said.

"Reasonable? Bah!" said Noel in disgust. "Erin Lark," he informed Cullen, "is the most unreasonable female I have ever met!"

"Which must mean she has refused to succumb to your charms," Cullen sagely observed. "Good for you, Brat!"

"You are a traitor to your sex," Noel darkly informed him.

Cullen grinned at him. "Friendship is thicker than testosterone."

"I am going to seek the company of the more convivial Henley twins," Noel informed them, stalking away.

"The hell he is," Erin said, beginning to follow him.

"Where are you going?" Samantha asked.

"*Someone* has to make sure the man doesn't wreck his constitution before the first day of competition. Cullen needs a healthy rival to keep him in peak form tomorrow," Erin said, striding off.

"What? My superior equestrian skills aren't enough of a challenge?" Samantha demanded.

"It's a guy thing," Cullen explained. "Speaking of guys . . ." he said, placing his hands on her shoulders.

She took a surprised step back, not quite meeting his eyes. "Boring topic. You should go recapture your Lady Fair and get on with your life. I've got people to mingle with."

He watched her go and experienced a little of the frustration Noel must be feeling with Erin.

He had wanted her to stay.

But he did as he was told, because he recognized good advice when he was hit over the head with it. He slowly worked his way through Whitney's masculine throng until he had reached her side and asked her to dance with him. But through it all, his eyes scanned the crowd until they found Samantha, then, satisfied, he gave his full attention back to Whitney, until he searched for Samantha again, uncomfortably grateful every time he found her *not* with Kaspar Reinhart.

An hour after his first dance with Whitney, they were standing near the fountain chatting about Senator Sheridan's re-election campaign while half of the Mackenzies' guests danced to a bluegrass tune on the patio. Keenan was holding court in the white gazebo, describing the glories of Trials past to nearly a dozen suitably deferential riders and their guests. Laurel sat on the arm of his wheelchair, sipping a beer and interjecting occasional factual corrections to her husband's elaborate stories.

Cullen's smile vanished as he watched Kaspar Reinhart begin to make his way toward Samantha, who was laughing with the Henley twins at one of the linen-covered rental tables.

"You know Whitney," he said hurriedly, "I've been a miserable host. I haven't danced with Sam once tonight. People are bound to talk. I'll be right back."

Unaware of the daggers that Whitney's blue eyes were shooting into his back, Cullen reached Samantha a good ten seconds before Reinhart got to her. He held his hand down to her. "Dance with me," he said.

Her eyes met his for a moment and then glanced away. "I don't—" she began.

He caught her hand in his and pulled her to her feet. "Dance with me," he said, holding her gaze captive with his.

"Okay," she said softly, looking pale in the lantern light.

A small sigh escaped him. He forgot all about Reinhart. "You're so beautiful," he murmured, loving the way her hand fit so perfectly in his.

She turned white. "The m-m-music's started."

He led her to the patio and pulled her into the middle of the dancers, and then into his arms. The night suddenly felt complete. "Anna one, anna two," he said, starting them off. They danced a vigorous country two-step, which brought the color quickly back to Samantha's cheeks and soon had them gasping with laughter as they narrowly dodged the other couples.

"Look out!" Sam shrieked as they nearly collided with David and Karen O'Connor, two of the top contenders in the Trials.

Cullen whirled them from the edge of disaster and then crashed them into the well-padded Helena Carmichael and her newest husband. She'd already had five.

"I'll be watching you most closely in the dressage test tomorrow," Helena threatened them.

"Now you've done it," Sam said darkly as they danced away. "She'll be inventing demerits throughout our rides tomorrow."

"Nonsense," Cullen said heartily. "Cousin Helena is as honest as she is well-married. Besides, I plan to bribe her with a five-pound box of Godiva chocolates."

"My hero!" Sam fluttered, which made him laugh, and that made her laugh.

Smiling down into her shining brown eyes, Cullen thought that she was more fully present and honestly herself in his arms than he'd ever felt her before, except perhaps for that one shocking kiss at Whitney's dinner party so long ago, and he loved it. He loved learning all of who she really was behind the jokes and the nonsense and discarding his one-dimensional image of her once and for all.

This summer had slowly peeled away the layers Samantha had used to hide herself, revealing her sensuality, and her drive, her fears, her guilt, her own shadows, and her pain. And her passion. Her passion for Skylark, and for horses, her passion for hiding herself as much possible, her passionate loyalty, and her passionate hold on life. That passion of hers spoke to the passion he had hidden so long within himself and was only now rediscovering.

Staring down at her, Cullen suddenly realized that his heart was pounding and his head was spinning and his mouth was aching for another of her fevered kisses.

The music ended in the next moment. Being the sensible man that he was, he excused himself and got the hell away from Sam and the other dancers and the music that had started once again. He hid in a corner at the far side of the patio and slowly brought himself back to a semblance of calm in a world turned suddenly upside down.

He was as depraved as Noel Beaumont. He wanted Samantha as much as he had ever wanted Whitney. And maybe, just maybe, he wanted Samantha more.

It was hard to catch his breath. How could so much change in a single summer? Was he mad? Was he drunk? Was he having a psychotic episode? Or had this summer peeled away layers from him as well, until he stood now staring at aspects of himself he hadn't even known existed?

"You look as if you could use a drink, my friend." Noel Beaumont—in black cotton slacks and a black short-sleeved shirt—stood before him.

"Thanks," Cullen said gratefully, taking the offered glass of scotch. He swallowed half of it, hoping it would remove some of the hunger from his mouth. It didn't. In fact, it seemed to make him want to kiss Sam *more*.

"What is wrong, my friend? You do not look at all like yourself."

Cullen sighed as he regarded the Frenchman. "I seem to be in the midst of betraying Whitney."

"Ah. Then you need not be so troubled," Noel calmly assured him, "because you cannot betray what you do not love, and you do not love Whitney."

"I beg your pardon?" Cullen said, outraged.

"You are infatuated with her merely."

"Of all the—"

"Trust me, my friend," Noel said, holding up one hand to silence him, "I am an expert in these matters and have long been accustomed to discerning the differences between the two. It is impossible to betray an infatuation, for it is itself merely heated air, so you have nothing to worry about now and may return to the party with good cheer."

Cullen stared at Noel. "There are times when I think you must be the maddest horseman on two continents."

"Ask your heart if I am not right," Noel advised, resting a hand on his shoulder. "And if your heart will not answer, ask Samantha."

Fourteen

"WHAT DO YOU THINK?" Whitney asked anxiously as she walked down the Sheridan staircase Wednesday morning in dark brown cotton slacks and a matching jacket that offered a partial view of her breasts.

"Great as always," Missy said from the oak chair near the front door. They were late, of course. But getting to the first day of the Mackenzie Horse Trials was far from Missy's greatest ambition or concern.

"I've tried Slut of the Universe, I've tried Puritan of the Year," Whitney said. "So, I thought maybe I should go for something more in-between today. Cullen's been acting so odd lately, I can't even begin to guess what he wants from me."

"Maybe he doesn't want anything at all," Missy said, idly flipping through the pages of *Town and Country* magazine.

"Don't say that!" Whitney said, marching up to her. "He's got to want me. He's got to give me the life I need. I have too much time and energy invested in that man for him to renege now. If he doesn't speak up, I'll just propose to him myself. I'll back him into a corner and *make* him marry me!"

"He's the square-jawed, honorable type. He might just let himself get trapped," Missy said, setting aside the magazine and standing up. "But Whitney, think a minute. Is it in your best interest to marry a man you don't love and who may no longer love you?"

"Of course Cullen still loves me! He's just confused and getting cold feet because he can sense I'm ready to marry him now. Every man panics when an altar is staring him in the face."

"I find it interesting," Missy said with an amused smile as she leaned back against the front door, watching her friend closely, "that you didn't challenge me on the you-not-loving-Cullen part of my question."

"Like you said once," Whitney retorted, checking her makeup in the mirror above the entrance hall table, "I've never really loved any man. But I like Cullen more than any of them, except Teague, of course. Cullen is rich, he's generous, he'll give me whatever I want. He'll more than do."

"Whitney, there are other ways to get the things you want besides marrying Cullen."

"I will not become a career girl," Whitney said, turning on her, hands on her hips, "I will not become some potentate's concubine, I will not hock even one piece of jewelry. What else is there?"

Missy smiled as she reached out and stroked her fingers through Whitney's loose blond hair. "Whitney honey, we have to talk."

Then she kissed her as she'd dreamt of kissing Whitney since sixth grade.

THE FIRST DAY of the three-day Mackenzie Horse Trials had dawned blue and pink. White cumulus clouds towered up into a sky also dotted with half a dozen hot air balloons, the sound of propane gas jetting into cavernous silk mingling with bird songs, the clatter of cars and trucks and horses, and the dull roar of conversations among the fifteen thousand spectators streaming onto Mackenzie Farm. They were expecting up to thirty thousand spectators on Thursday and Friday.

With over ninety horse and rider teams competing, every hotel and bed and breakfast inn within fifty miles was packed to the rafters, as were the long lines of stalls Cullen's grandfather had built behind the Mackenzies' main stables to house the equine competitors.

Horse trailers of every size and color filled the roads that dawn and crowded onto Mackenzie Farm where exercise boys and girls guided them to the temporary parking lot in the northeast pasture. Catering trucks offering everything from hot dogs and beer to quiche and white wine had taken over the lane fronting the Mackenzies' employee housing, while a huge white tent had been set up to the west of the main house for more formal sit-down dining.

Bleachers lined the dressage and show-jumping rings on three sides. Television cameras and crews were already set up for the first Trials competition: dressage.

"Well," said Keenan with a satisfied smile as he sat in his wheelchair on the front porch of the Georgian manor, a red plaid blanket covering his lap and legs, "we've done it again."

"I and a staff of eight have done it again," Laurel tartly corrected.

Keenan grandly ignored her as he surveyed his fiefdom. "Thank God the English crown believed in large land grants."

"Thank God Aidan Mackenzie was an ambitious son of a bitch," Cullen corrected, standing at his father's side as he surveyed this glorious legacy.

"That too," Keenan said, chuckling.

"I wonder if Grandfather had any idea what he was getting us into when he inaugurated the Trials sixty-three years ago," Cullen said.

"Your grandmother certainly did," Laurel wryly replied, as she clasped Keenan's hand in her own. "Many's the time she'd look at her husband across a crowded room and, far from fondly, inform me that Darby had the vision and she was left to somehow make it a reality.

"Look, there's Samantha," Keenan said, pointing down the driveway.

Cullen turned and saw Samantha leading Lark Magic up the driveway. Unlike most of the crowd, she was dressed casually in jeans and sneakers and an emerald green sweatshirt, its sleeves pushed up to her elbows. Her hair was far more formal. That copper flame had been pulled tightly back from her face into a formal bun at the nape of her neck, a telling metaphor, he thought suddenly, for all the passion she had held in check so ruthlessly these last five years. She stroked Magic's neck as he danced beside her, excited by all the horses and people and activity, an ear cocked to catch Sam's soothing words. She looked up at the Mackenzie front porch and waved at them with a brilliant smile.

Five years of stress and anxiety and overwork seemed to have been washed away in the night. She looked happier than he had seen her all summer, probably because she was doing what she loved. It came to him with startling clarity that Samantha represented everything he had been running away from these last twelve years. She was the culmination of three hundred and fifty years of his history. She was the land he loved so fiercely and the horses he loved so passionately. She was the joy and family of his childhood. Living the life she was born to, she had been a daily reminder of the life he had wanted for himself and insisted on denying.

Running away from guilt and pain and truth, clinging desperately to the fantasy future he had built around Whitney, he had wanted none of the lessons Samantha's very existence offered him. She'd been right about this, too. He *had* deserted her twelve years ago. Self-preservation, or at least self-delusion, had dictated that he ignore her and fend off the woman she was becoming. She would have awakened too many truths in his soul had he stayed.

Bobby Craig with Central Lark, Andy with Flora Lark, and Marybeth with Lark Ness followed behind Sam. Miguel Torres, with Erin and his sister Calida beside him, drove a blue Skylark pickup slowly past them and into the sea of campers set up in the pasture beyond the dressage rings where riders could store their gear, get out of the sun, and rest if need be.

"Where's Whitney?" Keenan demanded.

"Missy Barrisford is bringing her," Cullen replied, feigning disinterest when every day had been plagued by the mess of his own making and the constant refrain of 'what was he going to do about Whitney?'

"I can't believe Samantha Fay is competing on four horses," Laurel said, frowning as the Skylark entourage walked past. "She'll kill herself."

"It's done often enough," Keenan said reassuringly. "Arianna Shepard did it just last year and went on to become Rider of the Year. Something," he said with a stern glance at Cullen, "to keep in mind."

"Yes, Dad," Cullen replied with a grin. "Mind if today I just shoot for surviving my first advanced competition in twelve years?"

"Hell yes, I mind!" Keenan said. "You're to finish in the top five, Cullen, and that's final."

"Yes, sir."

"*I'll* be satisfied if you just survive," Laurel said, leaning over Keenan and kissing her son on his cheek.

"Thanks, Mom."

He would have said more, but he was silenced by the disgusting sight of Kaspar Reinhart in full dressage regalia, his hair practically glowing in the morning sunlight as he walked up to Sam and casually kissed her *on the mouth*. Cullen forced himself not to march down to the driveway and forcibly remove the offending lips from Sam's mouth and Reinhart's face. Instead, he glanced at his watch. "Your ESPN interview is about twenty minutes away, Dad," he informed Keenan tersely. "We'd best get you over to the main dressage ring."

He pushed Keenan's wheelchair down the ramp that had been added to the side of the porch and into the steady stream of horses, riders, and spectators that filled the driveway. Everyone had a greeting for Keenan. They knew him either through the Trials or from his years of competition. He knew all their names, of course, what horses they were riding today, where they were in the world standings, and had a word for each of them, like a beneficent king greeting his loyal subjects.

Cullen parked Keenan with the ESPN camera crew and commentators, then headed off to the stable to saddle Mackenzie's Pride himself. The dressage competition would start in forty minutes, promptly at eight o'clock. The bleachers where Whitney would be sitting with the Barrisfords were already three-quarters full. Cullen was slated to ride just after nine o'clock, but he wanted to take his time warming Pride up and working the kinks out of the gelding's legs and brain.

Already dressed in gleaming black boots, tan breeches, a black shadbelly coat ending at his waist in the front, with tails in the back, gloves, and top hat, his hair pulled back into a single braid to reflect the formality of this event, Cullen walked into the stable and saw Samantha settling onto the dressage saddle atop Lark Magic. Because of the Larks' favored status, the Mackenzies always found room in their own stable for the Lark horses during the Trials.

She had changed clothes. Samantha's black shadbelly coat and pristine white breeches seemed to have been molded to her body. Her new black riding boots and short blunt spurs gleamed even in the shadowed stable. He could just glimpse her copper hair beneath a black top hat. She looked every inch the pro she was. Still, her face was white and tense as she nodded at something Bobby Craig was telling her.

"Have you tried meditation?" Cullen asked.

She looked at him curiously.

"You'll do Magic no good if you ride into that ring stressed out," he explained.

She grimaced. "Tell me something I don't know."

"Have you even eaten?"

"I drank a little tea. Don't frown at me! I can't keep anything down this morning. Even thinking about food makes me nauseous. Maybe I'll be able to eat something after the first couple of rides."

He placed his hand on her slightly bent knee. "You're going to be great today, Sam. You're gonna leave us all in your dust."

She smiled down at him, a genuine smile that warmed her brown eyes. "My, you're sweet. Idiotic as they come, but sweet."

He chuckled. "You look great, Sam. Tense, but great."

She grinned at him. "I defy even Whitney to outshine me when I'm in my dressage best."

"That's the spirit! Lean down here a second."

Curious, she obliged. He pulled from his pocket a thin

gold chain with a tiny gold horseshoe dangling from it and slipped it around her neck. "For luck," he said.

Her smile took his breath away. "Thank you," she said softly.

"You're welcome. Now get out of here and show us how it's done."

She saluted him and walked Magic out of the stable toward the outdoor dressage rings. The dressage test in a three-day event was designed to demonstrate a horse's harmonious physique and ability, and the teamwork of horse and rider. The judges would be looking to see if the horse was calm, supple, loose, flexible, as well as confident and attentive, working in perfect harmony with its rider.

The horse's gaits, from walk to canter, had to be free and regular, the steps elastic and relaxed. The rider had to maintain a correct position and seat, using hands and legs so invisibly that the horse seemed to move of its own accord through the changes of gait and lead around the dressage arena in the prescribed patterns that every team of horse and rider followed.

During the six-minute test, they were penalized for everything from errors in executing a particular turn or gait or halt to failing to initiate a prescribed movement at a prescribed point in the arena. To get out of the dressage arena with less than fifty penalty points was considered a brilliant ride.

At the end of the day, Samantha had placed all four Lark horses in the top twenty-five in a field of ninety-three advanced horse and rider teams, a stunning feat on green horses that had every rider and owner in the Trials gravitating to the Mackenzie stable to look each Lark horse over carefully in the late afternoon and early evening.

"They're graceful for hybrids, I'll give them that," old Matthew Barrisford said at dinner that night.

The Mackenzies, the Larks, and the Barrisfords always

had dinner together on the first day of Trials competition. Even Whitney was there, seated next to Cullen, across from Missy, and oddly silent.

"How could they not be graceful when they were blessed with so talented a trainer and rider?" Noel said, raising his wineglass in a private toast to Samantha.

"I like to think that breeding had something to do with it," she wryly retorted, her copper hair freed from the prim bun and glowing beneath the crystal chandelier.

"You'd like to think that breeding had *everything* to do with it," Cullen corrected, "but we must give credit where credit is due."

"Says the man in third place," Samantha said with a grin.

He bowed his head as if receiving his due. "I rode brilliantly today, it is true."

"Yes," Keenan said at the head of the table, "but Noel outrode you all. First and fourth in the standings. You were wonderful to behold, Noel."

"You are too kind, my friend," Noel said without a blush.

"Yes, but he's got to watch out for Arianna Shepard," Erin cautioned at his side. "She and Witching Hour have been great all year. With them nipping at your heels in second place, I don't advise you to grow too complacent, my friend."

"Arianna and I have met many times in competition. It is a challenge I relish," Noel replied.

"Don't you go forgetting my granddaughter," Matthew Barrisford broke in. "Sixth place is an admirable beginning for anyone, even a Barrisford."

"Thank you, Grandfather," Emily Barrisford said with a grin at her curmudgeonly relative. Though only thirty-four, she had won Rider of the Year twice in the last five years. With two horses entered in the Trials, she had every reason to look and feel, if not complacent, then certainly relaxed and confident as she sat across from Matthew.

Cullen glanced across at Samantha, who had actually managed to eat most of her meal. She did not look relaxed as her slender fingers fiddled with a button on her sky blue silk gown, but she did exude her old confidence, and that, with all she had riding on this competition, was a major accomplishment.

Her brown eyes met his and she smiled. The air left his lungs in a long, silent sigh. It suddenly felt impossible to sit in the midst of all these people and utter polite chatter. As soon as Williams began pouring after-dinner coffee, Cullen escaped into the warm night, stars thick above him, horses lazily grazing in the paddocks in the distance. The world was resettling on a new axis. It was time he had a look around.

SAMANTHA SAT IN the Mackenzie family room, sipping perfect after-dinner coffee among people who loved the land and the horses as much as she did, and felt a contentment she hadn't known in years. It was amazing, really. Seven years of soul-breaking work had come down to these three days. She should be a gibbering idiot. But instead, the fear and the stress had fallen away, to be replaced by the sheer joy of competing on the best horses she'd ever bred against horses and riders that were testing the full limits of her and her horses' abilities.

She decided that she thrived on challenge. She thrived when asked to give the best that she had. She felt steady and calm and absolutely confident. If she'd been an Olympic swimmer, she'd have blown the competition out of the water. If she'd been a VP, she'd have pitied those above her on the corporate ladder to success.

Speaking of business . . . She looked around the room at the Barrisfords mingling with the Mackenzies, at Noel flirting with Erin, at Whitney talking earnestly with Missy. But his High and Mightiness, the master of the business world and her libido, was nowhere to be found. Slipping inconspicuously out of the conversation, Sam went searching, but Cullen wasn't in the drawing room, or on the opposite side of the house in the study that had been transformed into his office.

Staring out the study's French doors into the velvet night, she thought she saw movement. A flash of white, like Cullen's pirate shirt with the billowing sleeves. She was outside before she'd even made the conscious decision to open the door. A soft breeze blew silk against her arms and calves, feeling delicious in the warm night. For these few days at least, the world was magical once again and she was free of everything but delight.

She wandered over thick, silent lawn, the nearly full moon lighting her way as she followed brief glimpses of that patch of white to a string of paddocks in which Thoroughbred mares grabbed a last snack before sleep, or walked slowly across the bluegrass looking for just the right place to spend the night.

She saw Cullen in the middle of the second paddock, his long blond hair shimmering like fairy dust in the moonlight as, arms outstretched, he seemed to telepathically summon the four mares and their foals to him. Moving in slow motion so as not to startle them, his strong hands brushed soft black muzzles, stroked down sleek necks, slid across strong backs. He looked in love with the miracle that surrounded him with such grace. Cullen as Nature intended him to be.

None of his old ghosts hovered around him any longer. Cullen was truly home at last. Samantha's heart ached in its fullness. She felt stripped naked in the night air and open to every feeling the Fairy King felt and evoked.

"Hi, there," Cullen said softly.

Samantha jumped, her heart in her throat. She hadn't thought he'd seen her. "Hi, yourself," she managed. Had he seen the desire she'd hidden so long? They were silent a moment.

"You make me think of Scott's *The Lady of the Lake* standing there," Cullen said. " 'In listening mood she seemed to stand, The guardian Naiad of the strand.' "

Samantha blushed all the way down to her toes and hurriedly retorted, also from Scott, " 'There is a southern proverb—fine words butter no parsnips.' "

Cullen chuckled. "Ach, you're a handful, Samantha Lark. It's no wonder you're still unmarried."

"The same, sir, could be said of you."

"I am a great trial to kith and kin," he humbly agreed.

"But you're worth it."

"That, too," he said with a grin. "Come on," he said walking toward her, "we'd better get back inside before Whitney sends a couple of swarthy men with baseball bats to break our kneecaps."

"Miss Sheridan would never be so crass," Sam countered as he climbed through the paddock fence. "She's more of a strychnine or arsenic kind of gal."

Cullen laughed as he looped her arm through his and began leading her back to the house. "And what are your weapons of choice?"

"I am but a plain woman of the people. All I ask is a simple thirty-eight, a knotted garrote, or a well-sharpened Bowie knife to wreak my vengeance."

Cullen stared down at her. "I've been a bit slow on the uptake, I know, but I've finally come to realize that *you* are a very dangerous woman."

"Oh, I *am* dangerous, and in more ways than *you'll* ever know."

"Try me."

She stared up into eyes turned black by the night and tried to hear her own voice above the hammering of her heart. "Sorry, Mr. Mackenzie. You're not even in my league."

Fifteen

THE CROSS-COUNTRY COMPETITION took up most of the second day. The course was designed to prove the speed, endurance, and jumping ability of a well-trained and conditioned cross-country horse, as well as the rider's knowledge of pace and his or her horse. In advanced competition, there could be as few as twenty-five or as many as forty different obstacles on the two-and-a-half-mile course, all of which had to be cleanly jumped in a little under seven minutes. Time penalties were imposed for finishing too slow or too fast. Pacing was everything. Penalties also accrued for a horse refusing an obstacle, for run-outs (a horse avoiding an obstacle at the last moment), for circling before taking an obstacle, or for a rider's fall. If a horse fell, it meant mandatory elimination of that team from the competition.

Many of the world's best riders considered England's famed Badminton to be the premier cross-country eventing course. Of eighty-six starters in a recent competition, only forty-five had jumped clean, and only sixteen completed the course without time penalties. It had always been Keenan Mackenzie's ardent wish to raise the Mackenzie Horse Trials to Badminton's level of competition and prestige.

Consequently, many of the Trials' riders had damned Keenan and his cross-country course designer, Derek di Grazia, as devils incarnate as they had walked the course the day before. The American Horse Show Association rule book advised against overkill in the number and size of jumps in both the cross-country and show-jumping courses. So the Mackenzie Horse Trials had just thirty-two cross-country obstacles, but they ranged from uphill combination ramp jumps to a ten-foot-wide spread jump over Brandy Creek.

There were mandatory inspections of each horse by the Trials veterinarian, Dr. McClaren, before the start of the cross-country test, at its conclusion, and before the show-jumping test the following day. Any hint of ill health, strained muscles, or over-exertion and the horse was eliminated from competition. Usually, riders pulled their horses out long before they were scheduled to appear before Dr. McClaren. Eventing was a partnership of complete trust between horse and rider. It forged deep bonds that prize money and competition standings could not breach. For riders, their horses always came first.

On Friday morning, Samantha—wearing tan breeches, an emerald green sleeveless knit shirt, the necklace Cullen had given her, and the helmet and protective vest all riders were required to wear—started Lark Magic off at a controlled gallop just after eight o'clock in the morning. She was the fourth to ride the course. Cullen would be twelfth. He stood, Pride's reins in his hand, Erin at his side.

"She's looking strong today," he said, watching Lark Magic clear the first hedge effortlessly and disappear into the eastern woods.

"Atlas is a ninety-pound weakling compared to my big

sister," Erin replied. She stood in sneakers, jeans, and a yellow oxford shirt, watching Noel start the course on Annamarie, his gray mare, her gallop supple and brilliant and completely self-assured, as it should be for a world champion. "You've gotta give the man his due," Erin said. "He looks good on horseback."

"What am I, chopped liver?"

"You look very nice, too," Erin primly replied.

"Gee, thanks," Cullen said, turning to Pride and pulling the stirrups down their leathers. He'd be on the cross-country course in ten minutes.

"Try not to get yourself killed, will you, Neighbor?"

He swung himself into the saddle and grinned down at her. "I'll do my damndest, Brat."

She blew him a kiss. "Luck to you."

"Just you keep your toes and fingers crossed."

He rode Pride toward the starting line, which was less than a hundred yards from the finish line, where his father sat, vibrating with the energy of a man half his age and in far better health. Keenan was listening to the radio reports from the judges stationed at the different obstacles on the course while he watched the feed on a miniature TV he had conned out of the camera crews. Laurel, in a peacock-colored dress, sat beside him. Nurse Morgan, in her starched white pantsuit uniform, stood behind him, frowning. This was not part of the regimen Dr. Moorlock had prescribed.

"Give 'em hell, Son," Keenan said as Cullen rode towards them.

"Yes, sir."

"Let Pride have his head for a minute or two at the start of the course, so he can get the feel of the ground and the morning. Then pull him back and ride him carefully. He's got the stamina to finish this course twice, if need be, but only if you marshal his resources."

"Yes, Dad," Cullen replied, hiding his grin. Keenan had given him the same advice twice last night. This was the third time this morning.

"Samantha just cleared the brush combination at number twelve," Keenan said. "She and Magic are working well this morning."

Cullen had expected nothing less.

No fool he, Cullen followed his father's advice and let Mackenzie's Pride have his head a little as they galloped from the starting line toward the first hedge, pulling him back just enough to control the jump, loving the exhilaration of this brief flight, then giving him his head again as they galloped into the eastern woods and towards the second jump, a ditch and vertical log fence combination. The morning air was crisp and cool and scented with earth and horse and a touch of autumn. His body moved as one with the Thoroughbred, his heart pounding with excitement. *God,* how he'd missed this!

Pride cleared the ditch and log almost with disdain, as if it was beneath him even to notice that they existed; then Cullen pulled him back, reminding him they had a long course ahead of them. They'd need all of their wits and their stamina. He glanced at his large wristwatch. Right on schedule.

This was far from a silent or a solitary ride. There was the sound of the strong drumming of Pride's hooves on the ground, the squeak of leather from his saddle, the sound of Cullen's own voice urging Pride on. There were spectators at each obstacle, standing behind ropes to keep them off the course. Whitney would be with the Barrisfords on a low hill at the fourteenth obstacle that provided a good view of a quarter of the course, as horses and riders took the downhill triple combination of log vertical to ditch to log vertical.

Jump spectators applauded as horse and rider came into

view, cheered when they cleared a fence, groaned when a horse refused the fence or jumped it badly. There were obstacle judges at each fence as well, tallying every default, supervising after a horse crashed into a fence, making sure the obstacle was repaired in time for the next horse and rider, keeping the course traffic moving smoothly. It was more work for some fences than for others.

Cullen had heard before starting the course that riders were having particular trouble at the eighth obstacle, what should have been an easy jump up onto a three-foot-tall ramp bordered by brush, as well as at the sixteenth obstacle, a variation of the log maze Bobby Craig had constructed at Skylark, and at the twenty-second fence, a tricky log pile double combination *into* a covered bridge over Brandy Creek. He had adjusted his strategy accordingly.

For now, though, he opted for the shorter, more treacherous turn and jump up three feet onto the grassy ramp at number three, rather than the longer and easier approach around two ancient magnolias. Pride took it with ease. Cullen patted his neck and then wove the blue roan gelding in and out of the trees on a narrow trail that made the fourth obstacle, a triple combination of posts and rails, almost a blind jump until the very last second. It startled Pride and he wanted to balk and complain about such an unwarranted surprise, but Cullen was having none of it and spurred him over the jump, cringing slightly when he heard Pride's back hoof rub the final rail.

But there was no time to dwell as the winding trail led him to the fifth obstacle, vertical rails over a ditch, one of the more treacherous jumps, which was just seconds away. He had been trained from the first day his father had placed him on a horse to think about just one jump at a time.

Midway through the test, the cross-country route began doubling back on itself, not over the same ground, but parallel to the first half of the course, like fairways on a golf course. Cullen occasionally glimpsed the rider and horse ahead of him finishing the last half of the course behind Samantha. Galloping through Maggie's Meadow—a wildflower-strewn oval named for Aidan Mackenzie's wife—and toward the fourteenth obstacle, he suddenly heard shocked gasps and cries from spectators at number twenty-two. His heart leapt into his throat. Had something happened to Samantha? Had Magic refused the fence? Or crashed into the bridge? Or fallen in the river? Was Sam hurt?

There was no way of knowing as he cleared the meadow and rode into a series of jumps that led him to the log maze. He heard a dull roar from the crowd of spectators before he saw the obstacle. Something must have happened to the horse and rider ahead of him, but he had no time to see what, because the maze was upon him.

Pride easily jumped down the three levels and, just before he leapt into the water, Cullen saw the problem. The horse ahead of him had thrown his rider into the pond, nearly at Pride's feet. Pride wanted to jump straight into the air at this unwelcome obstacle to his happy descent into the water and Cullen let him do just that. There was a lot to be said for steeplechase experience. They easily avoided the rider before them and the horse dancing in the water to the right. Pride plunged forward, creating a fountain that drenched Cullen, then Pride was jumping up onto the opposite bank of the pond and stretching himself over the green gate.

Cullen gave Pride several strong pats on the neck as he galloped toward the seventeenth fence, a five-foot-wide, four-foot-high hay wagon, complete with hay. "Thatta boy, Pride. Show 'em how it's done."

He didn't mind being wet. He'd been too hot anyway. This was a welcome chance for them both to cool down and face the last ten obstacles. He glanced at his watch. They were about thirty seconds ahead of schedule. He pulled Pride back to a canter. "Easy boy. Don't spend it all in one place."

But Pride seemed only to grow stronger with each new jump. Adrenaline surged through Cullen. It was as if he could do no wrong. He and Pride moved in perfect harmony, breathing as one, seeing as one, flying over the ground and the jumps as one. Pride jumped over the twenty-second fence and into the covered bridge as if it was nothing, as if he'd been doing it all his life. Sheer exultation swept through Cullen as he gave Pride his head and they galloped toward a combination that went over a post-and-rail vertical down into a dry ditch and back up and out over a three-foot-wide log span. Who would ever choose an office in New York, or London, *or* Hong Kong when there was *this* to do?

Pride sailed over the log span and galloped on, Cullen holding him back just enough to keep his focus and his form. But when they cleared the final jump, Cullen leaned over his neck and, with a Rebel yell, sent him at a dead run for the finish line, loving the sheer power beneath him, the rush of wind deafening him to everything save the pounding of Pride's hooves on the ground and the pounding of his own heart in his chest.

He crossed the finish line with a loud "Whoop!" and then reluctantly pulled Pride down to a plain old walk, both of them breathless. "God, let's do that again!"

"Sorry, Mr. Mackenzie," the chief timer at the finish line said with a smile. She was marking the score sheet on her clipboard. "Each rider and horse gets just one shot today. By the way, that ride of yours just put you into first place."

"With dozens of teams still to ride the course," said Cullen with a wry grin as he patted Pride's strong neck. Then he remembered. "Sam! Samantha Lark, is she all right?"

"Fine and dandy," the chief timer said, watching the chestnut Trakehner and rider who'd had the spill at the log maze pond coming towards the finish line.

"But at twenty-two, I heard—"

"You probably heard Jamison Porter blow it," the woman said, glancing at her clipboard. "He was riding just after Samantha Lark. Sent his horse into the jump every wrong way you can imagine. Got his leg broken as a result. The horse is fine."

"Thank God," Cullen said, thinking of Samantha, not Jamison Porter's horse. He jumped off Pride, ran up the stirrups, and led him into an enclosed pen for a thorough inspection by Dr. McClaren. Once he got the all clear, he led Pride over to the family group a few yards away.

"That was quite a ride," Keenan said.

It was the greatest praise Cullen could have received. He grinned all over. "Thanks, Dad."

"You're a mess," Laurel pointed out.

"But I'm in first place."

"With dozens more riders to come," Keenan said.

Cullen tried to scowl at him, but his grin just wouldn't let him do it. "A pyrrhic victory, it's true, but I plan to milk it for all it's worth. I want Pride as a birthday present, Dad. I want him in a big way."

"If you're still in the top five at the end of tomorrow's competition, he's yours. Otherwise, you can go whistle."

Cullen laughed with the sheer joy of the day and the ride and his family and the adrenaline still pumping through him. "Yes, *sir*!"

THIRTY MINUTES AFTER she finished the cross-country course on Magic without a fault, Samantha was cantering Flora Lark toward the first hedge. By the time she had reached the fifth obstacle, a rails and ditch, Cullen had handed Pride to his groom and, still high on adrenaline and one of the best cross-country rides he'd ever had, joined his parents to watch and hear how Sam and Flora Lark were doing.

As the Skylark team reached the slippery ten-foot spread jump over Brandy Creek, Erin joined them. "How's she doing?" she asked.

"Great," Cullen replied, glancing at her. "Clean ride so far. Where have you been?"

"Wishing Noel luck. Somebody had to."

"Traitor," Cullen charged.

Erin sighed. "I'm just too nice for my own good."

Cullen watched Keenan's miniature TV monitor as Samantha steered Flora into the log maze. He held his breath as the roan mare jumped down into the pond, cleared it in the four strides prescribed, jumped up onto the bank and—Cullen's heart stopping for just a moment—cleared the green gate as if it was no trouble at all. "That's my girl," he murmured, breathing again,

A bad slip at number twenty—a steep grassy ride down into a spread jump over a broad exaggeration of a wooden picnic table—almost had Flora Lark sitting on her haunches before Samantha somehow pulled her upright in time to take the jump.

"Good girl!" Keenan murmured approvingly.

"Ow!" Erin said.

Cullen realized that he'd grabbed Erin's hand as Samantha had struggled to save Flora and herself from disaster, and was still crunching delicate bones that were necessary to his neighbor's livelihood. "Sorry," he said, hastily releasing her.

Hazel eyes glared at him. "A crippled cello player is not a happy cello player, Cullen."

"I apologize. Profusely."

"We tend to become homicidal, at the least provocation."

He raised the hand in question to his lips and kissed it. "There, all better now."

"Here she comes," Laurel said.

They all turned to watch Samantha and Flora Lark neatly clear the thirty-second jump, a ditch backing onto a centuries'-old rock wall, and then gallop to the finish line.

"Time?" Cullen asked his father.

"No faults," Keenan replied, studying the small television screen on his lap. "It was a clean ride."

"Thank all the patron saints of equestrians," Cullen murmured. "Come on," he said, grabbing Erin's unbruised hand, "let's go see how she's doing."

Andy, resplendent in black leather, his hair dyed turquoise blue for the occasion, was already leading Flora Lark away to her cool-down when they reached Samantha.

"That was some ride," Cullen said.

Samantha turned to them with a lopsided grin. "Sometimes I hate horses. They're just so damned unpredictable. Horses and riders are dropping like flies at eight, and sixteen, and twenty-two, and Flora acts like they're no trouble at all. Then she freaks out because of some *grass*!"

Erin laughed and hugged her. "That was quite a save you pulled off, Sammy."

"I was so damn mad, I'd have *carried* her over the jump if I'd had to!"

Cullen smiled. He'd felt like that on more than one occasion during his teenage years of competition. "When's your next ride?"

"Not until one," she replied.

He grimaced. "Lovely. The heat of the day. That should kill you off in nothing flat."

"What's a little heat and humidity to a Virginian born and bred?" she demanded.

"A death-stroke unless you take care of yourself beforehand. Come on," he said, placing his hands on her shoulders and steering her toward the house. "You can use a guest room to shower and rest and then *eat*. You do remember what food is, don't you?"

"I had breakfast," Samantha said defensively.

"A piece of toast is not breakfast," Cullen retorted, steering her through the crowd of spectators, riders, friends, and family. "It's bird food. Come on, Rose Stewart made pecan pie just for you."

"Calida will be jealous."

"Calida has Bobby Craig to distract her."

"Well," said Erin, "since you've got my big sister well in hand, I'll go and cheer our local Frenchman to the finish line. See you soon."

She trotted off as Cullen pushed Samantha toward the house, ignoring her repeated attempts to escape and her even more frequent declarations that she was perfectly capable of taking care of herself. As far as he was concerned, he was on a mission from God and no feminine jibes about his maniacal power trips were going to deter him.

AT EXACTLY ONE o'clock, showered, rested, and fed, Samantha started Central Lark on the cross-country course. Noel, who had knocked Cullen out of first place in the competition with his second ride on Chevalier, a nine-year-old French Anglo-Arab gelding, joined Erin and the Mackenzies beneath Keenan's green and white striped awning, listening to the radio reports from the course and watching the miniature TV.

"Emily Barrisford just cleared sixteen," Keenan informed

them. He glanced at Noel. "The way she's riding today, she could unseat you in the standings."

Noel shrugged. "It is a difficult course and she must ride without mistakes."

"Matthew wouldn't let her do anything less," Erin said with a grin.

"Damn!" said Keenan.

"What?" they all said as one.

"She's down," Keenan said, frowning at the TV.

"Emily?" Laurel asked.

"No. Samantha."

"What?" Cullen bellowed, grabbing the television from his father's lap. He stared, heart pounding, at the tiny image of Central Lark staring at the tangle he had made of the wooden ramp and brush of the eighth fence. Samantha was on the ground, just sitting up. She shook her head to clear it, then started to rise, and stopped suddenly. Cullen swore. "She's hurt!"

"Badly?" Erin asked, pressing against him to get a better glimpse of the screen. She was shaking.

"I can't tell." He watched Samantha try again to stand up and finally succeed. She limped badly up to Central and ran the reins back over his head. "It's her ankle, I think. She's twisted, or broken, her ankle."

"She can't ride like that!" Erin exclaimed.

"She's going to," Cullen replied grimly as the jump judge helped Samantha up onto the dun gelding. He winced watching her force her injured right foot into the stirrup. The repair crew finished rebuilding the fence. Samantha circled Central around and then sent him at it once again. He sailed over the jump as if he hadn't a care in the world. "Damn the woman," Cullen muttered. Twenty-four obstacles to go, and she had to be in more and more pain with every stride.

But she rode as if she wasn't hurt. It was solely for Central's benefit, of course. Any change in the way she rode, in the way she held herself or used her legs, would stress out a green horse on an advanced course.

It was a tense, silent little group that watched Samantha and Central Lark continue the course. Central tried to refuse the fifteenth obstacle, a long zigzagging fence of varying heights, but Samantha pressed him forward. He took it, awkwardly, but somehow he cleared it and galloped on. He took the log maze at number sixteen as if he was having the time of his life, ignoring Samantha as she nearly fell from the saddle on the final six-foot drop down into the pond, before splashing happily through the water and up the opposite bank and over the gate, Samantha clinging to his neck to stay in the saddle.

"I can't watch much more of this," Erin said.

Noel put an arm around her waist. "She will finish the course well. Watch."

And she did. Samantha crossed the finish line still on Central's back with 109 faults—twenty for Central's refusal at number eight and sixty-five for Sam's fall there, plus twenty-four time faults for finishing sixty seconds behind the optimum time. By anyone's standards, it was a good showing. Some of the veterans in the competition had not fared so well. A clean show-jumping round could keep her in the top thirty. But it was doubtful she was thinking of that as, ghost-white from pain and exhaustion, she pulled Central Lark to a stop.

Cullen elbowed his way through the two Lark grooms, and Bobby Craig, to reach Samantha and pull her down from the saddle and into his arms as Marybeth led Central off to be inspected by Dr. McClaren.

"What are you doing?" Sam demanded, albeit weakly.

"If you tell me you can stand, I'll gag you," Cullen

informed her as he carried her through a knot of judges, riders, and spectators. He reached the Mackenzie stronghold beneath the large awning and set her on Keenan's lap.

"Well, hi there," Keenan said with a smile, his arms going around her waist.

"Hey!" she protested.

"You have to sit and the other chairs aren't sturdy enough for this," Cullen grimly informed her as he knelt down and grabbed her boot.

"Don't you dare," she warned.

He pulled the boot off in one smooth tug, fully aware that Sam had jammed a fist in her mouth to stifle her scream and that it was only Keenan's arms around her that kept her with him in the wheelchair. The course doctor was busy with another rider's broken wrist, so Cullen examined Sam's foot and ankle with expert fingers, feeling her silent shudders of pain.

"How is it?" Erin asked anxiously.

"I don't think it's broken," he said, glancing up at Nurse Morgan. "What do you think?"

The dour nurse examined Samantha's foot and ankle carefully as Sam kept a hand pressed to her mouth. The examination was excruciating, Cullen knew. He'd twisted an ankle at the International Gold Cup, a steeplechase race, when he was sixteen.

"Certainly there are some torn ligaments," Nurse Morgan said when she finally stood up. "But I doubt if anything's broken. Still, I strongly recommend having it X-rayed."

"Not now," Samantha said tersely as Bobby Craig came up to them, dark eyes grim. "Tape it, Bobby."

"I knew you were going to say that," he said with a sigh as he knelt on the ground and opened up a first aid kit.

"*Tape it?*" Cullen exploded. "You don't seriously intend to ride again today?"

"Of course I do," she retorted.

"Come on, Sammy," Erin said coaxingly, "you just barely made it off that course alive."

"I'll be fine once my foot's taped," Samantha said firmly.

"*Look,* pea brain," Cullen said, grabbing her shoulders as his father looked on, "finishing decently on three horses will accomplish just as much as finishing on four horses. I promise. You need a doctor, and X rays, and professional taping—no offense Bobby—and drugs, lots of drugs if you have any hope of staying in the saddle during the show-jumping competition tomorrow."

"I could give you a mild pain-killer now," Nurse Morgan offered.

"Nothing stronger than aspirin," Samantha said firmly, despite the pain Bobby was inflicting as he firmly taped her foot and ankle. "Lark Ness needs me to have all my wits about me and I'm not about to let her down."

Cullen brought his face within an inch of hers. "I'll see you in Hell before I let you ride again today."

Brown eyes shot death rays right back at him. "You have no right to tell me what to do and no say in what I choose to do. If I want to ride *ten* horses today I will and you can't stop me! I dislocated my shoulder in a German competition seven years ago and I still placed first. I know what I'm capable of doing, Cullen Mackenzie, and I am capable of riding Lark Ness half an hour from now. So back off!"

Their little circle of family and friends watched this showdown with open interest. Neither Samantha nor Cullen blinked.

"I'll tie you to the banister," he said.

"I'll have you shanghaied to the Bermuda Triangle," she retorted.

He glared at her, and then laughed, easing the tension in their circle. "*Damn* you, Samantha Lark," he said.

Half an hour later she was galloping Lark Ness toward the first hedge on the cross-country course.

"If she breaks her neck, I will never forgive her," Erin said, trying not to watch her sister take the first jump, and watching anyway.

"Better have an ambulance ready," Cullen advised his mother.

"Now, now. Samantha Fay is stronger than you think," Laurel said quietly.

"Maybe," he conceded. "But she's not as strong as *she* thinks."

No one spoke as they listened to the radio reports and watched Samantha's progress over the two-and-a-half mile course on the miniature TV. Sam chose the easier approaches and jumps, losing valuable seconds, but jumping cleanly. The minutes moved like sludge on a winter's morning.

They held their collective breath as Samantha guided Nessie through the number sixteen log maze. She lost her right stirrup—which held her injured foot—on the plunge into the pond and was forced to take the opposite bank and the jump at the top without it. Somehow she stayed in the saddle. Somehow Nessie cleared the gate. Then the dun mare was galloping toward number seventeen and Samantha was leaning down, reins in one hand, catching the loose stirrup with the other and forcing her foot through it again. She moved upright just in time to set Nessie up for the hay wagon spread jump.

"I must have taped it too well," Bobby said.

"No," Cullen said, resting a hand on his shoulder, "it just hurt too much for her to twist it around in search of the damn stirrup."

His heart was pounding painfully in his chest. He felt as if his ribs were bruised. He was scared. Scared for Samantha.

But as she continued on the course, fear slowly turned to admiration. It was the most controlled cross-country ride he'd ever seen. Lark Ness wasn't taking a breath that Sam didn't instigate. She chose gaits for Nessie that required the least amount of movement on her own part. She chose jump approaches and clearances that were models of calm. While other horses and riders were ragged and scrambling, she and Nessie were the very image of serenity. Yes, they were racking up time faults, but not as many as might be suspected. The ride was controlled, but it was fast.

When Samantha and Lark Ness crossed the finish line, they'd had a clean ride with only 4.8 time faults. The dun mare had come out of the dressage competition in thirteenth place. This ride might even advance her in the standings.

"I am grateful our Samantha does not always compete against me," Noel murmured. "I would have far fewer points in the annual standings if she did."

But Cullen scarcely heard him. He was striding up to Samantha and Lark Ness, Bobby and Erin on either side, scattering riders and spectators in their wake and not caring. Bobby grabbed Nessie's bridle just as Samantha began to fall from the saddle.

"Sammy!" Erin cried.

Cullen caught her and pulled her the rest of the way down and into his arms.

"Time faults?" she whispered.

"Under five, you damn fool," Cullen retorted as he began carrying her to the house.

She twisted slightly in his arms, reaching behind her. "Nessie! What about Nessie?"

"Bobby's got her," Cullen said, badly shaken. She hadn't seen Bobby!

"Is Nessie okay?" Sam demanded.

"She's fine. Champion material. You'll have a bidding war for her before this competition is over. Now shut up."

"Yes, sir," she whispered, which scared him more than anything else had.

"I'll look at her," the course doctor—a shaggy lion of a man in his fifties—said as he strode up to them.

"That's okay, Doc," Cullen said, "we know what we're dealing with. You'd best stay here in case something more serious comes along."

"Well, call me if you need me," he said amiably, moving off.

"Put her in the guest room next to your room," Laurel called to Cullen, running ahead of them.

"Need any help?" Noel inquired solicitously.

Cullen scowled at him. "I've got her."

"Push, woman, push!" Keenan bellowed at Nurse Morgan behind him as she guided his wheelchair toward the house.

Cullen felt Samantha trembling and looked down at her white face, tears streaming down it, just before she buried it against his shoulder, her arms wrapping around his neck and clutching him tightly.

"It hurts so much, Cullen!" she whispered.

"I know, hon," he said softly. "Hang on just a little bit more."

Whitney ran up to them in a white summer dress and had to jog to keep up. "Sam, what's wrong?"

"It's nothing, Whitney, don't worry," Samantha managed in a carefully calm voice.

"Cullen, is she going to be all right?" Whitney demanded.

"I don't know," he said.

He carried Samantha into the house and up to the guest bedroom to find that Laurel and Margery Thompson, their housekeeper, had already drawn the curtains, pulled down the bedcovers, and produced several basins of ice. He set Samantha gently down on the bed, a sharp sob escaping her. She immediately brought herself back under control.

"No ice, thanks," she quipped. "I like my scotch neat . . . in the biggest glass you've got."

"Her foot's probably swollen inside the boot," Cullen said, ignoring her. "I'll have to cut it off. I'll be right back."

"Here you go," Laurel said, handing him the cutters she used to prune her rose bushes. She smiled at his surprise. "I've lived around horses and horse people all of my life, Cullen. I know what's needed."

He smiled back, then looked down at Samantha. "Even cutting it off is going to hurt like hell."

"I know," she said, her jaw clenched. "Just do it."

Laurel sat beside her on the bed, pulling her partially into her arms, her plump body absorbing Samantha's scream as Cullen began cutting.

"Why don't you just faint and make it easier on yourself?" Cullen muttered as he continued cutting down the calf-length black boot.

"Damn you, Cullen Mackenzie, Lark women don't faint!" Samantha shouted at him. "Even with corseted eighteen-inch waists, we never fainted." She buried her head against Laurel to muffle another scream.

"I can't watch this," Whitney groaned, hand to her mouth as she dodged out of the room.

"There we go," Cullen said with a sigh of relief as the boot fell to the floor. Quickly he untaped Sam's foot and ankle and for a moment stared down, appalled, at purple flesh swollen to twice its normal size. "Let's bury her in ice. Now," he ordered.

Noel and Margery Thompson quickly packed Samantha's

foot and ankle in ice a good ten inches deep on all sides, Sam shuddering from the cold and the pain, but saying nothing as Laurel held her. Nurse Morgan pushed Keenan into the room.

"How is she?" Keenan barked.

"Conscious," Cullen replied.

"She's a damn fool."

"That's what I said."

"If I was a violent man, I'd shoot that damned horse," Keenan said.

"It wasn't Central's fault," Samantha protested weakly as she pulled herself from Laurel's arms and collapsed back against the three deep pillows. "I didn't set him up properly for the jump."

"Here comes the cavalry," Erin announced as she walked into the room, followed by a man in his early thirties dressed in jeans and a tie-dyed tank top. His brown hair was held back by a leather tie and streamed down to the small of his back.

"Who the hell is he?" Keenan demanded.

Erin smiled at his bad manners. "This is Mr. Joshua Grant, our handy dandy local acupuncturist."

"Acupuncturist?" Noel exclaimed.

"Why doesn't someone just shoot me now and get it over with?" Samantha moaned.

"Oh, hush," Erin said. "Joshua is a miracle worker. He got Emily Barrisford back in the saddle two days after she twisted her knee and the doctors were talking surgery. More importantly, Sammy, he's the only shot you've got at being able to ride tomorrow."

Samantha raised herself on her elbows and stared at the acupuncturist. "If you can get me well enough to ride, I promise you my first born. And my second."

Joshua's smile was sweet and amused. "My usual fee and ample referrals will be reward enough," he said. "Let me read your pulses, and then we'll have a look at that foot."

He picked up her arm and began pressing his fingers up and down the inside of her wrist.

"The cavalry has changed since John Wayne rode with them," Noel murmured. "So, you are an aficionado of acupuncturists?" he said to Erin. "What else don't I know about you?"

"I'm also a big fan of chiropractors and massage therapists," Erin replied, watching Joshua work.

"She has never looked at me with such interest," Noel complained to Cullen.

"That's because you've never held her sister's future in your hands," he replied.

Noel glanced at him. "Completing the Trials is that important for Samantha?"

"Yes."

"And of course, she will accept no help from those who care about her most."

Cullen looked at Noel. A very perceptive man, this Frenchman. "None at all."

Noel looked back at Samantha. "We must be grateful, then, that she accepts the gift of Mr. Grant's services."

"I only hope he's as good as Erin claims."

He was better.

Just before eight the next morning, Cullen tossed Samantha up onto Lark Magic's back. Her foot and ankle were as tightly taped as before, but they were almost back to their normal size and she had even gotten a decent night's sleep in the guest room. It was amazing what they were doing with needles and herbs nowadays.

Sam and he were dressed nearly alike: glossy black boots with brown tops, white breeches, white shirts, canary-colored vests, a black frock coat for Sam, a scarlet frock coat for Cullen. She wore her gold horseshoe necklace, her hair in a French braid; his hair was tied back in a pony-tail at the nape of his neck.

"Erin will be on hand to make sure you let Joshua treat you after each ride," he warned.

"You people act like I'm adverse to self-care," Samantha complained as she gathered her reins.

Cullen scowled at her. "You've had a lousy track record these last few months and you know it. Stick to the program or answer to Erin, and Mom, and Dad, and *me*."

"Okay, okay. Don't you have a horse you should be warming up?"

He pointed a finger right at her nose. "I mean it, Sam."

"Alright already! Now will you stop worrying about me and start thinking about your own ride? You're in third place. You don't want to blow that off."

"I won't. I've got a better horse than Noel Beaumont ever owned riding on this."

Samantha shook her head. "Men and competition," she said disgustedly.

Which made him laugh out loud. "*You* should talk!"

She grinned sheepishly down at him. "Well, maybe I should rephrase that," she conceded. She suddenly leaned down and cupped his cheek in her hand. "Thanks for everything, Cullen."

He could still feel the warmth of her hand on his skin as she rode Magic out of the Mackenzie stable.

Whitney, in lavender Armani slacks and top, suddenly appeared, walking beside Magic, a hand on Samantha's leg. "Sam, are you sure you should do this?"

"I'll be fine, Whitney," Sam said soothingly. "Don't worry."

"You're sure?"

"Positive. Now get back to the bleachers and watch some world-class Lark horsemanship."

Sam rode on as Whitney stopped and watched.

"Your concern is touching," Erin said caustically behind her.

Whitney turned around and glared at her. "Just because Sam and I want different things for Cullen doesn't mean that I don't love her and don't want her to succeed."

Erin folded her arms over her chest. "Then why have you been late every morning when you know she's one of the first riders?"

"Look, you little toad," Whitney spat out, her cheeks stained pink, "Sam is my best friend and I love her and she knows it, and the one thing I don't give a *damn* about is whether you believe me or not!" She spun around and stalked back to the bleachers.

"Well, hell," Erin muttered.

"What's the matter?" Cullen asked, walking up to her and putting an arm around her shoulders.

"I may end up liking the goddess after all," Erin said disgustedly.

Cullen chuckled. "We all have our crosses to bear."

They followed discreetly in Whitney's fulminating wake.

Show-jumping was the final test in the three-day event. It was designed to prove the suppleness, obedience, and jumping ability of the horse, and the rider's knowledge of pace and horse. The course could have anywhere from twelve to fifteen jumps which had to be successfully negotiated in under ninety seconds. Unlike Grand Prix jumping events where fence heights could reach well above six feet, a Trials jump course was designed to show a horse and rider's ability after a grueling cross-country competition. Heights could be no greater than three feet eleven inches for solid fences, or four feet seven inches for brush fences. A spread jump could be eleven and a half feet wide if the horse did not also have to contend with height. If height was involved, a spread jump could be no more than five feet three inches wide.

Faults were easily accrued. Knocking down a rail or any other part of the fence, or placing a hoof in the water of a water obstacle or on the white demarcation line before or after a water obstacle, earned five penalty points. A first refusal at a jump racked up ten penalties. A second refusal collected twenty penalties. A third refusal meant elimination. Time faults were awarded for every second, or fraction of a second, a horse and rider team went over the time allowed to complete the course.

The first round of show-jumping at the Mackenzie Horse Trials had fifteen obstacles, varying from three feet eleven inches to five feet three inches in height with a triple spread jump at number eleven that was deadly. There was a spread water jump at number eight, flanked by plastic replicas of Shamu, the whale. There was a series of jumps at twelve, thirteen, and fourteen which the riders had begun referring to as the three little pigs. Twelve was a three-foot-eleven-inch jump made of yellow-painted plywood boxes that resembled straw. The merest wisp of a horse's hoof would send at least one box sailing to the ground and add five faults to the team's total score. Thirteen was a broad arching jump over a series of brown poles, each one eager to tumble out of its cups. Fourteen looked like a brick wall made of red-painted plywood blocks that loomed up after a sharp turn from thirteen, giving the horse just three strides to gather itself for the leap up and over.

It was a treacherous course that racked up faults throughout the morning. Of the more than ninety horse and rider teams, only nine horses jumped clean and made it into the jump-off. Samantha was riding two of those horses. She'd been dutifully receiving acupuncture treatments throughout the morning. But there'd be no time for an acupuncture break now.

The jumping officials reduced the number of jumps from fifteen to eleven, raised the heights and broadened the spreads on several obstacles, and then reduced the time allowed from ninety seconds to seventy seconds. The eight jump-off riders stood together along one side of the ring and stared at the course, mentally tracing the new route they had just walked together and in a moment must ride, gauging where to cut corners to save time, counting how many strides between each jump, calculating each millisecond in their minds.

"Well, crud," Emily Barrisford said, which made everyone smile. She'd pretty much summed up the situation.

"Why are Americans so sadistic?" Noel sighed as he swung himself back up onto his gelding, Chevalier.

"As I recall," Cullen retorted atop Mackenzie's Pride, "the Marquis de Sade was *French*."

"But a miserable horseman," Noel retorted.

"Probably too fond of the whip," Cullen said.

A gurgle of laughter escaped Samantha from atop Lark Ness. "Will you two shut up? I'm trying to concentrate!"

"We're just trying to psych you out, my little one," Noel said with a smile.

"Men," Samantha said with a wealth of disgust as she rode toward the entrance to the arena. She'd be riding first, a distinct disadvantage. Seeing how the other riders succeeded or failed at shaving time from their ride would have helped her strategy. Instead, they would use her ride to their advantage.

Lark Ness jumped clean but took a time fault. Sam didn't care. It had been a great ride, Nessie responding with everything in her when Sam had shouted "Up, Nessie!" at the taller house-of-sticks jump, clearing it and eagerly moving on. The next three horses amassed jump faults, everywhere from five to fifteen points.

There were five horses and riders left to go.

"Okay, boy," Samantha said, patting Magic's strong dark brown neck. "Let's see if I gave you the right name after all. I need everything you've got."

Magic jumped every fence cleanly and finished the course a full four seconds under the allotted time. The cheers and the applause from the spectators in the grandstand were deafening. Samantha loved it. Her heart pumping with joy and adrenaline, she didn't care if Magic finished first or fifth in the show-jumping, he'd done everything she'd asked of him and more, and every knowledgeable horseman and woman in the place would know it, and talk about it, and want a little of that magic for themselves.

The last four finalists rode clean. Now it was just a question of time, and there was little doubt who had won. Arianna Shephard had out-raced everyone else by nearly two seconds. She had won the show-jumping competition. But in a three-day event, the scores from all three tests—dressage, cross country, and show-jumping—determined the final standings and overall Trials winner.

Olympic silver medalist Karen O'Connor, with just 48.2 penalties, had taken first place overall, Cullen had placed a strong second with 50.4 penalties, Noel third, Samantha and Magic fourth, Emily Barrisford fifth, Arianna Shephard sixth overall, Sam and Nessie seventh, and Karen O'Connor's husband David eighth.

"It's a day of wonders," Cullen announced as he stood beside Noel at the jumping arena railing, listening to the scores read out over the loudspeaker. "Second. How in God's name did I manage to place second in my first major competition in twelve years?"

"I give the horse all the credit," Noel said.

Cullen burst out laughing.

"And you did have the home court advantage," Noel continued with a grin. "Come to Paris next spring, my friend, and ride against me in a *real* three-day event."

Cullen grinned back at him. "You're on!"

It took him nearly an hour to wade through the sea of friends and family who surrounded him and Pride to congratulate him and rehash the jump-off, and the rest of the Trials, but finally the crowds began to disperse. Erin was conferring with Joshua Grant, the miracle worker. Laurel and Keenan hurried up to the house to prepare a celebratory party that would, of course, include the Barrisfords and the top ten finishers, and the Trials judges and officials. Noel had taken Chevalier, his nine-year-old gelding, out for a celebratory gallop, a habit of his and a reward for his horse, who loved to run.

"That's okay, John," Cullen said to Pride's groom, who had begun to reach for the bridle, "I'll take care of him. You go find yourself some champagne."

"Yes, sir!" John said with a grin.

Cullen led Pride into his stall and removed his saddle and then his bridle with the second-place ribbon still attached. He stared fondly at it for a moment, then carried saddle and bridle into the tack room, returning with a bucket of different brushes and hoof picks.

The sound of weeping was a surprise.

He set the bucket down in front of Pride's stall and quietly began searching through the stable. Six stalls down he found Samantha, still in her breeches and black coat, clinging to Lark Magic's neck and crying as if her heart would break. He opened the door and stepped into the stall.

"Samantha, honey, there's no need to be sad," he said.

She looked up at him in surprise, her face wet with tears.

"What you've accomplished these last three days was nothing short of incredible," he said, gently drying her face with his folded handkerchief. "In a field of seasoned competitors, you placed four green horses fourth, seventh, fifteenth, and twenty-fourth. No one in the world could have pulled off a stunt like that except you."

"Cullen, you nit, I'm not crying because I'm sad," she said.

"You're not?" he said.

"No!" she said, taking his handkerchief and blowing her nose. "I'm crying because I'm happy. I'm ecstatic. I'm out of this world with glee!" She shoved his handkerchief into her jacket pocket. "You think it's incredible I placed four green horses in the top thirty? It's a miracle!" she yelled, and then hurriedly lowered her voice as Magic took exception to such volume. "There is no way in hell I should have finished so well. Orders are pouring in so fast for the new stock that Bobby can't keep up. Matthew Barrisford started a bidding war for Magic and Flora, which he won. He didn't even blink when he wrote out the check. Don't you get it? The Trials were the hat trick to end all hat tricks. I'll be able to pay off the bank in full within the next month!"

Cullen let out a whoop, grabbed Samantha, and swung her around in the air, her arms around his neck as she laughed and laughed . . . and then she began to sob.

Startled, Cullen set her back on her feet and stared down at her.

"How could he?" she demanded, and he realized they were tears of anger she was furiously brushing from her face. "How *could* he have put me through five years of *hell* like this? My own *father*! How could he just . . . just *deliberately* throw Skylark away to the banks and leave me to pick up the pieces? How *dare* he? How dare he treat three hundred and fifty years of history and love and blood and dreams like they were dirt? And why didn't Mom stop him? She had brains. Hell, she had influence! All it would have taken was one word from her and Skylark would never have been put in such mortal danger. Oh, *damn* them!" she said, pounding the side of the stall with her fist.

"It's all right, Sam," he said quietly.

"No, it's not all right!" she shouted. "I'm not supposed to be mad at them. They're *dead*!"

"Just because they're dead, doesn't mean they weren't wrong when they were alive."

She shuddered and wrapped her arms around herself. "When I was a kid, I kept dreaming of the day I'd be running Skylark all by myself. They turned that dream into a nightmare, Cullen. My own parents. I deserved a better legacy, Cullen. I did."

"I know," he said gently, cupping her taut face in his hands. "But you finally got the legacy you deserve, Sam. I mean, you *made* the legacy you deserve, in spite of them. In spite of the banks and the other creditors and impossible odds, you pulled off the hat trick to end all hat tricks. Maybe you should think of today as the end of the nightmare and the beginning of your true legacy."

She seemed to crumble as tears splashed down her face and across his fingers. "I-I-I'm sorry," she wept. "I can't s-s-seem to stop."

The breath left his lungs with a whoosh. He pulled her into his arms and held her tight. "Go ahead," he murmured. "You're more than due."

Which only made her cry all the harder. "I've just been so damn scared!"

"I know," he murmured softly. "I know."

He stroked her soft copper hair and her back and let her cry as if she would never stop. He shouldn't have been so surprised. All of the stress and the overwork of the last five years had finally overwhelmed her, now that she didn't have to fend them off any longer. All the years of hiding too many truths and feelings behind jokes and work had caught up with her at last. She cried and he held her. She clung to him and he murmured words of comfort into the delicate ear so close to his lips. She wept and he kissed her ear, the top of her head, her temple, her cheek . . .

Her mouth.

Her lips were warm and soft and salty from all of the tears and they lingered on his for a moment. He'd never felt anything so good. She pulled slightly away, startling him. He was about to protest, then her look of mingled fear and desire registered in his brain. He was staring at the truth. Sudden vertigo sent him spiraling down into her brown eyes. With a moan, he claimed her mouth with his, hard, demanding, taking everything his soul had hungered for.

Echoing his moan, she curled her arms around him and arched into him, filling every empty niche. Her mouth on his was hot and equally demanding and soul-satisfying. He sank his tongue into her heat, groaning at the intimate caress and her delicious shudder, groaning as her soft tongue met his. Words welled within him, half-formed and incoherent but vital to his very existence. He wanted to tell her so much.

Suddenly she jerked back out of his arms. She stood three feet away from him, breast heaving as she dragged in oxygen, the back of her hand pressed against her mouth, her brown eyes huge in her white face.

"I-I-I'm sorry!" she stammered. "It's all my fault. I don't know why I . . . It won't happen again, I promise."

"Samantha," he said, taking a step toward her.

"I m-m-mean, Whitney isn't even here to enjoy the performance," Sam babbled, backing up against the stall door. "Please don't look at me like that! I feel bad enough as it is. Of all the stupid things to do. I really should be committed somewhere. I'm so sorry, Cullen."

She was out the stall door and running.

"Samantha!" Cullen called after her, but she didn't stop. Torn ligaments and all, she was running out of the stable and away from him just as fast as she could.

Cullen stood in the cool shadows staring after her, considering.

Sixteen

THE MACKENZIE HORSE TRIALS always fell on a Wednesday, Thursday, and Friday, so that everyone could party Friday night and Saturday and Sunday. It was one of the reasons the Mackenzie Horse Trials were so popular.

Daily Samantha cursed the Mackenzies for loving fun so much.

It made avoiding Cullen and hiding her guilt and embarrassment almost impossible. Because of her injured foot and ankle, she had to sit through the Friday night party. She handcuffed a rotation team of Erin, Whitney, Emily Barrisford, Matthew Barrisford, Noel, and Kaspar Reinhart to her side so that Cullen couldn't sit beside her and strike up a conversation.

On Saturday, she hid in her office with Bobby going over pending sales, or hid in her room claiming the need for rest. On Saturday night, with Joshua Grant's help, she had advanced to a single crutch to support her right side and so hobbled continuously from room to room, and from clump of party guests to clump of guests, one hop in front of Cullen all night long. She got home exhausted, but safe.

During Sunday brunch, she huddled with Kaspar Reinhart, who had placed eleventh in the Trials, pretending to be happy talking over old times, well aware that Cullen was watching her—glaring at her, actually—from across the room. Unfortunately, she was working so hard at pretending to enjoy Kaspar's conversation that she didn't notice that most of the brunch guests had left the dining room until Kaspar excused himself to obey a summons from Emily Barrisford.

Then the absence of an effective screen struck her hard. She stood up to leave too, but it was too late. Cullen trapped her in a corner of the Mackenzie dining room.

"We have to talk," he grimly informed her, deftly blocking every move she made to escape.

Her mouth was dry. Her pulse was pounding against her wrists. Her brain went completely numb. Then rescue came from an entirely unexpected quarter.

"Ladies and gentlemen, if you please," Noel said, striding into the room. For some reason, he had changed into white tie and tails. "Your presence is requested elsewhere."

"Sorry," Samantha said happily up at Cullen, "gotta go!"

He grabbed her arm and held her in place. "Nothing doing."

"Come, come, my friends," Noel chided as he insinuated himself between them and then took an arm from each in his, "you will not wish to miss this, I assure you."

"Beaumont, you're intruding," Cullen informed him.

"Whatever you have to say to the so charming Samantha may be said later," Noel assured him, pulling them both through the Great Hall and into the drawing room. "*This,* however, cannot wait. If you will sit here," he said, shoving Cullen down onto a gold satin–covered love seat beside Laurel and Keenan in his wheelchair, "and you, my little one," he said to Samantha, tugging her toward a delicate white and gold chair beside Whitney, "will sit here."

Samantha looked around. The Barrisfords were sitting behind her and Whitney. The rest of the thirty brunch guests were scattered around the room on chairs, love seats, and sofas. She even spied Calida and Bobby and Miguel on the other side of the room.

"What's going on, Noel?" she asked.

Noel appeared the soul of innocence. "I am about to marry your sister and naturally thought you would like to attend the wedding."

All hell broke loose.

A modicum of calm was restored only when Erin, dressed in a slinky gown of white satin, her brown hair twisted into an elegant chignon, leaned into the room to announce that the judge had arrived and they could get this show on the road.

"You're really going to marry Noel?" Sam demanded of her sister.

Erin appeared affronted. "Of course I am. You don't think I'd squeeze myself into a dress like this just for kicks, do you? Come on in, Judge Parker. You know most of the major players, I think."

Judge Parker, a small, vastly amused woman in her late forties, strode into the room, clearly happy to be a pivotal player in this impromptu entertainment. "Certainly I do," she said with a soft drawl. "Mr. Mackenzie, good to see you looking so well. Don't you worry, Mrs. Mackenzie, the room is charming just as it is. And let me assure you, Miss Lark," she said to Samantha, "that I perform the most elegant civil ceremonies in Virginia."

"Just so long as the vows are binding, you may perform any sort of ceremony you choose," Noel said as he guided her to the head of the room.

"Oh my God," Cullen groaned loudly and plaintively, "I'm going to have the man as a neighbor!"

"Sammy, you're maid of honor," Erin called.

"Damn straight I am," Sam said, hobbling up to her in her peach silk dress.

"Keenan, will you give me away?"

"An honor, my dear," Keenan assured Erin, rolling his wheelchair down the room toward her.

"I can see the headlines in the social columns now," Sam said with a grin. "Two gimps and a bride."

Erin burst out laughing. "Stop! It's hard enough to breathe in this dress as it is. Laurel, I need someone to cry over me."

"That," Laurel said, dabbing her eyes with a handkerchief, "won't be a problem. Music! You need music!"

"Already covered," Whitney said, sitting down at the grand piano in the far corner of the room.

"Best man?" Noel asked Cullen. "I promise to return the favor."

Cullen clapped him on the shoulder. "I know how hard it was for you to finally admit that I *am* the best man, Noel. I'd be happy to stand by you in your hour of insanity."

"Hey!" Erin protested. "Marrying me is the sanest thing *any* man could do."

"But I thought of it first," Noel reminded her.

"Yes, but does he meet the intellectual and sexual requirements for marriage?" Sam demanded of Erin.

"That's what I've been led to believe," Erin said.

"What requirements are those?" Noel politely inquired.

Sam patted his cheek. "It's a girl thing."

He took her hand in his and kissed it. "I shall like having you as a sister, I think."

"Just you do right by her," Samantha said.

"That is a given," he assured her.

"Well, that puts my mind at ease," Erin said. "We all ready to go?"

Keenan sat laughing in his wheelchair.

"Good," Erin said with a grin. She pointed a finger at Whitney. "Hit it!"

Whitney hit it with a boogie-woogie version of "The Wedding March" that soon had everyone, including the bride and groom, laughing helplessly. Judge Parker came through with a simple, elegant ceremony that took ten minutes and ended with a kiss between the new husband and wife that lasted nearly as long. Williams, Rose Stewart, and Margery Thompson, informed just scant minutes before the nuptials that a celebratory party would be required, were already wheeling in carts of champagne and salmon mousse and apple tarts.

Samantha stood near the site of the vows for a moment, happily drinking in the scene. Calida and Bobby and Miguel had already offered their congratulations to the bride and groom and had begun to party hearty. Laurel was crying over Erin, Cullen seemed to be threatening his new neighbor with vivisection if Noel caused Erin a moment's pain or worry, Keenan was forcing a glass of champagne into Nurse Morgan's hand, Matthew Barrisford was surrounded by Kaspar Reinhart, Arianna Shepherd, and five other Trials competitors as he regaled them with the tale of his Depression-era wedding, Whitney and Missy Barrisford were huddled together, probably critiquing Erin's gown. Everyone else in the room was talking—loudly—as well, already high on champagne and laughter and Noel and Erin's love, which was apparently infectious.

"Champagne, Miss Lark?" Williams inquired with a barely suppressed grin.

"Absolutely," she replied, liberating a full champagne glass from his tray and winking at him.

Winking right back at her, Williams ventured forth to libate the rest of the wedding guests.

Samantha's survey of the room swept over Whitney once again and suddenly stopped. Her friend's beautiful mask had crumbled for just a second. She looked shell-shocked. Well of course, Sam thought, Whitney must be badly shaken by this sudden abandonment of what she had thought was one of her most ardent admirers. There were no two ways about it. The wedding had hit her pride and sapped her confidence. She was vulnerable, and it occurred to Sam that she really ought to take advantage of that.

With one strategic move, she could probably push Whitney from her position of reluctant compromise into devoted wife. She owed the friend she loved that much for all the grief she had caused her during the Great Plot. Equally important, Cullen loved her, Cullen wanted her, and Sam had it in her power to help him get the wife he had been miserable without. Besides, she owed him major recompense for that volcanic kiss in the stable Friday evening. All she had to do was reinstate the Great Plot now, and within the hour Whitney would be proposing to *Cullen,* she was certain of it. Limping only slightly, she made her way to the clutch of Mackenzies and Beaumonts standing near the head of the room with Judge Parker.

"But this is all so sudden!" Laurel was wailing.

"Ah, yes," Noel said, gazing lovingly at his wife as she sat on the arm of Keenan's wheelchair. "The love at first sight was very sudden, but the marriage has taken forever to arrange."

"Fought you tooth and nail, did she?" Cullen said with a knowing grin.

"Lark women are formidable, I was forewarned," Noel said with a sigh. "My love and my kisses she accepted with perfect equanimity, but my many proposals, *no!*"

"What made you finally succumb?" Samantha asked Erin.

"My husband can be very persuasive," Erin replied with a wicked smile, which actually made Noel blush.

"And where will you live?" Keenan demanded, sliding

a protective arm around Erin's waist. Blue eyes glared at the groom. "Erin's sister and career are here, you know."

"So I had observed," Noel said smoothly. "I recently negotiated an acceptable purchase price for Cormac Park, which borders the Barrisford estate. We will live there during Erin's concert season and on my farm in France for the other half of the year."

"Wonderful!" Sam said. "I just got you back. I sure didn't want to lose you all over again."

"Don't you worry. I plan to keep a close eye on you from now on. But we will be flying to France tonight," Erin warned her sister, "for our honeymoon and so I can meet Noel's family. We'll be back in two weeks."

"By then, the house will be renovated to our tastes, the concert season begun, and our married life may proceed without the hiccups," Noel concluded.

"I could really learn to hate you again," Cullen said disgustedly. "Why your love life should run so smoothly, while mine—"

"Smoothly?" Noel cried. "She turned down my proposal nine times. *Nine!*"

"I thought he was only interested in the chase, and I liked having him around," Erin said with a shrug, "so I figured the only way to keep him around was to keep him interested in the chase."

"She has learned better," Noel informed them as he pulled Erin off the arm of Keenan's wheelchair and into his arms.

She smiled happily up at him. "Yes, I have."

"It was a lovely wedding," Laurel said with a tearful smile, "even if I didn't get to help plan any of it."

"Speaking of which," Samantha said, well aware that Whitney was watching as she slid an arm around Cullen's neck and draped herself against him, "we should probably start planning *our* forthcoming nuptials. I think an outdoor wedding would be best. There'd be more room to invite more guests and—"

Cullen took her completely by surprise by removing her arm from around his neck. "You'll have to excuse us," he said to the others in the circle as, Sam's wrist held firmly in his hand, he dragged her out of the room.

"Cullen, what are you doing? Stop it, you're hurting me!" she cried, but Cullen ignored her.

He dragged her into the study he had turned into his office at the other side of the house, slammed the door shut behind them, locked it for good measure, and then practically threw her into the center of the room.

"What the hell were you trying to pull back there?" he demanded, glaring at her, arms akimbo.

She had no idea why he was so angry. "Reinstating the Great Plot, of course."

"What?"

"Cullen, you should have seen Whitney's face. I think this wedding has thrown her completely for a loop. It's the perfect opportunity to get her to not only compromise on the battle of the lifestyles, but to actually fall into your arms and your plans once and for all. All she needs is a push, and that's what I was trying to provide. A little twist of the jealousy knife and you could probably get yourself engaged before the hour is out."

"I see," Cullen said, slowly advancing on her.

He seemed suddenly very dangerous, very large, and overpowering. For the first time in her life, Samantha was scared of Cullen.

"In the future," he said, stopping less than a foot in front of her, "I suggest that you discuss your plans with *me* before you start managing my love life."

Samantha's heart was beating wildly in her breast. It was hard to breathe. It was hard to think. "I'm . . . sorry."

God, she'd never been so completely aware of another

human being in her life! She could feel the heat shimmering from Cullen's body, smell the hint of musky aftershave he used, hear each sharp staccato breath he took, trace every taut muscle beneath the white, loose-fitting peasant shirt.

"I was only trying to help," she whispered.

"There are other ways to help me."

Her heart was pounding in her throat, blocking all oxygen and blood flow to her brain as she stared up into gray eyes streaked with lightning.

She was suddenly plunged into the depths of her true feelings with a force and a clarity that were stunning. She felt the truth in her marrow and in her breath and in the frenetic pounding of her heart. *I love you, I love you, I love you, I love you,* sang within her over and over, but only one word came to her lips.

"Cullen," she said from far, far away as she fell into his heat and his scent, into his breath and his arms, her mouth finding his. She gasped with the onslaught of flame and vertigo and a voracious hunger that drove her deeper into him, shuddering as his tongue met hers, stroking her, stroking her until she was trembling against him.

She pulled her mouth free and began to trace with her tongue the white crescent scar that curved down his cheek to his mouth. He went absolutely still against her. She pressed soft kisses from the corner of his mouth back up the scar and she heard him gasp her name. She gently sucked the thin white scar, moving closer and closer to his mouth again. His groan reverberated through her as he cupped her buttocks, molding them in his hands, pressing her hard against throbbing iron and heat.

She cried out, an ache growing deep inside her, empty and hurting and enveloping her. She wasn't even aware that she had torn open his shirt until she felt her hands splayed in his thick mat of chest hair, her mouth blindly seeking and finding one hard male nipple, Cullen's moan reverberating throughout her body.

Oh, she wanted to drink him in and fill this aching emptiness. Drink in his heat and his taste and his scent. There was no world beyond this room, and no one. There was only this man whom she loved past bearing. Her mouth claimed his other nipple and she felt him jerk with shock, heard his groan of pleasure, his hands shaking as they sifted through her loose hair, before suddenly cupping the back of her head and pulling her mouth back to his.

She'd never known such a taking. It was savage and hot and wet as he sucked at her, sucked her deeper into him even as his tongue thrust into her, hard and rhythmic, his hips moving against hers in the same rhythm until she thought she would shatter with wanting him.

He began to suck and feast on her throat as one hand pulled down the zipper at the back of her dress. Then it slid back up over her exposed skin, the heat of his hand raising goose bumps on her flesh. "Yes," she said gratefully. Her hands had already wrestled open his belt and now were at work on his black slacks, opening them, pushing them down, before she did her own taking.

He was hot and hard and pulsing in her hands. She felt him jerk at her touch, heard him moan *"Samantha,"* and she had to have him. She was tumbling to her knees, stroking him, whispering his name. Her mouth claimed him then, his shocked, ragged cry filling her as she sucked at him, loving the feel of him and the taste of him and the heat of him.

"No!" she cried out in protest when he suddenly dragged her upright. "Oh *yes!*" she gasped when he pushed the thin spaghetti straps off her shoulders and shoved her dress to the floor. She was naked except for a pair of panties. Naked and pressed against his naked body. "Yes," she whispered again as she drank him in, her hands stroking over his warm broad back and taut buttocks, her breasts heavy and aching against his chest.

Their thighs and hips were locked together, moving together, his heart pounding against her mouth, his hands sweeping over her flesh as he whispered in her ear, whispered all the ways he wanted to take her, until she couldn't stop shaking, until she was pulling him down to the floor and telling him to do it, to do everything, again and again, until they both lost their minds, until they each begged for mercy, until this fire burned them both to ashes.

"That's right," he murmured, pushing her back against the thick Chinese carpet and stretching out over her, resting his weight on one arm as he licked and teethed her ear, his free hand stroking one of her restless legs, "give me everything I've ever wanted, see if I care."

His hand swept up to cup one of her breasts, which grew heavy and aching at his touch. "C-C-Cullen!" she gasped as his mouth claimed that cupped breast, his wet tongue sliding over the now painfully sensitive nipple, soothing it, teasing it, until he sucked it sharply into his mouth. Her body bucked against his, her cry incoherent, her smooth leg stroking up and down the hair-roughened leg between her thighs.

His mouth took her other breast and she bucked again, crying out, her fingers sliding feverishly through his long blond hair, holding his head to her, her body shaking with the erotic tension he was building.

He raised his head long enough to smile into her eyes. "No mercy," he promised.

She moaned all the way down to her toes.

He followed her moan with his hands and his mouth, moving slowly down her body. "You need to gain a little weight here," he said, sucking at her hip, "and here," he said, lapping at her concave belly, "and here," he said, biting and sucking at her inner thigh.

"Anything. Anything!" she vowed, her head restless on the floor, her hands reaching vainly for him as he worked his way down her legs, tugging her panties off as he went.

He pulled the sandals from her feet and tossed them away before raising her taped foot to his mouth and pressing kisses to the side and to her surprisingly sensitive toes, sucking them gently until she began to writhe from the unexpected pleasure. Smiling, he slid his hands up the back of her legs until he was cupping her buttocks, lifting her slightly.

"This, of course, is perfect," he murmured, just before his mouth sank into her wet flesh, his tongue circling and caressing the delicate folds until she convulsed against him, her cry sharp and shocked at the speed and the force of her climax. His fingers dug into her buttocks for a moment. "So passionate," he said, almost reverently.

Then he was sucking, hard and without mercy, as he had promised, and Samantha was spiraling away into a never-ending series of climaxes that kept building, harder and stronger, until she felt mindless and formless and helpless. Until she grabbed his head with both hands and dragged his mouth to hers, half-sitting up to take him, sinking her tongue into him, tasting herself and him, not knowing where one left off and the other began.

He pulled just slightly away and smiled into her eyes. "Was that a plea for mercy?"

Slowly she shook her head, feeling time stop and the room dissolve around them. "No," she said softly. "I want more. I want you to stop this damn ache that keeps growing stronger every moment you're not in me."

"Show me where it hurts," he murmured with a wicked smile.

She took him with both hands, loving the way his eyes darkened at her touch. *"Here,"* she whispered. She arched, drawing him suddenly into her, catching him off guard, his cry shocked, his body shuddering in her arms as she slid back down to the floor pulling him with her, pulling him deeper into her, until she was gasping in his arms and the blood was flaming in her face.

"Oh . . . my . . . God," she said, her whole body expanding to welcome him home.

His hand was shaking as he brushed his fingertips over her cheek. "Feel better?"

Her mouth quirked in a startled smile. "Lots."

He pulled almost all the way out of her and then slid slowly, too slowly, back in. "And now?"

"Y-y-you're definitely on the right track," she said, the blood pounding in her ears.

"I just wanted to be sure," he said, pulling back again, smiling and shaking his head no as she tried to reach for him. "Sometimes these natural cures require a little adjustment." He thrust into her suddenly, deeply, and she cried out, clinging to him, almost weeping with the blessedness of this joining. "There now," he murmured, "that's much better."

And it was. He moved in her with deep, rhythmic strokes that stole her breath and then her sanity as his gray gaze held her in thrall, binding her to him in ways she had never imagined, drawing her into secret places she had never guessed were within him. Each stroke filled the ache deep within her and at the same time steadily tore through a wall she had hidden away long ago, driving against it, again and again, making her hunger and thirst for its disintegration so she could have whatever lay beyond, so she could give whatever it was, take . . . she didn't know.

She only knew she was becoming more and more frantic, a frenzy and desperation building inside her, until she was arching up against Cullen, trying to take him harder, deeper, farther into her, his ragged moan only fueling the need within her.

She gasped when he suddenly pulled her up into his arms. She was straddling him as he sat back on his heels, his hands sweeping hungrily over her back, his mouth taking hers again and again as she writhed against him. Then his hand knotted in her hair and pulled her head back.

"Your turn," he said.

She took his mouth, pouring her moan into him. Then she began to move, driving him deeper and deeper into her, a wail rising in her throat as he lowered his head and sucked hard on one breast, the pleasure shooting down into her, igniting her. She became a frenzy in his arms, pitching, and driving, and hurling herself on him, drawing him up into the very marrow of her soul.

Her mouth was on his now, sucking at him, fusing him to her in every way that she could, her arms holding him tight, his chest hair rasping her nipples raw with her frenzied movement. She was taking him with everything she had. He was giving her everything she demanded and needed and didn't even know she needed, and she loved it. She loved him.

That wall within her shattered and she couldn't stop. It shattered and she was calling his name. It shattered and light and joy and peace cascaded through her.

She clung to him, feeling his strong arms holding her tight, hearing him tell her how beautiful she was and how glorious. Then the world was tumbling over and she was staring up at him, seeing only Cullen, not the room, only Cullen, and gray eyes turned nearly black with the storm raging within him, his beautiful face taut and hungry, the heat from his body burning her arms and her legs as they held him tight.

"Yes," she said on a long breath that was suddenly cut off by her sharp cry as he thrust into her. "Oh *God*," she sobbed as he drove into her again and again, his eyes never leaving hers. He drove through her climax, and then another, taking her without mercy, until all she could feel was this shattering pleasure and Cullen, his heat and his need and his hunger, which were hers, and she gave herself up to all of it.

He was storming into her, a hurricane consuming everything in its path, and she was laughing and sobbing and telling him "yes" and telling him "anything" and telling him *"more"* as she rode this storm, as he rode her, plunging into her. He was ravaging her, bombarding her with truths and glory and ecstasy and she was telling him, even though there weren't words, she was telling him as his eyes held hers, as she saw it begin, felt it sweep her up and crash into her, tumbling her over, flooding the world as Cullen called her name again and again and again.

Then he was holding her and pressing kisses to her face and murmuring words she couldn't quite hear as she slid into a deep sleep, pulling him with her.

SHE WAS ENFOLDED in warmth. It was her first conscious sensation. Then she heard the slow, steady thump of a heartbeat against her ear, and she woke up with a vengeance, stifling her horrified cry. *She was in Cullen's arms.* She had just made love to Cullen when Whitney was in the same house!

Her immediate impulse was to scramble to her feet, grab her clothes, and run. But Cullen would wake up and then there'd be a scene and she couldn't face him now. She just couldn't. Skin cold with fear, heart pounding in her throat, Samantha slowly, inch by inch, eased herself from Cullen's arms, creeping away from his warm, glorious body, holding her breath, terrified of making any sound, any sudden movement that would wake him.

She stared at his face still close to hers, so peaceful, so beautiful, and she nearly wept. *Oh, what had she done?*

Her legs were free, and her belly. Carefully she eased the last few inches out of his arms, then held herself immobile, watching to see if the absence of her heat would wake him. He didn't move.

With a gasp, she rolled to her feet and, moving silently, her injured foot throbbing with a dull pain that had nothing on her heart, she began frantically picking up and putting on her clothes, damning herself with every hateful word she had ever learned.

"Sam?" Cullen murmured sleepily. *"Sam?"*

Oh God, how was she going to survive this? "L-l-let's just agree that it was all my f-f-fault, and that I'm so sorry, and that it'll never happen again, and I won't tell Whitney if you don't," she babbled as she began backing toward the study door.

He was on his feet, naked and stalking her. "What the hell are you talking about and where the hell do you think you're going?"

She couldn't stop the tears from spilling out. "It was the worst mistake of my life, okay? I don't know why I did it. I've never seduced anyone before. I've never done anything so wrong in my life. I just—"

"Are you telling me that you think what we just shared was a *mistake*?" Cullen growled.

She gaped at him through her tears. "Well of course it was! You love Whitney, she loves you. I shouldn't be messing that up."

"Samantha—"

Something shattered inside her. "Oh God, how could I have betrayed Whitney like this? How could I have betrayed *you* like this? You trusted me and I turned that trust against you, seducing you into what I've dreamt of night after night for weeks, when it was the farthest thing in the world from what you wanted."

"*How* can you think I didn't want what we just shared?" he asked in disbelief. "I loved every millisecond of it."

She was shaking her head, fending off his words, fending off knowing that all she had to do was reach out and she could touch him. "It doesn't matter that you were willing. It doesn't matter that you . . . enjoyed me. It was my fault. It was all my fault." Tears were cascading down her face. She couldn't see him clearly. "*I* threw myself at you, Cullen. *I* kissed you, *I* stripped off your clothes, *I* pulled you to the f-f-floor! I betrayed you. I'm a monster to have done this to the people I love."

"Samantha, honey, you're no monster," he said gently, cupping her face in his warm hands.

His scent was on every inch of her skin. She could still taste him on her lips and her tongue. She could still hear his wild cries in her ears. His touch was invading her heart. He was all she had ever wanted and she'd just driven him away forever. "I swear, Cullen, I swear that I'll make amends. I'm going to do everything in my power to bring Whitney to her senses and get her standing in front of Judge Parker with you at her side."

"Excuse me?"

"Of course, if you want a church wedding, that's fine, too," she hurried on. "Whitney won't care, just so long as she gets to wear the most drop-dead wedding dress on this or any other continent. She used to make collages from pictures she had cut out from bridal magazines. She'll want hundreds of guests, of course, and—"

Cullen pressed his thumbs to her lips to silence her. "Samantha, my love, shut up. I don't want to marry Whitney. I want to marry you."

She stumbled back, freeing herself, wiping the tears

from her face. "Don't be stupid," she ordered. "That's just guilt, at least, or lust, at worst, talking. You don't owe me anything, Cullen. We goofed. End of story. Now let's get our lives back to normal. You love Whitney. You are going to marry Whitney, just like you've always dreamed."

"No," Cullen said, tenderness in his gray eyes that seemed to reach out and enfold her, "I've always loved *you*."

"Cullen," she said in her most reasonable voice, "you can't have always been in love with me, because you've always been in love with *Whitney*."

"No," Cullen said, "I've been infatuated with Whitney. There's a difference. You taught me that."

"Oh, I did not."

"Yes, you did," he said with a smile, brushing his fingertips across her cheek before she had a chance to jump back. "I love you, Samantha. I have always loved you. You are perfect for me and I can be perfect for you if you'll just let me try. All I want in the world is to spend the rest of my life with you."

"No," she said, her hand fumbling for the study door lock. "Try to understand that this was just temporary insanity on both our parts, okay? It didn't mean anything. We don't ever have to talk about it again. You'll marry Whitney and go on a month-long honeymoon and when you get back I'll be the hardworking neighbor somewhere off in the background and everything will be back to normal again."

"Sam—"

She tore the study door open and ran out into the hall. Cullen lunged and grabbed her wrist, but she pulled free, her thoughts focused on a single goal: to get out of this house and away from Cullen *now*, before she gave in, before she let herself believe that this was anything but her worst nightmare.

She heard him swear violently behind her as she ran.

He had probably just figured out that he could not chase her naked through the house when there were friends and family all around. But she was taking no chances. She redoubled her speed as she raced through two parlors and into the rose marble Great Hall which was, blessedly, empty for the moment.

She was outside, the sun blinding her through her tears, before she quite realized she had opened the front door. She ran down the driveway, sobbing until she collided with her car in a multitude of the other guests' cars. She slid onto the front seat of the Audi, shaking badly, pulled the keys from the glove box, and fumbled for the ignition. How fast could an angry man get dressed?

She looked wildly around, but so far Cullen had not appeared. Thanking every god, she started the car, backed up, narrowly missed ramming the Barrisford Mercedes, and then sent the Audi hurtling down the Mackenzie driveway at eighty miles an hour.

Seventeen

CULLEN DRAGGED ON his clothes, fury, fear, and exultation warring within him. He reached the front door just in time to see the black Lark Audi disappear around the last curve in the driveway. Damn the woman! He stood there glaring into the sunshine, Samantha's scent on every inch of him, the taste of her on his mouth and tongue, the warmth of her body encoded on his.

This was twice now that she had run from his arms. He wasn't about to let her get away with it a third time. Sam had been wrong at the beginning of summer when she'd insisted that a woman could keep a man completely in the dark when she didn't want to reveal her true feelings, because he knew the truth now.

She loved him. It had been in her eyes and her voice and in every caress, though she'd never said the words. Though she'd run away from saying the words, she loved him. He knew it as surely as he knew that he loved her and he'd be damned if he was going to let her hide from him anymore.

He stalked into the family room and stood glaring at the phone, glancing at his watch every eight seconds, until he was sure Samantha had had enough time to drive home. He dialed the Lark number and heard a Lark day maid answer on the second ring.

"This is Cullen Mackenzie," he said, forcing himself to sound calm. "Did Samantha just come home?"

"No," she replied. "There isn't a soul in this house except me."

Damn! "Okay, thanks." He hung up the phone, vibrating with frustration. She could have driven anywhere, so he couldn't go looking for her, particularly in the middle of a wedding party.

Cullen groaned. *Erin and Noel.* The last thing he wanted to do was pretend he hadn't just made love with Samantha Fay Lark. But if he ran out on them to look for Sam, his absence would distract the wedding party from Erin and Noel's moment in the spotlight. He figured that every man, and many of the women, in that party would know exactly what he'd been doing—if not with whom— the minute he walked back into the drawing room. Damn! All he wanted was Samantha—a sane Samantha—in his arms at this moment and for many more moments to come. Instead, he'd have to shower and regroup and play the happy host.

Fifteen minutes later he walked into the drawing room, relieved a glass of champagne from the tray Williams was holding, and surveyed the party. It was like seeing the world with brand new eyes. Seeing himself with new eyes, too. He liked this new view, except for the tornado on the horizon that was Samantha in full retreat.

And there was something else. . . . He searched the room until he saw Whitney, standing with Missy Barrisford as usual, but there was a reserve in Whitney, and a look of fear in her blue eyes as she stared at him a moment that he'd never seen before. She looked like she was standing on the edge of some giant cliff, toes clinging to the last inch of earth, and he knew with absolute certainty that he could rescue her, that he could pull her back from that cliff, whatever it was. But he couldn't decipher the message in her eyes. Did she want to be rescued, or for once in her life did she want to jump?

He walked over to the two women. "Hi," he said gently, because Whitney seemed suddenly fragile.

"That's quite a secret Erin's been keeping," Whitney said too brightly. "Didn't any of you guess?"

He looked at her with his new eyes. She was as beautiful as ever in a strapless white dress. But that was all. She felt exactly like . . . a friend. Cullen almost laughed out loud. Was there a bigger fool in all creation? "I never had a clue," he said.

"I've got to hand it to Erin," Missy said. "This is one of the few weddings I've actually enjoyed attending."

"I've always loved weddings," Whitney said. "All the pomp and ceremony and theater of it, the hundreds of people watching, the flowers, the family—" Her eyes suddenly welled with tears. "Laurel cried nonstop, did you see?"

Missy slid a comforting arm around her shoulders. "There are all kinds of happily-ever-after, Whitney."

"I know," she said, blinking back the tears. "I think I'd like some more champagne."

"Allow me," Cullen said. He headed back into the party, wondering why Samantha had blamed herself just a short time ago. *He* was the monster. He had long affirmed his undying love for Whitney, lying to her, lying to himself, vowing to shower her with all the blessings of wealth and power and status, and then he had systematically broken each one of those vows as he had held Samantha in his arms.

Cullen got Whitney her champagne and then, to get away from the suffocating horde of wedding celebrants and Whitney's troubling blue eyes, he volunteered to drive Erin and Noel to the airport so they could catch their honeymoon flight to Paris.

"YOU'RE NOT ALTOGETHER HERE, Cullen," Erin said as she and Cullen and Noel stood at the Washington Dulles departure gate, crowds of passengers and incessant airport pages creating a solid wall of background noise. "What's got you so distracted?"

Cullen dragged himself into the present. "I've just been imagining the horrors of having Noel for a neighbor for the rest of my life," he retorted.

"I thought Samantha left the party very early," Noel commented innocently.

Cullen glared at him. Damn the man for being so perceptive. "We had something of an argument."

"Was that all?" Noel murmured.

"An argument?" Erin said, one hand resting on her cello case, the other on her hip. "On my wedding day? Was that why you two disappeared for so long? Of all the inconsiderate men—"

"I'll make it good, Erin, I promise," Cullen said.

"Yes," Noel said with a lazy smile, "I rather thought you would."

"Oh, just get on the damn plane and let me get on with my life!" Cullen erupted.

Noel laughed as he took his wife's arm and began to pull her toward their plane. "Good-bye, my brother. Good luck."

"Brother? What brother?" Erin demanded.

"I'll tell you over the Atlantic Ocean, my love," he promised.

Feeling like a black thundercloud, Cullen stalked back to his car and headed home, oblivious to the roar of planes taking off and landing as he thought about years wasted, brown eyes that had never lied to him, and silky copper hair spread across a Chinese carpet.

> *"True love's the gift which God has given*
> *To man alone beneath the heaven:*
> *It is not fantasy's hot fire,*
> *Whose wishes, soon as granted, fly;*
> *It liveth not in fierce desire,*
> *With dead desire it doth not die;*
> *It is the secret sympathy,*
> *The silver link, the silken tie,*
> *Which heart to heart and mind to mind*
> *In body and in soul can bind."*

Scott had been describing Samantha Fay Lark when he wrote *The Lay of the Minstrel* in 1805. If Cullen had paid attention to those early nineteenth century truths these last twelve years instead of to "fantasy's hot fire," he wouldn't be alone right now.

But he had wasted too many infatuated years pursuing Teague's bride, ignoring the bride preordained for him, and now he was paying the consequences: a woman who didn't love him but meant to have him, a woman who did love him and refused to have him. It would have been funny if it didn't hurt so damn much.

He held on to the heat of Samantha's body burned into his, the scent of her, the taste of her, like a talisman. In her arms he had found himself and a depth of love and peace that were unimaginable only yesterday. They were worth every heartache, every painful truth, every roadblock she threw in his way.

He drove through the late-afternoon Sunday traffic

trying to figure out how to make things right, no matter how badly Whitney got hurt, no matter how hard Samantha fought him.

He had his home. He had his business. It was time and past time to get his woman.

SAMANTHA SLID OFF Sky Rocket on Monday afternoon, handed the reins to Guadalupe, the mare's groom, and watched her lead the roan away. She stared after them, sighed, then turned to the house and sighed again. The home she loved. The land and the horses she loved. They were all safe now. But it wasn't enough. After all she'd been through to hold on to them, after all the terror and stress and sleep deprivation, they had let her down, because even they could not assuage this throbbing ache in her heart. She hurriedly blinked back tears and headed for the front porch.

She was back on a reasonable eight-hour work schedule, which meant a two-hour lunch break, and she didn't know what to do with herself. All she did, in the house, on horseback, on the phone with potential customers, was think about Cullen, relive their lovemaking again and again, long for him, weep for him.

She loved him. She had *always* loved him, just as she had once told Whitney in the interest of furthering the Great Plot. When she had thought she was making jokes for the amusement of others these last twenty years, she had in fact been in earnest about wanting to marry the man. She just hadn't let herself know it . . . until yesterday.

She thought of her other lovers, all blonds—Phillippe, Marceau Giscard, and Kaspar—and realized that they had been pale imitations of the man she really wanted to take to bed and spend her life with. She realized now that Sky-lark's debt wasn't the only reason she'd tried to work herself into the ground these last five years. She'd also been trying to avoid the aching absence of Cullen in her life.

Like she was trying, and failing, to do now.

It was a miserable existence. She'd much rather be working herself to the bone to avoid some of this misery, but there'd be revolt on the farm if she tried it. She walked into the house, and just stood there, not knowing what to do next.

Calida poked her head through the swinging kitchen door. "Lunch is ready."

"I'll be right there," Sam mumbled.

Calida didn't move. "You look like you just lost the farm."

"I haven't."

"And I haven't seen you this sad since your parents died," Calida said, walking up to her. "What's wrong?"

"Nothing," Samantha said with a sigh as she started for the dining table. "What's for lunch?"

"The truth," Calida said, arms folded across her chest as she blocked Sam's escape.

"That doesn't sound very filling," Sam said, trying to sidestep her.

But Calida was quick on her feet. Maybe it was the athletic shoes. "You might as well tell me what's wrong, Miss, because I won't stop hounding you until you do."

"Oh, hell," Samantha said, tears welling in her eyes. But she wouldn't let them fall. She wouldn't. "I'm in love," she said, not looking at Calida.

"Have you told Cullen?"

"Of course I haven't told—" Samantha stopped and stared at Calida in horror. "How do you know it's Cullen?"

"I've known it's Cullen for years now," Calida said, patting her cheek. "What are you going to do about it?"

"Nothing!" Samantha said, startled by the suggestion. "He came home to marry Whitney, remember?"

"This isn't like you," Calida said, frowning with severe disapproval. "You're a fighter. Get in there and fight for what you want and what you need!"

"No," Samantha said firmly. "I won't do that to either of them. I'd never know a moment's peace, Calida. My conscience would hound me to the grave."

Calida shook her head in disgust. "You've been working so hard these last few years, it's made you stupid. Are you really going to consign the man you love and the friend you love to a loveless marriage? Are you going to martyr your heart in the name of a teenage fantasy that should have died long ago?"

"But—"

"Whitney would run you down like a rabbit if you stood in *her* way."

"That's an awful thing to say!" But it was true, and Sam knew it.

And when push came to shove, wasn't Cullen worth fighting for?

"I think I'll go have a chat with Whitney," Sam said, heading for the front door.

"Thatta girl," Calida said.

Sam pulled open the front door and there was Whitney, about to ring the doorbell.

"Hi," Sam said, her courage shot all to hell by this unexpected encounter.

"Hi, yourself," Whitney said, looking pale but lovely as she stood before her in a floral print silk jumpsuit. "May I come in?"

"Sure," Sam said, stumbling backwards into the house. "I was just coming to see you, actually."

Whitney walked past her and into the living room. She sat down on the green Edwardian sofa and then immediately stood up again. "There's something I have to tell you," she said, a dark blush creeping right up to her scalp, stunning Sam. She'd never seen Whitney blush before. "I'm leaving for Europe in a few hours."

Sam's head felt filled with helium. "With . . . Cullen?" she asked.

"No," Whitney said, her hand shaking as she traced the woodwork on the back of the sofa. "With Missy."

"Missy?"

"That's right."

"B–B–But what about Cullen?"

"He'll have his horses. He'll be fine."

Samantha grabbed Whitney and stared at her, trying to understand just what in the world was going on. "You don't want Cullen?"

"Sam, you're hurting me," Whitney complained.

"You don't want Cullen?"

"No, I don't," Whitney said, pulling free.

"B-b-but—"

"I know," Whitney said with a shaky smile. "I can't believe it either. I thought I loved him, Sam. I really did. I'm not completely mercenary, you know. But it turns out I was just telling myself one more lie to avoid a reality that didn't fit in to the pigeonhole I thought I believed in. But you don't have to worry about me. I'll be fine. Missy has promised to give me everything I've ever wanted, and more."

Samantha stared at her friend for a moment as the full implications of this conversation hit her. Then she collapsed onto a nearby arm chair and laughed. "This can't be happening. This just can't be happening."

"Don't you dare laugh at me!"

"I'm not laughing at *you*, Whitney, I'm laughing at *me*. Of all the idiotic . . ." Sam's smile faded. "But are you *sure*, Whitney? Are you sure this will make you happy?"

"It has been pointed out to me, rather forcefully, that there was a reason I waited for Cullen all these years. It kept me safe. It kept me from betraying myself by tying myself to a man. I'm scared witless, Sam, but I *am* happy."

"But do you really love Missy Barrisford?"

Whitney looked pale but resolute. "I've never loved anyone except Missy—and you, of course, but you don't count."

Samantha gaped at her.

"Oh, you know what I mean," Whitney said crossly.

In between gasps of laughter, Samantha assured her that she knew exactly what she meant.

Whitney studied her a moment and then slowly relaxed her taut body. "This is not exactly the reaction I expected."

Samantha leapt out of her chair and enfolded her in a bone-crushing hug. "Oh Whitney, how could you think I'd be anything but thrilled that you've found real love? I hope you are happier than any human being on earth has ever been happy! Send me lots of postcards and give my love and my everlasting thanks to Missy! Calida," she shouted as she ran for the front door, "bring Whitney our best bottle of champagne!" Heart pounding, she ran outside. She had some major back-pedaling to make amends for.

She was halfway to the garage when she saw Marybeth Hill walking Lark Ness across the driveway.

"Marybeth," she yelled, *"stop!"*

Marybeth stopped.

"I'll take Nessie," she said, pulling the halter rope from her hands, looping it through the halter and pulling it back into makeshift reins. "Give me a leg up."

Puzzled, Marybeth gave her a leg up. Sam set Nessie galloping down the driveway before she had even straightened on her back. "Run, girl, *run!*" she shouted, and Nessie eagerly obliged.

It was only the superb brakes of Cullen's BMW and Nessie's ability to stop on a dime that prevented a head-on collision near the end of the driveway.

"Sam, are you out of your mind?" Cullen shouted as he lunged out of the car.

"Cullen!" Samantha yelled gleefully as she threw herself off Lark Ness.

"You could have been killed," Cullen said, grabbing her shoulders and shaking her.

"Don't be ridiculous. We'd have jumped you if we'd had to. Now listen, we have to talk."

"That's my line. Give me your hand," he said, grabbing her left wrist and raising her hand in the air. He slid a ring with a slim silver band and a small perfect pearl onto her ring finger. "Do you see that?" he said, holding her hand in front of her face. "That is an engagement ring. You are wearing it because I love you, not Whitney, and I am going to marry you, not Whitney, and that's final."

"Yes, Cullen," Samantha demurely replied, hiding her euphoric grin. He'd been telling the truth! He *did* love her!

"What?"

"Whatever you say, Cullen," she said, just before she grabbed him and kissed him, hard.

He was stunned, there were no two ways about it. But Cullen had always had good reflexes. He kissed her back until she couldn't feel the ground beneath her feet. He kissed her until she felt ready to spontaneously combust. He kissed her until Lark Ness got bored and wandered off the driveway and onto the lawn to grab a snack.

"What the hell happened?" Cullen demanded when they came up for air.

"I kissed you," Samantha said, fully aware she had a beatific smile on her face and not caring. It was time she started getting mushy with Cullen.

"Before that," he said.

"I agreed to marry you."

"Yes, but why?"

Samantha couldn't decide whether to laugh or to weep with happiness. She settled for cupping his beautiful face in her hands and staring up at him, drinking her fill of him, nearly rapturous with the knowledge that she would be able to do this for the rest of their lives. "Because I love you, Cullen Mackenzie. Because you are perfect for me and I will try to be perfect for you."

Cullen closed his eyes for a moment and seemed to have trouble catching his breath. "I love it when I'm right," he said. "But what about Whitney and all your fears of betraying her trust?" he demanded suspiciously.

"Ah. Well, that's kind of a non-issue. Whitney has discovered that she's in love with Missy Barrisford, and apparently Missy loves *her*, so . . ."

"You're kidding," Cullen said.

"Nope."

"Wow," he said, leaning against the red BMW, Samantha firmly locked in his arms. "I'd heard a few rumors about Missy, but this . . . No wonder Whitney looked so scared yesterday! She was getting ready to change her entire life!"

"You're not crushed," she observed.

"Hardly," he said with a smile. "I've been agonizing over how to let her down easy."

Sam shook her head. "All that nobility wasted. What a pity."

"I should probably still talk to her."

"Later, Calida's busy getting her drunk."

"Alcohol could only help," Cullen agreed. "Okay, okay, let's get down to what's *really* important. I spent hours choosing that ring. Do you like it?"

Samantha looked at the engagement ring on her hand and then grinned up at him. "I *love* it," she assured him.

"Good," he said with an answering grin, "because you're gonna have to wear it for several decades to come. October wedding?"

"You're on." She received a kiss for her answer.

"Mom gets to help plan the festivities?"

"Of course." She received another kiss.

"Wow. I seem to be on a roll here. So, ever thought about trying to get onto the U.S. Olympic equestrian team?"

Samantha stared up at him a moment. Then she grinned. "Hey, you've helped me fulfill my fantasies, I'm more than happy to help you fulfill yours."

"See?" he murmured, kissing her again and again and again. "I told you we're perfect for each other."

"Cullen?" she said in between kisses.

"Hm?"

"I am not going to make love to you in the middle of my driveway."

He raised his head, a slow, sexy smile crooking his mouth and making her heart skitter. "Your place or mine?"

"They're both a bit crowded, don't you think?"

"True." He considered a moment. "Well, if Nessie doesn't mind us riding double, I'm sure we can find some place private." He pointed a stern finger at her nose. "And no running away this time."

She laughed, a low silky laugh. "Oh Mr. Mackenzie, that is something you *don't* have to worry about. Think of me as super glue."

He cocked his head. "Kinky. But I'm game."

Her smile widened. "See? I knew you were perfect for me."

"And it only took me twenty years to figure it out," Cullen said, kissing her arched throat.

"Trust me," she gasped, melting into his arms, "you were worth the wait."

About the Author

MICHELLE MARTIN is the author of eight other novels. She lives and writes in Albuquerque, New Mexico.

Bantam Books by

Michelle Martin

Stolen Moments

___57649-6 $5.50/$7.50 Canada

Stolen Hearts

___57648-8 $5.50/$7.50 Canada